As Ansalon struggles for survival
during the War of Souls,
the empire of the minotaurs is
about to enter a new Golden Age
. . . or perish forever.

"I am your *emperor.*"

"No more," said Hotak. "No more."

The axe came down.

✝ THE MINOTAUR WARS ✝

RICHARD A. KNAAK

THE MINOTAUR WARS
VOLUME I
NIGHT OF BLOOD

RICHARD A. KNAAK

NIGHT OF BLOOD

©2004 Wizards of the Coast, Inc.

Distributed in the United States by Holtzbrinck Publishing. Distributed in Canada by Fenn Ltd.

Distributed to the hobby, toy, and comic trade in the United States and Canada by regional distributors.

Distributed worldwide by Wizards of the Coast, Inc. and regional distributors.

Cover art by Matt Stawicki
Map by Dennis Kauth
First Printing: June 2003
First paperback edition February 2004
Library of Congress Catalog Card Number: 2003111902

9 8 7 6 5 4 3 2 1

US ISBN: 0-7869-3196-5
UK ISBN: 0-7869-3197-3
620-96539-001-EN

U.S., CANADA,
ASIA, PACIFIC, & LATIN AMERICA
Wizards of the Coast, Inc.
P.O. Box 707
Renton, WA 98057-0707
+1-800-324-6496

EUROPEAN HEADQUARTERS
Wizards of the Coast, Belgium
T Hofveld 6d
1702 Groot-Bijgaarden
Belgium
+322 467 3360

Visit our web site at **www.wizards.com**

For my mother, Anna, with thanks for her constant inspiration and support.

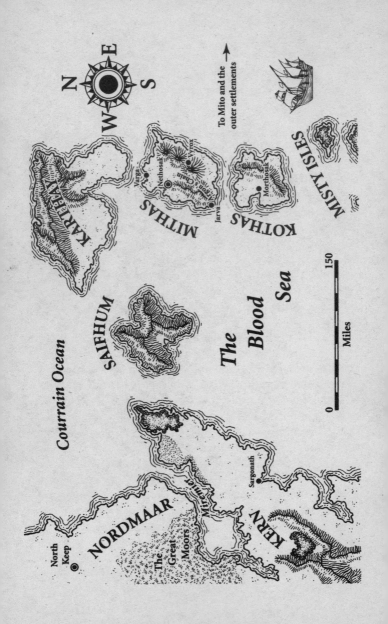

PROLOGUE
By MARGARET WEIS

Following the devastation of the War of Souls, the people of Krynn will look to a future that is uncertain, unknown. Of course, one might say that the future is always uncertain and unknown to those who cannot see into it. In the history of Krynn, however, every event that occurred in the world had some basis in history. The future of Krynn was built up on the secure foundations of the past. Events may have been catastrophic, but—looking back—one could say that they were predictable based on what had gone before.

When Takhisis ripped the world from its moorings, she set it adrift in time and space, so that what was is no more and what will be is unfathomable. Not even the gods can see what is to come.

They call this time the Age of Mortals. At the beginning it was so named because the gods had departed. After the War of Souls it will keep its name because the gods themselves are in turmoil. The river of time has overflowed its banks and washed away the stars.

The gods will have some say in the future of the world, of that there can be no doubt. But they will grope and feel their way through the darkness, the same as mortals. Evil will flourish in this atmosphere of fear and uncertainty. But the deeper the darkness, the brighter the light will shine.

This is the time for minotaurs to make their mark upon the world, a time for new villains and heroes.

Richard A. Knaak's trilogy is the first step into that future.

A Chronicle of the History of the Minotaurs
(Excerpted from the Archives of Palanthas)

Although the minotaur race has spoken little of its past to outsiders, fragments of history have been gathered that speak of a realm fraught with upheaval and rejuvenation, collapse and survival. Despite their violent existence, the minotaurs have endured and even prospered.

Legend disagrees on their origin. Most believe that in the waning days of the high ogres' civilization, when decadence began to corrupt them, a more immediate danger materialized in their realm—the Graygem, an artifact of fearsome magic with the power to transform anything and anyone. In the case of the ogres, it twisted their bodies, remaking more than a quarter of the race into the horned behemoths feared to this day.

In contrast, the minotaurs' account paints a stark portrait of the ogres' decline and the benevolence of one god. Sargas took the form of a giant condor, gathering up and flying those ogres he found worthy to a land on the eastern edge of Ansalon. Here they would start anew. He then placed upon each his sign, transforming them into minotaurs, and by doing so ensured that never would they and their cousins be one again.

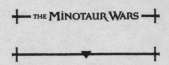

Historically, the minotaurs appeared three thousand years before the First Cataclysm. They settled on the eastern coast of Ansalon and named their home Mithandrus, the Land of the Bull. From their beginning, they dreamed of their own empire, one resurrecting the early glories of their forebears, but marked by their own particular beliefs.

But the minotaurs made the blunder of invading the dwarven realm of Kal-Thax. The dwarves took umbrage. They razed Mithandrus and dragged thousands of minotaur slaves back to Kal-Thax. For over two hundred years, minotaurs worked the dank mines, suffering under the yoke of harsh dwarven rule. Only when civil unrest split Kal-Thax in two—creating the rival kingdom of Thorin in the process—did the slaves, under the leaders Ambeoutin and Belim, revolt. They slaughtered the dwarves and destroyed Kal-Thax.

With Belim dead, Ambeoutin led his people back to their homeland, which his followers named after him in his honor. Yet, fearing for his people, Ambeoutin prayed to his god for guidance.

It is said Sargas appeared to Ambeoutin in a vision as a giant, fiery minotaur seated upon a throne carved from an extinct volcano. The god raised Ambeoutin into the air, the king drifting like a leaf in the wind.

"I have heard your pleas, Ambeoutin, and understand your fears. They are the grounded fears of a worthy warrior, and so I shall answer them. I will teach you, and you will teach my children."

Honor was given as the first and foremost virtue of the Horned One's children, for without honor there could be only savagery, as indeed had happened to the ogres.

"Honor without the strength to defend oneself is nothing more than an empty, fragile shell, easily crushed," the deity said. "My children must be strong, for they will endure much hardship as they struggle toward their rightful destiny."

The rest of the vision is lost to time, but Ambeoutin, once pale brown, is said to have stepped out of his chambers that next morning colored as black as soot. He had met the god of fire and volcanoes face-to-face, and the mark of it would stay with him forever.

So Ambeoutin taught the minotaurs the codes that shaped every aspect of their existence: Honor to one's family, one's clan, one's race. A minotaur's word was inviolate, something he would sacrifice his life to defend. Those who lacked resolve brought dishonor to all.

To teach the physical strength necessary to defend one's honor, the king introduced the first of the armed tournaments. He then decreed that all major decisions be adjudicated through formalized duels. For this purpose, he had the first arena—a simple, round structure—built.

After a reign of sixty years, Ambeoutin died. Despite his declaration that all minotaurs were equal and might rule, the people turned to his twin sons, Mithas and Kothas, who agreed to meet in the arena to decide who would lead. Yet, despite battling for over a day, they were too evenly matched. In the end, both fell, exhausted.

The people clamored equally for each to be proclaimed victor. Fearing civil war, the brothers split the kingdom in two, with Kothas ruling the southern half and Mithas the northern. They also agreed to regular tournaments between the two new kingdoms, ensuring that the fates of their realms, named for them, would forever be entwined.

Yet the twin kingdoms did not last. Kothas perished ten years later, his neck broken in a fall. Mithas moved to maintain stability in the south, but his actions were misinterpreted as an invasion. As he marched his forces there, he left his other borders thinly-defended. The ogres, recently reconstituted under a charismatic khan, invaded in great numbers, crushing the minotaurs and sweeping away both realms.

After overthrowing the ogres at the end of the Second Dragon War (2645 PC), the minotaurs rebuilt the twin kingdoms. However, this time the gathered leaders agreed that, for better security and coordination, the minotaur people needed one absolute ruler. With this in mind, they launched the first Great Circus and declared that within a year an inaugural imperial duel would decide the first emperor.

After days of struggle, Bosigarni Es-Mithas seized victory in a duel that left him with the appellation "Bos of the Blood." Avidly promoting the minotaurs as the future rulers of Krynn, Bos set up the temple of Sargas to spread the god's word. He then created the Supreme Circle, the governing body overseeing the everyday workings of the empire.

With Bos's death, the minotaurs commenced on a series of disastrous forays. Repulsed by dwarves and humans, the empire collapsed again. For several generations, the race suffered as slaves to first the dwarves, then the ogres. To better control their servants, the conquerors maintained the pretense of an emperor, but one who would answer to them, not any god.

Freedom came again in 2485 PC, when a gladiator named Makel succeeded in slaying the Grand Khan. Leading his people on a bloody swathe through their masters' domain, Makel—later called Ogrebane—nearly wiped out the ogres.

As emperor, Makel made Nethosak, the largest northern settlement, the permanent imperial seat. Within a year, construction began on a palace. Makel ruled for forty years, dying—in a manner uncharacteristic for a minotaur—in his sleep.

His death ushered in the Age of the Pretenders, so termed because of their brief reigns. Not until the archer Jarisi did the minotaurs have a true leader again. Jarisi defended her crown for fifteen years and expanded sea exploration. In 2335 PC the minotaurs claimed their first island colony, naming it Jari-Nyos in her honor.

Jarisi's successors once more tested the resolve of a neighbor. They looked to the lush eastern border of elven Silvanesti, which was entangled in conflict with the human empire of Ergoth to the west. But chaos erupted within the border. Mapped paths changed. Patrols vanished. The emperor died on horseback, strangled when a vine wrapped around his throat. Unable to cope with such magic, the minotaurs retreated. The defeat again weakened them, and a reinvigorated ogre realm crushed the empire, enslaving the race for another two hundred years.

Coinciding with the defeat of Ergoth by Vinas Solamnus in 1791 PC, a minotaur named Tremoc appeared. Tremoc had crossed Ansalon four times to hunt down his mate's killer. His dedication stirred the realm, so much so that when Tremoc entered the Circus to challenge for the throne, his adversary conceded without combat, the only time in minotaur history.

An unprepossessing ruler, Tremoc changed forever one night when, alone in the temple, he was disturbed in his prayers by a booming voice.

"Tremoc . . ." the voice called, echoing from everywhere. "You pray for your lost love, but do you love enough?"

Tremoc rose and shook his fist at the condor icon above. "There is no love more true than mine, neither on Krynn nor in the heavens!"

"Love of a mate is honorable," the god said, "but what of your people? They are without an emperor. My chosen have free will, but with it comes responsibility. As ruler, your responsibility is greatest. Honor your mate, but love your people. They are your family now!"

A glorious red light touched the emperor, filling him with the blessing of Sargas. Tremoc emerged determined. He had a newer, vaster Circus built and strengthened the realm. Once again minotaurs established themselves on outlying islands. The kingdoms prospered.

Tremoc desired a passage through ogre lands that would give his people access to the richer, fertile human realms. The temple and the Supreme Circle preferred to avenge themselves against the elves, but Tremoc would not listen. He prepared his armies, certain of victory, but the day before battle, Tremoc was found dead, an elven dagger in his chest. He was brought in state to a grand pyre set before the palace. It is said that the skies thundered for vengeance as the body burned.

A series of imperial duels quickly followed, as many sought the legacy of Tremoc for their own. But before the minotaurs could go to war, fresh disaster swept over their homeland.

The earthquake of 1772 PC is chronicled as the worst in minotaur history. A huge fissure split Nethosak in two. The arena caved in, killing thousands in attendance. Aftershocks ravaged the region. Despite minimal damage, Morthosak fell to disease and chaos as refugees filled it. Rebuilding would take years. Tremors continued to besiege the realm, leaving it ripe for conquest by a new nation—Istar.

Desiring trade routes, labor, and resources, Istar invaded in 1543 PC. Nethosak was razed again. General Hymdall, Istar's military commander, headed south, certain that Morthosak would easily fall.

Instead, two days from his goal, a small army commanded by the minotaur Mitos awaited him. Hymdall sent in his massive cavalry to cut down the weak lines, but from the ground suddenly arose camouflaged framework barriers covered with sharpened stakes. The swift-rising barriers gave the cavalry no escape. Horses and soldiers were impaled or thrown. Men panicked. The enemy cavalry splintered.

General Hymdall urged his infantry to the rescue, but after his men crossed the field, minotaurs emerged from hidden pits behind them. The Istarans had marched right over the enemy and now stood trapped.

Hymdall was forced to surrender. Ransoming the surviving enemy, Mitos obtained the release of the minotaurs already taken to Istar.

Beginning with Mitos's reign, the minotaurs withdrew from the rest of Ansalon. Their art and their culture were forgotten by the outside. Most recalled only their monstrous image. Terrifying tales spread. Without raising a weapon, minotaurs became more feared than ever.

When the dark goddess Takhisis unleashed the Third Dragon War in 1060 PC, her commanders saw the minotaurs as the perfect beasts of war. Serving as slave soldiers, the minotaurs became the right arm of the Warlord Crynus's legions as he swept toward Solamnia. But there the advance came to an abrupt halt as the heirs to the legacy of Vinas Solamnus mounted a steadfast resistance.

In a unique sidelight of history, one minotaur, Kaziganthi de-Orilg, slew his ogre captain and fled into the Solamnic lands. There he was saved by the legendary knight, Huma Dragonbane. An unlikely friendship developed. Kaz followed Huma through the war and would be the one to carry his body from the site of battle after Huma defeated Takhisis.

There are many tales of Kaz's later life. It is said he returned home and battled a fearsome red dragon who had secretly manipulated the minotaurs in the name of Takhisis. However, the legend takes place eight years after the Third Dragon War. As records prove, all dragons vanished at the end of the war. Still, minotaurs insist on the credence of this tale.

Once again, the minotaurs returned to their isolation. But, though the minotaurs wished to avoid the outside world, the world would not ignore them. In a dispute with the elves over sea routes, Istar inadvertently aroused the minotaurs. The empire refused to accept the presence of either side and, in 645 PC, launched an aggressive drive in the Courrain, sinking both human and elven vessels. However, by 460 PC, with all but a few regions now bowing to its dominance, Istar pushed the imperium's sea power back to its own territories, penning in the minotaurs.

With the Proclamation of Manifest Virtue in 94 PC, the Kingpriest, absolute ruler of Istar, declared nearly all other races inherently evil and commanded that they either be exterminated or brought into the Light. Sargas's chosen were again led from their homeland in chains. A handful of colonies survived independently through piracy, but as a nation the minotaurs ceased to exist—until the disaster that all other races lamented returned to them their birthright.

To any other land, the First Cataclysm is a time of godly fury and earth-rending horror. In response to the Kingpriest's declaration that he be worshipped as the supreme god, the heavens burned and a flaming mountain plummeted from above, plunging Istar into the depths. The Blood Sea was born. Disease and famine ravaged the continent, and war erupted.

Yet, amidst the horror, the minotaurs rejoiced. Many perished with Istar, but the majority, working distant mines and fields, survived. They overthrew their remaining masters and in fragmented groups headed home.

Home was now two vast islands on the eastern edge of the Blood Sea. Nethosak and Morthosak were nearly intact, a sign, so all believed, that Sargas had delivered his children from the Cataclysm.

Under their new leader, Toroth, the minotaurs looked to the east. Toroth expanded the new island empire, claiming stretches of the Courrain never before explored. Even after his death in 21 AC while fighting sea barbarians, Toroth's vision guided his people for generations to come.

Emboldened, the minotaurs also began to resettle the coast of Ansalon. Unfortunately, contact with the continent would bring them to the attention of a new tyrant, the dread Lord Ariakas.

A servant of Takhisis, the charismatic Ariakas gathered disenchanted humans and others into the dragonarmies in 340 AC. Ogres, goblins, and more joined his ranks. The minotaurs, too, came under his sway, albeit more reluctantly. Taken in as "allies," their position was more that of the slave-soldiers of old.

As Ariakas advanced over Ansalon, the minotaurs pushed through Balifor and, in 353 AC, prepared to attack the elves. They struck several times at the border, but were stopped short. With Ariakas's death that same year, the dragonarmies collapsed and the elves routed the minotaurs.

Left in flux, the empire did not stabilize until the rise of Chot Es-Kalin in 368 AC. Chot tightened the reins on the legions and reestablished ties with the temple of Sargas. He built the most elaborate Circus ever. Following Toroth's lead, Chot expanded the empire's reach. By the fifteenth year of his rule, minotaurs had spread to fourteen colonies.

But in that fifteenth year came the Summer of Chaos.

In 383 AC the very gods battled amongst themselves. Horrors never before seen walked Krynn. Dragons of molten lava, shadows capable of erasing a person from time—these and other monstrosities ravaged Krynn. The Maelstrom, the whirlpool in the midst of the Blood Sea, ceased to be.

For the empire, the threat manifested in the form of the crustacean Magori and their serpentine master, the Coil. The Magori swarmed over ships and slaughtered colonies. Not until Mithas did the creatures encounter resistance. There, Sargas, god of the minotaurs, and Kiri-Jolith, the bison-headed god of just cause, put aside their differences and protected their people. The Knights of Neraka, who had come as conquerors, joined the minotaurs. Mortal heroes appeared, most notably Aryx Dragoneye. From the east came the Kazelati, followers of the legendary renegade, Kaz.

Sailing to Ansalon, Sargas and a small band of minotaurs and humans vanquished the demon serpent, but in the terrible struggle Sargas vanished and was feared slain. Bereft of the Coil's control, the Magori were easily routed. The minotaurs had won, but at the cost of half their people.

However, distrust between the humans, the imperium, and the Kazelati grew quickly now that no threat bound them together. Chot sought to force the Kazelati into the empire but failed. The Kazelati sailed off to their uncharted homeland, vanishing. An unsteady peace existed between the empire and the knighthood.

Any dreams of expanding its tiny hold on Ansalon were shattered by the coming of Malystryx, only a year later. Even the minotaurs knew better than to face the great leviathan. But, for reasons unexplained, the isles went virtually untouched by the dragon, and the minotaurs turned ever more to the east and the unchecked growth they might find there.

The most recent history of the empire is known only from hearsay. Chot still rules, but his reign has grown corrupt. Despite his age, he has succeeded in dispatching all challengers.

A new sect has arisen in the absence of the gods, who departed after the Summer of Chaos. The Forerunners have expanded their numbers rapidly throughout the imperium. Their vague tenets suggest that the lost loved ones of a minotaur remain around them, guiding them. The high priestess claims to speak directly to the dead and bear their messages.

There is contact with Neraka again. Much of it may rely on the health of the emperor, though, for others of rank do not trust the humans.

With the dragon overlords in control, Ansalon need not fear the minotaurs. No doubt they will be content to continue spreading east and, if so, they will become less a factor in Ansalon, eventually perhaps vanishing from the continent's history forever.

Martinus of Palanthas
35 SC

CHAPTER I

NIGHT OF BLOOD

Zokun Es-Kalin, first cousin of the emperor, Ship Master of the House of Kalin's merchant fleet . . .

They found Zokun at his estate on the wooded, northern edge of the imperial capital of Nethosak. He was fast asleep in his plush, down-filled bed. Although in command of a mighty fleet of some two hundred ships, he himself had not gone to sea for years and had no desire to do so. Zokun preferred the rewards of power to the work, and many of his tasks were handled by well-trained subordinates who knew their proper place in the imperium.

A bottle of rich and heady briarberry wine, one of the finest produced in the empire and coveted even by the lesser races beyond, stood empty next to three others previously-drained. A slim, brown form beside the fat, snoring minotaur turned over in her sleep. This was not his mate, Hila, but a younger female who hoped soon to take Hila's place.

And so she did, dying along with the Ship Master. The helmed assassins dispatched her with one stroke—compared to the four needed to gut her drunken lover. Both perished swiftly.

No servants heard them cry out. None of Zokun's family came to his aid. Most of the former had been rounded up and taken away. The latter, including Hila, had been slain at exactly the same time as the venerable Ship Master and his mistress.

The feminine hand took the long quill pen, dipped it in a rich, red ink, and drew a line through Zokun's name. The wielder of the quill took care not to spill any of the ink on her silky gold and sable robes. She moved the pen to another name—

Grisov Es-Neros, councilor to the emperor and patriarch of the house most closely allied with that of Kalin . . .

Grisov was a scarred, thin minotaur whose fur was almost snow white. His snout had a wrinkled, deflated appearance, and over the years his brow had enveloped his eyes. Despite his grizzled countenance, the patriarch was hardly infirm. His reflexes were still those of the young champion of the Great Circus he had been years before the bloody war against the aquatic Magori. His well-schooled, well-paid healers encouraged him to sleep at a proper hour, but Grisov continued to take his late-night walks, a cherished tradition to him and others in this area of Nethosak. Grisov liked to survey his fiefdom, reminding himself that, as long as Chot was kept in power, the children of Neros would profit. He had no qualms about what part he had played over the years in propping up the emperor; the strongest and most cunning always triumphed.

The street did not seem as well tended as when he was young. Grisov recalled immaculate streets of white marble with nary a sign of refuse. These days, all sorts of trash littered the avenues. Bits and pieces of old food, broken ale bottles, and rotting vegetation offended the patriarch's sensibility. One large piece of trash, a snoring, drunken sailor, snuggled against the high, spiked wall of the abode of one of Grisov's nephews, a wastrel who lived off the hard work of his uncle.

It was all the fault of the young generation. The young could be blamed for everything. They had never learned the discipline of their elders.

Two able warriors clad in thigh-length, leather-padded metal kilts, colored sea-blue and green—the official clan colors—accompanied the robed minotaur. Each carried a long, double-edged axe shined to a mirror finish and etched with the Neros symbol—a savage wave washing over rocks—in the center of the head. Grisov thought the guards a nuisance, but at least this pair knew not to speak unless spoken to. The guards knew his routine well, knew what stops their master would make, knew what comments he would murmur and how they ought to respond.

Yet, there was one change in the routine this night. Grisov had no intention of letting drunkards invade his domain.

"Kelto, see that piece of garbage on his way. I'll not have him sully this street!"

"Aye, patriarch." With a look of resignation, the young warrior headed toward the snoring sailor.

A whistling sound made the patriarch's ears stiffen. Recognition of what that sound presaged dawned just a second later—a second too late.

A gurgling noise made the elder warrior turn to see his guard transfixed, a wooden shaft piercing his throat.

As the hapless warrior fell, Grisov turned to Kelto—only to find him sprawled on the ground, his blood already pooling on the street.

Peering around, the elder minotaur discovered that the drunken sailor had vanished.

A decoy.

Grisov reached for his sword and cried, "Villains! Cowards! Come to me, you dishonorable—"

Two bolts struck him from opposite directions, one piercing a lung, the other sinking deep into his back. Blood spilled over his luxurious blue robe, overwhelming the green Neros symbol on his chest.

With a short gasp, the patriarch dropped his blade and collapsed beside his guards.

A young minotaur, clad in plain, ankle-length robes of white trimmed with red, approached the senior priestess, bringing a silver flask of wine for the empty chalice sitting next to the pile of parchments. The priestess looked up briefly, then flicked her eyes toward the half-melted candle by which she checked her lists. The servant glanced that way but saw nothing. The servant finished refilling the goblet, then quickly backed away.

"Tyra de-Proul?" asked the senior priestess. She was a chestnut-colored female, still attractive in the eyes of her kind. Her words were whispered to the open air. She fixed her gaze in the general direction of a lengthy silk tapestry depicting a white, almost ghostlike bird ascending to the starry heavens. "You are certain?" the priestess asked the emptiness.

A moment later, her ears twitched in clear satisfaction. She nodded, then looked over the lists. Many lines were already crossed out, but she soon located the one she desired.

A smile crossed her visage as she brought the quill down. "Another page complete."

On the island of Kothas, sister realm to Mithas and a two-day journey from the capital, Tyra de-Proul stirred from sleep. Her mate had been due to return this evening from his voyage to Sargonath, a minor minotaur colony located on the northeastern peninsula of Ansalon, but he had not yet arrived. Feeling pensive, Tyra pushed back her thick, gray mane and rose.

Jolar's ship might just be late. That shouldn't bother her at all, yet some vague dread insisted on disturbing her asleep.

The tall, athletic female poured some water. As appointed administrator of the emperor's interests, Tyra made constant sea trips between the imperial capital and this island's principal city of Morthosak. Jolar's lateness could readily be attributed to any number of innocent causes, even foul weather.

A muffled sound beyond her door brought her to full attention. At this hour, no one in the house other than the sentries should be awake, and the sentries knew to make their rounds without causing clamor of any sort.

Tyra seized her sword and scabbard, then headed toward the door. Weapon drawn, she opened it—

And was stunned to see a frantic struggle taking place between Jolar and three helmed minotaurs at the foot of the steps.

One of the intruders had a hand over her mate's muzzle, but Jolar twisted free and shouted, "Flee, Tyra! The house is under siege! There is no—"

He gasped, a dagger in his side. Jolar fell to the floor.

Like all minotaurs, Tyra had been trained from childhood first and foremost as a warrior. As a young female, she had helped fight back the vile Magori when the crustaceans rose from the sand and surf, the destruction of all minotaurs their sole desire. Never in her life had she turned from a battle, whether on the field or in the political arena.

With a savage cry, Tyra threw herself down the steps, her sword cutting the air as she descended.

The nearest foe stumbled against her mate's corpse. Tyra thrust the blade through the helmed assassin's unprotected throat. Before he had even dropped to the floor, she did battle with the second, a young female who moved with the haughtiness of one who thought that before her stood merely a decrepit elder. Tyra caught the intruder's blade and twisted it to the side. She kicked at her opponent and watched with satisfaction as the latter went flying back into a nearby wall, knocked unconscious.

In the dim illumination, she made out two dead bodies in the lower hall. One also wore a helm, but the other Tyra recognized even though he lay muzzle down.

Mykos. Her eldest son. In three days he would have become the newest addition to the Imperial Guard. General Rahm Es-Hestos, the commander of the emperor's elite, had personally recommended Mykos, a moment of great pride for his mother.

An axe had done him in. His blood still pooled beside his hacked torso.

Tyra screamed, swinging anew at the last of her attackers. He continued to back away from her.

"Stand still so I can smite the head from your body, you dishonorable dog! My mate—my children!—demand your blood!"

Still edging away, her opponent said nothing.

Too late did the obvious occur to the outraged minotaur. Tyra de-Proul wheeled quickly, but not quickly enough.

The female assassin whom she thought had been knocked unconscious stabbed Tyra through the heart.

"Stupid old cow," the assassin muttered.

Tyra slipped to the floor and joined her mate in death.

So many names crossed out. So few remaining.

She looked over the pages, noting the survivors. Some looked to be of no major consequence, but a handful tugged at her, urgently.

A chill wind suddenly coursed through the stone chamber that served as her private sanctum. She quickly protected the candle.

My Lady Nephera . . . came a voice in her head, a voice rasping and striving for breath.

Nephera glanced beyond the candle, seeing only glimpses of a shadowy figure at the edge of her vision. At times, she could make out details—such as a hooded cloak—and within the cloak a minotaur unusually gaunt of form. Of the eyes that stared back at her, she sometimes made out the whites, but this monstrous phantasm had no pupils.

The cloak hung in damp tatters with glimpses of pale flesh beneath. Whenever this particular visitor appeared, the smell of the sea always seemed to accompany him—the sea as the eternal graveyard.

As she reached for a grape from the bowl set by her side—the only sustenance she would permit herself this glorious night—the elegantly clad High Priestess of the Temple of the Forerunners waited for the ominous figure to speak again.

The shade's decaying mouth did not move, but once more Lady Nephera heard a grating voice. *Four of the Supreme Circle now join me in death.*

She knew three names already, but the addition of a fourth pleased her. "Who? Name all four so that I can be certain!"

General Tohma, Boril, General Astos . . .

All names she had. "Who else?"

Kesk the Elder.

"Ah, excellent." Pulling free one of the parchments, Nephera located the name and gave it a swift, inky stroke—as lethal to the council member in question as the axes and swords that had actually killed him. The elimination of the highest-ranking members of the Supreme Circle, the august governing body under the emperor, gave her immense satisfaction.

They, more than most, she held responsible for all that had happened to her and her husband—and to the empire.

Thinking of her mate, the Forerunner priestess scowled. "My husband's hand-picked warriors move quick, but not quick enough. This should be finished by now!"

Send out your own, responded the gaunt shadow. *Your trusted Protectors, mistress?*

She would have dearly loved to do so, but Hotak had insisted otherwise. This had to be done without the temple. The military would not look with favor on her husband if it appeared that the Forerunners influenced his actions.

"No. We shall leave this to my husband. The triumph must be his and his alone." Lady Nephera picked up the stack of parchments, her intense black gaze burning into each name. "Still, the temple will have its say."

Throughout the length and span of the empire, the Night of Blood continued relentlessly.

On Mito, three days' journey east of the imperial capital, the governor of the most populated island colony rushed forth to greet two massive vessels that had sailed into port. An honor guard had quickly been arranged, for who but an important dignitary would arrive without warning and with such a show of force? The captain of the first vessel marched a squad of helmed warriors down to salute the assembled well-wishers—and then executed the governor where he stood.

On the island of Duma, the home of General Kroj, commander of the empire's southern forces and hero of the battles of Turak Major and Selees, became the scene of a pitched battle. The fight went on until dawn, when the barriers of the general's estate were finally broken down by his own troops, who joined the attackers. Kroj committed ritual suicide with a dagger even as helmed fighters burst down the door to his study. They would find his family already dead, their throats slit by Kroj just prior to his own demise.

In Mithas, Edan Es-Brog, the high priest of the Temple of Sargonnas, would be discovered dead in his sleep, a mixture of poisons in his evening potion.

Veria de-Goltyn, Chief Captain of the eastern fleet, drowned as she sought to escape her burning ship. Her own captains had been paid to turn on her.

Konac, imperial taxmaster, was stabbed more than a dozen times at the door of the emperor's coffers. A stronger figure than his rotund appearance indicated, Konac would outlast his guards and two assassins, making it to just within a few yards of the Imperial Guard's headquarters before dying. No one within heard his final choked warning.

A massive fleet, organized quickly and secretly over the course of weeks and combining the might of over three dozen turncoat generals and captains, spread out over the expanse of minotaur interests. Some of them had been on their journeys for days already. Before the night would conclude, twenty-two colonial governors, their principal officers, and hundreds of loyal subordinates would be executed. All but a handful of the major territories and settlements within a week's reach of the main island would be under the iron control of Hotak's followers.

All of this, Lady Nephera saw as it happened. She had eyes everywhere. She knew more than her husband's lackeys. Even the emperor, with his complex and far-reaching network of messengers and spies, knew but a fraction of what the high priestess knew.

Thinking of the emperor, Nephera turned her brooding eyes to one particular page, reading the only name still listed. No furious stain of ink expunged this name's existence, yet by her estimate, only minutes remained before she would have the ultimate pleasure.

The high priestess read the name over and over, picturing the puffy, overfed countenance, the vain, ambitious, clownish visage.

Chot Es-Kalin.

In his younger days, the massive, graying minotaur had been the scourge of the Circus, the unbeatable champion to whom all had deferred in admiration. Chot the Terrible, he was called. Chot the Invincible! Over the span of his life and decades-long rule, scores of would-be rivals had fallen to his bloody battle-axe. No minotaur had ever held the title of emperor for so many years.

"More wine, my lord?"

Chot studied the slim, dark-brown female lounging next to him on the vast silk-sheeted bed. She had not only the energy of youth, but the beauty as well. Chot's last mate had died over a decade ago, and since that time he had preferred enticing visitors to a regular companion. The much-scarred emperor knew that this added to the list of grievances his political foes spouted about him, but he did not care. His foes could do nothing so long as he accepted the imperial challenges and faced down his opponents in the Great Circus.

They could do nothing so long as each of their champions fell dead at his feet.

He shifted his great girth and handed his mistress the empty goblet. Years of living the glory of an emperor had taken some toll on his body, but Chot still considered himself the ultimate warrior, the envy of other males, and the desire of all females.

"Is that enough, my lord?" his companion said as she topped off his drink.

"Enough, Maritia." Chot took a gulp of the rich, red liquid, then looked the female warrior over, savoring the curve of her lithe form. Some female minotaurs looked too much like males. Chot preferred curves. A female should look like a female, especially when she had been granted the glorious company of her emperor.

His bed companion replaced the squat wine bottle on the carved, marble table. The well-cleaned remains of a roasted goat sat atop a silver tray next to the bottle, and beside that stood a wooden bowl filled with exotic fruit shipped to the capital from one of the farthest and most tropical colonies.

Maritia leaned forward, rubbing the soft tip of her muzzle against him. Curiously, the image of her father flashed into his mind. Chot had recently solved the problem of her insufficiently loyal and increasingly irritating father by sending him far, far away on a mission of some import—and some danger as well. If he succeeded, his glory would reflect on Chot. If he died in combat—a more likely outcome—so much the better.

Chot belched, and the world briefly swam around him. The emperor rolled onto his back, snorting. Enough entertainment for tonight. Time he got some sleep.

There was a fuzzy sound in the distance.

"What's that?" he rumbled, trying to rise.

"I heard nothing, my lord," replied Maritia. She rubbed her graceful hand over his matted brown and gray fur.

Chot relaxed again. It would be a shame when he had to banish her, but she would never forgive him once she found out what he had done to her father.

"Sleep, my lord," Maritia cooed. "Sleep forever."

He jarred awake—in time to see the dagger poised above his head.

Drunken, tired, and out of shape, Chot nonetheless reacted with swiftness. He caught her wrist and managed to twist the blade free. The dagger clattered on the marble floor.

"What in the name of Argon's Chain do you think you're doing?" he roared, his head pounding.

In response, she raked her long, sharp nails across the side of his muzzle.

Roaring, Chot released the fool. Maritia scrambled away from the bed as the emperor put a hand to his bloody face.

"Vixen!" Legs protesting, the immense minotaur rose. "You little cow!"

She glared at the last insult, one of the worst things anyone could call a minotaur. Chot stood a head taller and still carried much muscle under his portly girth, but the female seemed strangely unafraid.

The emperor snorted. Maritia would learn fear.

Then he heard the same fuzzy noise as earlier, only closer.

"What's that?" he mumbled, forgetting her for the moment. "Who's fighting out there?"

"That would be your Imperial Guard, my lord," Maritia said, pronouncing his title as if it were excrement. "They are busy falling to the swords and axes of your enemies."

"What's that?" Chot struggled to think clearly. His guards. He had to call his guards. "Sentries! Attend me!"

Maritia smirked. "They are otherwise detained, my lord."

The emperor's stomach suddenly churned. Too much wine, too much goat. Chot put one hand on the bed. "I must think. I must think."

"Think all you like, but my father should be here shortly."

"Your . . . father?" Battling against the nausea and the pounding headache, Chot froze. "Hotak's here? Impossible. I sent him to the mainland weeks ago!"

"And despite your treachery, he's returned. Returned to demand the justice due to him, due the entire imperium!"

With a roar, Chot lunged for her. Maritia eluded his grasp. The emperor turned, seized his favorite axe, and swung wildly. He came nowhere near the treacherous female, though he did drive her back.

"Assassin! Traitor! Traitors!"

Maritia attempted to retrieve her dagger, but Chot swung again. The heavy blade of the twin-edged axe buried itself in his bed, cutting through expensive sheets, through the rich, down padding, and even through the oak frame.

As the bed collapsed in a heap, the emperor stumbled back. Through bleary eyes he glared at Hotak's daughter.

"Slay me if you can," Maritia sneered. "But you'll not live more than a few minutes longer." Her ears twitched toward the window behind Chot. "You hear that?"

Keeping his gaze on the female at all times, Chot stepped back to the balcony. He glanced over his shoulder just long enough to see that the palace grounds swarmed with dark figures heading toward the building.

"Father will be here very soon now," Maritia called to him.

"Then he'll find you begging him to save your life . . . cow!"

Chot stumbled toward her, reaching clumsily with one hand while with the other he threatened her with the axe. Maritia dodged readily, leading Chot on a merry chase through the room, mocking his growing rage and taunting him with her derision.

He swung wildly. Rounded crystalline vases, minotaur statuettes of emerald, tapestries of spun gold, marble icons of dragons and other fearsome beasts—the treasures he had accumulated through his lengthy reign—scattered in shards.

His own body finally rebelled. Even as fists began to pound upon the door, Chot the Invincible fell against the broken bed, his head spinning, his insides a maelstrom.

"Chot the Magnificent," he heard Maritia mutter. "Rather you should be called Chot the Pathetic."

"I'll . . . I'll . . . ." The emperor could say no more.

He heard her open the door, heard the sounds of armed and armored figures marching into his chamber.

"And this is supposed to be the supreme warrior, the epitome of what our people seek to be?"

The emperor fought to raise his head.

They wore the traditional silver helms. Nose guards ran along their muzzles. Their breastplates were also silver, with the ancient symbol of the condor clutching the axe emblazoned on the chest in deep crimson. Well-worn, padded-metal kilts with red tips at the bottom completed their outfits.

These were his soldiers, warriors of the legions—and they had dared such treachery!

In the forefront of the traitorous band stood their leader. Although otherwise clad as his companions, he also wore the richly crested helmet reserved for the highest generals of the empire. The crest, made of thick, excellent horse hair, hung far back. Over his shoulders hung a long, flowing crimson cape.

Dark brown of fur, slightly over seven feet, well-muscled, and with very angular features for one of his race, the leader glared down at his lord with distaste. A pommel-handled sword hung in the scabbard at his side; a large battle-axe was in his grip.

"Chot Es-Kalin," announced the newcomer, nearly spitting out the name.

"Hotak de-Droka," responded the emperor. The de- before the clan name indicated House Droka had its roots on the island of Kothas, considered, especially by those who bore the more regal Es-, the lesser of the two kingdoms making up the heart of the empire.

Hotak looked to his daughter. His expression turned even grimmer. "You've sacrificed far too much, daughter."

"But it wasn't so terrible a sacrifice, father," she responded, turning back to smile coldly at Chot. "Only passing minutes."

"You . . . damned vixen!" Chot struggled to rise. If he could just get his hands around her throat—

The emperor fell to his hands and knees again. "I feel sick," he murmured.

General Hotak kicked at Chot's side. The immense, graying minotaur dropped flat, moaning.

Hotak snorted. He took a step toward his emperor. "Chot Es-Kalin. Chot the Invincible. Chot the Terrible." The one-eyed commander raised his weapon high. In the light cast by the torches of his followers, the symbol of the rearing horse etched into the axe head seemed to flare to life. "Chot the *Fool*. Chot the *Lying*. Chot the *Treacherous*. Time to put your misery and our shame to an end."

Chot could not think. He could not stand. He could no longer even raise a finger. This had to be a mistake! How could this happen?

"I am Chot," he mumbled, looking down in utter bewilderment. He felt the contents of his stomach finally coming up. "I am your *emperor*."

"No more," said Hotak. "No more."

The axe came down.

When it was over, the general handed the bloody weapon to one of his aides then removed his helmet. Dark brown hair with a touch of gray flowed behind his head.

Nodding toward the body, Hotak commanded, "Remove that blubbery carcass for burning. Make sure nothing re mains. As for the head . . . see to it that there's a high pole set up at the very entrance to the palace grounds. Make certain that anyone who passes by will be able to see it from some distance. Understood?"

"Aye, General—aye, my lord!" the warrior said, correcting himself.

General Hotak de-Droka looked at the soldier, then at his daughter. Maritia smiled and went down on one knee.

One by one, the rest of those who followed him knelt before he who had slain Chot the Terrible, knelt before the new emperor of the minotaur race.

CHAPTER ÏÏ

TRÏUMPH AND DESPAÏR

In the depths of the vast, marble-columned Temple of the Forerunners, the thick, oak door to the high priestess's sanctum swung open, and a deep but anxious voice called out, "Mother!"

The two veiled acolytes stepped quickly to the side. Nephera turned from her desk to see a tall, young minotaur charging toward her. His blunt, fearsome muzzle and blazing, crimson-tinged eyes reminded Nephera of her father, who had perished in the great war some decades before.

Ardnor, her eldest son and, in many ways, her personal favorite, strode through the chamber like an angry bear. He was clad in a simple, ankle-length robe of plain, gray cloth, befitting his high rank in the temple. Ardnor had been among the first to join her black-helmed Protectors and had been appointed First Master of the armed sentinels of the Forerunner faith. Her son had transformed the faithful into a legion fanatical to his mother's cause.

"Calm yourself, Ardnor. What is it?"

"I'm asking again. Let me take the Protectors out! We've been chafing for action, chafing to do our part! Let Chot understand that his enemies are not only Father's troops but the unparalleled might of the temple!"

The high priestess dismissed her servants with a glance. Heads bowed, the two young females withdrew.

Nephera rose, walked over to her son, and looked up into his eyes. One hand caressed the rough hide on the side of his muzzle. Like Hotak, Ardnor bore many small scars from previous combats.

"You need not concern yourself over Chot, my son. He is dead. Dead at your father's own hand."

"Dead?" His eyes lit up. "Dead? It's over, then?"

Lady Nephera led him back to her desk. She poured him wine then replied, "Nearly so. Some names remain, but I expect those to be crossed out before long."

He gulped the wine, his eyes momentarily fixing on one of the tapestries in the room. A half-seen figure clad in a free-flowing robe, seemingly made of mist, guided a pair of young minotaurs over an old wooden bridge underneath which lay an ominous, black gap. The image had been rendered in such fine detail that, although barely visible, the ghostly guardian looked almost ready to step out into the real world.

The images portrayed on the other tapestries were just as vivid. They had been sewn under the guidance of the high priestess herself. They represented the tenets of the Forerunner faith, how the spirits of the past generations interacted with the living, guiding them through crises. Tapestries similar to these could be found throughout the temple, but also in the private homes of the faithful, who donated dearly for the honor of owning one that had been blessed by the Lady Nephera.

"Anyone of significance?" asked Ardnor.

"A few. General Rahm Es-Hestos, commander of the Imperial Guard. Governor Zen of Amur. Lord Hybos on Kothas. Kesk the Younger and Tiribus—"

"The Chief Councilor of the Supreme Circle," muttered Ardnor. The empty goblet in his hand crumpled under his tightening grip. "He should've been the *first* one to die. He'll cause trouble."

"There still remain elements of House Kalin," the high priestess went on, ignoring his interruption. "The younger brothers of our late, unlamented emperor and his—" She looked up abruptly, staring in the direction of her eager son. "What's that?"

"I didn't say anyth—" Ardnor broke off as he realized that his mother spoke not to him, but rather to something over his shoulder . . . something beyond his mortal ken.

She heard a whisper, a child's frightened whisper, though Ardnor could hear nothing. Nor could he see what his mother saw—a floating form, a faint shadow of a young, very pale female. Her face was ravaged, nearly furless and full of pockmarks. The high priestess sensed the vestiges of some great sickness.

"The house afire," Nephera murmured, her eyes rounding. The words she spoke repeated what was told to her by the shade. "Axe . . . death in every room. Blood on the staircase."

Well-versed in the ways of his mother, Ardnor kept silent, his eyes narrowing.

"The names!" Nephera demanded. "The names! All of them!"

She seized a quill, dipped it in ink, and began scouring the pages. One by one, Lady Nephera drew lines through those of House Kalin, each crossed-out name punctuated by a grunt of satisfaction. The list grew shorter.

"More," she warned the flickers of darkness surrounding her. "There should be more."

Ardnor leaned forward.

"Fire above . . ." the high priestess murmured, her gaze staring off into the distance. "Trapped. Axes clashing . . .

the dead . . . young . . . old. Fire everywhere . . . fire everywhere . . ."

A throaty chuckle escaped the priestess. Her hand moved
as of its own volition and struck out a few more names.

"They are gone," she said, looking up at Ardnor and smiling now. "They are no more. Clan Kalin is no more."

"All dead? Including his brothers?"

"Each of the estates is surrounded, and most are engulfed
in fire. By morning there will be nothing but ash. Any not
slain by the sword shall be purified by the flame . . . and so
removed from this mortal plane." A fervent look crossed her
handsome features. "And with them goes the last blood traces
of the old regime. The capital, the island, belongs to us!"

Ardnor stood there for a moment, letting it all sink in.
Finally, Ardnor asked, "And what about Kothas?"

"As secure as Mithas, my son. Even as we speak, the
net tightens on the greater colonies. Amur, Mito, Tengis,
Broka—they and all the major settlements that make up the
shield of the empire! The smaller colonies and even those
beyond the secure borders will also fall into line. They
cannot survive otherwise. They will all acknowledge your
father as the new emperor . . . and at his ascension, you shall
be named heir."

This, more than anything, he wished to hear. "He'll do it,
then? He'll end the imperial combats? Make the succession
by blood?"

"Of course. Have I not promised that from the beginning?"

Ardnor could barely contain himself. The crimson in his
eyes burned. "Emperor . . ." A grin crossed his coarse features. "Emperor Ardnor the First."

"After your father, of course."

"Of course."

She stretched out her hand, the gold-trimmed sleeve of
her sable robe sliding back past her wrist. "Now be good and

go calm your Protectors. Their part in all of this will come soon enough."

He knelt before her and kissed her tapering fingers. The high priestess touched the top of his head, giving him the blessing of the temple. At last, Ardnor rose and, with one final bow, departed her sanctum.

Returning to her lists, Lady Nephera resumed scouring the pages, silently reveling at the sight of each victim of this night's work. With special pleasure she again read the name of Chot and his family.

Her gaze paused at Rahm Es-Hestos.

The high priestess looked up. "Takyr . . . ?"

From the faint, shifting patches of darkness surrounding her tall, wooden desk, a single swirl of shadow separated itself. As it neared her, Lady Nephera caught an almost imperceptible glimpse of the cadaverous form under the tattered cloak.

"Find out why Rahm or Tiribus haven't been destroyed by now. Kesk the Younger, too, although he is not as important as the first two. How is it possible that they've escaped our net? Someone faltered in their duty! Go! Find the truth!"

She felt rather than saw the shadow depart. General Rahm and the others would not long remain at large. There was nowhere they could hide from her. Nowhere at all.

Faros stumbled out of the seedy tavern, his head filled with too much drink and his money pouch emptied from gambling.

Dull light shone from the tavern and the raucous sounds of merriment continued inside. Two axe-wielding members of the State Guard, their armor—all gray save the crimson condor symbol worn on their breast plates—marched quickly by, despite the late hour and the long-standing decrees concerning noise and violence. The proprietor had agreements with certain high-ranking members of the Guard, agreements for which he well paid. The pair ignored Faros, barely glancing at the seedy structures lining the grimy avenue, as they hurried on their way.

Three young minotaurs burst through the entrance, the one in the middle dragged by his companions.

"What'll we do with him?" muttered one of the able pair.

"We'll leave 'im by the gate to the house. Old Majar's not someone I'll face with his son like this! He's liable to ask us how Luko got his ear shorn off."

The first snorted. "I told him not to join that game. You saw that one with the patch. He had a necklace of ears on him! I still say he set Luko up."

Their conversation faded away as they hurried on.

Over Faros's pounding head, the half-decayed sign marking the dank establishment as Challenger's Roost swung back and forth, the loud squeaking of the rusted metal adding to his misery.

He groaned as the pounding multiplied. "Great Sargonnas," the bleary minotaur prayed, calling upon the god who had sacrificed himself for his people more than a generation ago. "Let me find my way home to my bed without my father finding out. And if you can manage that miracle . . ."

Once a major avenue, the street upon which the tavern stood still had a grimy, sputtering fountain in the center. The triumphant minotaur warrior posed atop it had lost the upper half of his axe, and his features had been chipped away by drunken vandals. Below, two of the dragonhead spouts dribbled rather than gushed and, in the daytime, the water all six spat would have had a markedly mossy tint to it. Still, Faros stuck his head under one set of stone jaws and let the cool liquid rush over him.

The water stank slightly and did little to soothe his throbbing skull. Pulling free, Faros shook his head, sending his lengthy, waved mane flying. He snorted a few times to disperse excess liquid from his nostrils then trudged toward his horse.

"Hold still," he told the beige charger waiting for him. He slumped forward onto the neck of his steed. The horse knew the way home, just as it knew the way to the Challenger's Roost. The animal had made the journey back and forth many, many times.

Half in a stupor, Faros paid little attention to his surroundings. Because of that, he did not notice the eerie emptiness of the most popular thoroughfares, nor the fact that most of the lamps along the way had been doused. Nor did he notice the lack of sentries and torchlight as he neared the gates of his home—the vast, walled estate of the emperor's youngest brother.

Even though he was the least favored of Chot's siblings, Gradic Es-Kalin benefited from his connections to power. High, stone walls surrounded the plush, three-story villa, and within those walls was a garden of sculpted trees and beautiful stone paths. Servants kept everything trimmed. Among the elite of the capital, Gradic's estate was considered a prime example of sculpted perfection.

If his master did not notice much around him, his horse did. As they drew closer, the trained steed slowed, growing hesitant. At last the horse stopped and whinnied nervously. Faros looked up, trying to focus blood-shot eyes.

"What's gotten into you?" he demanded of the animal. "Move!"

Even for so late at night, the estate—the entire vicinity, for that matter—was deathly quiet. There were no sentries at the gates, and all the torches had either been doused or removed. In fact, the only illumination from in the house itself was a wildly flickering light in several upper windows that looked like nothing less than—

Fire!

His first thought was to turn the horse around and ride back to the security of the tavern.

Hands shaking, Faros urged his reluctant mount toward the burning edifice.

Just within the walls of the estate, several helmed figures armed with swords and axes watched the flames. Curiously, none of the onlookers made any move to fight the fire or to aid those who might be left inside. In fact, to Faros's horrified gaze, they actually looked happy, laughing and clapping each other on the back.

They did not notice him as he steered the horse away.

Sweating with fear, Faros rode cautiously along the perimeter of the stone wall until he came to a section recently damaged by a fierce storm.

Securing his horse and taking one last anxious glance around, Faros scrambled up and over the wall. As he landed, he drew his sword and, crouched over, scurried toward the burning building.

While most of the exterior consisted of handcrafted stonework, much of the interior was covered with lavish wood paneling imported from the outer colonies, extravagant cloth tapestries sewn by notable artisans, and other highly flammable material. The luxurious decor was now the building's downfall. The fire might leave the exterior nearly untouched, but the inside would burn like the charred belly of a potter's oven.

As he slipped through a battered side door, smoke from within caused his eyes to tear and his throat to constrict. Blinking constantly, Faros stumbled forward—and in the process tripped over a large object lying just inside the entranceway.

The unarmored guard had perished quickly, the shaft in his chest having struck his heart. Just beyond lay another sentry, her death caused by several thrusts of a blade. Both were distant cousins hired because of their high proficiency in combat, which made their deaths all the more unsettling.

"Father!" Faros shouted. "Mother!" The loud crackle of flames made it doubtful that anyone would hear him unless they stood very near. "Crespos!" he added, trying for his elder brother. "Where are you?"

No one responded.

Everywhere lay bloody, contorted bodies wearing the black, crimson-tipped kilts of the Kalin clan, but none were Faros's family. His anxiety growing, he continued to call out, but the only sounds he heard came from the fire.

The stained, cedar railings of the winding stairway leading up to the family quarters had been shattered and many of the steps were chopped to ruins. The thick red carpet at the base of the stairs lay twisted around the limp body of a helmed figure. Scattered nearby, three other assassins sprawled in various poses of violent death.

Struck dumb, Faros edged up the steps. Halfway up, he found the bodies of his brother and sister. Tupo, two years younger than him, had been stabbed through the throat. His eyes still gaped in astonishment. Resdia, his darker-furred younger sister, who so often had listened earnestly as he regaled her with his stories of wild nights out, lay half draped over Tupo, as if her final act had been to try to comfort him. One of the assassins had apparently caught her from behind, between the shoulder blades. Her short sword lay unbloodied on the ground.

Tearing himself away from the pair, a shaking Faros came upon his mother. He knelt down in shock.

An axe had done her in, the fatal blow delivered to her chest after she had already received several lesser wounds on various parts of her body. At least two of the intruders had perished at her hand before she was overcome. Faros laid his sword down and cradled her head, brushing back the blood-matted hair from her face.

An ominous creak from above the stairway made him stiffen. The next instant, the ceiling over the bottom portion of the stairs collapsed—timbers, plaster, and charred stone falling in a blazing inferno.

Ducking as he ran, Faros fled up the curving path of the ruined stairway. At the top of the steps, he came across two more family guards who had been hacked to death by zealous opponents.

Trying to see through the thickening smoke, Faros called out again. "Crespos! Father! Can you hear me?"

The heat had grown more intense. He had little time left to search. Soon the fire would eat away at the last of the supporting timbers.

"Father! Cres—"

From far to his right came a strangled sound that might have been a voice.

Starting down the hall, Faros saw little more than smoke. The smoke grew so thick that he could barely see a single pace ahead. His eyes teared. His lungs burned with each strained breath.

An obstruction on the floor hidden by the thick smoke sent him tumbling forward, his sword flying from his grasp.

His muzzle collided with something soft.

A hand.

Faros frantically pushed away—and found himself staring into the vacant eyes of his elder brother.

Crespos, the brother everyone admired, the brother whom their father had always held up as a true and honorable minotaur, had died from a single axe wound across the neck. The vicious blow had nearly decapitated the muscular fighter.

Burying his face in his brother's blood-matted chest, Faros wept. His mother, his brothers, his sister, had all been slain.

Someone coughed.

Startled, Faros looked up. Clearing his throat, he shouted, "Who's there? Who's there? Father?"

Someone coughed again.

Eyes hopeful, Faros pulled himself away and advanced through the choking smoke. Yet a third time, someone coughed.

Unfortunately, the kneeling figure that suddenly materialized in the smoke proved not to be his father.

"Faros!" the other gasped. "By Kalin's Horns, I'd hoped it was you!"

"Bek?"

The tawny, well-groomed minotaur with the broad, ever eager expression was more than a servant to Faros. He was almost another brother, loyal and caring.

Yet any pleasure at finding Bek faded as Chot's nephew looked down at the limp figure cradled in the kneeling servant's arms.

An axe had caught Gradic Es-Kalin at the shoulder and nearly torn away his arm. Sinew and bone were visible, hacked into a pulp. The wicked cut almost went to the breastbone. Blood caked the wound, drenching most of his father's torso.

Eyes staring, Faros came forward and knelt next to Bek. Up close, he saw that, in addition to the heavy shoulder wound, Gradic had suffered a pair of deep sword thrusts to the abdomen.

And then he saw his father's chest rise and fall, Gradic's entire body shuddering as he fought to breathe.

"Don't be hopeful," Bek said. "The traitors did their work well. He'll be dead soon. I'm sorry, Master Faros."

"What . . . what happened here?"

"They came from the darkness," replied Bek, gazing down at his honored lord. Bek had adored his master. "The sentries never gave the alarm. They must've died quickly. Everyone but the night watch was in bed. Everyone save me. I'd gone down to keep an eye out for you as you wanted, Master Faros. Went to the place I waited for you last time."

"I should've been home."

"Then you'd be dead, too. You would've, master." Bek gently rocked Gradic. "They were thorough. They knew where to find everyone, how best to strike. If not for your mother waking, they would've caught all asleep. I arrived in time to see the mistress die, her face already filled with tears for the dead children at her feet.

"Master Gradic spoke to me when I found him. He called out your name. 'Is that you, Faros?' he said. I almost said yes, to give him some last hope, but then he recognized me. 'Come to me, good Bek,' he pleaded. He told me how the cowardly fiends separated him from your mother and siblings, how they slew Master Crespos. Master Gradic fought against five and made them pay, as you can see."

Faros followed Bek's pointing finger and saw that two more of the treacherous intruders lay sprawled inside the chamber. One was headless, while the other had Gradic's trusted axe buried deep in his chest.

"Why?" Faros whispered.

"Only . . . only the lost gods know . . . why . . . my son."

They stared at Gradic, who had stirred to consciousness. A hand touched Faros's arm. "I prayed to . . . Sargonnas and Kiri-Jolith . . . that I would l-live . . . long enough . . ."

"Hush, Father. Rest. Bek and I will get you to a healer. You'll be—"

"Dead. Hear me . . . Faros. The House has . . . fallen. These were not . . . were not brigands. These . . . were soldiers! Imagine!"

"Never mind that, Father." Faros looked around, trying to find something to stanch the flow of blood. The thickening smoke boiled over them.

"Listen . . . to me!" Gradic gasped, coughing. "I fear . . . I fear that if . . . an attack . . . takes place here . . . it takes place . . . everywhere! I fear that Chot . . . himself may have fallen."

What his father said left Faros speechless. Gradic and Chot had little enough love for one another, but Chot could rely on his youngest brother's political loyalty and, in return, the emperor had rewarded Gradic with House Kalin. Chot would never permit such a heinous act against Gradic, which meant those who had done this no longer feared the emperor's wrath.

"F-Faros! You must . . . flee Mithas. A friend . . . Azak . . . you can trust. H-his ship, *Dragon's Crest* . . . sails to . . . Gol."

"Gol!" exclaimed Bek. "Your father spoke of this place the other night! One of the outermost colonies! The governor there is a former comrade of his."

Gradic touched his son's arm again. "Aye. Jubal will . . . hide you and Bek. Jubal will—" he coughed, pain contorting his battered features— "protect both of you lads."

"I'll not go without you, Father!"

"Y-you must! You *are* . . . the House now! The honor—" The elder minotaur suddenly twisted in his son's arms. Eyes closed, mouth agape, he slumped, more a rag doll than the imposing titan he had always been to his children.

Shivering, Faros knelt, staring at his father, his eyes glazed.

Bek seized the shocked minotaur by the arm. "Master Faros, listen! The house is nearly done in! Come! We must leave here now!"

Together, they started toward the hallway. Urgent voices arose from elsewhere in the vast villa.

The sharp-eyed Bek looked around. "This way! Our only chance, Master Faros!"

He led them toward a staircase at the rear. Around them, centuries-old tapestries went up in flames, prized antique weaponry melted. Faros dimly noted a jeweled axe, awarded to his grandfather for service to the empire, glittering brightly in the growing flames.

A tremendous roar shook the entire area. Both turned in dread. The floor behind them cracked then completely collapsed.

Clouds of smoke and fiery talons rose above them. Faros and Bek ran.

A figure burst through the smoke to block their way—a helmed soldier armed with a long sword.

The pair dodged into a ravaged doorway. Trying to stifle their coughing, they watched as the fearsome figure stalked past. The newcomer stood taller than either of them and appeared about half again as wide. His silver kilt with red tips marked him as a member of one of the elite legions that should have been protecting the empire, not slaughtering its highest-ranking citizens.

The hulking minotaur turned toward the half-destroyed doorway, squinting. He took a step toward them—then shouted something that was drowned out by an explosion.

"Hurry, Master Faros!" Bek pulled the dazed Faros toward the stairs, half running, half-tumbling down the steps.

The top floor caved in.

The staircase dropped. Faros caught a last glimpse of the flailing assassin just before the ceiling crushed him.

The portion of the staircase crashed to the bottom floor, and the shock sent them tumbling.

"Look out!" Bek shouted, grabbing Faros and pulling him to his feet.

A flaming timber crashed past them.

"The kitchen!" Bek shouted, pointing. He picked up a long piece of hand rail, then another, and handed it to his master.

They ran for the kitchen. The door leading to the rear of the estate had been broken and now hung loose. They stumbled out, fully expecting to be assaulted, but, to their surprise, no one awaited them.

"Your horse, Master Faros! Where is it?"

"By the broken wall. I secured him there."

"Praise Kalin's Horns! We've a chance, then. He can easily carry the two of us."

The pair reached the half-mended wall unhindered and found the well-trained animal waiting. The stench of the fire was all around them. They heard shouts and cheers.

"Stand where you are!" roared a voice.

Two helmed figures emerged from the shadows, one armed with a sword, the other with an axe.

Bek shouted a command, and the horse reared, catching the two assailants completely by surprise. The horse's heavy hooves struck the pair, sending them to a tangled heap.

"Come!" Bek shouted, jumping on the horse and reaching down for Faros.

Needing no further encouragement, Faros leaped upon the horse after Bek, and they raced off, leaving the home of Gradic to its death throes.

CHAPTER III

FALL OF AN EMPEROR

It had been a grim night. Grim but necessary, in the eyes of Bastion.

Tall, sleek, black of fur—a throwback to his father's grandfather—the second son of General Hotak de-Droka watched from horseback as his weary soldiers herded the surviving servants from the house of this particular branch of Chot's family into the barred wagons. Behind him, yet another opulent villa of the old regime burned bright with flames. The sculpted trees near the front entrance had become massive torches, and the stables to the side of the main house could not even be recognized. Fortunately, all the horses had first been herded out, for why waste such magnificent animals?

A helmed soldier prodded an elderly servant into the wagon. Impatiently, the warrior shoved the gray minotaur, sending him stumbling to his knees.

"You there!" Bastion roared, startling those around him. Penetrating eyes of coal-black glared down over a muzzle long and narrow. "Cease that! He moves as fast as he can!"

The guard in question bowed, then stammered, "A-aye, my lord! F-forgive me!"

Bastion's expression turned more understanding. "We have all had an unnerving night. The worst is over. All that matters now is the cleanup. The sooner that is done, the better."

"Yes, my lord."

Snorting, the black minotaur turned his horse and found himself facing a much more welcome sight.

"You look done in," a hulk of brown-furred muscle remarked cheerfully. "Taking too much on your shoulders as usual, brother?"

Although shorter than his brother by half a horn's length, Kolot made up for it in width, but none of his extra mass was fat. His shoulders were intimidating. Bastion had seen Kolot lift an opponent over his head using only one hand. Once, when their eldest brother Ardnor had taunted him about his appearance one day when they were younger, little Kolot had picked him up and thrown him across the room.

His squat muzzle gave Kolot a piggish appearance, and his intelligence was rumored to be as dim as that of those animals. Yet looks were deceptive.

"Doing what must be done, Kol. I want this business settled by morning. The stability of our nation demands it."

"You worry too much. When they find out what Father's done, they'll fill the streets, cheering."

"You are probably correct," the older minotaur admitted. "I just prefer to be cautious."

"And would you still be my brother if you were any other way? Always thinking too much, that's you!"

Bastion bristled. "You must be here for a reason. What is it?"

"Hmm? Oh! Aye! Father wants you. Says I can surely handle the simple matter of carting these poor fools off to the mines. He wants you back as soon as possible."

"Did he say why?"

"No." Kolot leaned closer. "I think he's just nervous about all that's happening. Not everyone steals an empire overnight."

"It's not over quite yet. I hear that Tiribus and General Rahm are still at large."

Behind them, one of the guards shut the gate on the first of the prison wagons then signaled the driver. The horses strained forward.

The mountain of muscle snorted. "You worry too much."

A sudden, harsh, cracking sound alerted them. Kolot pulled his axe out even as Bastion reached for his own weapon.

But it was nothing—only the wagon. One wheel lay splintered, the spokes scattered everywhere. The wagon bulged and tipped, the prisoners pressing against the bars.

Bastion started forward, but Kolot moved in front of him. "Father wants you. I can handle this."

The soldiers had begun unloading the prisoners by the time Kolot reached the wagon. Bastion paused to watch for a moment.

Dismounting, Kolot shouted, "That's good enough! Leave the rest inside! Time's wasting!" He went to where the wheel had broken off, inspecting the axle. "Looks fine!"

As everyone watched, Kolot squatted and, with still more than a dozen servants locked in the wagon, lifted his end up off the ground.

"Get the spare wheel ready!" Every muscle strained, but even in the faint light of the coming dawn, Bastion and the others could see the pride in Kolot's face as he flaunted his strength.

The black minotaur chuckled quietly and rode away.

That morning, the citizens of the imperial capital awoke to find their world turned upside down.

Merchants with wagons of goods heading for vendors in the city found the gates to Nethosak barred. Entrance was permitted only after careful inspection of each consignment. Wagons leaving were also carefully checked for stowaways. At the port, no ship was allowed to unload or take on cargo without a search of the vessel.

Shopkeepers and workers stood transfixed at their doors and windows, watching as rank upon rank of armed units under the proud banner of Hotak's Legion marched through the streets. Their silver armor—with red insignia—gleamed in the morning sun. Some citizens realized that these emblems should not be flying over Mithas or anywhere else in the empire, but rather on the mainland. The knowledge of their presence quickly spread through the populace.

Throughout Nethosak, throughout Mithas, throughout the majority of the more than three dozen established colonies, mounted officers flanked by sturdy lines of seasoned warriors unrolled scrolls. Crowds of wary and curious faces stared in silence as the announcement was read.

"Hear this, all good people of the empire!" each officer said. "Hear the words of General Hotak de-Droka, Hotak the Sword, Hotak the Avenger. A wrong has been righted. Justice has been served. The corruption within has been lanced!"

Wherever the scrolls were read, be it the vast square near the imperial palace or the modest streets of the more primitive colonies, crowds gathered. Tunics and kilts sporting every house pattern and color created a sea of myriad designs. Every citizen of the far-flung empire knew the name and reputation of Hotak.

"Let it be known that the vile, corrupt Chot Es-Kalin, whose deceits in the Great Circus are understood, whose betrayals of honor have been legion, whose reign has been marked by the murders of rivals, the ruinous taxation of his subjects, the imprisonment of innocents, and the moral decay of the imperial capital itself, whose treacherous pact with the humans known as the Knights of Neraka would have delivered his own kind back into slavery—"

"Never!" rumbled one scarred, brown-furred veteran, his muzzle cut and twisted by an old wound.

In different places across the realm, others, too, called out.

"No more masters!" cried a leather-aproned woodworker.

"No more slaves!" a muscular, young female wearing the sea dragon emblem of the Imperial fleet on her breastplate added.

"—said Chot has been declared a traitor, unfit to command the respect of his people, unfit to rule. Therefore, he and those who aided in the corruption, dishonor, and downfall of the glorious minotaur race have been sentenced, and that sentence has been carried out. House Kalin and other allied Houses have been condemned, their holdings seized. In addition, those House names shall be forever expunged from the lists of honored clans."

The chosen officers, as they had been trained, rolled up the proclamations, stared at the awe-struck crowds, and proclaimed, "Chot is dead! Long live the Emperor Hotak! Long live the Emperor Hotak!"

The helmed soldiers who had assembled to protect the heralds in case of a riot, took up the cue, shouting the same in their deep, stentorian voices. "Long live the Emperor Hotak! Long live the Emperor Hotak!"

Others raised long, curled horns and blew hard. Cries from the crowds celebrated the new lord of the realm. The din was heard in all the islands and colonies.

Of course, not all were quick to curse the deposed emperor. In every crowd, a few pairs of eyes looked warily about. A few faces struggled to look unconcerned. Those loyal to Chot kept quiet or even pretended to join in the merriment.

Everywhere, soldiers armed with thick, sturdy rope swarmed over the tall, painted statues of Chot that lined nearly every major avenue and stood in front of each imperial site. The emperor had made certain that each colony had received at least one such statue, and through the years most had accumulated many more.

The great, looming statue in the spacious central square of the capital, the very site where Chot had given his inaugural public appearance as emperor some four decades before, was the first to tumble. The gigantic, elaborately chiseled figure had survived storms, tremors, and even war. Bloody, twin-edged axe raised high, it depicted the young, burly champion who would become the despot, lustily roaring his triumph as he placed one foot upon the slaughtered and remarkably lifelike corpse of a hairy ogre clutching a thick club. The ogre, his flat face contorted, his tusk-filled mouth open in a final grimace, had one hand up to plead for mercy.

Surrounding the statue of the titan was a vast, deep fountain with great marble waves of wild froth. Water sprayed high. Fanciful horses with the tails of fish where their hindquarters should have been furiously raced around the outer edge.

Around the fountain, marble benches had been arranged on all sides. Huge axes of black stone, each sculpted as meticulously as the fountain, stood with their heads pointed toward the water spray. The axes, three times the size of the tallest warrior, stretched toward the immortal Chot. The pure white stone filling the rest of the square added to the overall magnificence of the scene.

The people, swept up in the triumph of their new emperor, cheered as the eager soldiers secured ropes to the marble leviathan. Some threw rotting cabbage, tomatoes, and other vegetables at the icon, defacing and staining the statue.

Children threw mud. A common cause stirred all. Several of the younger onlookers moved to help with the binding of the painted goliath. In a scene that was repeated all over the realm, members of the citizenry offered strong rope and gave use of their own leathery hands.

At one time this vision of Chot had been near truth. These days, everyone knew better the graying, round-bellied bull with the bloodshot eyes and scraggly fur slumping on the throne. The glories Chot had once stood for had been over-shadowed too long by his stupidities.

The titan in the capital square, which stood the height of five minotaurs, was gripped by six of Hotak's warriors—four pulling on the sturdy waist and throat, two more for the up-raised arm—using lines of good storm-tested rope.

The mounted officer on duty, face emotionless, made a cutting motion.

"Pull!" shouted a subofficer on foot, his expression more lusty.

As one, the soldiers tugged, straining the muscles in their arms, legs, and necks. While some pulled to bring the statue toward them, others pulled in the opposite direction so that the huge monument did not simply crush their comrades.

"Easy!" shouted the subofficer. "More slack back there! Hurry!"

Finally, they had Chot leaning far forward, his vast muzzle looming over one of the benches.

Those under the threatening shadow of the stone emperor scurried away to avoid being flattened.

"Remaining squads, release!"

As one, the other minotaurs obeyed, the ropes fairly fly-ing from their hands as gravity seized command.

With a final groan, Chot the Invincible tumbled forward.

By the scores, by the hundreds, all throughout the minotaur realm, the many statues of Chot were toppled and destroyed.

Not one sculpture survived. Not satisfied, the incensed crowds began to tear down or deface anything that bore Chot's likeness. Reliefs carved into imperial buildings, banners hanging high over the rooftops, tapestries draping meeting chambers—little escaped the orgy of destruction.

The soldiers of Hotak watched all, noting those who did not seem to enjoy their master's victory sufficiently.

And while soldiers watched the citizenry, shadows observed all, reporting to their mistress in the temple.

Yet, with all these eyes, living or dead, not one noticed General Rahm Es-Hestos, late of the Imperial Guard.

The lone ship, her sails full, plied the high waves. The three masts strained but held under the power of the harsh winds, enabling the lengthy vessel to course swiftly through the turbulent water. Built foremost for cargo, *Dragon's Crest* nonetheless was also streamlined to match speed with any foe.

Patches here and there spoke of the ship's checkered history, one not only of profit but war. The repairs had all been made with great skill, but each scar spoke proudly of a legacy of brutal seafaring.

Sturdy of limb despite his age, the graying brown captain watched his sole passenger stare at the violent waters and boiling sky. They had left the Blood Sea hours ago, but the compact figure at the rail still gazed behind them.

"Have no fear, my good friend!" Azak de-Genjis called, his gravelly voice rising above the roar of the sea. "Your family is safe elsewhere, and we are well away from danger!"

His passenger turned. In contrast to many minotaurs, General Rahm Es-Hestos was barely over six feet, not including his horns. He made up for this with a musculature worthy of a champion of the arenas. Above his broad muzzle glared two penetrating blue eyes. Like most of his race, his fur was a brown shade, but a streak of black jetting over his eyes gave him a bit of an exotic look. Few who met Rahm forgot him, not only because of his appearance, but also because of the sharp, commanding tone of his voice.

"We're never out of danger, Azak. Never." The renegade officer wore only kilts. The kilts were not even his, but had been borrowed from one of the captain's kin. Its design had marked Rahm as a member of Genjis clan, thereby saving his life.

"Well . . . perhaps not," agreed the captain as he hobbled toward his friend. A long-ago duel had left his right leg permanently injured. His opponent had not fared as well. "But that hunter ship turned off more than three hours back and there's not been a sign of any other pursuit since then."

Rahm considered his friend's words. With a snort, the commander of the Imperial Guard finally commented, "I wonder what that captain would think if he knew that he just allowed a major enemy of the state to flee under his very snout?"

Azak's thick brow crinkled. "You are no enemy of the state, my good friend! It is the state that has become the enemy."

"Hotak . . . I knew his ambitions, admired them even, but I never dreamed he would do this."

"This travesty will haunt him, Rahm. You will see."

Thunder rumbled. *Dragon's Crest* pushed on. The crew all knew who sailed with them, knew that the lone figure they transported had been marked for death and that by aiding him they joined in his fate, yet they gave their loyalty to their captain.

The unsettling blue eyes glanced at Azak. "I've thought it over," said Rahm. "We've got to forget Gol. They'll head there first, suspecting Jubal's friendship. Even if he survived this coup, he'll be under watch, I'm sure."

"Not Gol? Then where? You don't want to join your family on Tadaran. I know that. Where then? Mito? Aurelis?"

The captain rubbed the underside of his muzzle. "Aurelis is farthest, but there are others—out of the way. Quar?"

The ship rocked violently, sending both grasping for the rail.

"Hotak would know them all. Make no mistake, Azak, he's everything an emperor should be, and if he'd defeated Chot in the Circus, I would've been the first to cheer his name. No, we must go somewhere that Hotak would not even consider as a possibility, and yet gives us a vantage from which to strike back." A crafty look seized Rahm's face. "I'm thinking it has to be Petarka."

"Petarka?" The wizened sea captain could not recall any island by that name, much less a colony. "I've not heard of it."

For the first time since boarding *Dragon's Crest*, General Rahm almost smiled. "No. And neither will have Hotak. I hope."

CHAPTER IV

CORONATION

The original structure of the Great Circus had been oval in shape, built of simple, sturdy, gray rock, and unadorned, for in those days the minotaurs were a utilitarian society. It had been built, in part, to celebrate the minotaurs' liberation from the rule of the ogres, and those who led the rebellion created it so that it could also serve, under extreme conditions, as a walled fortress. The slits in the uppermost level of the stands served not only to allow circulation of air, but also as positions from which archers could fire. Within the walls themselves, enough storage space had been set aside so that those inside the arena could theoretically survive a siege of up to three months. That the structure would fail miserably in this regard, barely half a century later, the designers could not predict.

The decision to choose their ruler by combat—with guile as much as strength and skill playing a hand—was overwhelmingly popular, and the initial imperial combat had taken place in the Great Circus in the first year of the empire.

When the ogres enslaved the minotaurs again, they tore down the coliseum as a mark of their contempt. When the minotaurs regained their freedom, they built a larger, more extravagant structure, this time circular, reflecting the fact that the Circus was the center of the minotaur world.

Through the dragon wars, the cataclysms, enslavement a dozen times and more, the *Great* Circus, as it came to be called, changed and grew. One coliseum fell, and a more spectacular one took its place.

And no more spectacular Circus had ever been built than the one in which the crowds gathered by the thousands early this day.

Still circular in shape, with lovingly carved lifelike statues representing the greatest of those champions who had graced the fields of combat, it made those who recalled the previous edifice feel at home, yet the changes and embellishments could all be traced to the ego of the Emperor Chot.

Forty-thousand minotaurs could have seated themselves in the coliseum that had stood before the war against the Magori. Twenty-thousand more could fit here now; both the diameter and the height of Chot's monument to his own glory had been increased by his architects. Ten stories tall and with a playing field alone that measured six hundred and twenty-five feet in diameter, it filled more space than any of its predecessors. The finest white stone had been transported from distant reaches and upon each carefully honed block had been carved the history of the minotaurs. Epic battles of both sea and land, explorations and discoveries, and major events of minotaur history—all found their place on the walls of the now-overthrown emperor's Great Circus.

More than a few reliefs, including those most strategically placed, represented the emperor himself. Over each of the twenty-five entrances—five was considered a lucky number and thus five times five made the Circus a place of good fortune—the proud visage of the emperor was displayed. There loomed Chot the Proud, Chot the Just, Chot the Fearsome, and many more Chots.

But it was appropriate that images of Chot dominated this Great Circus, for it had been the site of his greatest victories and had helped keep his people pre-occupied even during the worst times of ruinous finances, disease, failed conquests, and more.

However, the great structure had deteriorated under the reign of Chot. Years of insufficient scouring had created a deep moist moss, an accumulation of grime and dirt, and a permanent smell.

The aging emperor, in his imperial box, saw only the dusted marble benches, the painted statues, and the hundreds of banners waving in the wind. Chot never entered by any but one passage, and that single passage, reserved for him and his guests alone, was kept pristine.

Nor had Chot seen—in truth, he would not have cared to see—those who lurked in the rank corridors, as at home in the stench and grime as all the rats and cockroaches. On the lowest levels of the coliseum could be found the shadow sellers, who did all their work in the deep inner corridors and rarely saw the light of day . . . or even the dark of true night. Oil lamps and torches set into the walls served as the only light for these less-than-respectable merchants who sold everything from trinkets and souvenirs to the powders and herbs that many found so refreshing, despite their eventual devastating toll.

There would be no shadow sellers today. Not only had Hotak commanded that the underdwellers be rounded up and the Circus cleansed of their malignant presence, but anyone caught seeking to buy their diverse wares would likewise be imprisoned. The core of minotaur life, the true heart of the empire, the Great Circus, must be purged of its ugliness. Today would begin the renewal of its glory, a return to purity.

Today, a new emperor would be crowned.

Bastion, Maritia, and their brother Kolot stood on a hastily-erected wooden dais in the center of the Great Circus. The brothers wore fresh, knee-length, leather kilts studded with tiny silver stars. The axe harnesses strapped diagonally across their torsos shined bright from seal oil run lovingly over the leather. Their military badges displayed the rearing horse symbol of their father's legion. The twin, curved heads of the battleaxes strapped behind the two minotaurs also gleamed and had been turned sideways to emphasize their massiveness. Each blade had been honed sharp. Both brothers wore silver, unadorned, open-faced helms whose lower front edges curled around their cheeks and whose backs slid down to cover their necks.

Their sister wore a simple, low-cut tunic of gray cotton and a kilt, identical in design to Bastion and Kolot's. She favored a slim long sword over a heftier axe.

The vast arena was filled to overflowing. Everyone within riding distance of Nethosak came if they could. After the assassinations and the rejoicing of the people in the streets, Hotak had immediately ordered a lavish coronation. He felt he needed to seize the moment. Wait too long, even a day too long, and the people might begin to question the tumultuous events.

"Still no word on Tiribus, Kesk, or Rahm," Maritia whispered in Bastion's ear.

"I told Father he should have waited until they were all taken care of," her elder brother murmured back. Squinting, the black minotaur peered up at the top of the massive arena, where the statues of past champions—excluding Chot's now—stood guard. Next to each stood an able archer, the finest in Hotak's legion.

In addition, soldiers armed with either twin-edged axes, long swords, or sharp, needlelike lances stretching ten feet from base to tip, lined each level and every exit.

"How long—?" Maritia began.

At that moment, heralds, their silver dress armor gleaming, raised their long, curled horns. The Circus acted as a natural amplifier and, positioned as they were on small square platforms overlooking the playing field, the heralds created a wave of sound that rose up like thunder.

The emperor-to-be and his consort had arrived.

Through the main gate on the floor of the arena—the high, barred gate used to unleash wild animals or fighters onto the playing field—burst a pair of charging chariots, each drawn by four horses of the purest black. The gilded vehicles, also black but with brilliant gold scrollwork and etched with the profile of a fearsome minotaur, raced around the field. Behind the chariots, two helmed warriors rode.

Reaching the middle of the arena, the chariots spun and came to an abrupt and, to the crowd, quite startling halt. As the crowd held its collective breath, General Hotak de-Droka and the Lady Nephera strode majestically into the vast center of the Circus.

Hotak's breastplate gleamed brighter than anyone's and had, in fact, been finished this very day. Ornate scrollwork marked the shoulders, and on the chest no longer did the crimson condor fly. Instead a savage black warhorse reared.

Baring his teeth in a smile, Hotak stared out from under an open helm. The emperor-to-be wore a long sword whose gold handle was encrusted with a circular pattern of red rubies and upon whose blade had been etched the single word: DESTINY.

Hotak's mane had been neatly trimmed and his dark-brown fur treated with palm and olive oil to make it glisten. He waved to the crowd, and the air filled with cheering and the stomping of feet.

At his side, Nephera, too, greeted the throngs. Ever elegant, the high priestess had for this ceremony foregone the stately robes of the Forerunner faith—which brought great relief to her husband—in favor of shimmering, silken ones dyed silver, then trimmed at the sleeves, waist, and throat with emerald green lace. They were caught at the waist by a silken belt with a pattern made of true emeralds. As with Hotak's cape, her robes trailed behind her, where they were held steady by a pair of young female fighters.

Three stunning necklaces composed of silver strands of intertwining serpents adorned her throat, and between her horns Nephera wore a slim, coiled headband encrusted with small emeralds and rubies patterned like stars. Her hair had been cleansed and oiled, and her fur scented with lavender, the last a favorite not only of high-ranking females, but a perfume which reliably enticed her husband.

Behind the pair came Ardnor. Hotak's eldest son had foregone the robes of the temple for an outfit virtually identical to those of his brothers, with the minor addition of a clean, gray tunic without sleeves under his axe harness. But he also wore an imposing black helm, which everyone in the coliseum would instantly recognize as the symbol of the Protectors.

Trailing the new emperor's family were his closest allies—generals, naval officers, and the patriarchs of powerful clans. They came clad in their finest, well-crafted robes or brightly polished breastplates. All waved to the roaring crowd.

The absence of some notable Houses was glaring. This included prominent Houses that had escaped the bloody lists. While some of their leaders sat among the vast audience, others were missing and observers wondered about their future and the future of their clans.

The platform had been draped over with a massive banner, displaying a monstrous shadow of a horse. At the uppermost point of the makeshift dais sat, for all to see, the imperial throne, removed from the palace for this occasion. The tall, oak chair was stained a deep, deep red. The head of a fierce minotaur with lengthy, curved horns was carved into the top. The savage countenance evoked the lost god Sargas—or Sargonnas, as others called him—as imagined in the favored form of his chosen people.

Hotak and his wife stood before the throne. An elegant chair had been brought from the temple for the high priestess. The arms of the second chair curved like waves on the sea and the legs resembled those of a dragon, even down to the clawed feet. Neither the general nor Lady Nephera sat, however. They continued to acknowledge the crowd while the other dignitaries took their places.

Ardnor, ignoring his brothers and sister, took up a position close to Nephera, then surveyed the crowds as if he, not Hotak, stood ready to be crowned.

The emperor-to-be nodded to a trumpeter, who quickly thrust the horn to his mouth and blew to signal a new figure approaching from the main entrance.

The hair on Bastion's neck rose, and both Maritia and Kolot stirred uneasily. All three had expected the gaunt, hooded minotaur clad in plain, gray robes and a simple, unadorned breastplate, but still the sight of him disturbed them. Lothan came as the only member of the Supreme Circle to survive the overthrow of Chot.

Five of the Supreme Circle were dead. Lothan had worked hand-in-hand with his fellow councilors to the very end. Councilor Boril, an unassuming but capable administrator, had even gone to the traitor to warn him of rumors of danger. In return for that warning, Lothan had let the very assassins Boril had feared enter his own home, slaying his guest.

Flanked on each side by five soldiers wielding the banners of the new emperor, Councilor Lothan walked solemnly toward the steps leading up to Hotak. The cheers and stomping grew incessant.

Joined by two of Hotak's officers, Lothan ascended the steps until he stood before the general. Only then did Hotak, now unhelmed, and Nephera seat themselves.

The throngs grew silent. The councilor turned to face them, holding up for all to see two objects. *"The Crown of Toroth!"*

The stomping and roaring erupted anew. The first artifact resembled a helmet, but jeweled and with a condor's head as the crest. Its ruby eyes were worth a fortune in themselves. The entire crown glittered with so many and varied jewels that some in the crowd had to turn their gaze or be temporarily blinded.

Up thrust Lothan's other hand. *"The Axe of Makel Ogrebane!"*

No one truly believed that the sleek, golden axe with the diamond runes spelling out Makel's name was the same one wielded by the hero—later emperor—who had freed his race from slavery, any more than that the crown had actually been worn by Toroth, the ruler instrumental in expanding minotaur maritime interests beyond the Blood Sea. Both artifacts had been created much later when such symbols were needed—as they clearly were now.

"There is no greater honor," Lothan continued, "than to be found worthy of wearing this fabled crown and wielding this legendary weapon! There is no greater honor than to sit upon the throne of the ancients, to be acknowledged as the one who, by right of strength and wit, has been chosen to rule!"

The hooded figure turned to Hotak. " 'We have been enslaved, but have always thrown off our shackles,' " Lothan proclaimed, beginning the ancient litany that each child learned early on. " 'We have been driven back, but always returned to the fray stronger than before!' "

Those in attendance began murmuring the same words, thousands of deep, minotaur voices speaking in unison.

Lothan's voice rose. " 'We have risen to new heights when all other races have fallen into decay! We are the future of Krynn!' "

" 'The future of Krynn . . .' " chanted the crowd.

" 'The fated masters of the entire world!' " the councilor cried.

" 'The entire world . . .' "

" 'We are the children of destiny!' "

" 'Destiny . . . destiny . . . destiny!' " the people repeated. The stomping began again.

With the one hand, Lothan held the crown over the general then, with horns blaring, reverently set the elaborate headpiece down on Hotak's head.

The crowd stilled.

The general adjusted the crown slightly, then, his good eye gleaming, nodded for the councilor to proceed.

"General Hotak de-Droka, I place in your hands the Axe of Makel Ogrebane, so that you may rule with strength, determination, and honor!"

Hotak gripped the axe in his hands and rested it across his lap.

"Hotak de-Droka, let none call you general from this day forth, for that enviable rank is now beneath your grand status! Let it be proclaimed here and now—" the hooded minotaur turned back to the crowd— "on this day we honor the rule of Emperor Hotak! All hail Emperor Hotak!"

Bastion, Kolot, and Maritia roared their approval along with the crowds. Long, thin cloth streamers of red and black, the new imperial colors, flew from every section.

The former general slowly rose, saluting with the ceremonial axe. He took a moment to lean down to his mate and nuzzle her hand, then turned to the crowd once more.

"I am not your emperor!" Hotak shouted.

Complete stillness overwhelmed the onlookers.

"I am not your emperor," he continued, turning his single-eye gaze from one row to the next, "if it means treating you with the respect, the honor, with which one treats a gully dwarf! I am not your emperor . . . if it means holding in contempt the traditions by which our people have thrived for generations!"

The crowd seemed mesmerized. As they listened, Hotak's soldiers herded in a small, disheveled group of surly prisoners.

"I am your emperor," the scarred commander cried, not once glancing down at the newcomers, "if you seek a return to honor and glory! To end decay! I am your emperor if you truly believe, as I do, that we are indeed the children of destiny!"

The roaring and stomping renewed.

Hotak let it go on for more than a minute. Below, the prisoners, set in two groups of five apiece, were forced to their knees. Some wore the raiment of warriors, one that of a general. Others were clad in muddied and tattered garments that had once been wealthy robes marking a patriarch or a high-ranking councilor. The faces bore bruises and scars. All kept their muzzles to the sandy ground.

Hotak descended. The new emperor paused before the first of the prisoners, then signaled his subjects for silence.

"For the past several decades," Hotak said with a snort of contempt, "a shadow has enshrouded the throne. Corruption, the worst since the days of Polik the Pawn! Minotaurs have risen in power through bribes and favors. Filth litters our streets! Our once-proud structures have fallen into disarray, and justice has become a mockery. These before you are a few of those responsible—and for their crimes they shall now pay!"

Hotak whirled upon the prisoner behind him and brought the polished head of the axe down upon the kneeling figure's neck.

The decapitated body slumped forward, blood pooling near the emperor.

Hotak marched to the second prisoner. Once again, the axe rose high . . . and once again it came down.

When the last of the ten lay sprawled at Hotak's reddened feet, he held the axe up for all to see. Fur covered in sweat and an expression of intense satisfaction on his face, the emperor cried, "Under Chot and others before him, that which chose who should lead, the *imperial combat*, has become a mockery! For four decades, it served only to lengthen Chot's foul reign and keep our race stagnant!" Hotak snorted in righteous fury. "Never again! I declare here and now that the imperial combat is no more, that no emperor will rule through subterfuge and treachery! Honor shall be restored to the throne—and with your help, I shall see it done quickly!"

Again the crowds cheered, most not realizing that Hotak had just informed them that he intended to be ruler for as long as he desired. The choice of emperor had been taken from them forever.

"I hereby declare a three-day celebration—not to honor my own glory, but to mark the rebirth of the empire, to mark the dawning of a new age! The Age of the Minotaur!"

Hotak's name became the audience's collective cry over and over. The former general ascended the dais again. Hotak did not sit, instead once more taking his mate's hand. Nephera stood next to her husband.

Trumpets blared. More streamers fluttered to the arena floor. They landed everywhere, merrily decorating the headless corpses or sinking into the swelling puddles of blood.

With the confidence of one whose every word was law, the emperor led Nephera off the dais.

Maritia glanced at her brother. "Bastion! What—?"

"Quiet!" he returned. "Just follow along as if everything has gone as planned!"

Ardnor and Lothan also were caught by surprise, but quickly joined the others. The procession continued into the corridor beneath the public areas. The stone walls bore decades of scars and the thick doors on each side hinted of the many beasts and prisoners held there. Crimson stains marked the length of the corridor.

Four guards unbarred the heavy outer doors as Hotak neared.

Hotak waved cheerfully to the people beyond, saluting them with the still-dripping axe. His name could be heard from every direction. *Hotak! Hotak!*

Well-guarded, the horses of those who had participated in the ceremony awaited. For the emperor and his consort, a huge, black war chariot drawn by ebony steeds sat ready. Hotak helped his wife up into it, then joined her, waving again to his subjects.

The others took to their mounts. Horns blared. Armed soldiers began clearing a path before the imperial family. Slowly at first, then faster as the onlookers dispersed before it, the magnificent vehicle pushed on toward the palace.

As Kolot and Maritia urged their own mounts on, Bastion paused, glancing at his eldest brother. Ardnor's expression was solemn, but the eyes of his sibling made Bastion's hands tighten on the reins, for the whites had turned completely blood red.

Despite the fury obviously welling within him, Ardnor rode on as if nothing was amiss. Bastion stared after him, wondering why their father had not done as planned and announced Ardnor as heir.

The Knights of Neraka never had a chance.

Before the patrol's incursion into the rocks and hills of southern Kern, dragonriders had flown over and verified that no ogre activity was taking place in the region. The beast-men had fled before the superior might of the Knighthood.

So the ogres had wanted the Knights of Neraka to believe.

The ogre leader's plan was to let the patrol wend its way through the area, let them return and report that the way was clear, that paths existed for the larger army, then, when the army returned, catch an entire column while they were confined to one of the narrow passes crisscrossing the harsh landscape.

But ogres were never patient, and when one impetuous warrior rose up to throw his spear, the rest followed suit, waving clubs and tossing boulders down on the dozen hapless humans.

"Keep order! Keep order!" shouted the patrol commander.

The humans briefly fended off the attackers. One ogre was decapitated. The hooves of a warhorse cracked the rib cage of another.

Although the knights fought well, surrounded by a hundred ogres, they had no real hope. One after another, they were dragged from their horses. Heavy clubs bashed in armored skulls. Brutish hands crushed throats or broke necks. The lead knight managed to slay two opponents before a spear drove through his breastplate, leaving him dangling in the air like a stringless marionette.

Two of the patrol managed to escape the ambush, urging their steeds back the way they had come. Dust rose high in their wake, but their flight was short-lived. Ahead of them, more ogres shoved tremendous boulders down. The massive rocks crashed into the horses, sending riders and mounts toppling.

Savage, tusked warriors rushed down and battered the two stunned knights with their clubs until little remained recognizable, bringing their struggle to a quick, horrific conclusion.

One of the ogres seized a bloody helm and propped it atop his spear. Harsh cries arose as the victors celebrated the deaths of their enemies.

Overlooking the slaughter from atop the highest ridge, a short, slim ogre clad in a cloak and garb more suitable for an elf spat angrily in the dust. The scent of blood and the cries of battle stirred him as they did all his kind, yet he held himself in check. The others could revel in their victory, but he knew how little this skirmish counted. The army that should have been easy prey would now be warned by the disappearance of their scouts. The knights' relentless advance into Kern would continue.

Despite this dire fact, he grinned. "All will change," he promised himself in almost perfect Common. "All will change soon, yes."

CHAPTER V

HUNTED

Under Nethosak, a vast series of rounded tunnels let the water waste of the imperial capital flow out to sea. Built of sturdy stone, this marvel of engineering had survived eruptions, earthquakes, and even the Cataclysm that ripped Mithas from the mainland. A fast-flowing river coursed through the tunnels, diverted by the work of more than one generation. A pair of yard-wide ledges ran across each side of the water flow, enabling workers to enter and keep the sewers in good order.

However, the reign of Chot had seen little maintenance. The water now moved sluggishly, restricted by trash accumulation. The tunnels suffered from the same lack of care; massive cracks littered entire areas. In some sections through which the fugitives ran, huge chunks of masonry and rock had collapsed into the river. The stench of rotting matter was everywhere.

There was little light. Faros had nearly fallen in the water once. Worse, rats abounded, more rats than could have been imagined.

They had taken to the sewers after being forced to use the horse as a decoy to throw off pursuers. Twice during the night Bek and Faros had also eluded soldiers searching the tunnels. The darkness had aided them . . . as had the stench. None of the searchers wanted to remain for very long, even with torches and oil lamps.

With great relief, they crawled out of the sewers within striking distance of their goal. To be above ground gave them some semblance of hope again.

"I wonder what that cheering earlier today was about?" Bek muttered, trying to rid himself of the scent of the tunnels.

"What does it matter?" came Faros's sullen reply.

The wind picked up, a moist, chill bite coming in from the Blood Sea. Both froze as several soldiers came into sight just down the avenue. Bek pulled a staggering Faros back into the shadows, and the two watched as the figures marched past.

"They seem to be leaving the area, Master Faros."

"Does that mean that they've finished searching around here?"

"Maybe. If so, then we've hope of reaching Captain Azak." Faros glanced around. "But there's still light."

"The longer we wait the harder it'll be."

The pair had removed their clan emblems and hoped no one would wonder why. Few minotaurs went around without some symbol of their House, but someone might recognize their outlawed clan.

Another band of minotaurs appeared, laughing among themselves. They had been drinking. They shouted at a pair of females carrying goods, then laughed again when the latter turned up their muzzles and gave snorts of offense.

At the same time, a pair of veteran soldiers armed with axes came toward Faros and Bek from another direction. These two had wary expressions and when one noticed Faros, he muttered to his partner.

Some of the revelers also noticed the fugitives and waved at them, shouting, "Long live Emperor Hotak!"

Bek immediately shouted back. "Long live Emperor Hotak!"

The two soldiers neared. Faros greeted them with a cheer, putting on the face he normally wore during bouts of drinking and gaming.

One chuckled and gave him a mock salute. The other nodded.

Bek and Faros moved on. As they walked, they jested loudly with one another, speaking of the good times to come under the rule of the one-eyed general.

At last they spotted the first tall sails jutting over some flat-roofed buildings. All they needed now was to find Captain Azak.

Life went on in the port much the way as it had before the bloody coup—except that armed soldiers patrolled everywhere. Mariners in kilts of all colors and clan patterns fixed lines, repaired hulls and worked to ready ships for sea. Others unloaded cargo. Urged on by their keepers, rough-furred goats from Kothas scurried noisily onto land. Huge barrels were rolled up gangplanks by straining sailors. A band of workers under the watchful eyes of a pair of soldiers scrubbed away at the moss, gull droppings, and grime covering the stone buildings.

Faros froze in his tracks, startled by what he saw. Under the direction of a grizzled minotaur with a wooden leg, an armed escort had begun removing from a Kalin ship everything that signified its ownership by that clan. Two warriors on the deck took special interest in ripping the Kalin banners to shreds. Other soldiers swarmed over the vessel, seizing anything of value.

Atop the highest mast, the rearing warhorse now danced.

Bek nudged his companion in the ribs. "Master Faros," he whispered. "It can't be helped. We must go on."

Faros trailed after him, and it fell to the servant to inquire after Captain Azak. The first mariners he asked did not know his name, but eventually an elderly sailor pointed ahead up the dock.

Thanking the weather-scarred mariner, the two pushed on. Soon they sighted what appeared to be the sea captain's home, a clean, block-styled building with little adornment other than the tell-tale trident and ship symbol marking the captain's clan.

Bek knocked hard on the arched wooden door. Faros braced himself, expecting a legion of soldiers to come bursting out.

No one responded.

The servant put an ear against the wood. "There's no one in there. We'll have to find a place nearby where we can hide. We'll try the captain again when it's dark."

"I saw some storage houses nearby," Faros offered.

"They'll do. Some of them should be unused. We can find a way inside and wait. Sunset's not that far away."

Trying their best to maintain an air of normalcy, the two headed off. Soon they came to a series of tall, gray structures with wide, bolted and chained doors and small slits near the top for windows.

"There should be a way inside," murmured Bek, checking the doors. "Maybe we could climb up to the roof. We only need—"

A shadow loomed behind them.

"Who are you?" demanded a steely voice. "What business do you have here?"

Five figures clad in black, crestless helms confronted Faros and Bek. They wore sleek ebony breastplates, shoulder armor, and gauntlets. Each wielded a sturdy mace. Their knee-length kilts consisted of black segments of leather and metal. Yet nothing unnerved Bek and Faros as much as the symbols emblazoned in gold upon both the breast plate and helm. A twin-edged axe broken at the midpoint and folded upward. Above it, seeming to rise to the sky, the shape of a majestic bird—the insignia of the Temple of the Forerunners.

As the Forerunners had grown in numbers and power, so, too, had their martial arm, the Protectors, expanded its scope. Now they sent out their own patrols and pursued—and often punished—those lawbreakers they caught. The Protectors swore their lives and their existence to the temple. Only the mistrust of Chot had kept them from seizing more authority on the streets. But Chot was gone, and their mistress sat as consort to the new emperor.

"I asked a simple question," the barrel-chested leader proclaimed. He used the multi-barbed head of the mace to prod Faros's chin up, so that he could look him in the eyes. "Have you no simple answer?"

Bek came to his master's aid, replying, "We are guards sent to mind House Delarac's holdings." The clan symbol of Delarac, a close ally of House Droka, hung above several nearby buildings. "There are those who would use the emperor's coronation as an excuse for theft."

The leader said nothing, instead staring intently at both fugitives.

"I see no badge of your House," he said, using the mace as a pointing stick. "Nor on you," the Protector added, shifting the mace to Bek. "In fact, they look to have been ripped off, and that begs further questions. I think perhaps you two should come with us to the temple, where this matter can be sorted out."

One of the other Protectors put a hand on his superior's shoulder. The latter turned to listen.

Bek used the distraction to grab Faros by the arm and run.

Their inquisitor whirled about. "Stop them!"

To the fugitives' horror, three more Protectors came into sight from the opposite direction. Brandishing their maces, the armored trio charged toward them.

Bek pulled Faros into a narrow alley. Four more figures materialized ahead of them. These, though, wore the silver armor of soldiers.

"You there!" shouted the officer in charge. "Identify yourselves immediately!"

Faros opened his mouth, but Bek pushed him back.

"You wish to know who I am?" the servant cried. "Ask not my lowly servant, Bek, then! Hear it from me! Hear it from Faros Es-Kalin, son of Gradic, nephew of the true emperor, Chot!"

"Kalin?" The officer's eyes lit up and he snorted with anticipation. "A bonus for us! Stand still and—"

Bek hurled himself at the soldiers. He managed to knock the officer to the ground, even wrench the axe from the other's hands. "My family—my honor—will be avenged!"

Before he could do anything, a sword caught him in the chest. A second followed, skewering the brave servant.

"Kalin—!" Bek managed to gasp, dropping the axe. He fell back, dead.

Horrified, Faros turned from the soldiers—only to run into the oncoming Protectors.

They pummeled him, used the blunt end of their maces to hit at his unprotected body. Faros collapsed. Even then the temple sentinels did not pause, but continued to strike him.

"Stop that! In the name of the emperor, cease that at once!"

Half lost to the world, Faros could not even look up at his savior, the legion officer.

"This is an enemy of the state," rumbled the Protector commander. "We are ordered to show traitors no mercy."

"He's half-beaten to a pulp! Even a temple lackey should be able to see that."

Dark muttering arose from the Forerunner faithful. "Watch your tongue. Our master is Lord Ardnor, the emperor's eldest."

"Then he should've told you of Emperor Hotak's own command. The servants of the condemned Houses are to be rounded up, not slain. This wretch doesn't even carry a weapon."

"Such a worthless hide should not be saved."

"That is not ours to decide, Forerunner. We are to deliver his kind to the officers of Lord Bastion or Lady Maritia. Those are our orders and therefore yours, too!"

"Take him, then," the Protectors' leader said, "but we lay claim for the discovery of the nephew."

"You could've just as easily lost him if we hadn't been nearby, but we'll talk about sharing, shall we?" One of them prodded Faros. "He'll be going nowhere on his own. You two! Get him to his feet. Drag him along."

As the soldiers pulled him up, Faros saw the Protectors seize hold of Bek's body. The black-helmed figures lifted Bek's limp form as if he were a sack of wet grain. Faros's vision cleared enough to enable him to stare into the slack face of the one who had saved his life, who had sacrificed everything for a futile cause.

Once more, they were pursued.

Where the two huge, three-masted ships had come from, neither Rahm nor Azak could say. The vessels appeared from the south, small dots that grew rapidly. The precision with which the two ships broke through the choppy waters and maneuvered so near to one another spoke of the discipline of the empire's naval force.

"To port! To port!" cried the captain of *Dragon's Crest*.

Sailors worked the lines, trying to feed their own ship the

wind it needed. *Dragon's Crest* flew over the water and yet still could not escape the fast-approaching pursuers.

"There should have been no other ships in these waters," Azak growled. "What's to be found here that would interest a pair of hawks like that?"

Eyeing the newcomers, the general muttered, "Us, apparently."

"We could stand and fight," the captain suggested. No minotaur desired to run from battle, even a hopeless one.

"Neither can use their catapults in these mad waters," Rahm reminded the elder captain. In calmer seas, *Dragon's Crest* would have been in range of an expert shot. "Can't we make better use of the wind? You've always said this is one of the swiftest ships in the empire."

The graying mariner looked down his muzzle. "And she is, but we'd need to head south to catch the wind, and that would bring us even closer to that ugly pair."

Rahm made a desperate calculation. "Make a shift, anyway, if only by two degrees."

Azak gave him an incredulous look. "Has madness taken you? We'll only guarantee swift capture—*if* they don't sink us!"

"Do as I say!" The general peered at the cloud-covered skies to the east. "Give it everything you can! Cut through the water and never mind that pair! I think we're near!"

"Near to what? That island of yours cannot be around here! Islands just don't pop up on well-charted waters."

"Just trust me, Azak!"

With a shake of his head, Azak shouted the change in course.

At that moment, what sounded like thunder burst from the closest enemy vessel.

A massive, spherical object flew into the air, arcing clearly towards the Crest.

"Starboard!" roared Azak. "Starboard!"

A rock as large as a minotaur crashed into the water just off the port side. The sea welled up, sending a wall of water over the rail.

One sailor was swept away. Another barely held on. *Dragon's Crest* rocked back and forth violently.

The captain swore. "That was too damned good a shot for the first try! The next one's bound to be a hit!"

While the first ship reloaded, the second vessel, charging forward, angled for a clear shot.

Rahm glanced ahead and saw nothing. No, was that a dot on the horizon?

"Azak! Hold your course!"

A second dot appeared, then a third. Moments later, the general counted five distinct forms.

One of the crew spotted them and called out, "Pirates!"

No sooner did the cry go out than another crack of thunder sounded.

"Damn it! Two degrees port! I said port this time!"

The sudden veering saved *Dragon's Crest* from a direct hit. Unfortunately, the massive rock did not miss completely, smashing into the crow's nest with such force that splinters rained down. The hand on watch never had a chance to jump to safety. Rahm heard him scream, and then no more.

"We're done for either way, but we'll give them a fine fight!" Turning on his good leg, the graying mariner called out, "All hands to stations! Prepare to repel boarders!"

Rahm put a hand on Azak's shoulder. "No! Do nothing! I think . . . I think they've come to meet us!"

"They what?"

The two pursuing ships had finally noticed the five new vessels approaching. For a moment, it appeared that the pair would stand and fight, but then the two imperial vessels turned, abandoning their prey.

The other five closed in.

"Are you sure of this, lad?"

Rahm's throat constricted. "No."

"Lovely to hear." With reluctance, Captain Azak called for his crew to stand down.

One of the strange ships veered toward them while the other four sailed at a swift pace after the bulkier imperial hunters.

"Look at those lines!" the first mate, a heavy, jovial male called Botanos rumbled. The black giant leaned over the rail, disregarding the target he made for any expert archer as he stared at the approaching ship. "Look how she cuts the water!"

"She travels the open sea like a fish!" returned the bosun.

"Just who are they?" Azak asked.

Rahm, his hands gripped tight on the rail, said nothing. The imperial vessels could not escape. As they and their adversaries shrank in the distance, the general heard a short, familiar crack and saw something fly toward the slower enemy ship.

Limping next to him, Captain Azak wore a grim expression. "They'll never make it. If those low-slung wolves mean to end them, it'll happen, mark me."

"Captain!" called a hand up on the ropes. "She flies no banners!"

"You sure these are not pirates?"

"No, they're not." Rahm muttered. The fugitive commander bent his head low, keeping his horns down and showing the back of his neck. "I've not told everything, I admit that now, Azak."

The frustrated captain shook his head. "Raise your horns and tell me what's going on. I can always take your head later if I do not like what I hear, eh?"

The general pointed at the nearing ship. "I didn't say so before, but we could never find Petarka on our own. He said that a ship would come and guide us. I had every reason to believe he told the truth."

"And who is 'he'?"

"An associate."

"An associate. That's it?" Azak rubbed the underside of his muzzle then gave his friend a cautious nod. They both knew that Rahm had not only staked his honor on this, but all their lives as well.

As the mystery ship neared, more details could be made out. Lower and narrower than their vessel, its hull was painted a dark sea green and built with such precision that it was difficult to see where one plank ended and another began. The sails were arched. The masts, shorter and slimmer than the *Crest*'s, showed no strain at all as the sails filled. The bow sliced the waves, its elongated, narrowing point thrusting forward like a lance.

"That thing could do a lot of damage," commented the captain uneasily. "It's built sturdy, and as low as they sit, a ship rammed by them would take on water quick."

Several figures moved about the mysterious vessel.

"They're minotaurs!" someone roared.

While that in itself was no tremendous surprise, the strangers caused some curiosity. The crew stood tall and slim. They moved with more the grace of acrobats than warriors. Their fur tended toward light brown, and most wore their manes in a tail. Snouts were angular, less pronounced. The mysterious mariners wore knee-length, seagreen kilts.

Instead of a catapult, the new vessel carried near its bow a ballista that could launch two wooden, iron-tipped javelins eight feet in length. A long, flexible piece of timber hauled back by the windlass—a drum-shaped winch—would, when released, strike the javelins with such ferocity that they might pierce a hull. Like the imperial fleet's ballistae and catapults, this one rested on a flat platform that enabled its users to turn it in any direction.

The unknown ship slowed, taking up a position alongside *Dragon's Crest*. Both Rahm and Azak noted that the ballista was aimed in their direction.

One of the green-clad figures pointed southeast.

"Follow them," Rahm urged.

"They'll lead us to Petarka?"

"I'm staking my life on it."

"You're staking all our lives on it," Azak grumbled. Turning, the wrinkled minotaur shouted out Rahm's instructions.

As *Dragon's Crest* turned to follow the other ship, its captain could not help commenting, "Interesting allies you seem to have picked up, my good friend. Interesting, indeed."

Gazing at the vessel in front of them, General Rahm shook his head. "Not allies," he corrected, with a touch of anxiety. "Enemies."

The two helmed minotaurs swung their axes lustily, both gasping from continued effort. Sweat caked their fur and stung their eyes.

One flung off his helm, the better to wipe his brow. The other tried to take advantage but failed. The axes clanged together, resounding.

Above them, the crowd cheered and thumped their feet.

Hotak had declared an end to imperial combats, but he had not declared an end to the Great Circus. No emperor would be so foolish. The Circus was the imperium.

And this, being the first day of events since Hotak had been crowned, was a time of intense excitement. This was something that the minotaurs, having experienced so much upheaval, not only needed, but demanded. The Circus was now the outlet for their pent-up tension, each gladiator the living representation of their anxiety. The cheers were almost manic.

The once-sandy field now lay drenched in sweat and blood from earlier combats. One of the duelists put his foot down in a slick, red puddle and lost his balance slightly.

It was all the helmless fighter needed. His axe came in under the first minotaur's own weapon, then cut upward. A horrific, crimson slit opened up the length of the gladiator's torso. With a snort of pain, the helmed minotaur wobbled and dropped his weapon. He took a step toward his foe—then twirled and dropped to the ground.

The roar of the throng echoed beyond the Circus. The victor raised his axe and turned in a circle, stopping before the imperial box.

There, Hotak, accompanied by Nephera and surrounded by an entourage consisting of his senior officers, stood and acknowledged the fighter with an outstretched fist. The victor knelt in tribute as horns blared and drums rumbled. Behind him, others hurried to drag the carcass of the loser away.

"Another excellent duel," the emperor commented as he sat again. "A promising omen after the coronation—and just what the citizens need! A good day's entertainment to remind them that the realm is secure and stable, that they have nothing to fear."

"But they know that already," Nephera replied. "After all, you are their leader now."

Banners whipped in the strong wind coming in from the Courrain Ocean. Horns blared, sounding the next combat.

A blunt-nosed veteran seated near Hotak's other side shifted at the sound. The emperor looked his way. "This is Kyril's duel, isn't it, Commander Orcius?"

"Aye, my lord."

Hotak looked somber. "He had command of those ordered to secure or slay General Rahm Es-Hestos. It was imperative his force succeed, yet the general evaded capture rather too easily, did he not?"

"Aye, my lord."

"A tragic error of command. My officers represent me. When they fail, I fail in the eyes of the people. You know that." When the other minotaur nodded, Hotak added, "He chose to take this path. Kyril chose to enter the arena to atone."

The horns blared again. From the gate nearest the imperial box entered a young, sturdy minotaur with brown fur and a determined expression. He wore no helm, no armor. For a weapon, he carried only a short sword and a dagger.

Hotak rose, his entourage following suit. The Circus grew still.

Eyes unblinking, Kyril saluted his leader. "For the honor of my commander and emperor! May the stain of my disgrace be this day erased!"

With a nod, Hotak acknowledged the words, then re-seated himself.

Stepping to the midst of the field, Kyril took his position.

The drums beat, and the horns unleashed two harsh, foreboding blasts.

From the disgraced officer's left and right two gates opened. Out of each marched first one, then two, then three massive, armored figures. The newcomers wore not only helms and breastplates, but additional protection on the forearms and shins. Three even carried round wooden shields.

And where Kyril had only a short sword and dagger, his adversaries wielded twin-edged axes, long swords, and even maces. Kyril was not expected to survive this combat. What was important was that he die valiantly and redeem himself.

In ominous formation the six surrounded their lone foe, leaving between them a gap twice as large as a minotaur's reach. Kyril turned in a circle once, evaluating his foes. By the emperor's decree, the six gladiators had been chosen from the best fighters, and while that further increased the odds against the officer, it made his expected demise all the more honorable. The greater a minotaur's enemies, the more glory he attained, regardless of the outcome.

A lull swept over the Circus, adding to the suspense.

Then a single horn sounded.

The moment it did, Kyril reacted. With an astonishingly swift but graceful turn to his left, he flipped the dagger around and tossed it at one of the axe-wielding figures.

The dagger embedded itself in the unprotected throat of the minotaur.

With a gurgle, the stricken gladiator fell to his knees. Dropping his weapon, he made one feeble attempt to draw the blade from his throat then fell, blood spilling from the wound.

The throng, momentarily stunned, had its cheering cut off, but a second later the cheering erupted louder than before, and many stomped their feet to honor the first kill.

Even before his opponent had dropped, Kyril had already begun running toward his fallen foe. His hand came within inches of securing the lost axe before a sword lunge from the next nearest fighter almost severed his fingers. Kyril rolled over his victim, then rose in a crouch, short sword ready, as the other five charged him.

Two with shields moved in first. Kyril deflected a mace. He backed away continuously, trying to keep his eyes on the other three, who sought to circle him.

Then, with a snort Kyril astonished his attackers by charging headlong into the pair. Instinctively they moved their shields to create a wall, but Kyril used his forearms to push the shields up into the faces of the gladiators.

Momentarily blinded, they were not prepared when he raced around behind one of them. As he passed, Kyril swung wildly at his foe. He failed to wound the gladiator, but the force of the blow against his armored back nonetheless sent the fighter stumbling forward.

The audience roared its approval of the condemned one's cunning. He was giving them the best of shows.

Kyril shoved the sword through the belt of his kilt then scooped up the huge, double-edged weapon on the run.

No sooner had he done so then another axe blade sliced into the ground next to him, raising up a storm of sand. Coughing, the lone minotaur spun about, using his new weapon to deflect a second attack. The formidable weapon dug into an attacket's shield and by sheer brute force Kyril ripped the shield away.

The shield went flying into the audience, unleashing a new gasp of admiration and pleasure. In the imperial box, Hotak nodded proudly and patted Nephera's hand. He glanced at Orcius, giving him an approving smile.

Keeping his enemies at bay, Kyril backed toward the far end of the arena. The five fighters steadily approached him. They seemed content to let him guide the battle now—not what the hungering crowd expected.

The ground behind the dishonored officer shifted. A trap door slid open, sand trailing into it.

A ten-foot high burst of flame shot up, spreading out as it ascended.

With each succeeding generation, minotaur overseers of the Circus devised more surprises. From the passages built underneath the artificial floor of the arena, workers could send up beasts, new fighters, and an array of deadly traps. The blossoming inferno was the latest stunt. It was created by feeding oil into a fire and, with the use of bellows, funneling it upward.

With a cry, Kyril threw himself to the side, rolling in the sand. Smoke rose from his back, where his fur had been singed black.

Now two of his boldest adversaries closed in to finish him off. Yet as the first neared, Kyril, still on the ground but aware of the danger around him, dragged the axe in a wide arc.

He caught the first minotaur in the calf, a glancing blow but one that upset the fighter's balance. As he stumbled, Kyril rose and swung, burying the blade deep in the gladiator's thigh.

Even as his latest victim roared in agony, Kryil backed away. Already the flames were dying, but there would be other surprises, and he had to stay cautious.

The four remaining imperial gladiators retreated in unison back to midfield. Kyril's brow furrowed. He looked around for the next surprise.

The floor to his right slid open, revealing a much wider trap door. A ferocious roar stilled the crowd.

A hulking, horrific form appeared. Although chained tight to the platform that had raised it up, the monstrosity tugged with such frenzy that some in the crowd involuntarily leaned back as far away as possible— despite the fact that they were protected by high walls.

It roared again , , . with both mouths.

Manticores, with their brutish, almost human faces and vestigial wings, were rare in Krynn. This twin-headed beast resembled a manticore in some ways. Its two muzzles were flat and thick; black manes framed each macabre, savage visage. Its body was that of a muscular, leonine creature almost as large at the shoulder as a horse. The beast's spiked tail snapped back and forth as the heads strained to be free of their iron collars.

The minotaur adventurers who, after several grisly losses, had captured the first of these monsters had named them *chemocs*, or "the feeders of Chemosh" in the old tongue. The overseers of the Circus liked to promote them as the "Twin Deaths."

Under either name, they spelled doom for any combating them.

Onyx eyes glittered wildly in the daylight. The chemoc snapped its two heads in the direction of the crowd, then one set of eyes noticed the fighters. The beast strained again, causing the braces in the platform to groan ominously.

Although chained by the throat to each corner of the platform, the chemoc's paws were free. Talons half a foot long slashed at Kyril.

The four armored fighters now advanced again, forming a tightening half-circle around Kyril. They would drive the officer toward the beast, forcing him to choose one death or another.

The crowd roared happily at this newest turn of events.

Kyril moved to within just a few feet of the chemoc's savage reach. The talons came close, and its two heads snapped at him again and again, teeth as long as the minotaur's fingers seeking their target.

The two remaining axe wielders prodded at him, trying to push him toward the chemoc. A gladiator with a mace and shield moved in on his left.

The blood that had already been spilled drove the chemoc wild. One head began gnawing at a chain. Another concentrated its stare on the fresh meat so near.

Kyril deflected the stabbing axes, but in doing so he took one step too close.

The chemoc's claws tore at his back.

The first strike was glancing yet left four long, red tracks in his flesh. The crowd gasped, expecting a quick finish.

But Kryil again maneuvered away from the beast, forcing the gladiator with the mace and shield away from the rest.

Fresh blood on its paw, the chemoc grew mad with frustration. It pulled and chewed at its bonds. Its talons ripped at the platform.

One of the rear braces gave, and then the others failed. The chemoc tore itself free.

A stunned cry arose throughout the throng. The combatants, caught up in their duel, did not at first notice the surprise of surprises.

The chemoc was free, and like the manticore it had vestigial wings. The leathery appendages did not let it fly, but gave its leap more speed at short distance.

It leaped straight for Kyril, but the flux of battle awarded it a different victim. Down went the mace-wielding gladiator, his wooden shield a useless defense against the hulking beast.

One head thrust forward, and the beast took in the minotaur's head and neck and snapped them free. The other sniffed the air and sized up the remaining figures. Any of them would do. It was not choosy. The three remaining gladiators glanced at each other. They hadn't counted on this. Only Kryil seemed calm. The chemoc's breath came in rapid gasps. Its handlers had not fed it for days.

None of the fighters broke. The gates through which they could escape were too far away, and to turn one's back on the chemoc invited its attention.

The upraised head roared, which seemed to bring it to the attention of the other one feeding. Jaws drenched red, the second joined the first in seeking new prey.

Nostrils scenting blood, the chemoc again leaped toward Kyril.

He jabbed at it with the axe as it descended, catching the bloody head just under the throat. The chemoc landed clumsily, but the wound it suffered only stung.

The other minotaurs backed away. Kyril was the show here, and they would be glad to escape the chemoc's attention.

But Kyril fought fiercely, driving the chemoc back, swinging the axe again and again. Once the huge creature almost snagged it from him, but Kyril pulled his weapon away.

He managed a blow to one head's snout, drawing more blood. Both heads snarled.

Movement caught the chemoc's eyes. Forgotten in the struggle, the minotaur whom Kyril had wounded in the leg was seeking to drag himself to safety. In attempting so, however, he only marked himself as an easy victim.

The leonine fury whirled from Kyril. For a brief moment, the disgraced officer hesitated—and then rushed the beast from behind.

Kyril had been intended to die, but with the threat to their comrade, the other minotaurs joined the fray. They, however, came from farther away and would have been too late to save the wounded fighter.

Kyril was not.

He leaped upon the monster's back, barely grabbing hold. In the process, Kyril lost his axe.

The chemoc reared, the heads trying to twist around enough to bite. The wounded gladiator, forgotten again, pulled away as best he could.

Straddling his horrific foe, Kyril struggled to free his sword. He raised it up, but the violent thrashing by the twin-headed horror kept him from making any use. The other gladiators stood near, transfixed and uncertain.

The crowd was caught up. Hundreds of minotaurs now stood and shouted. They raised their fists in the air. Many of those seated thumped their feet.

In the imperial box, Hotak sat poised at the edge of his seat. Unlike the crowd, he held his emotions in check, but his eyes blazed with anticipation.

The chemoc's wings flapped wildly, and the spiked tail sought Kyril. If not for its wings, the leonine beast would have rolled over and simply crushed the minotaur.

Brandishing their axes, the two other fighters now stepped in front of the snapping heads. They did not move to assist

Kyril, but rather to shield their fallen comrade. Another gladiator seized the injured fighter and pulled him to safety.

One head sought Kyril while the other bit at the two gladiators standing before it. One of the armored minotaurs got too close. A paw suddenly lashed out. It caught warrior and axe together and sent the gladiator smashing against the nearest wall. The clang of metal against stone was drowned out by the screaming thousands.

Taking advantage of the distraction, Kyril plunged his blade into the back of one of the chemoc's skulls.

Shrieking, the creature rose on its hind legs and tossed its undesired rider off the back. Kyril crashed hard and rolled onto the sand. As he tried to rise, a chance slap of the spiked tail caught him in the stomach.

No one heard his scream over the roars of the crowd, but his pain was evident to those in the royal box. As the wounded chemoc stumbled back and forth, Kyril forced himself to his feet. His entire torso was drenched in blood and three gaping wounds could be seen.

Twirling around and around, the other head of the chemoc sought in vain to remove the sword from the wounded one. Its blunt snout, however, did not give it reach.

Blood flowing over its mane, the injured head bobbled. The onyx eyes dulled and, its tongue lolling, the one head stilled.

Seeking something on which to vent its fury, the chemoc started after the surviving gladiators. Kyril, unsteady, used the moment to stumble toward the axe he had dropped.

The chemoc saw him, and, forgetting the others, roared and turned on the one who had caused it so much pain.

Kyril seized the weapon.

The chemoc leaped one last time.

Hands slippery from blood and sweat, the young officer knelt and planted the back end of the axe like a pike.

The savage beast fell upon Kyril. Already terribly wounded, the minotaur could not brace the axe well enough. The immense mass of the chemoc crushed him.

But his axe sliced into the creature's lower throat and chest. Had that not been enough, the minotaur's long, sharp horns impaled the chemoc just below the jaw. The head snapped up so hard that the beast's neck cracked.

With a groan, the twin-headed fury collapsed.

An uncertain silence enshrouded the Great Circus. This had been a most unusual battle. Hotak leaned over the edge of the wall.

Armed handlers rushed out to the scene. After some prodding and poking of the chemoc, they nodded to the emperor.

The crowd let out a booming cheer. Over and over they repeated one name. *"Kyril! Kyril!"*

Hotak and the others watched as the body of the beast was pushed over. Other minotaurs bearing a wooden stretcher hurried to the site.

The young officer was dead. Had his monstrous opponent not crushed him, his wounds would have killed him soon enough. Yet still the throng cheered him. They stood and waved their fists and cried his name.

Kyril's body was brought before his emperor. With a glance to the dead minotaur's superior officer, Hotak rose solemnly from his seat. An attendant handed him a small sheaf of horsetail grass.

Hotak held the sheaf high so that all might see it, then with horns blaring, he tossed it respectfully down onto the prone form.

Again, the crowd roared approval. The honor bestowed upon Kyril restored to the officer his place among his people. His failures were erased from memory. The stain that had reflected upon his emperor was no more.

The bearers held the stretcher and body over their heads as they circled the perimeter of the field once. Small banners and more sheaves alighted onto the corpse, signs of admiration for the passing of an honorable warrior.

Their circuit completed, they vanished with Kyril through the main gate. Orcius had already made arrangements for the remains with his young protege's clan.

"Not as expected," Hotak commented to Orcius, as he seated himself again. "but still a glorious end for Kyril. His name will be spoken of by all for some time to come. He will be a model for those who follow him."

"As you say," Orcius responded.

"Consider this, too, commander," Lady Nephera added. "He now becomes a guide to his kin and loved ones. He takes on a mantle greater than any in his mortal life."

"As you say, my lady. I am not of the Forerunner faith, though."

"Perhaps with time."

Hotak quieted them both. "Let us be content to honor young Kyril. He even saved the lives of his foes. He lived and died well. Truly, a symbol of minotaur honor." He leaned back, awaiting the next event.

CHAPTER VI

DREAMS AND NIGHTMARES

As his grip on Nethosak tightened, so did Hotak's demands over the empire. From rocky Kothas to lush Selees, from wheat- and corn-rich Amur in the northeast to wooded Broka at the heart of the realm, imperial units took over the local government and placed the colonies under the absolute control of appointed military liaisons, the provost captains.

On Mito in the port city of Strasgard, the militia commander stepped into the provost captain's office. The three gold rings he wore in each ear—symbolizing his authority—jingled as the beefy minotaur went down on one knee.

Behind the desk of the late governor, the brooding gaze of Provost Captain Haab swept over the local commander. Born in the capital, the slim-snouted Haab was a soldier dedicated to his emperor.

"What is it, Commander Ryn?" the provost captain asked, tapping his long fingers on the desk. Haab accented almost every statement or question with tapping of his fingers.

"The shipwrights've gathered supporters. They're marching through Strasgard, demanding that their masters be released and management of the facilities be returned to local sovereignty."

Three days earlier Hotak's legionaries, in conjunction with the imperial fleet, had marched in, seizing the port operations. Mito was not only the third largest island in population, but also third largest builder of ships. To have its autonomy revoked had created shockwaves throughout the colony.

"I warned them that the emperor would brook no opposition," Haab responded with a tap.

" 'Tis hardly a rebellion. Mostly a show of raised arms and shouts, provost captain. My . . . *the* people are upset. This is not how the empire works!"

"This is the way it works now, Ryn." Haab leaned forward. "The realm will be put in order. This latest edict by the emperor is meant to help that happen."

Keeping his horns very low, Ryn suggested, "If the ship masters were set free . . . with new restrictions placed on them perhaps. . . ?"

He let his words sink in. If the masters swore to uphold the new edicts, things could go back to normal. Ryn liked normal. Dramatic change unnerved him.

Haab tapped the desk. When he spoke, it was in a tone that made the fur on Ryn's neck stiffen. "Your desire to keep Mito stable is commendable. The emperor looks to this colony as one of the vanguards of expansion. Mito's ships will supply our forces with transportation, defense, and supplies. It is essential that Strasgard, the largest port, be up and running at full strength."

At that moment, a messenger entered. He handed Haab a small scroll, then departed. The provost captain read it.

"Right on schedule." He tossed the message aside and leaned back, quite satisfied. "Our worries are over, Commander Ryn."

"Sir?"

"Reinforcements from Broka and Dus have just arrived. They're coming to shore south of Strasgard, as we speak."

A sick feeling swelled in Ryn's stomach. "For what purpose, provost captain?"

Haab bared his teeth in a smile. "For the purpose of putting our house in order."

The stunned militia officer could say nothing, understanding exactly what his superior meant. He lowered his head and tried not to think of his friends among the protesters.

The new arrivals joined the units stationed on Mito and quickly beat back the surprised protesters. Scores of colonists perished under the unforgiving onslaught, and soldiers dragged away dozens more, now identified as enemies of the state even though they had borne no love for Chot. Packed aboard a vessel built in Strasgard itself, the chained losers were sent off to—as Haab put it—"serve the empire in the only way fit for such as them."

Although the rebellion in Mito proved rare, the changes led by Hotak shook the empire. Ships laden with salted goat meat from Kothas, wheat from Amur, or breadfruit from Tengis were now under a special tax to aid the reorganization of the state. All foodstuff—whether fish, goat, grain, fruit, or even wine—was to be distributed under guidelines drawn up by the emperor. A portion of the profits of each shipload would go directly into the coffers of Hotak, there to be distributed to his chosen projects.

Several elders from clans who had looked with favor upon the coup now added their voices to the dissent—until the first of their numbers were led away in chains.

Emboldened, Emperor Hotak made his next move. All minotaurs received combat training from almost the time they could walk, and a good portion of those later served in the military. But few served for very long, most leaving to pursue their own destinies. The legions and the fleet were constantly in flux, their strength erratic and, especially during the past decade, general readiness declining under Chot.

Hotak intended to reverse all that. He envisioned a race of trained soldiers, a grand force consisting of every male, female, and adolescent, capable of organizing at a moment's notice. Thus came down the edict declaring that all young minotaurs would be conscripted. Every corner of the realm was expected to contribute their finest prospects, even though for some remote colonies this diminished their entire labor force. On major islands like Mithas, squads from the State Guard raided unsavory establishments and pressed into military service all the revelers. The game houses, considered another foul legacy of Chot, were then burned to the ground.

In just a few months, the new emperor declared to his loyal staff while signing the conscription edict, the imperium would boast a force twice as large, twice as well-trained, as any that served in ages past. A force to be reckoned with across all of Krynn.

Lady Nephera glided through the towering, stone corridors of the temple. To either side of her, set in marble block alcoves, huge figures three times her height stared down at her. Ephemeral forms clad in shroudlike garments, they seemed to take an intense interest in Nephera as she headed to her chambers.

Rounded, brass oil lamps whose flames arose from a curved spout hung suspended over the heads of the statues. Little other light illuminated this corridor. The horizontal slits near the outer ceiling were designed for ventilation.

Revealed in light and shadow by the flickering lamps, the huge stone figures represented the ghosts, the *forerunners* of the present minotaurs—those for whom Nephera had named her sect.

Acolytes in white robes with red trim from the shoulders to the cuffs bent low in homage. Two female attendants, their manes tied tight, prostrated before Nephera. Protectors in full black and gold regalia kept to their positions near the walls, eyes straight ahead, multi-barbed maces held ready.

The shadows and wind shifting around Nephera represented a force beyond the mortal plane. When the priestess passed by, the statues seemed—just for the briefest of breaths—to stir. A rustling of cloth here, the shifting of a masked gaze there. Even the fanatical Protectors peered anxiously over their shoulders when passing through.

Two brawny, female guards, chosen from among her own priestesses, raised their axes in salutation as Lady Nephera approached her quarters. Clad as the Protectors save for helms, they lived to serve her and no other.

Falling to one knee, her horns pointed down and her ponytail pulled to one side so as to bare her neck, the senior guard announced, "Mistress, your son awaits you within."

Nephera hid her displeasure at this news as she entered. Even after many days, Ardnor had been unable to forget his disappointment at the coronation.

Clad in gray robes and slung over the curled arms of an elegant oak and leather chair, Ardnor had a bottle of temple wine in one hand. In his other hand, he held a half-crumpled parchment that the high priestess immediately recognized as having been taken from her desk.

Nephera's dark eyes widened, and her shoulders stiffened.

"Stand up! What sort of mockery do you think you make of yourself when you appear in such a state?" She ripped the sheet from his hand. In truth, Nephera cared not so much about her son's drunken appearance, but that he had dared go through her papers.

"So old Nymon's found himself on one of your lists, has he?" Ardnor rumbled, the smell of fermented fruit washing over his mother. "What's he done?"

She turned from him, returning the precious paper to her desk. "Nothing, but his character has come into question. He is being . . . observed."

"Observed." Ears twitching in mirth, the massive minotaur let loose with a short, barking laugh.

Her hand pressed against her chest, Lady Nephera turned on him. "Put that bottle down, and act your station! Do you want to exasperate matters? What would happen if your father saw you?"

"Father'd never step foot in this room, and you know it." Ardnor pushed himself to his feet, then tossed the empty bottle on the chair. Drops of wine dribbled onto the leather. "Father's ashamed of this place . . . and us!"

Nephera slapped him.

Their gazes did battle, and Ardnor looked away.

"Speak not like that again."

Sullen, he nodded. Nephera saw that wine had stained his gray robes.

"Forgive me for my words, Mother." Ardnor took a deep breath, then exhaled. The high priestess tried to ignore the new wave of sour fumes. "They were rash and unfounded."

"And dangerous, too. I've just come from the palace."

All trace of sluggishness vanished. Ardnor leaned toward her like an eager puppy. "Did you speak with him? Did he explain why he shamed me?"

"I spoke to your father, yes. He explained quite reason ably why he chose to do what he did. He needs a bit more time to solidify political support and to prove the stability of his rule. You'll be declared heir yet, my son, but the announcement will have to wait a little. That's all."

"How long? A few days? A week?"

She grew exasperated. "Not long. You must learn to live with that answer, Ardnor. Trust in your father."

"I trust in you, Mother. If you believe him, then so do I."

He still raged inside, but Nephera could see that the fight had started to go out of him. Still, she would be happy when Hotak announced Ardnor as the next emperor.

"It's late, my son," she said softly. The same hand that had struck so violently now caressed Ardnor's muzzle. "I've work still to do."

Ardnor took the hint, bowing before her and responding, "Then I wish you good night, Mother. Thank you for everything."

"I do what is right—as does your father."

With reluctance, he nodded. "I know."

As Ardnor turned to leave, his mother recalled something else she and Hotak had discussed. The high priestess gritted her teeth, knowing this would prompt another battle.

"Ardnor, I want you to pull the Protectors from the searches."

A snarl escaped him. "He told you that?"

"I agree with him." With some reluctance, but she did.

The veins in his thick neck grew taut. Ardnor's grip on the door handle tightened, the wood groaning. In the end, though, he simply nodded, then silently departed, leaving in his wake two unnerved guards who quickly moved to shut the door.

Lady Nephera clapped her hands. "I require two attendants. Summon them."

Within seconds, a pair of anxious priestesses knelt before Lady Nephera and raised their slim, folded hands toward her.

Staring down at the two awed faces, Nephera commanded, "See that the meditation room is prepared. Then alert all Protectors that under no circumstances am I to be disturbed once I enter. No matter what they hear. Is that understood?"

"Yes, mistress!" they piped in unison.

While the two scurried off, Nephera stepped past her desk, past the vital lists that Ardnor had disorganized, and into her most private rooms. Darkness enveloped her as she entered.

The high priestess whispered a single word. A candle near her bed sputtered to life.

A slight shifting in her eyes represented Nephera's only pleasure at this achievement. She had progressed far beyond basic skills and, if her hopes held true, tonight she would cross yet another threshold.

When the temple had served the followers of Sargonnas, this room had been reserved for their high priest. Polished, silver-gray marble tiles covered the floors. Each piece had been cut into the shape of a five-inch wide square and inlaid with design by skilled workers. The import costs for such fine-quality stone would have paid a legion commander's wages for a year.

Built into the floor of the adjoining chamber and decorated in the same prime marble, was a vast bath. Servants did not have to tote buckets of cold or hot water to it; instead, in a separate portion of the building, they kept a set of giant cisterns—one heated, one not—filled to the brim with water. Through a set of pipes, Nephera herself could manipulate the temperature she desired, filling the bath—eight feet in width and double that in length—whenever she so desired.

The bath called to her, but the high priestess could not rest. She turned to the wall closet, carved, just like the wide bed beside it, from cedar imported from Sargonath, and reached in for a garment never seen outside of the temple. Utter black, almost shroudlike, and with a voluminous hood lined at the front edges in silver thread, the floor-length robe made its wearer resemble one of the dead. To further the effect, a black, shimmering veil of silk obscured the wearer's features.

As she dressed, her eyes drifted to the savage condor symbol, set in the wall across from the bed, which seemed to glare vengefully at her. The artisans had created the fiery bird from special marble, then touched it up with paint resistant to the constant scrubbing by her attendants. Eventually Nephera would have to have the wall replaced, but for now this last vestige of a lost god would remain.

Mistress.

Nephera glanced toward the bed, where a flickering shadow had separated from the others. With each dancing movement of the candle flame, Takyr's cadaverous, green-gray form faded in and out of sight. The tattered mariner's cloak billowed as if caught in a great gale. A faint scent hinting of the open sea and rotting vegetation touched the priestess's nostrils.

"I've a spell to cast. I'll need you."

Aye, mistress.

Lady Nephera adjusted the upturned collar of her robe then departed the room. As she passed her desk, the high priestess paused to pick up the parchment her son had been perusing earlier.

"What of Itonus? Anything observed?"

The mistress is not mistaken.

She reached for a quill, quickly adding the name to the parchment. Her expression grew triumphant. "The emperor will be very surprised. He didn't believe me. Now, he must."

The ghost said nothing.

With immense satisfaction, the high priestess returned quill and sheet to her desk then departed for the meditation room.

The two brooding Protectors on duty slapped their right fists on their breastplates then opened the doors. Nephera gave both an approving nod then stepped inside and waited for the doors to close behind her.

Once a place of secret rites, the high, arched chamber had fallen into empty ruin before Nephera had claimed the building ten years earlier. With the vanishing of the old gods, the great temples had been abandoned. Only a few small temples of Sargonnas and his rival, the bison-headed god of just cause, Kiri-Jolith, still remained here and there throughout the empire.

The tenets of the Forerunner faith had been inspired by the dream she had one night while her mate was away winning battles and glory for his undeserving master. Lady Nephera had no name for the mysterious power she wielded. Perhaps it had to do with this One True God she had heard of, perhaps not. Her only guidance came from dreams—and the voice that still spoke to her during her slumbers.

In the first dream, Nephera, clad in the robe she now wore, had found herself in a vast white nothingness standing upon a misty path composed of tiny bones. The path led into forever. An endless line of gray, shrouded figures made of smoke trod the path—the dead on their journey after life.

More curious than afraid, Nephera had dared join that monstrous line. The dead had paid her no mind. When she reached out to touch one, her fingers passed through shadowy mist. Her ethereal companions made no sound; they simply trudged along to their destiny.

Then, suddenly, the unearthly trail had ended, and Nephera had discovered herself at the wide steps of a gleaming, ivory temple. The gargantuan bronze doors, covered with the symbols of an ascending bird hovering over an axe of gold, opened readily. Lady Nephera stepped forward—

A blinding light burst forth. Nephera blinked until her vision returned and had found herself inside the temple.

Glittering tapestries three stories high covered every wall of the vast chamber, fluttering in a wind she could not feel. The marble floor beneath her feet shone. Ridged columns towered over her.

And there, set upon a waist-high, bone-white pedestal in the very center of the chamber, she had found the golden axe depicted on the doors—lying broken in half. Before the shattered weapon, there stood another new line of spectral forms. The first one touched with dry, transparent hands the head and the base of the handle.

The axe flared bright.

The ghost vanished. A second followed suit, then a third and on.

An inexplicable desire to put the two broken halves together compelled Nephera to step forward. But when she touched the pieces, nothing happened, and the weapon remained broken. This infuriated her beyond measure.

With a growl, Nephera slammed the two pieces together, forcing them to meld even as they shook, flared, and burned like fire in her hands. A hundred times she considered letting go, but a hundred times she held on, *fusing* the two parts.

In death is the axe broken, intoned a voice without gender, a voice without emotion—a voice that came from within and without. *It is lain upon the chest of the dead warrior, a symbol of his or her passing on to the next great battle.*

Then the golden weapon began to shrink, growing so small that within seconds Nephera could cradle the artifact in her arms.

When the axe is broken, it can never be made one again; so it is written, continued the genderless voice. *But if there is one who can mend that which cannot be made whole, then that one holds power over death itself—and the world beyond.*

All the while the ghosts floated around her, each wanting to touch the weapon but unable to do so because of her. They watched her with awe and fear. Their gray, washed-out features contorted in silent pleas.

Nephera realized that she had complete command over them.

By now, the once-great golden axe was but a tiny amulet.

The minotaur raised it to her breast, touched it to her skin just below her throat—

And there it sank into her flesh, melding with her body, fusing with her soul.

More from surprise than fright, Nephera had screamed, and that scream had shattered the dream. Hotak's wife had leaped from their bed, certain that she had imagined all.

But in the mirror, the tiny axe buried in her flesh still burned as bright as fire—and erased any doubt.

From that day forward, Nephera had become a different being, one who constantly walked not only the plane of the living, but also the realm of the dead. Ghosts—true ghosts, not the faded figures of her dream—gathered around her, obeying her every word and bringing her news and information. With her newfound powers, Nephera drew others to her and proclaimed the birth of the Forerunners.

Hotak had not welcomed her change, not until one of her ghosts had informed her of the ambitious officer spying on him for Chot. An accident had readily dealt with that situation, and from then on Lady Nephera had ensured the loyalty of all those around her and her husband. She took a more active hand in his campaigns, aiding his victories with her unearthly spies.

Now, years after that fateful night, Nephera stood in the meditation room, staring at the symbol of the Forerunners— the golden axe broken in two and, above it, the magnificent bird of prey, a hawk, also of pure gold. The axe represented death, with the ascending bird symbolizing the spirit rising from the mortal plane.

Nephera opened her collar, revealing the tiny golden axe still embedded in her skin just below her throat.

Only those who stood highest in the temple hierarchy knew of its existence, and they were sworn to secrecy. Even her husband did not know of the axe bestowed on her by the dream, for Nephera had discovered the ability to mask it from the eyes of others. Any who stared at her would see only the usual fur and flesh.

In contrast to the massive icon on the wall, no other images and no furniture decorated the great room. A single torch set in each corner gave sufficient illumination, and no more. For what Lady Nephera did here, she wanted no distractions.

Looking now to Takyr, the high priestess nodded.

The ghost raised one transparent, skeletal hand and the chamber began to fill with the dead.

All around her stood green-gray forms forever locked in their moment of death. By fire, blade, sickness, infirmity, and other causes they had perished. All were minotaurs. These and more each day came to serve her.

Some wore rags, others fine gowns and uniforms. If their death had been peaceful, then the spectre looked intact, almost alive—save for the hollow eyes and hungering look. However, if their end had come through catastrophic means, then that ghost carried with it the horrific image of its demise. Ripped and torn flesh, skulls opened by axes—the variety was endless.

Here stood one male who had been slain in violent battle, his head barely upright on his shoulders, his breastplate slashed wide. Blackened blood covered his chest, oozing slowly from his vicious wounds. Beside him drifted a child who had perished from the scarlet plague, a scourge on all races since the Dragon Wars centuries before. The dead youngster was constantly caught up in fits of pain and coughing. Pustules covered her muzzle.

Scents mingled around her—the smell of burned ash, the deep sea, and flowery fragrances. The fire was that which consumed agonized flesh, the sea that which swallowed a life whole, and the flowers those left to decay with the dead.

"Attend me!" Nephera commanded the shades.

They encircled her, a ghastly, grasping horde whose presence might have driven another mad, yet their nearness only made Nephera's heart pound with joy, for they were her key to glory.

Placing her hands upon the icon on her chest, she began to hum. The ghosts—with the exception of Takyr—crowded near, their fleshless hands reaching. They were drawn to the axe.

One by one, the shades passed through the high priestess's body and disappeared.

With each intrusion, Nephera shivered. She muttered and drew symbols in the air, symbols from both the dream and her subconscious.

Above her, a cloud formed, a cloud that writhed, as though alive. A faint sound like the breathing of a beast touched her ears.

"Barakash!" Nephera shouted, using the words of a language she knew only from her dreams. "Verisi Barakash!"

The cloud blackened, thickened. Within the monstrous, growing mass, two fiery orbs appeared. They stared down at the ecstatic high priestess, and Lady Nephera stared back, undaunted.

"Takyr! Attend me!"

The dark shade drifted over to her. The cloud creature remained near the ceiling, writhing.

Now Takyr stepped into the priestess's body.

She shook like a puppet whose strings have been jerked. When Nephera spoke, her voice came out both female and male, alive . . . and dead.

"Rahm Es-Hestos!" her own strange voice called. "Tiribus de-Nordmir! Verisi Barakash!"

Armlike appendages sprouted from the sides of the cloud. The eyes focused on something the high priestess could not see, then moved toward the icon on the wall, momentarily lost all cohesion—and drifted through the wall as if no obstruction existed.

Takyr, looking very faint, emerged from Nephera's body.

The priestess gasped and nearly fell. Her body was drenched in sweat, and her heart was pounding . . . but she had done it! She had passed a threshold of spellcasting that once had been beyond her. Nephera had summoned into being a hunter, an avenger, a shade that would end her anxiety.

"I did it," she muttered. "Hide. Hide wherever you like. You cannot escape."

Regaining her breath, the high priestess looked up to see the ghosts reappearing. Like Takyr, they seemed drained. From experience, she knew they would recoup their strength and grow in numbers.

Nephera, too, had to recoup. Her body ached, and her head pounded. Ignoring the unearthly stares of the spectres, Lady Nephera made her way from the meditation room. The Protectors snapped to attention, and although they watched her as she passed, she found herself amused that they could not see the swarm of ghosts escorting her.

And well beyond the confines of the temple, a dark, inhuman searcher with eyes of fire now drifted throughout Nethosak.

Above the Blood Sea and the Courrain Ocean, clouds began to form—thick green-gray clouds such as not even the most grizzled mariner could recall. Gradually, they filled the skies.

The seas grew choppy, and wary captains kept one eye on the darkened skies as the heavens transformed.

CHAPTER VII

HARSH MEASURES

Several days after Hotak's coronation, a smaller ceremony took place late one evening in the headquarters of the eight members of the Supreme Circle—a vast, rectangular building flanking the palace. With retinues greater than some small Houses, the Circle saw to it that the imperial armies were fed, the fleets kept in good repair, and the lives of the citizenry safeguarded. In the past, the Supreme Circle had kept the minotaurs united during even the most violent eras. Emperors came and went, but the Circle persevered.

Until recently. Now the Circle itself was tainted. All but one member had been replaced. Now the Circle existed to serve Hotak, not the people.

It was well after dark when Maritia and her escort of six arrived at the headquarters. Unshuttered square windows lined the upper levels and half a dozen unadorned columns flanked the entrance. Her party strode up a short flight of steps where they were met by a contingent of the State Guard, which saluted her smartly, then led the party inside.

As she entered the great gallery, rows of robed elders stood to acknowledge her. The gallery had been created for important debates concerning the Circle and the major Houses. Today, somber minotaurs filled the five hundred seats, more standing than sitting.

On a high, wide platform the members of the Supreme Circle sat. One step below the rest was the seat of the council scribe, who set down the words of the gathering and, therefore, the words that became law. Only those with the sharpest ears and quickest hands could do this job.

Protocol demanded that no weapons were allowed in the chamber save those wielded by the guards, but neither Maritia nor her companions had been asked to remove theirs. Only when the emperor's daughter faced the assembly did the eight elders of the Supreme Circle finally take their places. The council scribe seated herself and took quill in hand.

Nearby stood a dais upon which a tremendous pyre had been set. The immense, bronze bowl was set afire at the start of each session to symbolize the vitality of the empire. A guard waited, torch in hand. The fire this day would burn higher and brighter than ever.

High above hung the banners of each clan, but a good many of the poles now stood bare.

Lothan, his hood pulled back, joined Maritia in the center. A hush fell over all as the gaunt councilor bowed to the emperor's daughter.

"The wisdom of the throne is welcomed by this assembly," he intoned, using the traditional greeting.

"The throne gratefully accepts the invitation of its most learned and trusted servants," Maritia replied.

To the left of the Circle, a single trumpeter sounded three short, deep notes, and the guard thrust the blazing torch into the oiled wood. A fearsome fire shot up, briefly engulfing the gigantic bowl.

The scribe rose from her seat. "The horn is sounded! The flame is lit! The words spoken now, the actions taken hence, will be set for the record, for the future of the empire! Let those gathered recall this, for there shall be no more warning!"

As she seated herself again, guards shut and barred every door.

The formalities concluded, Maritia handed a scroll to the councilor.

Lothan quickly perused it then surveyed the audience. "Attend me, brothers and sisters!" he shouted. "I hold in my hands a proclamation delivered unto me concerning those Houses who, by their own acts, chose freely to align themselves with the regime of Chot the Corrupt!"

Rumblings arose as the assembled patriarchs and their retinues made a show of how much they despised those clans. Their feet drummed hard. Never mind that almost everyone there had willingly engaged in business and political transactions with House Kalin over the years.

"It is the righteous and knowledgeable decision of the emperor," the senior councilor went on, "that these clans suffer the greatest penalty for their treasonous behavior!"

A guard standing to the right of the platform beat on a large, brass kettle drum. He repeated the same short cadence, one hand striking, then two heartbeats of quiet, then the other hand striking, two more heartbeats and so on.

To the far side of the pyre stood a long, plain table upon which several immense, folded cloths lay stacked one upon another. Lothan nodded his head slightly as a guard lifted one cloth up in the air.

The members of the Circle rose and moved toward the table.

The drum beats ceased.

"On this day," continued the gaunt councilor. "At this august hour, and by signed declaration of the emperor, let the following Houses suffer all loss of recognition. Their holdings will be assumed by the throne, to be distributed among the people. Those who served their base causes will be removed from minotaur society, their names erased forever. All records concerning these clans shall be stricken. They and theirs shall be shunned. It will be as though they never existed."

A new rumble of approval met these words, the surviving patriarchs bowing to the wisdom of Hotak.

"Let it begin!" Lothan raised his hand, and the cadence began anew.

The first elder stepped forward, taking the tightly folded banner from the guard. The gray-robed minotaur carried the banner up a set of short steps until he stood before the dancing flames. He then let the banner fall open for all to see. Upon a field of green stood a menacing orange crab.

The drumming ceased.

"Let forever be forgotten—House Ryog!" Lothan roared.

With a look of disdain, the elder threw the banner into the inferno, where it was engulfed. In seconds, nothing remained but ash.

The minotaurs in the audience bared their teeth and hissed their hatred of all things Ryog.

A second member of the Supreme Circle ascended. She repeated the steps, letting all see the clan symbol—a brave silver warrior wielding an axe, his body highlighted by a golden sun.

"Let forever be forgotten—House Hestos!"

Once more the crowd responded, and once more the next elder took his place at the pyre.

Lothan almost evinced pleasure as he proceeded through the names. "Let forever be forgotten—House Neros!"

On and on it went until more than a dozen major clans and double that number among the lesser families had been banished and incinerated. The toll staggered even some of those loyal to Hotak.

Only two banners remained, one already in the hands of a councilor.

"Let forever be forgotten—House Proul!"

Into the flames went another clan's history, its life. Finally, Hotak's daughter stepped forward with the last banner A hush fell over the crowd.

Maritia climbed the dais slowly, holding her prize before her. At the top, she turned and flung open the banner.

A crimson dragon bearing twin axes in its claws stretched over a field of black.

Louder than before, Lothan shouted, "Let forever be forgotten, forever be damned—*House Kalin!*"

With a contemptuous shout, Maritia sent the last vestiges of Chot's clan to a fiery destruction.

The congregation clapped, pounded their feet, and did whatever they could to enhance their own trivial roles in this ceremony. Never before had so many been cast out. Today marked history, marked a branching in minotaur tradition and beliefs.

But whether for good or ill only time would tell.

"Out of the wagon, you wretched lot!" roared the titanic, mud-brown bull Faros had heard the other soldiers call the Butcher. Like his compatriots, he was clad as a member of the State Guard, but the gray of their kilts came as much from the dust on them as the material itself.

In the days since the prisoners had been turned over to this monster, the Butcher—whose true name was Paug— had so far whipped three weak prisoners to death. Paug's brutality left Faros chilled, for he had never come across the likes of it. The slightest infraction set the monstrous figure off, and even the other guards did their best not to attract his ire.

A harsh rumbling drowned out all other sounds. A short distance to the north, a volcano spewed black smoke.

He and his fellow prisoners had been carted southeast to the edge of the mountain range called Argon's Chain. A dismal, soot-covered land, Argon's Chain boasted not only the tallest, most wicked peaks, but also several live craters. Faros coughed, the air thick not only from the heat but from the dark-gray ash constantly blown around by the fierce winds.

"Sargas preserve us," whispered a gray-furred elder, who had served as steward in the home of Kesk the Younger. "What do they want with us here?"

Even Gradic's son knew the answer to that mournful question. "We've been sent to the mines, old one."

Rich in fury, terrible in strength, the volcanic regions around the Chain were also rich in minerals valuable to the empire. Iron, lead, zinc, and copper were mined here, and even diamonds could be found. However, the slaves and prisoners had to dig hard and deep, and try not to let the suffocating, poisonous sulfuric gases and dangerous conditions kill them in the process.

Faros had been sent to the Mines of Vyrox.

Once Vyrox had been a promising mining community. The soil had been good for growing wheat and barley. Pear and apple trees had thrived, and a river whose channel had been cut by an ancient flow had provided all needs. Herds of goats were raised here, and occasional hunts had garnered deer, rabbit, and other woodland game. Vyrox had threatened to grow into a city second only to Nethosak.

The volcanoes had been dormant in those days.

And then, the volcanoes had erupted.

Of old Vyrox, there remained no trace. The community and nearly a thousand minotaurs lay buried under layers of ash and lava. Within the nearby mountains existed numerous shafts that had collapsed because of tremors or been crushed under the eruptions—burying many more bodies.

But the empire still needed the riches of Vyrox. Humans were the first to send their slaves to work the mines, but when they gained their freedom, the minotaurs had created a special class of felons and unwanted to supply the mines with expendable labor. It was always claimed that any minotaur sent to Vyrox could redeem himself by entering the Great Circus, but none earned that opportunity.

A few gnarled oak trees and some patches of sickly, brown wild grass made up the only plant life. Faros paused as the raspy sounds of large birds caught his attention.

"Birds," he muttered. "What can they feed on in this forsaken place?"

With a harsh laugh, the Butcher rumbled, "They find plenty, calf!" he replied, using the term for a new prisoner. "See that real big one up there?"

Perched on a branch, a huge crow eyed Faros.

"Looks like he's already marked you for later pickings—if the rats inside the mines don't get first choice!"

The younger minotaur shivered and quickly turned his gaze from the damnable bird, but it was only to see a more vile sight—the mining camp.

Surrounded by a tall wall of stone, the camp consisted of row upon row of colorless, windowless, block-shaped buildings. A single, thick wooden door with a heavy brace to lock in the occupants stood in the center in each structure. The only ventilation came from narrow slits at the top of each building.

Ash covered everything, even the ground trampled by generations of laborers. Everything looked as though all life had been drained out of it, especially the haggard faces of the prisoners.

Here were minotaurs bereft of the vigor and hot blood that marked their race. Their eyes were hollow. They had lost patches of fur, and their rib bones were visible. They stared without blinking.

Guards eyed the arrivals with open hatred. To be a guard at Vyrox was a punishment, and those who watched over the prisoners had little more hope than Faros of ever escaping.

The weather-worn, weary-looking officer with his right arm cut off at the elbow limped out of one building to stare at the new arrivals.

"I am Krysus de-Morgayn, commander of Vyrox," he said in a resigned voice. "You will address me as Commander. You will obey all orders and work your shifts without fail. You have been given one last chance to serve the empire. Work hard, and you may earn the opportunity to return to Nethosak." Paug snorted, but Krysus overlooked it. "That is all. The guards will show you where you sleep and eat. Sleep well, for tomorrow you work."

"That's it! Move along, now!" Paug and the other guards herded the new arrivals toward the dour buildings. Dust swirled with each trudging step. None of the soldiers offered water, and no one was so foolish enough to ask.

The prisoners were divided up. Faros and the steward were assigned to a building. No prisoners awaited them inside. Other than those on cleaning duty, the rest were working in the mines.

"Inside!" growled Paug. He raised the whip, but Faros and the other prisoner had already hurried in. The Butcher laughed, then shut the door behind the pair.

"We are dead," muttered the steward. "We will catch the breathing sickness and die."

The breathing sickness came from inhaling the noxious fumes and dust thrown up by the volcanoes. Victims lost fur and developed a pallor. Breathing was reduced to hacking coughs. The coughing grew incessant, and the inflicted spewed blood. Eventually, most simply wasted away, finally falling dead in their tracks.

"Shut up!" Faros snapped. He looked sullenly around at the aged, two-level bunks. Some had a few tattered belongings on top. Faros finally chose a couple a few spaces apart that appeared to be vacant.

He left the lower one to the old minotaur then took a nearby upper bunk. With great distaste and not a little anxiety, Faros shook off the stained blanket.

"What do we do now?" his fellow prisoner asked.

"I don't know," Faros grumbled, lying down. "Stop asking questions! Just . . . just try to sleep." His stomach rumbled. He shut his eyes.

The door swung open, squealing.

The snarls of several exhausted and ill-tempered figures rattling chains jolted Faros to attention. He blinked, realizing that he actually had dozed off. Forcing himself up on his elbows, Faros glanced at the shadowy forms.

"What's this?" bellowed a black behemoth. "New calves to the slaughter, eh?" He stepped up, and with one shackled hand nearly swept Faros from the bunk. "So clean! So spotless! Yeah, new calves all right! Bring anything with you to pay for your room and board? Costs plenty to stay at a fine villa like this!"

"I have . . . nothing!" gasped Faros, trying to peel the massive fingers off his throat.

"You'd better have somethin' good, or I'll—"

A lean figure pushed through the ash-covered mob. In the dim illumination, it looked as if splotches of oil covered his fur. The newcomer stood taller than either Paug or Faros's assailant, though the top of his horns had been cut off. He wore his mane in two tight pony-tails.

"Leave 'un be, Japfin."

"I'll leave him be," the one named Japfin grumbled, turning toward his rival. "Leave him be just long enough to break what's left of those stubs of yours!"

He swung a meaty fist toward the other prisoner.

The splotch-covered miner with the curious accent caught Japfin's fist and twisted it back. The burly minotaur swung hard with the other hand.

His adversary dodged the blow, then, with Japfin off-balance, swept one fettered foot under the heavier prisoner.

Japfin fell and struck the floor with a thud.

The lean minotaur jumped on Japfin and smashed his head to the floor. When his foe did not move, he leaped to his feet. For the first time, Faros saw that tattoos covered the minotaur's shoulders, torso, and even his legs. The tattoos somehow colored his fur as well as his skin.

"Take 'un to his bunk!" the tattooed one commanded. He turned to Faros. "I am Ulthar. Your name, new one?"

"B-Bek. Bek."

The strange minotaur quietly repeated the name, then nodded. With a grand sweep of his arm, he added in a more affable voice, "Welcome, Bek! Welcome to our humble abode! May you enjoy being a part of our good family—" some of Ulthar's humor fled— "for what little be left of your life."

In the Courrain Ocean the clouds had built up so much over some areas that they now seemed to push down, as if seeking to squash anything jutting above sea level. Thick fogs covered some islands and ships sailed slowly, fearing obscured rocks.

The first storm struck without warning.

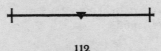

Waves grew swiftly to giants three times the height of the main mast. Lightning played across the sky, yellow and red flashing amidst the ominous green gray. A howling wind ripped at the sails, and hands strained to keep lines set. For hours the crew of the *Gryphon's Wing* did battle without any seeming end in sight.

"It's not natural!" cried Captain Hogar to his first mate. "Sailed the Blood and the Courrain for thirty years and never saw a gale rise up so sudden and violent, even around the Maelstrom! Not natural at all!"

Barely had the burly, brown minotaur finished when a wave struck the lower deck. One sailor screamed as he was washed over the opposite rail. Another was tossed against the mast with such force that his back cracked like a twig.

"To starboard! To starboard! Cut into it!" Something flew into Hogar's face. "What, by the Sea Queen—?"

His first mate, Scurn, ducked as thick, fat forms almost a yard long pelted the vessel and its crew. Hogar seized one that almost struck him in the chest, then had to struggle to hold it long enough to identify it.

" 'Tis a dartfish, captain! A whole school of dartfish!"

"I can see that, you fool!" The minotaur eyed the gaping mouth and pointed nose of the fish. Dartfish were deep sea creatures, seldom caught because of the depths they preferred. "Must be a violent storm indeed if it dredged these hunters up!"

Even as he spoke, another wave of fish leaped through the air, falling on the decks and wriggling frantically. Now they consisted of all shapes and sizes, one of them almost as big a minotaur.

"I don't like this one bit, captain," muttered Scurn. " 'Tis like the entire ocean is churning up so much even the fish are scared to be swimmin' in it!"

"Then let's get ourselves to a port as quick as we can!"

Unfortunately, the nearest island was another day's journey. All the crew of the *Gryphon's Wing* could do was hope that the storm would let up.

Another monstrous wave rose up, washing over the struggling vessel. This time, the minotaurs were prepared. They were soaked down to their skin and half-choked on sea water, but they held on, breaking through the wave.

Hogar was encouraged. They were still on course. If they could handle the other waves as good as the last . . .

From the crow's nest came a shout.

"What's that?" The minotaur's ears stiffened. "What'd he say?"

Scurn sounded incredulous. "He said, 'Land ho!' "

"There ain't no land in this area!" Both officers strained to see ahead. The first mate shook his head.

The sailor in the nest shouted again. "It's gone, captain!"

"A trick of the fog," suggested Scurn.

"Aye, but let's—" He broke off as something became barely visible ahead.

The huge, vague silhouette of an immense, rounded land mass stretched before the ship, dwarfing it.

"That's not on the charts!"

Another storm of fish bombarded the *Gryphon's Wing*. All around the sea-wracked vessel, dark shapes leaped out of the water.

"Do we make for it, captain?"

"Any port in—" Hogar cut off.

Had the island *moved*?

Ears taut and the fur on his neck stiff, the captain cried, "Hard to starboard! Turn! Turn!"

The dark mass before them rose higher.

Lightning flashed.

All Hogar could think was *By the lost gods! What teeth!*

It was a fish, a monstrous beast with two white eyes and a mouth capable of swallowing five *Gryphon's Wing*s without noticing.

It was likely the strange leviathan did not notice them at all. As his crew tried desperately to get their craft away, Hogar watched it, noting that it seemed to move just like all the other fish—as if seeking to escape.

The *Gryphon's Wing* moved with remarkable swiftness, considering the storm. It cut through the water like a knife, but still not fast enough to maneuver out of the way of the gargantuan beast.

The waves struck first, hitting with a force a hundredfold of previous assaults. More hands were washed overboard. Scurn tried to hold on but was dragged loose. He disappeared over the back rail.

Utter blackness enshrouded the swamped ship.

The minotaur captain dropped to his knees, staring.

The leviathan came down on *Gryphon's Wing*. It shattered the proud vessel like brittle pottery. Masts, rails, and pieces of hull flew in every direction.

Momentum carrying it on, and the sea beast vanished under water again. With it went all that remained of the *Gryphon's Wing* and her crew. The body of Captain Hogar was one of the last bits of flotsam to be sucked down into the black depths.

CHAPTER VIII

SHADOW OF THE TEMPLE

Two months into Hotak's reign, the first of the new colonial governors were assigned. Many were provost captains already in command of those colonies. Adopting the example of Mito, the new governors of Broka, Tengis, Dus, and Selees restructured their local militias and consolidated their power.

Under a proposal by Governors Haab of Mito and Zemak of Amur, the system of justice underwent radical change. Sanctioned duels in local arenas gave way to tribunals consisting of three officers appointed by the governing administrators. Those found guilty were chained and made ready for the next ship sailing to the mining colonies.

Hotak needed miners as much as he needed soldiers. To expand, the empire required vast quantities of copper, iron, and other valuable minerals. Several previously uninhabitable islands became new colonies and were peopled by those who had found themselves on the wrong side of the new regime. With few natural resources, the only hope of the island workers was finding and digging out enough high-grade ore to satisfy their overseers. Gask and Warhammer Point, both to the east of Mito, and iron-rich Firemount, one day south from Kothas, were among the newest additions.

Where once there had only been one Vyrox, now each day it seemed that yet another colony of death sprang up.

The axe's curved edge swung toward Ardnor's head—a certain deathblow should it strike. Nephera's eldest grunted and shifted his twin-edged axe into a defensive posture.

In his eyes, the other minotaur moved with the speed of an animal caught in tar. His adversary's round face distorted, the eyes bulging out. Droplets of sweat slowly seeped to the floor. Every muscle of his foe strained, but still the axe came slowly.

Ardnor almost grew impatient with the entire matter.

The First Master shifted his own weapon. The world around him moved faster, but still not fast enough to match Ardnor's impatience. His adversary attempted to kick the leg of the emperor's son out from under him, but Ardnor dodged that attack, too.

Distorted, stretched-out roars of encouragement arose from the other fighters forming a square around them.

With a savage grin on his face, Ardnor stepped back, causing the other minotaur to stumble forward. As his foe sought to regain his balance, the First Master brought the haft of his axe around, thrusting it into his opponent's stomach. At that point, Ardnor let his concentration relax.

Like a madcap dream, the world resumed its normal pace—and the unpadded hilt of the axe buried itself deep in the other minotaur.

Ardnor's opponent gasped and doubled over. A hush fell over the audience. Ardnor wasted no time now, bringing up the flat of the heavy axehead and striking his opponent squarely on the temple.

His attacker dropped to the floor.

Laughing, Ardnor brought his weapon high, then swung down with all his might at his defenseless foe's neck.

The blade's edge paused within an inch of its target.

Pulling back, Ardnor raised his axe over his head and, with a triumphant expression, looked around. The gathered Protectors applauded the skill of their leader. More than a hundred warriors stood, clapping—each secretly giving thanks that they had not been among his sparring partners this day.

The defeated minotaur kept his head close to the floor, the tips of his horns touching the worn, almost black stone.

"My life is yours," he announced, not only to his leader but all ears. "My death is yours, too."

"Ever and always," Ardnor returned, finishing the short oath that all Protectors made to him upon becoming one of the blessed champions of the temple. Those who failed to complete the final trials—five days of fasting, followed by hand-to-hand combat with a Master and, lastly, an ordeal by fire—generally had nothing else to say, for many died in the process.

"On your feet, Jhonus!" Ardnor barked. Nephera's son felt especially satisfied with this duel. Jhonus had a reputation for being one of the temple's best. Defeating him, even through use of what might have been called sorcery, pleased Ardnor.

The assembled warriors continued to cheer. The walls of the chamber made their shouts reverberate.

One of his servants brought him a towel and a mug of water. Ardnor took a sip then rubbed himself with the rough towel. He decided he would bathe later. Too much demanded his attention.

Tossing the towel aside, Ardnor faced his followers, who had formed up in five lines. They stood at attention, their breathing coming in almost perfect unison.

Ardnor matched their stance, and his euphoria gave way to ritual solemnity.

"The people are the life of the temple!" he said.

"The people will be protected!" they shouted back as one.

"The temple is the soul of the people!"

"The temple will be protected!"

Nostrils flaring, the First Master continued, "By the rites performed, by the trials conquered, you have proven yourselves worthy to fulfill that sacred duty. Your lives, your deaths, belong to the Forerunners forever. You are its eternal servants, its eternal defenders."

Each struck the center of their chest with a closed fist. "We are the Protectors of the faith!"

As they lowered their fists, they displayed for Ardnor the symbol of their utter dedication.

At the center of each warrior's chest, seared into the flesh and fur, was the distinct outline of a twin-edged axe. All Protectors wore the emblem.

"Keep a wary eye," Ardnor concluded. "The day is coming. . . ."

They filed out in silence, leaving only the First Master and his attendant. Ardnor accepted another mug of water from the older male and swallowed it in a single gulp.

"Where's my mother?" he asked, wiping his muzzle.

"She still rests, First Master," the attendant replied.

"Still? It's nearly noon!"

"She said she wants to be well-ready for the special service, First Master. She says she still has many, many preparations to make and that, despite there being yet another month before the event, the preparations take time."

Ardnor grunted. "I see. A good idea, then. Wouldn't want her fainting before the sheep, would we?" Ignoring the look of dismay on his elderly servant's face, Ardnor turned to other subjects. "Any messages for me?"

"Your brother Bastion desires to speak with you at first opportunity."

"Bastion? Wonder what he wants." Ardnor saw his younger sibling as a tedious but efficient link in the running of the empire. "Did he say where he'd be today?"

Here the wizened servant showed some perplexity. "He said you would find him overseeing the colossus, First Master."

Ardnor paused, looking at the servant with wide, wondering eyes. "Have they begun work already?"

"One would assume so," replied the lowly figure.

"Then I'll go see him at once."

He threw the cup to the servant then hurried to his quarters. A short time later, clad in the full garb of a Protector, Ardnor called for his horse. Accompanied by four dedicated guards, he headed toward the northern quarter of the capital.

The small party drew the attention of those on the streets. Whether or not one followed the teachings of the Forerunners, all knew the First Master. True believers bowed or cheered as he rode past, while the ignorant quickly glanced away or shrank back.

Ardnor's band rode for some time, leaving the central district—home of not only the palace and the Supreme Circle, but also that of the legion and naval commanders—for the first of the districts where high-ranking citizens and prominent clans made their homes. Some villas had been burned to the ground here, others ripped apart. Huge four-wheeled wagons pulled by teams of muscular workhorses still carted away refuse.

The villas gave way to rectangular buildings, smaller but neatly ordered dwellings. Then there were gray, communal houses, and beyond them, at last, the larger, more utilitarian structures of one of the crafting and business districts.

At a tall, drab stone building buried deep in the district, the First Master finally reined his horse to a halt. Two sentries stood at attention. Leaving the horse with one of his own, Ardnor and the three other guards approached.

"My brother's inside?" he asked, removing his helmet.

"Lord Bastion awaits you, Lord Ardnor," one sentry replied.

Ardnor barged through the door, glancing briefly around. Scores of minotaurs of varying ages, dressed in dust-covered aprons, persistently worked at marble blocks, gradually chipping into existence stalwart minotaur champions, majestic steeds, and sundry other forms. With few exceptions, those at work were members of House Tyklo, whose tradition in stonework had made them one of the most respected clans in the history of the race. Since Tyklo himself, the clan had carved the majority of monuments for every emperor, victorious general, or great House.

Under Chot's reign, Tyklo had carved reproduction after reproduction of the late ruler's image. The hard work of a generation of sculptors had been shattered after his fall. However, Hotak's coup had opened new doors, new commissions—projects such as the colossus.

It stood twice as tall as the massive statue that had once commanded the central square, a towering marble behemoth clad in breast plate and kilt and holding a double-edged axe high in one hand and the head of an ogre in the other. Even as Ardnor watched, a powder-covered young minotaur chiseled away at the wild-maned ogre's toothy, grimacing features, turning the face into a helmeted human, a Knight of Neraka.

With shifting alliances came shifts in art.

His brother stood near the statue, pointing at the ogre's head and saying something to the master artisan. The other minotaur nodded sagely, then noticed Ardnor. He spoke to Bastion, who glanced over his shoulder. Bastion went to greet his elder sibling.

"We can thank his Imperial Majesty Chot for saving us some time and trouble," said Bastion, coming as close to humor as Ardnor thought possible. "After all, Chot planned to have this great statue unveiled on the next anniversary of his overly long reign."

"Well worth seeing." Ardnor briefly pictured his own face atop the gargantuan monument, then decided that when he assumed the throne he would have an even more massive statue commissioned.

"I'm glad you came. I need to speak with you."

The brothers moved to the far side of the great workshop, the constant chipping from the sculptors protecting their words from prying ears.

"Well, what is it, Bastion?"

"Ardnor, I must insist that your Protectors stop interfering with the duties of the Imperial Guard and the legions."

The First Master stared, not believing the other's audacity. "Interfering? My Protectors? You've some gall, Bastion! If not for the temple's warriors, at least one fugitive might have escaped! We've kept order when rioting would've brought even more damage to Nethosak! Father had the Imperial and State Guards completely over-committed and the legions spread over most of the empire. *Interfering? We saved* the day!"

Workers nearby paused, stealing looks.

Bastion held his ground, his expression maddeningly calm. "What you say has merit, Ardnor, but hear me out. However wonderful the people act toward Father, it doesn't look good if the Forerunners take too active a part in the policing of the capital. Your temple is strong, but most people still follow the old gods or none at all. The Temple of Sargas always tried to rule the emperors through either force or guile. No one wants that any more."

"You're talking nonsense!"

"The temple has a critical role to play, Ardnor. Let it fulfill that role and leave other matters to those better suited."

"And what about General Rahm and Tiribus? The longer they remain free, the more trouble they might cause. You know that. They need to be found—by any means."

"They'll be dealt with."

Ardnor's eyes grew crimson, and the vein in his neck throbbed. With a deep breath and a curt nod, he replied, "Very well, brother, I'll take your suggestion under advisement. That's all I can promise."

Bastion nodded.

"I'll tell you one thing, though, brother," Ardnor said, eyeing the colossus. "When I'm emperor, such stupid fears won't exist any more. When I'm emperor, no one will ever worry about whether the empire is run by the throne or the temple, because they'll be one and the same."

With that, the First Master pushed past Bastion. His bodyguards gathered around him as he barged out of the Tyklo work place and headed to his horse.

Thrusting on his helmet, Ardnor mounted and, without so much as a backward glance, rode off. Still seething at his brother, Ardnor calmed himself by picturing his own mighty statue being unveiled and the throngs cheering his succession to the throne.

Tiribus's dealings with Chot had served him well, but the lean, crafty councilor had known that one day a new emperor would assume the throne. That emperor would look with question upon those closest to his predecessor. Thus it paid to have a contingency plan.

Tiribus had never trusted Lothan, yet he had not expected the gaunt minotaur to take such an active role in plotting the overthrow of Chot. Lothan's treachery had caught even Tiribus's best spies by surprise, much to their fatal regret.

Rumor had it that a few others had escaped Hotak's net, but only General Rahm interested Tiribus. A practical officer, just the kind the councilor would need if he staged an overthrow of the usurper. Rahm could rally the military.

A knock stirred the councilor. The desolate cabin, which lay two hours' journey from the nearest town, had been purchased by Tiribus through an intermediary long ago. It had been kept well-supplied, and a guard had always watched over it.

"Enter, Nolhan."

Nolhan resembled his master somewhat, both having long, narrow snouts and high brow ridges. However, Nolhan had silver-brown fur, a rarity. "Frask's just returned. Arrangements have been finalized. The ship will meet us on the northeast coast. If we leave here in the morning, we'll be on our way to the mainland three days from now."

"Good. Once there, we can send word to Lord Targonne."

"Excuse me for asking, my lord, but is this attempt at an alliance with the human a wise one?"

"Of course! Targonne needs minotaur support for his military campaigns. I will make certain that this pact is more balanced than the one Chot tried to negotiate."

"I meant no disrespect, my lord."

Tiribus waved away his apology. "Never mind. Is there any other news of import?"

"Kesk the Younger is dead. Caught trying to leave the imperial capital disguised as a hand on a ship. The captain and officers were also taken away."

The councilor snorted. "Scant loss! At least General Rahm still lives. He will have Hotak wasting resources looking for him, which helps our own situation." Tiribus clasped his hands together. "I will dine in one hour. Until then, I wish to be alone."

"Yes, my lord." The aide bowed, then backed out.

The elder minotaur turned back to the notes he had been compiling. Names of contacts, offers to Targonne, a schedule of future events . . . Tiribus left nothing to chance. He even had plans for the downfall of the Forerunners, whose beliefs disturbed him.

Nephera was a charlatan, but a clever charlatan. She had turned what Tiribus thought was childish madness into a powerful, rich sect that grew stronger with each passing day. Soon, though, Tiribus would see to it that the high priestess joined her vaunted spirits. Her rumored powers did not trouble him. He had no fear of ghosts. After all, what harm could the dead do?

At that very moment, the room darkened. Tiribus rose to light a lamp—and noticed that daylight still prevailed outside.

The elder councilor paused, feeling as if malevolent eyes watched his every move.

"Nolhan?" he called, suddenly not comfortable alone.

Despite the fact that the other minotaur should have been well within earshot, Nolhan did not respond.

Tiribus started toward the door, but as he did, the darkness grew so thick that he could not even see in front of him. He pushed forward, but each step became a struggle. A sense of foreboding made him look over his shoulder.

In the deep, misty darkness, two fiery orbs stared back.

"Nolhan! Frask! Josiris!"

No one came.

Tiribus peered again at the monstrous eyes, knowing that only one power could control such an abomination.

"Nephera . . ." he muttered. So the high priestess of the Forerunner temple was no charlatan after all.

The minotaur drew his sword and swung at the inhuman eyes, but the blade passed through them. Backing up, Tiribus seized the door handle.

The door would not budge. Dropping the useless blade, Tiribus gripped it with both hands.

Something seized him by the shoulders and spun him around to face those horrific orbs. Four monstrous limbs composed of smoke dangled Tiribus more than a foot above the floor. He tried to shout. The fiery eyes thrust forward—and filled his mouth. Tiribus gagged. He brought one hand up, but his desperate fingers clutched only emptiness.

The cloud poured into his mouth, down his throat, filling his lungs. The councilor's struggle turned frantic as the need to breathe became paramount. His eyes bulged as he strained.

Then his arms dropped to the side. The councilor's legs twitched once, then hung loosely. The eyes of Tiribus stared, but no longer saw anything but death.

His body dropped to the floor with a thud.

"My lord!" Nolhan called as he swung open the door. "What was tha—?"

He and the others gaped at the twisted body of his master.

Nolhan stood at the doorway for an instant, then hurried forward, seizing Tiribus's notes. Eyes on the corpse, he backed out.

They were warriors who would have sacrificed their lives to defend their master against any ordinary foe, but the fear and horror stamped on Tiribus's face shook even the hardened fighters. With Nolhan in the lead, the trio mounted and raced off, never looking back.

As they disappeared into the woods, a dark fog emerged from the dead minotaur's mouth, a dark fog with eyes that now looked beyond Mithas for its next prey.

CHAPTER IX

THE MINES OF VYROX

The horns woke the prisoners just before dawn. Their mournful notes were quickly followed by the harsh pounding of the guards at the doors. As he had for three months, Faros struggled to his feet, his body screaming. Despite the exhaustion with which he had fallen onto his bed, he had been unable to sleep well. In addition to the mites and splinters, the stifling heat made it impossible to find any comfort.

Though life was now constant pain and exhaustion, Faros was stronger and leaner. The daily, bone-wrenching labor had burned away his soft belly and tightened his loose muscle. He looked indeed like a younger, tougher version of his father.

The old steward offered an example of the fate befalling those who were not tough enough. By the third morning of his imprisonment, the elderly male had been unable to push himself up onto his feet. Paug had seized the weakened prisoner by the throat, demanding he get up and go to work or suffer the consequences. When that threat failed, the Butcher had wasted no more words. As the others watched,

Paug had casually taken the steward's head—and twisted it sharply until his neck snapped.

That memory still fresh after so many months, Faros climbed down from the bunk. Another prisoner who moved too slowly received a shove from a guard. In a rare act of kindness, Japfin helped the other steady himself.

One by one, the prisoners, clad only in ragged linen kilts and overworn sandals, lined up in front of the first of two wooden doors of the foul-smelling, soot-blackened building to the right of Commander Krysus's quarters. Each were given a small bowl. From huge, battered iron pots, a crew of cook's assistants dolloped out the day's fare—sometimes thick, pasty oatmeal, other times a similar, sticky substance culled from barley, corn, and leftover grains.

The prisoners ate their meager fare before the horns sounded again to begin their journey to the mines. In rows of thirty, the miners were packed into creaking, canopied wagons where they were seated on two long benches facing one another. In order to keep the prisoners from leaping out of the wagon, their ankle chains were secured to a sturdy iron bar running along the middle of the floor.

The sun rarely shone here. The constant smoke from the craters kept the sky covered with thick clouds, and the incessant winds stirred up showers of ash that coated everything.

About a mile north lay a companion camp with female prisoners. To the east and perforating the various peaks and volcanoes were the countless mine shafts where the majority of the laborers toiled. Many had been played out or simply abandoned as worthless, but more than forty shafts were still active.

Located centrally between the camps and the mines was the processing station, where teams of minotaurs unloaded the open wagons that brought ore. After separating the best finds, especially the copper-rich malachite and azurite, the sweltering routine of freeing the precious metals from the rock began. Afterward, the raw metals were transported to other facilities in Nethosak, where they would be refined for use throughout the empire.

For the first four weeks, Faros had worked as an ore gatherer, pushing the heavy, square carts in which the rock broken up by the other laborers was dumped. After that he was transferred to a shaft rich in copper, where he and Ulthar had battered away with pickaxes at a vast blue azurite vein.

Today, however, he and his group were assigned to a shaft dangerously close to the most active volcano. The guards called the shaft by its number, seventeen. The prisoners had their own name for it: Argon's Throat.

Argon's Throat was reputed to be the most dangerous of all the mines. The sulfuric fumes were constant. Miners were often forced to bind moist cloths over their muzzles. Every two hours the prisoners were allowed to step into the relatively fresher air outside the mine. However, after only a few minutes they were sent back to work.

Despite all that, Ulthar continued his merry demeanor. His axe struck harder and faster than anyone's. He hummed and even sang a little, as if the noxious atmosphere had no effect on him.

"... for the sea's my blood and blood'll call, over the highest mountain I might roam. Die I in a desert or castle fair, to the waters I'll return home..."

Faros tried to draw strength from Ulthar. He had learned some about the tattooed minotaur. Ulthar came from Zaar, a remote island colony that had for several generations lost contact with Mithas and Kothas. Left much to their own devices, the people had picked up habits from the docile, human natives. The art of tattooing, for instance, was a custom of the original islanders.

"This 'un here," Ulthar had pointed out one tattoo during a rare break. "The sun with the ship inside it. That's my father's vessel. That's where I was born during the voyage." He had pointed to one on his chest. "This 'un, the trident with the crab, that's when I killed the sea monster!"

Ulthar was not the only prisoner from beyond the shores of Mithas and Kothas. Some came from islands as far away as Gol or Quar. A middle-aged cart pusher from Quar bore a ceremonial scar on each side of his muzzle. Two other prisoners, shorter and stouter than the rest, had bright green eyes, a trait dominant on the wooded isle of Thuum in the southeast edge of the imperium.

Faros cried out as the tongue of a whip lashed out at his shoulder. A soot-covered guard shouted, "Get back to work or no break for you!"

Faros swung his pick harder. So far, they had found little ore, but still the prisoners dug into the smoldering mountain. The thick, hot air had caused one prisoner to pass out. After that unfortunate had been dragged away, the guards pushed the rest even harder.

Ahead, a group of workers set into place more thick oak beams in order to forestall a collapse. Their hammering echoed louder than the countless pickaxes.

Through heroic effort, the floor of the shaft had been scraped smooth by shovels so that the ore carts could be maneuvered. When full of ore, a cart was a burden even for muscular, seven-foot-tall minotaurs.

From the mouth the ore was brought to waiting wagons. After each open wagon had been filled to the brink, prisoners under armed escort guided it away. Faros had not yet seen the processing station, and Ulthar had warned him to stay away from it, hinting that death in the mine was preferable to being sent there.

"Bek!" called one of the guards "Over here!"

Faros rushed over to the guard, who handed him a bucket of water and a ladle. "Everyone gets one swallow only. Understand?"

"Aye." Faros began giving drinks to prisoners. Most gratefully took what he offered them, although each stared with eyes that begged for more.

"Come here with that," a familiar voice muttered.

Faros turned to discover Paug. For so massive a minotaur, the Butcher moved with surprising stealth.

Paug took the ladle.

"You can't—" The glare he got silenced the younger minotaur. The overseer tossed the ladle aside, then gulped down almost the entire contents of the bucket.

Faros said nothing, but simply moved on to the next miner. It was Ulthar. The bucket held only enough water for one more drink.

Ulthar raised the bucket to his mouth. He paused for a moment, then appeared to drink heartily as Faros watched with puzzlement.

"Aah! So good! Refreshes 'un, eh?" After Faros's listless nod, he added, "Thank you, Bek! You drink now!"

Frowning, the younger prisoner tilted the bucket.

Water sloshed at the bottom, nearly all that Paug had left.

Faros looked up, but Ulthar had already returned to his labors, striking with gusto and humming. He acted refreshed.

Desperate, Faros tilted the pail and let the cool liquid dribble down his throat. Ulthar continued to ignore Faros's efforts to catch his eye, even turning away.

The day dragged on. Faros fell into a trance, his mind drifting away. Some of the pain dwindled.

The mine trembled.

"Eruption!" somebody shouted.

Rocks from the ceiling broke off, pelting the startled miners. A crossbeam cracked in two, one bulky section striking a slow-moving prisoner. Some of the workers tried to run, but guards blocked their path.

"No eruption!" Ulthar cried. "Wait! See!"

The tremor passed, leaving most shaken but unharmed. Thick dust filled the narrow chamber, causing most to cough.

One of the overseers finally ordered everyone outside. Faros and the rest moved as quickly as their chains allowed. An officer on horseback, his mane wildly disheveled and his fur covered in dust, arrived just as the last gasping workers spilled out.

"Any casualties?"

"Just one, sir. The tremor knocked some rock loose, but nothing much else. Air just got too thick with dust. I'll have 'em back inside soon, I swear."

"Never mind that now!" The officer made a futile attempt to brush himself off. "Get any with strength left lined up. Eighteen's collapsed. There may be survivors."

"Aye!" The stunned overseer turned. "You, you, and you!" Faros, Ulthar, and Japfin found themselves among those chosen.

Dug into the far side of the crater, the other shaft required a lengthy trek over a cracked, boulder-strewn path. Ahead of Faros, other prisoners were working their way up the slope, stumbling because of the loose footing. A wooden ore cart lay to the right of the path, its sturdy side crushed by good-sized rocks.

As Faros and the others neared, they noticed the wall of rubble clogging the mouth of the shaft.

"No one could be alive in there," Faros whispered.

"No one," returned Ulthar, wearing the most solemn expression Faros had yet seen. "Still, we must try."

"Let's go!" shouted the officer who had brought them. "Get those lines moving!"

The magnitude of the collapse became more apparent with each passing minute. The devastation had been thorough.

No one truly believed they would find anyone alive.

Yet still they worked frantically. Faros dug alongside Ulthar and Japfin until at last they came across the first of the dead.

The stench was recognizable even in the sulfuric air. A hand materialized under a lifted rock and more of the grotesque find came to light. Hardened minotaurs swallowed and swore under their breaths.

One had been a guard, that much his kilt and the sword by his side indicated. His head was crushed beyond recognition. The sight shook Faros. Ulthar had to take him by the shoulders and push him past the mangled corpse.

An overseer came to investigate. With practicality, he retrieved the dead guard's sword. "Get the body out of here! Now!"

Each penetration brought to light a new corpse. Most were prisoners, but now and then a guard joined the growing list of casualties. None of the workers expressed any pleasure when finding the latter; in death, all minotaurs were the same.

As he dug, an occasional lightheadedness took hold of Faros. He noticed it start to affect others. Even Ulthar appeared a bit disoriented.

The tattooed figure sniffed the air—and almost lost his balance. He shook his head. "Bad. Very bad."

"What is it?"

Ulthar coughed. "The breath of Argon. The death of the air. Kills you as you breathe it."

"What do we do?"

Ulthar started to answer then paused at a distant, mournful sound. A moan . . . from within the ruined shaft.

Faros and Ulthar looked around. No one else had noticed the moan.

At that moment, an overseer neared. He started to say

something, then began to cough uncontrollably. A horrified look spread across his face and he raced away.

"Hurry!" insisted Faros. "We've got to hurry!"

"The air is dangerous, Bek," Ulthar whispered, backing up. "They be dead before we reach 'em . . . and if we stay, so may we."

Faros stared, dismayed. He recalled his own dying family. "You go, then, if you like."

Ulthar faltered. Finally, with a frustrated snort, he bent down to help. Redoubling their efforts, they made headway.

Once more came a brief sound from within the wall of rubble.

"Ulthar!" Faros shouted. "Did you—?"

"All right! Everyone out! This shaft is a death trap! Stop your work and get out! There's nothing left to do!"

Guards began pulling prisoners back. Ulthar and Faros continued.

Paug appeared, brandishing a whip. "You heard! Move! Don't think I won't use this!"

"But someone's alive in there!" Faros insisted.

Paug pushed him aside, then put an ear to the rock. He quickly pulled back. "I don't hear anything! Everyone's dead in there—" he coughed— " and I don't care to join them."

Faros hesitated. Paug snapped the whip at him, its sharp sting sending the prisoner stumbling. With the overseer pushing them along, the prisoners abandoned the ruined shaft.

The officer who had led them to this place eyed Paug. "That the last?"

"Aye! Caused some trouble this one did," Paug indicated Faros. "Needs to be punished, I think."

"We'll deal with that later. Are all the guards accounted for?"

Another guard spoke up. "No one left alive."

"And the prisoners?"

"Five bodies unaccounted for."

The mounted minotaur nodded his satisfaction. "We'll waste no more time here, then. Have the guards' bodies brought back, the others we'll burn. I'll make out the report."

"But there's still someone in there!" spouted Faros.

The officer glanced at Paug, who shook his head.

"Just as I said, then. You guards have your orders. I'll report this all to the commander."

He rode off. Paug and his comrades rounded up the miners and loaded them into the creaking wagons.

As they rode back, Faros muttered to Ulthar, "I thought they wanted to dig everyone out."

Japfin snorted in derision. "What did you expect? They needed to make certain about the guards." He leaned forward, eyes red. "They can always get more miners. The only lives they value are their own. We're the refuse of the empire! We're of no worth to it save as hands to dig!"

Faros looked at Ulthar, who nodded agreement.

They rode on in silence.

Drums beat, and the call was sounded. Across the hot, rock-strewn land and into the crumbling, nearly buried remains of a once-proud city abandoned long before the rise of the elves, poured ogres by the hundreds.

Huge beastmen from the mountains, their tusks broader and their eyes constantly trying to adjust to the lowland sun, dragged their hook-edged clubs behind them. Shorter, squat ogres with splayed feet emerged from the direction of the sandy regions. Musclebound, round-chinned hulks with jagged, curved swords and bronze breastplates—elite warriors from the area surrounding the nominal seat of power, Kernen, glared around haughtily at all.

They came in unprecedented numbers, a sign of just how important this gathering was. They came from all points in Kern, and some even dared journey across the harsh border from rival Blöde. Each group that entered the ruined amphitheater—a hollowed-out, oval structure built from chopped blocks of granite—was led by a chieftain. So many unwashed, lice-ridden bodies together quickly created a stench that aggravated even the dull senses of the ogres, stirring up already-taut nerves.

Old enmities die hard, and among ogres they linger longest. As the fierce, tusked warriors packed together, squabbles and feuds were resurrected everywhere.

Two bands that had just entered began exchanging harsh growls and grunts. One ogre brandished a club at his more heavyset counterpart. The other responded by swinging his brutish weapon at the first. In moments, a pitched battle broke out between the pair.

The clubs met with thundering cracks. Animalistic roars of encouragement raced through the throng, as each side urged their champion to further violence.

The hirsute figures battered away at one another. One landed a blow on the other's shoulder that would have cracked the bone of any human or elf, but only caused a small grunt of pain from the victim. Eyes blazing crimson, the heavier ogre barreled into his taller foe, sending both plunging into the stone pathway. Dust rose as the two grappled.

Suddenly, two towering ogres clutching swords broke through the howling crowd while others similarly armed pushed the mob back. The new pair went to the two combatants, kicking at the dust-covered fighters. As the ogres on the ground paused, the guards put the tips of their hefty blades against the duo's throats. One guard growled harshly, and the pair on the ground separated and returned to their respective bands.

The guards steered the two groups away from one another, then moved along. They and others had the unenviable task of keeping some semblance of order. It would literally be their heads if this gathering collapsed into violent chaos.

The drums continued to beat madly. A hundred of them had been set around what had once been an elegant walkway at the top of the amphitheater. The rhythm stirred the ogres' blood, for it spoke of victory, of conquest. Generations had passed since ogres had held sway over any other race, but the dream never died.

Which was why so many had come here, even with the Knights of Neraka encroaching so near.

Under lonely, cracked columns that once had supported a vast roof upon whose ceiling had been etched the glories of the ancient ogre race, a race whose beauty and perfection had not left even a shadow on its barbaric descendants, the gathering horde roared its impatience. They had been summoned, and they had come. Where now, was the one who had demanded their presence?

As the drumbeats reached a crescendo, a single, cloaked figure stepped up onto the dais at the eastern end, the marble platform where ages before enlightened ogre rulers had greeted their subjects. Of them all, he was the only one who dressed remotely as his ancestors had, and he was the only one who sought to make himself resemble the wondrous beings whose weather-eaten statues lay scattered in pieces throughout the lost city.

The latest debacle against the knights remained fresh in the memories of all, but the cloaked ogre did not let this show on his face. He raised fists high and roared loud and long. Although his features were less monstrous and his form slighter than his fellows, his fearsome shouts overwhelmed both the drums and the cries of the throng.

He had used the questionable authority of the Grand Khan, symbolic ruler of Kern, to bring so many together, even those from hated Blöde, but his reputation had stirred the others to make the trek during this dangerous time. The knights were slaughtering ogres left and right. Warriors were needed at the fronts. A gathering like this took precious might from the flanks.

But for him, they had come.

The sun hung high overhead, scorching the amphitheater. Despite his voluminous cloak, the emissary from the Grand Khan did not look at all overheated. He roared again to his fellows, in his people's barbaric tongue haranguing the ogre warriors. Morale grew lower with every day, every slaughter. Ogres as a rule used brute force and berserker fury to pummel their foes into submission and death. The careful, organized strikes by the humans had left them in doubt and disarray. The knights had shown once again why an ogre empire was only a fantasy, a dream of a lost era, a dream as ancient and as lifeless as the city surrounding this assembly.

The tempo of the drums shifted, accenting his fresh stream of words. The heartbeat of every warrior in attendance matched the cadence. Not all cared for the notions of this strange ogre, but they were caught up in the excitement with the rest.

"Garok lytos hessag!" He shouted, pointing in the general direction of Neraka. Ogres roared and beat their clubs or ends of their spears on the amphitheater's steps. Warriors on each end of the structure raised curled goat horns, blaring out harsh, sinister notes—a symbolic warning from all ogres to any from Neraka who would dare invade their lands.

The emissary bared his sharp teeth and pointed to the east, making the waving motion that to his kind signified the sea and all that lay within it. *"Queego! Garoon teka ki! Garoon teka—Uruv Suurt!"*

A protesting roar erupted from the listeners. Several chieftains rose, brandishing their war clubs in response to the audacious words. A few began to leave, their retinues following. Those still seated repeated the last words over and over, each time with growing vehemence. *"Uruv Suurt... Uruv Suurt..."*

Uruv Suurt. Few words from Ancient Ogrish had survived the ages, but these two together had been a part of the race's dwindling lexicon from the beginning. *Uruv Suurt*—the ogre words meaning minotaur.

The cloaked speaker signaled the guards. Immediately a band of loyal warriors blockaded the exits, snapping at the exiting bands and threatening them if they did not return to their seats.

Most obeyed, but one large faction refused. The leader, a huge gray monster, rumbled angrily at the guards then, with one lightning sweep of a club almost as long as his arm, shattered the skull of the one standing nearest to him.

Renewed howling erupted. Those who had alliances with the murderous protester moved to take his side while others prepared to vent old grievances on them. Pitched duels exploded all over the ancient arena, all semblance of order abandoned.

Above the chaos, the imperial emissary quickly snapped his fingers. One guard raised a horn and blew three notes. Below, the mob barely noticed the urgent call.

Then, suddenly, the guards blocking the entrances stepped aside. Through the gaps the other ogres plunged—only to back up with shouts of surprise and dismay.

Long tongues darting out, huge reptilian forms pushed into the amphitheater. Their red, inhuman eyes shifted hungrily. One hesitant ogre screamed as massive, toothy jaws snapped shut on his leg, and he was wrestled to the ground. The horse-sized lizard, a meredrake, raked its eight-inch claws through his chest, ripping it open.

Guards with whips and tethers moved other meredrakes forward, restoring order in brutal fashion. The battles in the stands broke up. Only the original chieftain and those who followed him still stood defiant.

Club dripping, the former glared up at the neatly clad figure and growled, *"Neya! Neya Uruv Suurt fenri! Uruv Suurt hela barom! Neya Uruv Suurt!"*

The smaller ogre shook his head and shouted back, *"Neya Uruv Suurt? K'cha! F'han Uruv Suurt . . . Garoki Uruv Suurt fenri! F'han!"*

"F'han?" The chieftain blinked, utter confusion just another ugly expression on an ogre's visage.

"F'han."

In the stands, an opposing war leader rapped the end of his club on the step. His escort took up the signal. The act spread throughout the crumbling arena. Above the racket, many rumbled over and over, *"F'han . . . f'han . . . f'han . . ."*

Still the one chieftain refused to accede. He shook his head. *"F'han bruut! Bruut!"*

He turned back to the entrance, still obstructed by the wary guards and the salivating lizards.

Atop the dais, the cloaked figure waved the guards aside.

Meredrakes snapping at their flanks, the defiant chieftain led his band out. A handful of smaller groups descended hurriedly from the seats and joined him. From his perch, the elegantly clad ogre watched as they filed out and vanished.

Those remaining behind were his entirely. Cries of *f'han* continued long after the departures. The drums recommenced, matching the grating voices. Ogre blood stirred, ancient desires burning bright.

Seizing the momentum, the emissary nodded to another guard, who waved to a comrade well below.

Through the eastern entrance, two lumbering warriors pushed forth a disheveled, beaten figure. The lone Knight of Neraka had been captured during the ogres' latest rout, a single prize in an otherwise disastrous day. Gone was the brilliant black armor, the arrogant expression. Legs weak, right arm held tight, the knight stumbled out into the arena. He wore only the tattered kilt given to him by his captors. Bruises covered his body.

The ogres howled anew, swinging clubs and stomping their feet. The guards kicked the pathetic figure into the middle of the amphitheater, then stood watch over him.

From their seats arose the strongest, most dominant of the chieftains and war leaders. They barged their way through the wild crowd and leaped down onto the field. The meredrakes hissed and strained to join, but their handlers whipped them into silence.

"Garok lytos hessag!" roared the cloaked emissary, pointing at the human. *"Lytos f'han? Lytos ferak?"*

The throng's reply was instantaneous. *"F'han! F'han!"*

He nodded, satisfied. Horns blared.

The ogre leaders had lined up in two ranks of twelve apiece, a passage six feet wide between them. They stood in alternating fashion, each warrior facing the gap between two of his counterparts. The ogres hefted their clubs, waiting.

Drums pounding, the guards shoved the panting knight into the passage.

The first ogre struck him on the injured arm. The blow was hard enough to send the human stumbling, but not enough to kill him.

Just as he stepped out of reach of this attacker, the knight was struck by the first of the opposing line. The human's cry was matched by an audible crack as the ogre's club crushed in his other arm at the elbow.

One by one, the chieftains beat the prisoner, slowly battering him to a pulp. If he hesitated, they hit him so that he fell toward the next warrior. When the knight slumped on the ground, spears prodded him forward.

The ritual was an ancient one signifying the supremacy of the ogre race over its enemies. The sacrifice of a prisoner in such a way spread the strength and glory to all involved, and promised those in attendance good fortune in future battle.

Each succeeding chieftain took aim, striking where none had yet made contact. By the time he neared the end of the horrendous passage, the dark knight's legs were broken and only one arm functioned at all. His chest and back were black and scarred and he was coughing blood. Prodded to the end of the line by his tormentors, he lay in the dust, barely breathing through ruined lungs.

As the other ogres stepped back, the one who had summoned them leaped down from the dais and trod toward the human wreckage. One of the guards handed him a club. The slight figure continued on, taking his place before the gasping prisoner.

Teeth bared, the emissary crushed the knight's skull.

Roars of *F'han!* boomed through the crowd. The drums beat harder, pumping the blood of the ogres faster and faster. The chieftains on the field saluted him.

He stepped back, leaving the limp, mangled body for all to see. Then, satisfied that the sight had served its purpose, he nodded to one of the handlers. The handler released both his leashes.

Driven wild by the smell of fresh blood, the two meredrakes rushed the corpse. The ogres retreated, watching warily.

The great lizards tore at the knight, quickly reducing the body to something even less recognizable. The ogres cheered.

As the savage reptiles feasted, the cloaked ogre saw an anxious messenger approach. He turned from the gory spectacle to meet the newcomer, taking a goatskin parchment from him.

Stepping away from the others, he studied the contents, words written in Common by a hand not of ogre origin.

A predatory smile spread across his features, eradicating any last hint of civilization. His eyes narrowed in satisfaction. "Yes!" he snarled. "It is done!" He looked to the east and saw in his mind beyond the shore to an island realm. "Yes. Come *Uruv Suurt*, come! Come . . . to me."

CHAPTER X

ENCOUNTERS

The emperor paraded through the capital. The warhorse banner flew proudly and decisively over the entire realm. The people loved him, and he felt absolutely secure after three months of rule.

Bastion was more cautious. "You should not ride up front, Father. You should be in the center, where you can be defended."

"I am their emperor. I must show myself to be a confident leader, not a knave who hides behind the shields of others. Besides, we've nothing to fear from the people. See?"

He waved at the citizens, and they waved back. Minotaurs from all walks of life—from the brown-smocked, cloth-booted street laborers to the fur-cloaked, silken-robed shipping merchants—hundreds cheered him. Behind the crowds, armed soldiers kept watch, just in case.

"General Rahm still lives," Bastion pointed out.

"One renegade in a sea of loyal followers. He'll be dead eventually, just like Councilor Tiribus."

It had been a month since Lady Nephera had brought the news of the councilor's death. That left only Rahm Es-Hestos, who continued to evade justice. Even Nephera could report no news of the elusive renegade. Undaunted, Hotak had dispatched messengers to the nearest colonies. Efforts had been hampered by the peculiar weather dominating much of the imperium of late, but sooner or later Rahm would be captured.

More cheering arose as the column turned onto a larger street. The emperor bared his teeth in a grin. "Try to smile a little, Bastion! It might do you good! Besides, I want the people to see you at your best."

Bastion gave him an apologetic look. "Forgive me, Father. Perhaps events are moving too fast for me."

"Well, they're likely to continue like that. Kolot should be reaching the mainland soon, which means our offer will be in Golgren's hands." Hotak patted his son's arm. "You have a lot on your shoulders, Bastion, and I thank you for all you've done. You just need to take a day to recoup. I understand."

"Aye."

The crowds continued to build. Hotak was giving them a show. Flanked by two polished warriors bearing shining axes over their shoulders, he and his son, clad in hip-length, midnight purple cloaks and wearing helms with the long horsehair crests, led the finest of his crack guards. Behind the emperor, two soldiers held high the rearing horse banner. After them came four archers, their long bows held steady in one hand, and finally two short columns of mounted fighters, one with axes, the other swords. The soldiers all wore the unadorned uniforms of the legion, but now they, like their lord, had the black warhorse emblazoned on their breastplates.

From the tall, flat-roofed buildings overlooking the area, minotaurs threw down tiny sheaves of horsetail grass, revered by the race as an herb granting strength of bone and heart. After the procession, the sheaves would be swept up and salvaged for practical use. In addition to its herbal abilities, the hardy grass served well for polishing woodwork and shining metal, and was also used for green dye.

The sea of well-wishers increased as the imperial party neared the great square. In preparation for the installation of Hotak's colossus, the damage caused to the fountain by the tearing down of Chot's statue had been repaired and the benches cleared away.

As Hotak and Bastion neared the fountain, Captain Doolb, the senior officer, rode up, his expression impatient. "Your majesty, these crowds are too thick for my taste. I think it might—"

His words ended abruptly. The captain clutched his head. A rock had struck his helmet. Doolb slumped in the saddle. A trickle of blood escaped from under his dented helmet.

All there realized that the missile had been intended for Hotak.

"It came from there!" roared sharp-eyed Bastion, pointing into the crowd.

A lithe, dark brown male with chipped horns broke away from the crowd, as onlookers and guards swarmed after him.

Four of the honor guard rode off in pursuit. Startled bystanders darted out of their way.

His path blocked, the fugitive tried to break into a house, but the door would not give. Angry hands seized him.

"Stop!"

The emperor's voice echoed loud and strong. Startled, the mob gave way to the soldiers. Two seized the rock thrower and dragged him to Hotak. His face bruised and some of his fur ripped away, the young minotaur gazed down sullenly.

"The kilt of my legion," commented the emperor, gazing at the attacker's garment. "I daresay you never gained the right to wear it proudly." Hotak glanced at his son. "How fares Captain Doolb?"

Two riders supported the officer, whose head was still bleeding. Doolb's helmet had been removed, revealing a red welt on the upper side of his skull. The captain seemed dazed.

"I would recommend sending him to a healer immediately, Father. This one may not be legion-trained, but he appears to have a good, strong arm and excellent aim."

"Aye." The emperor's good eye fixed on the miscreant. "And that good arm will be put to better use for the empire." Hotak's nostrils flared. "The mines can always use a hot-blooded, healthy worker."

Bastion cleared his throat. "I should like to question him first."

"Do it. Then see he ends up where he belongs." Baring his teeth, Hotak added, "The mayhem of the past will not be tolerated. The empire will have order, discipline!"

The crowds cheered his words. Hotak flashed a smile.

Captain Doolb and his attendants rode by. The emperor's smile became a frown. "Be sure he's treated with the utmost care." He glared at the rock thrower, whom the guards had begun to drag off. "And by all means," continued Hotak, "be sure that this one is treated as he deserves."

Hotak rubbed the underside of his muzzle with the back of his fist. The emperor's eyes had a touch of crimson around the edges.

"Make certain that the captain is medaled for this. Something befitting his years."

"Yes, Father."

Hotak turned his horse back. "Now, let us continue our procession, eh?"

"You want to continue? Even after this?"

"After what? A lone hooligan? If not for Doolb's injury, I would think nothing of the incident. You saw how the people reacted! They turned on the miscreant. Can you imagine what they would think if I fled? I would lose face. Of course, we'll finish. Why shouldn't we?"

"Father—"

Shaking his head, the emperor continued, "You shouldn't be surprised. I used to make myself visible to the rank and file before every battle. Walked among the troops, rode where the enemy could see that they faced a commander unafraid of them. This hardly compares to that."

"This is not war now," Bastion reminded him.

"No. No, it isn't." Hotak urged his horse forward, forcing the others to keep pace. "No. War was simpler."

Captain Azak admitted to the general that without guidance he would have never have found Petarka. Not only did it look like an unremarkable series of rock formations, but a perpetual haze covered the region for miles around, making navigation difficult. Reefs and shallows surrounded the island, making the place challenging to reach even after one spotted it.

Yet the other vessel guided them in easily. *Dragon's Crest* sailed into a small, hidden harbor, finally safe.

Petarka had, at least at one time, been colonized. Crumbling wooden structures had been built into the tiered cliffs, with thick rope ladders and narrow bridges between buildings. Forest covered the inner hilltops. The tiny colony of eight buildings had a short dock for loading and unloading, but little more.

For the next two months they waited there, restoring the buildings, foraging for breadfruit, fishing, and trying to formulate some plan. The sky grew strangely menacing, but although storms threatened in the distance, none struck near. The ship that had guided them departed without even anchoring, but all knew that it would return.

And so it did at last—along with a ship from the empire.

Almost identical to Azak's prized *Crest*, the newcomer slipped into the harbor, followed closely by Rahm's rescuers. Once the imperial ship docked, several weary figures disembarked, their kilts a varied mix of colors and clan symbols. Rahm recognized one immediately.

"Jubal!" Hearing his name, an elder minotaur with black fur rapidly turning gray raised a crooked arm in greeting.

"Jubal?" murmured Azak. "Governor Jubal?"

"Almost the *late* Governor Jubal," the minotaur replied in a scratchy, rasping voice, the permanent effect of a powerful blow to his throat years before. His crooked right arm had come from the same struggle, a battle against ogres. "I escaped just before the doors fell to the pretender's lackeys."

As they talked, a slim boat colored like the sea and carrying five figures slipped into the dock. Four kept the boat in place while a fifth, wearing only a gray kilt cut above the knees, climbed up the rungs of the wooden platform. Angular of features and with a thin coat of fur, he stood a head taller than anyone else.

"Captain Gaerth at last," Rahm announced.

The slim giant bowed his head. "I am pleased you received my warning."

"As, I see, did the governor."

"Not just me," rasped Jubal, his eyes never leaving Gaerth. "There's a dozen of us that wouldn't be here otherwise."

"We alerted those we could, though it cost us some secrecy," said Gaerth.

Rahm nodded. "Why, though? You've no love for Chot."

"Chot presented stability, however corrupt his throne. Hotak . . . Hotak sows unease in all of us."

Captain Azak had been quiet so far, but finally spoke. "And who are all of you? What clan? I recognize no ships like that built in Nethosak or Mito! Who—?"

The general silenced his friend. Meeting Gaerth's gaze, he told Azak, "They helped us. Leave it at that."

"I did not misjudge you," the tall figure commented.

"Don't assume that, Captain Gaerth. Our paths have the potential for conflict—but it's true I owe you much right now. Thanks to you, we have the opportunity to strike back."

Azak scanned the two vessels nearby. "With only three ships? Rahm, my good friend, I have committed myself to this enterprise, but we cannot fight Hotak with such small forces."

Gaerth made matters worse. "My ship will not be at your service, captain. I and mine have already risked ourselves enough. Your empire is your own to win back."

Rahm was disappointed. "I'd hoped . . ."

"We allied ourselves once. We regret that to this day." Gaerth bowed to the general. "I now leave you to your fates."

Azak's eyes flared red. "You cowering—"

"Azak!" snapped General Rahm. "Let him go."

Gaerth paused at the rungs, one hand on the dagger at his waist. His nostrils flared and the calm assurance with which he had held himself had given way to a tightening of his own eyes.

"Captain Gaerth," continued the shorter minotaur, holding back Azak. "You speak honorably. You saved my life and that of others. You sacrificed much for us. I thank you. I wish you'd stay and help, but I understand." Rahm turned his head to the side so that his horns pointed away from the departing minotaur.

Gaerth repeated the gesture. Both he and the general had marked that no conflict lay between them.

"Azak . . ."

The captain snorted, but he duplicated the others' action.

Gaerth descended to the waiting boat. The trio watched it slowly depart.

In the distance, Captain Gaerth called back, "You will not be without allies, general! I did not lie!"

"What's that mean?" the governor rasped. "What's that mean?"

Rahm's eyes were ablaze with triumph. He went to the end of the dock, calling out, "Veria? Is it Veria?"

Gaerth shouted back, but his words were lost.

Azak leaned close to his friend. "How long have you known this Captain Gaerth?"

"Only days before the slaughter and mostly through messages. He had suspicions about unrest, but even he did not foresee Hotak until the last moment despite his network of spies."

Hesitating, Azak then asked, "Is he a Ka—?"

Rahm glared at him. They watched as Gaerth's vessel got underway. The crew of the ship moved with astonishing efficiency.

"We'll see them no more, Azak. Just remember that."

Jubal turned from the ship. "I heard you say Veria. If you mean Veria de-Goltyn, she's dead. The Eastern fleet fell, betrayed from within. If that's our hope, then our plans are crushed already."

General Rahm bared his teeth in a smile. "But it's not our only hope. We have the greatest ally of all working with us, one that even Hotak wouldn't suspect." His eyes narrowed. "Captain Veria's dead, but she'll aid us yet . . . and there'll be others as time goes on, the dead demanding their justice. I swear it!"

The fur on Azak's neck stood up. "By the old gods, you sound more like a Forerunner with this talk of the dead."

"But these dead will stir the living more than the high priestess's hollow words and conjuring tricks." The general seized his comrades by the arms, trying to make them see as he did. "Wait a little longer, and you'll see! We have new hope now! Captain Gaerth must've meant what I think. Veria will bring us aid, and thanks to our other ally, more will come."

"Who is this other ally you speak of?" demanded Jubal, patience clearly at an end.

Rahm snorted and once more bared his teeth. "Why the greatest ally of all, Hotak himself!"

The weather over the length and breadth of the empire continued to grow more savage and unsettling. A scorching heat wave covered the island of Amur, and just beyond its shores rain poured relentlessly. A swarm of large, black locusts appeared out of nowhere and infested one of the outer farming colonies, stripping it of its entire crop before vanishing over the turbulent ocean.

And then . . .

The small colony had survived hurricanes and worse in the past, and so the unpredictable weather tossed at them by the sinister, green-gray clouds had not much disturbed the hardy minotaurs of Tadaran. Boats still dared the choppy waters to fish, while farmers tended their crops or herded their goats.

But Mogra, a more recent arrival to the island, worried as she watched the sky. The clouds were dark, threatening, and if she stared close, the slim, chestnut-brown minotaur thought they looked crimson around the edges, almost as if they burned or bled.

Pulling her cloak tight, she hurried toward the cabin she shared with two other females and their children. Like the other females, her mate was absent, and so the three adults shared the chores. It was Mogra's turn to barter with the fishmongers, and the full basket she carried marked her skill.

A tall, muscular male of advancing years strode toward her. Mogra tensed, then recognized Han, the blacksmith. Soot covered his arms and legs.

"Good evening, Mistress Mogra," he said.

"Good evening to you, Han."

The burly male paused, glanced quickly around to see if anyone was near. Satisfied, he asked, "You're well?"

She also stole a look around before answering. "Good, Han. Good."

"The new governor's not bothering you?"

"He's more concerned with crops. I'm just another face to him. One he doesn't know, fortunately."

The sky rumbled.

"You come to me if there's even the slightest hint he's pestering you, Mistress Mogra. We'll get you and Dorn out of here."

Mogra dared put her hand briefly on his arm. "Thank you."

Again the sky rumbled. Lightning flashed.

"Bad storm," her companion declared. "Best to get inside. Probably be pouring rain any second."

Sure enough, the first sprinkles wetted the pair. The wind picked up.

Han clutched her, over the wind calling, "I'd better walk you home, mistress!"

The two hurried toward her cabin, which lay purposely on the outskirts of the colony. Mogra and Han pushed up the uneven path, struggling against the increasing wind and drizzle.

Despite the weather, Mogra felt hotter with each step. The very air burned her lungs.

"Han, do you feel the heat?"

"Bit warmer, mistress," he replied. The blacksmith was used to working around fire. A little more heat did not bother him.

Her skin tingled. Mogra's eyes also stung. She spat rain from her mouth and noticed that her tongue burned oddly.

Beside her, the male grunted. "Something's stinging me!"

The drizzle grew stronger, and so did the burning sensation. "The rain!" she said. "The rain stings!"

He did not argue with her, instead grabbing Mogra by the arm and pulling her at a quicker pace toward her home.

But the quicker they moved, the harsher the rain. Mogra bit back cries of pain as long as she could, but each droplet now felt like tiny hot embers searing into her flesh.

The cabin lay in sight. The wind tore at them, ripping her free from the blacksmith. Han cursed and reached for her, only to slip in the mud.

She started back towards him, but he shook his head. "Go on, mistress! I'll be all right! You get out of this hellish—"

He gaped, staring at his arm, where smoke had arisen.

"Han! Wh—?"

With a roar, he tried to rise up but slipped again. Mogra took a step toward him then pain wracked her entire body. The scent of burning fur—her own—assaulted her nostrils.

"Run!" Tendrils of smoke rising all around him, the blacksmith made it to his feet. "I'll catch up!" He patted at his smoldering arms. "Go to your son!"

Mogra left, but only because of her concern for Dorn. What if he was caught outside in this unnatural storm?

All around her, the landscape smoked, even sizzled. The rain did not seem to douse anything, but rather stirred it up. Everything smelled of burning.

And then the first true flames burst to life.

The dry bush to her right blossomed into fire. A moment later, a broken branch did the same. Through stinging eyes, Mogra swore that even a *rock* ignited. Everywhere, flames burst up without warning, quickly intensifying.

Mogra's basket erupted. She barely had time to fling it away. Even so, tiny sparks singed her arm. She smothered them, but her fur smoked and her body was wracked by pain.

The cabin beckoned to her. Mogra pushed forward.

Her cloak caught fire.

Fumbling with the strings, she managed to free herself from it. With a gasp, she threw herself against the door, pushing it open and falling inside.

"Mogra!" called one of the other females. "What's happened to you?"

"Shut the door!" she cried. "Quickly!"

But as the other minotaur hurried to obey, they all heard a scream. It was quickly followed by another and another.

Pulling herself up, Mogra joined the other adults by the door and stared in horror.

The colony was in flames. Everything. Cabins, storehouses, the docks, even the very land. . . .

"We have to go help!" blurted one of the others.

"No!" Mogra roared. " 'Tis the rain that caused the fire! The harder it pours, the worse the conflagration!"

"But that's nonsense! How could—?"

"Look at me!" Mogra snarled, showing her scorched fur. "Look at—" She had been about to tell them to look at Han, but the blacksmith was still outside.

Still outside . . .

Mogra scanned the area near the cabin, but saw only fire. The bushes, the trees, even the rocks were clearly ablaze.

"Han . . ." Mogra muttered, knowing his fate.

Her nostrils caught a whiff of something burning. The top of the cabin groaned. The minotaurs glanced up and saw smoke.

Mogra leaped to her son, who sat perched anxiously on the edge of his cot. She scooped up the two-year-old and threw both of them to the back of the room.

Screams filled her ears as the front half of the burning roof caved in, killing the others. The rest of the ceiling creaked ominously. Rain poured in, setting the front aflame.

Crouched in the back corner of the cabin, Mogra looked around for some escape, but everywhere she saw only fire. Droplets drenched pots and utensils. Even metal burst into flames when this unnatural rain touched it.

She could do nothing. Clutching her son, Mogra waited for the inevitable. The image of her mate, so very far away, came to her.

"Rahm," she murmured.

The ceiling groaned, and the rest of the place collapsed.

CHAPTER XI

THE FORERUNNERS

The faithful came to the temple by the hundreds, drawn there by an announcement made several days earlier. The dead had important words for their kin. All the faithful needed to attend. It was paramount that everyone hear.

Members of the State Guard, many of them followers, kept watch. Protectors lined the steps of the building and the grounds. They watched warily, Ardnor's fanatical force certain that some unbeliever would attempt to harm the high priestess.

The temple was a vast, domed marble building whose rectangular center encompassed more than half its width. The huge condor relief that once stood over the wide, high entrance had been replaced by a massive representation of the Forerunner symbols. Beyond the grounds, a tall iron-bar fence encircled the temple's property.

Several thousand worshippers could attend services in the main chamber. The walls, white with red trim, had been covered with tapestries like those that hung in the high priestess's chambers. At the far end of the room stood the gold lectern, decorated with Forerunner symbols, from which Nephera generally preached. Many private sections—chambers where the acolytes, clerics, Protectors, and the high priestess lived—flanked this public area.

With so many expected, the high priestess had decided to move the event outside. The temple grounds were covered in a mosaic upon which the pilgrims could kneel, their horns pointed toward the earth in humble deference to their ancestors and loved ones. Because so many faces would be focused on the mosaic, the high priestess had ordered masons to design each tile in the outline of the bird and axe. Ever would the faithful be reminded.

"It's the largest crowd yet, Mother," Ardnor rumbled almost gleefully, "and they're still pouring in. The grounds are nearly covered!"

"The people want to know the truth. They have faith that they will hear it from me."

"I doubt all of them are the faithful, Mother. I'd be willing to bet that a good number are just the opposite."

Lady Nephera held her position while two priestesses affixed the high hood of her gold-trimmed, sable robe. The aureate emblem of the Forerunners decorated both the front of the overlapping hood and the back of the robe. The lamplight caused the axe and bird to look as though they were moving.

"Then perhaps we shall gain a few converts. You must always see the positive, Ardnor."

"I'm positive that some of them want nothing more than to see you make a fool of yourself—even if they do support Father."

"But I shall not fail. So the only thing that can come of their being here is good for the temple." She stretched out her hand so that one of her assistants could latch on a gold-braid bracelet. "Have you prepared the Eye?"

Ardnor nodded.

Nephera smiled. "Then we shall begin."

She snapped her fingers and the two acolytes, clad in plain black robes with red-trimmed shoulders, stepped behind her. One carried in her hands an exquisitely crafted, lifelike model of an ascending hawk made of solid silver, the other a foot-long golden axe bent at the mid-point of the shaft.

Clad in a robe similar to his mother's, Ardnor took his place before her. From the shadows emerged four silent Protectors, each clutching a mace whose wicked head rested above their shoulder. The grim sentinels formed an honor guard.

The small group exited the high priestess's quarters, where they were greeted by a procession of other acolytes, both male and female. As Lady Nephera and her retinue swept past, the acolytes joined the rear, forming two columns. All wore expressions of rapt devotion.

Protectors lining the way to the entrance came to sharp attention as their mistress passed, their eyes fixed directly ahead. Even the ghostly statues seemed to straighten.

As the procession passed, the spectral legions surrounded, even intermingled with, the living. Now and then one acolyte with keener senses would catch a whiff of the sea or hear a murmuring voice from an empty alcove, but that was all.

A quartet of well-muscled acolytes wrenched back the two high, bronze doors leading outside. Horns resounded as the procession stepped into the open. Nephera experienced a euphoria outstripping even what she had felt during Hotak's coronation.

One shade separated itself from the unseen legions, as Lady Nephera and her entourage took their places. Takyr, his moldering face and form more distinct, more malignant than the others, paused near his mistress, ready to heed her slightest command.

Standing to the side of Lady Nephera's party, two rows of attendants began beating with the flats of their hands on bowl-shaped copper drums. The drums created a hollow, thundering effect.

Nephera raised her arms, beckoning to the audience. The drums slowed, sounding like the steps of a weary giant.

Strong hands brought forth the Eye.

A perfect pearl of momentous proportions, it had earned its name from the way the light played upon its surface. All were left with the same impression—that an eye of rainbow blue gazed from within, looking outward and seeing inside of people. Years before, a mariner had discovered it in his catch. There had been no explanation to its origin, but the discoverer—one of the first of the faithful—had felt compelled to make a gift of it to Lady Nephera.

It took four acolytes to carry it to the silver, pyramid-shaped stand. The monstrous pearl became the centerpiece for special sermons. It glistened in even the slightest light like a miniature sun, terrible and brilliant at the same time. The colorful flashes of light reflected by it played across Nephera's face, too.

Nephera placed her hands atop the artifact.

The drums ceased.

"Honored are those who have preceded us!"

A stillness swept the crowd.

"Honored are our ancestors, who cut the paths upon which we now tread!"

Expression unchanging, Lady Nephera drew power from the shades around her. They resisted, but her will was stronger. She fed some of their energy into the pearl, amplifying its radiance.

"Honored are the Forerunners, they who crafted our people's history, our world's history, with each action of their lives!"

A dozen horns blared a single strong note.

Meeting the eyes of the crowd, she continued, "We, too, play a part. We craft the future for our children with each breath we take, each decision, until at last death claims us!"

The drums beat. The attendant who held the silver bird solemnly stepped up and placed it in her mistress's right hand. The second attendant followed, setting the golden axe in the other.

"But our work does not end with death!" Nephera shouted, thrusting forth the latter icon. "Though the axe might be broken, the physical form laid to rest, the spirit within knows no bounds!" She brought the silver bird toward her audience. "Born again, it rises forth, free of all infirmity, and sets upon a new path!"

The drums grew more insistent.

"Limited no more, the spirit may influence what flesh could not!" Her arms to the side, Nephera waited for her assistants to take the talismans away before adding, "We join the Forerunners, gaining the knowledge privileged only to those beyond the mortal plane! We see the paths that could be taken and the results of each step! We guide those who are still a part of the world, those blind to possibilities and dangers!"

"We give thanks to our ancestors!" Ardnor shouted, his booming voice heard by all in the crowd.

"Blessed are we to follow their wisdom," intoned the captivated throng, taking their cue.

"We pray for their guidance, understanding that with it there is no enemy too strong, no task too great for us to overcome."

The worshippers repeated their thanks. Many pressed their muzzles against the stone, honoring their predecessors.

Smiling to her favored children, Lady Nephera called out, "When the gods abandoned us, our kin did not! When the gods betrayed us, our kin stepped forth from the shadows of the otherworld and sought one who could bring their messages to those they held dear!" She bowed her head. "And I thank them for having chosen this poor vessel as their voice."

The high priestess stepped around the pearl, sending a wave of surprise through the sea of kneeling figures. She had always given the messages of their loved ones from behind the Eye.

The dead she had summoned stood ready next to Lady Nephera. They stared at the crowd, unblinking gazes fixed on particular figures among the faithful.

"This day, I have been charged to give a select few a message that must be spread to all. A message of our future and the duty it entails! You will not hear the message from me, though. No, these words of import will come from others nearer to you, nearer to your hearts and souls!"

Takyr glided over to her. Nephera felt her power swelling.

"Hear now the words of your ancestors, your kin!"

With that, the ghostly forms drifted forward, seeking those who had links of blood or love to them. They drifted near enough to touch some in the crowd—and with the power of the high priestess, they became visible to the chosen.

A young adult female floated down to a pair of identical twin males, her sons left orphaned twenty years before. A child with one twisted foot descended on an elderly couple, the parents who had lost him right after the Flight of the Gods. A handsome male in the bloom of youth whose breastplate had been pierced by a lance walked through the bodies of onlookers, pausing at last in front of a mature female, the mate left behind when he died in battle a few days after their bonding.

Gasps and shrieks erupted throughout the crowd. While onlookers stared in bewilderment, the chosen faithful tried to come to grips with the stunning visions.

"Mirya!" one cried. "Oh, Mirya!"

"My brother! I tell you my brother stands before me! I know his face as well as my own!"

For those who could see, the sights before them inspired awe. Their lost loved ones, marked by the circumstances of their deaths. Yet, the ghostly figures greeted their kin and mates with gracious, caring smiles.

Nephera focused on her puppets and made them speak.

"My time is short," each said in voices strong and steady because their mistress willed them accordingly. "I wish so much that I could be with you, but that moment must wait."

Although the chosen could see and hear their particular shades, they could not see or hear the others, and the vast majority of the faithful saw and heard nothing.

"Hear me," the ghosts went on, pointing at their kin and friends. "I bring you knowledge that must be passed on to all. A moment has come in our history that must not be lost."

"What? What is it?" more than one of the living cried out, their eyes wide with expectation.

"Chot the Terrible is dead! Hotak de-Droka now sits on the throne, a true emperor born," the spectres said. "This is the moment of destiny. Hotak is the emperor awaited for generations, the warrior who shall lead our people to victory, to domination! He is the ruler who shall see to it that no lesser race shall enslave us again!"

Lady Nephera grew excited as she sensed the words touching the minds and hearts of the chosen. It was time to finish and let word spread of those from beyond the mortal plane.

Raising a fist, each of the shades cried, "All hail Hotak! All hail he who shall shape the empire! All hail he who is the hand of destiny! All hail Emperor Hotak!"

With that last cry, the apparitions vanished.

It took a moment for most of the crowd to realize that some profound event had just played out in their midst. Those who stood around the select ones bombarded them with questions. The latter, in turn, repeated everything they had been told.

Nephera felt as though someone had knocked all the breath out of her. Ardnor seized her to keep her from falling. Her sudden weakness did not go unnoticed by the faithful, but they took it as a sign that the powers who had visited through her had taken their leave.

From a murmur the voices of those in attendance grew rapidly to an excited rumble. Those who heard the chosen compared their messages.

Let them spread this tale, Lady Nephera thought with intense satisfaction as she straightened and surveyed her excited flock. Let the fools know that no greater power serves the throne than the temple.

Chapter XII

Golgren

"Is that it?" Kolot asked, sizing up the treacherous peak in the distance. He shook to rid himself of dust. "Looks like a draconian's taloned thumb. We'd better not have to climb that thing."

One of the two warriors with Kolot looked over the parchment upon which directions were written. "Aye, my lord. It could be none other. We do not have to climb it, but we need to make our way around its base to reach our destination."

" 'Fraid you'd say that."

The inhospitable terrain of southwesternmost Kern made even the worst regions of Argon's Chain seem inviting. Savage cliffs and abrupt fissures dotted the rocky landscape and rarely could one find cover from the sun. A stone arch carved by some ancient phenomenon loomed over their path—an arch from which chunks of earth dropped. Some of the larger pieces fell with enough force to cave in the head of a thick-skulled minotaur.

Only an ogre could call this place home. Hotak's youngest son did not like being here, but Kern had agreed to talks

only if someone of close blood to the emperor acted as nego-
tiator—as a symbol of Hotak's trust. The task had fallen to
Kolot. Hotak had wanted to send more than two unarmored
guards, but that had been forbidden.

"I don't like this land," Kolot muttered. "We go much
more south and we'll be in Blöde."

"Kern and Blöde are allied at the moment, my lord," reminded the younger of his two guards.

The two ogre realms had managed to put aside their feuds
long enough to combine forces against the hated Knights of
Neraka. If not for the humans' incursions into both lands,
the ogres would have continued to pound one another to a
pulp. The Grand Khan of Kern and the Lord Chieftain of
Blöde had happily sworn out blood warrants on one another
in the past.

"They were allied at last report," Kolot retorted with a
contemptuous snort. "By this time they could be at war again!
This would've been better set up in the northeast by old Kern-
en," he added, referring to the ogre capital. "At least there
we'd see forest and rivers, even if it meant hordes of blood-
thirsty mosquitoes! We wouldn't have to worry about running across rogue bands of ogres sneaking in from Blöde."

The two subordinates did not respond, in part because
they knew that Hotak's son simply spoke out of frustration—
and also because everything he had just said was true.

On and on the minotaurs rode. Around them, the harsh
monotony of the landscape continued. Midday came and went
without any further utterance by the hot and weary trio.

Pausing to sip more water, Kolot blinked. He lowered the
sack casually, eyes studying the jagged formations ahead.

A two-legged shape edged out of sight among the high hills.

Kolot resecured the sack. "There's someone—"

A bestial figure emerged from atop one of the nearest rock
formations, deep-set eyes glaring down at the three.

Legend said that the ogres and minotaurs shared a common ancestor, the golden Irda. To Kolot, though, the ogre above resembled the offspring of a maniacal human and a raging bear. Teeth filed sharp ground in defiance of the minotaurs, and two chipped and jagged tusks protruded from the ogre's bottom lip. The wide, flat features twisted into a look of hatred. An unruly mop of tangled, dust-encrusted hair framed the horrific countenance.

"Stay," growled the ogre in a grating voice like that of one who chewed rocks for candy. The creature squatted atop the crusted formation, his only garment a half-ragged kilt likely scavenged from the corpse of a victim.

"This is our ally?" muttered one of the guards.

A clatter of rocks alerted the minotaurs.

More than a dozen equally grotesque warriors blossomed into sight around them.

Kolot managed to stop his companions before they unslung their axes. "No! Wait!"

They might have questioned his wisdom, but at that moment yet another ogre joined those surrounding them--an ogre like no other.

He wore a long, well-sewn cloak of brown cloth over an elegantly tailored forest-green tunic of similar fabric and a matching leather kilt that might have been minotaur-made. Unlike the others, who moved about on calloused, thorny feet, the newcomer wore padded sandals bound far up the ankles. Half hidden by the voluminous cloak was the lower tip of a shining silver scabbard.

The face most interested the minotaurs, for it resembled little the countenances of the other monsters staring at them. Although wide, this one's features were not so squashed, and the blunt, squat nose would have passed on a human. His teeth were sharp but did not protrude, and of tusks only nubs could be seen.

"My greetings to you," the newcomer rumbled almost pleasantly. Under a thick brow, almond-shaped green eyes watched with anticipation, wit . . . and cunning. "Son of Hotak."

"My greetings in return, Grand Lord Golgren."

A scent of musk pervaded the air, causing one of the guards to snort. Ogres did not smell of musk; they reeked of sweat, rotting meat, and the accumulations of a lifetime's lack of bathing. Golgren not only looked as if he bathed, but his thick, black leonine hair had been cared for.

"Never felt shabby in front of an ogre before," muttered the veteran guard to his younger counterpart.

"Forgive my ignorance," Kolot said. "I assumed that we were to meet over there." He pointed at the jagged peak.

"Some miscommunication, yes?"

There had been no miscommunication. Kolot had read the instructions correctly. The ogre had set up this little surprise to seize the advantage.

The barrel-chested minotaur shrugged. "Here's as good as anywhere." He patted a wide, leather pouch strung up on the side of his saddle. "What you want is in there."

Golgren nodded. With careful movements, Kolot removed the tightly rolled parchments, bound by thick leather string and sealed in wax by Hotak's signet.

Golgren glanced at one of his warriors. Club gripped tight, the bestial figure leaped from his perch then trotted toward Kolot. As the ogre took the missives from Kolot, the minotaur's nostrils flared. Unlike the emissary, this ogre smelled exactly as he looked.

Golgren paused to study the wax impression. "Ah, yes," he murmured in what sounded like amusement. "The horse."

To the trio's surprise, he did not open the parchments but rather tucked them safely in his belt.

Kolot almost bared his teeth. "My father told me you'd look them over on the spot. Is there another miscommunication?"

Golgren waved his hand and his forces began to melt back into the rocks. The Grand Lord of Kern smiled. "Your trip has been a long one, yes?"

"Yes. Lord Golgren, what—?"

The ogre went on. "My own trip . . . it also was difficult. The humans of Neraka plague all parts of Kern—even Kern-en, from where this humble one began his journey."

Kolot tried again. "Lord Golgren, my father's offer . . . you've not even read it."

"I will guide you myself, son of Hotak," Golgren went on. "The way into Blöde is treacherous." He smiled wider, revealing teeth very much like those of his savage warriors. Kolot saw that Golgren had actually had his tusks scraped down to produce such tiny nubs.

"The way into Blöde? What are you talking about, Golgren?"

"Some . . . changes . . . in our course of action must take place, son of Hotak. Blöde we must enter."

"I've not come to help you start a war with Blöde."

The ogre leader laughed, a harsh, brutal sound. "We plan no war, son of Hotak! Just the opposite. His glorious Grand Khan wishes you to meet with Nagroch, subchieftain of the Lord Chieftain of Blöde!" The monstrous smile stretched, becoming more bestial. "Nagroch will swear the allegiance of Blöde to our cause . . . if he does not slay us all first, of course!"

Each day the list of dead lengthened, most perishing from the sickness of the lungs. Despite cloths to wrap over their snouts, almost everyone inhaled dust constantly. Many of the slaves could not keep up with the punishing quotas. When they finally could not take it any more, they simply collapsed.

And when death claimed a worker, it befell on those who had labored at his side to dispose of the body. Paug made Faros and Ulthar the bearers of the corpses.

This day, they carried the body of a young male. He had come to Vyrox only two weeks before, arriving with some breathing ailment. The suffocating tunnels had simply hastened his death.

The two had to drag the corpse all the way to the old processing station. A gaping hole, over fifty yards in diameter, had been dug out generations ago. In it had been thrown charcoal and other fuel used to separate copper and other minerals from the rock. When a rockslide had completely devastated the station itself, a new, larger facility had been built some distance away at a safer location. The old pit had been left empty.

Its interior scorched black and smooth by years of gorging flame, the pit now held in its bowels the charred bones of all those prisoners who perished at their jobs.

"Throw it in!" shouted the Butcher. Shattered skulls, a half-burnt rib cage, a pile of mixed, black bones . . . Paug was unaffected by the ghastly sight of jumbled remains.

Ulthar muttered a prayer. Faros heard the names of the old sea gods, Habbakuk the Fisher King and his volatile counterpart, the dark and sinister mistress of the depths, Zeboim.

The pair heaved the body into the depths of the black pit. Halfway down it struck the side with a dull thud then cascaded deeper into the hellish realm.

"You! Barbarian! Take the tinder!" Paug looked to Faros. "You, take the oil! Be quick about it!"

Ulthar started a small fire while Faros dumped oil into the pit. Finished, Faros tried to back away, but Paug pushed him back, forcing his charge to look into the pit.

Ulthar sent a blazing torch into the air. It arced high, the wind causing the flames to dance merrily, then began an abrupt and swift descent.

The torch struck the well-oiled bottom. Flames erupted.

Everything within was engulfed in raging fire. The entire party, even Paug, retreated from the intense heat.

Faros glanced at Ulthar and saw that the mariner's hands were clenched tight. Again, his companion mouthed a prayer.

"All right!" the Butcher shouted. "Enough of a break for you two! Back to work!" The fires would burn until nothing remained upon which to feed.

The memories would burn far longer.

As they returned, Faros noticed Ulthar muttering under his breath. He was listing names, including the dead youth's. The list went on and on.

"Ulthar?" he whispered. "Did you know him?"

"Nilo? No," the other returned. "Knew Halrog some. Before him Yarl. Before that Ilionus, Gorsus, Tremanion, Kaj . . . knew Kaj and Gorsus. Before them was Urs—"

"But why?"

The mariner kept his eyes on the uneven ground. "I remember them."

Faros blinked, astounded. "All of them?"

"As many since I—"

"Silence there!" Paug gave Ulthar a brief taste of the whip.

The pair resumed their digging. Faros chipped away at the stone. Fragments flew in every direction. The fragments came not just from the work, but from the ceiling, loosened by the constant pounding.

Faros beat away at a huge rock, determined to reduce it to rubble. He struck again and again.

A groaning sound caught his attention. Startled, Faros looked up at the ceiling.

A rain of earth fell on him. The mountain roared. Faros tried to call for help, but dirt filled his mouth. The frantic minotaur fought his way toward the entrance, although he was blinded and could not tell if he was heading in the right direction.

Thunder shook the shaft, sending Faros to his knees. He tried to stand, but the collapsing earth pressed down on him. Giving in, he fell to his knees, letting dirt and rock bury him.

Strong hands seized his arms. Unable to see, Faros tried to speak but could only cough and sputter.

"Take 'un by the other arm!"

"I can't . . . there! Now I've got a grip!"

Two figures lifted him to his feet then dragged him outside Argon's Throat. Even the burning air of Vyrox tasted good. Faros sucked in great lungfuls, gulping and gasping.

His sight cleared, revealing Ulthar and Japfin. "What . . . what happened? Another tremor?"

"No. Supports not all in place. Walls too weak to hold themselves together, much less ceiling, too."

"Should've secured the whole area better before we started," Japfin grumbled. "But they couldn't wait, could they? Had to make the new quota."

"This quota they'll not make," Ulthar murmured. "Means tomorrow we'll be harder at it."

A shadow came up behind Faros. He looked up to see Paug's ugly muzzle. "He breathing good enough? We're falling behind! I want you all back in there. Hear me?"

"We hear," Ulthar said.

They reached the site of the collapse and quickly joined the others at work. Paug fell behind in order to speak to another overseer.

"Thank you, Ulthar," said Faros. "I appreciate you and Japfin helping me. You shouldn't have done it. You could have lost your own lives."

Ulthar tossed aside a rock, then shrugged. "Saw a chance and took it . . . this time. Maybe next time, I have to leave you." He snorted. "Besides, too many names to remember already, Bek."

Faros came to a decision. "Ulthar," he whispered, tossing another rock away. "I need to tell you something."

The other prisoner eyed him but did not pause in his labors. "What?"

The younger minotaur hesitated. I'm the nephew of Chot, he wanted to blurt. My name is Faros Es-Kalin!

But no words came out. Of all those in Vyrox, Faros should be able to trust the mariner.

Instead, different words finally tumbled from his mouth. "Never mind."

Ulthar shrugged and returned to his task. Faros stood there for a moment, teeth bared in frustration. He watched the other prisoner's back for several seconds then in bitter silence resumed his own digging.

Chapter XIII

House Droka

Four months after the overthrow of Chot, the palace sent word of a gathering of all those deemed the most respected of supporters. Invitations were delivered by messenger to the chosen clans. Most answered readily that they would attend. A few found reason to hesitate, however.

Lady Nephera kept a list of those.

Two weeks before the gathering, the House of Droka, Hotak's clan, received a visit that made all within the extensive, walled estate uneasy. Arriving at the clan house just as the sun peeked over the horizon, Hotak, from his horse, informed the surprised guards at the iron gate that he wished to see the master.

The guards opened the gate for him and his retinue of two dozen strong. Held up by the two soldiers riding behind the emperor, the warhorse banner flew defiant below the flags of Droka, which hung from posts set on the angled roof of the six-story tall, rectangular building.

An armed honor guard of ten soldiers met Hotak and his followers at the front steps.

"Your horses will be safe in the stables, my lord," said the leader of the guard.

"Two of my own will watch the animals. This will not be a long visit."

The guard bowed then, eyes warily surveying the dismounting figures, suggested, "Your warriors can wait in the common room. It's to the left as you enter—"

Hotak's ears twitched slightly. "I recall the layout of my old home quite well, and my soldiers will wait where I decide."

A corridor covered in mahogany greeted Hotak and his warriors. Within filigreed frames had been set life-size reliefs honoring the deeds and history of the venerable clan. Heroes of epic battle, stalwart champions of the arena, and three emperors had their images and achievements memorialized for all who visited.

Among the images was Hotak himself winning a glorious battle against ogres near the colony of Sargonath. The relief showed him at the head of a determined charge, face in profile, teeth bared as he cleaved the ogre leader with his axe.

At the end of the corridor, two Droka sentries opened the arched doors leading into the great hall, where the patriarchs held court.

Within, the other senior members of the House, dressed in collarless, ankle-length robes of gold and black, took their places on the five cordoned rows of benches lining both sides of the chamber. Every elder of Droka had come.

At the far end of the chamber, atop the crimson-carpeted dais, the patriarch's chair remained empty.

"Where is Itonus?" Hotak asked, keeping his voice level.

The guard to whom he spoke blanched. "I couldn't say, my lord."

"I see."

Itonus had been patriarch for twelve years, and he had supported Hotak in the past, yet the large, gray-brown minotaur was absent. Hotak had to wait in silence in the presence of the other elders. His mood darkened. Itonus obviously sought to remind him of the rules set by the first lords of the empire, that in one's own clan house, the patriarch reigned supreme.

Hotak removed his helmet and handed it to his second. As his gaze flickered impatiently around the room, he noted with hidden pleasure that the elders eyed him with not only deep respect, but a little uncertainty.

On his blind side, a rustling of garments warned him that someone had entered. A whiff of lavender, Nephera's scent, caused Hotak to smile. The guards stationed along the benches straightened.

Itonus had finally arrived.

Clad in a floor-length robe, the patriarch strode past Hotak without a glance. Pausing briefly to glance at the huge clan banner hanging above, the patriarch lowered his impressive frame into the mahogany chair. Itonus finally looked down his long, tapering snout at Hotak.

The thick-browed minotaur gave his visitor a gracious smile—baring all his teeth—then, in the most polite of voices said, "Welcome, son of Nemon, son of House Droka! What brings the progeny of my old comrade humbly seeking my guidance?"

The patriarch had purposely phrased everything to remind the new emperor of his place in the clan.

Choosing magnanimity over outrage, Hotak returned just as politely, "I come not seeking guidance, elder, but to speak with you of a matter of import. I have made a request of you that you have not seen fit to respond to properly."

The patriarch's right hand clutched the curved end of the chair arm tightly. Itonus looked past Hotak. There, in the far corner, the Lady Nephera stood, smiling.

"And what is it you do not understand about my response, Hotak?" Itonus rasped.

That he avoided the emperor's title did not go unnoticed. Hotak pretended to overlook it. "Most likely it's just a matter of misinterpretation. Surely I am mistaken to hear that the elders of our clan, yourself among them, will not be attending the gathering honoring my most loyal subjects? That cannot be true."

"You read correctly, my son. House Droka supports your ascension to the fullest. However, it has come to my attention that you intend some further . . . *changes* in the realm that cannot be condoned. I think you know what I mean."

Itonus had heard that the new emperor intended to create a hereditary crown. Rule by bloodline had always been considered a path of madness, fit only for the lesser races. That House Droka would be the clan from which all future rulers sprang had not changed Itonus's mind.

"All was made clear in my response, my son," the graying patriarch continued. "I see no confusion. The clan must draw the line for the sake of future stability. Having you on the throne will make Droka one of the foremost powers of the realm, but now you seek to flout all tradition! You will bring chaos on us all. And I will add that your desired dynasty, if one dares call it that, will not last past the second generation."

Hotak's wife made a slight hissing sound. The emperor swept back his cloak and stalked up to the dais. "I offer the greatest stability to the empire, to our people, that could ever be possible. I put an end to the reign of a fool who led us into utter disaster. I'm eradicating the corruption, disease, and crime birthed by his rule." He glanced at the surrounding elders. "I will lead our people to their rightful place in the world!"

Several in the crowd stomped their feet in a display of support for the one-eyed commander. Itonus glared, silencing them.

"And your clan shall support you in your efforts—to the point of reason," Itonus countered. "It is one thing to topple a corrupt emperor, but another to oppose the rights of the people. There have always been limits to the power of the throne, and the imperial combat has always ensured them. A hereditary system goes against the word of Sargas himself!"

"The word of a god who abandoned us," Nephera quietly remarked.

Hotak took up her words. "Yes, abandoned us! Fled with the other gods after leading the world to destruction! We're far better off without him, I'd say." He put a foot on the first step. "And I think House Droka would do just as well without a leader long past stepping down."

Six legionaries started toward Itonus, weapons ready.

Rising, the patriarch roared, "Halt!"

They continued toward him.

He looked to the clan guards. "Remove them!"

Instead of obeying, the majority of the sentries turned their weapons on the seated elders. The few loyal guards quickly found themselves disarmed.

Hotak's voice boomed throughout the chamber. "Elder Itonus, I declare you unfit for the role of patriarch and, by the precedent of history, I order you removed from your position, your role to be filled by imperial edict this very moment." He pointed at a heavyset figure sitting in the front row. "Master Zephros!"

Zephros, long Itonus's chief rival among the clan elders, stirred. "My emperor?"

"I appoint you acting patriarch! Will you accept?"

Zephros pushed his massive bulk out of his chair. His jowls shook when he spoke. "Your majesty, for the sake of the clan and realm, I accept the duty you thrust so unexpectedly upon me." He lowered his horns. "I will try to fulfill the role honorably."

Looming over Hotak, Itonus declared, "You cannot do this! It is beyond the bounds of your power! The elders of the other Houses will not allow—"

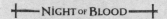

A sword point touched his throat, cutting off any further protest.

Hotak turned to the assembly. "Zephros is declared lawful patriarch! I leave it to you to ratify his position as permanent. What say you, clan elders?"

As Itonus gaped, the assembly swiftly hailed his rival and successor. Satisfied, the emperor turned to Itonus. Of all Houses, Droka had been expected to show its support of him.

The ousted clan leader was led down the steps. Hotak watched as they approached.

"How would it look," he asked the prisoner quietly, "for the emperor's own kin not to show a united front? I can't let questions arise as to the strength of the throne. You should have considered that carefully, cousin."

"I have never denied you!" the ousted patriarch gasped. "Only some of your insane changes! You seek a pact with the ogres, our taskmasters of old! Worse, you move to declare Ardnor as your heir, the first emperor to gain the throne by birth alone! That, more than anything else, cannot be permitted!"

"Everything I do," Hotak said, "I do for the good of the people."

Snapping his fingers, he sent the arrested elder on.

Nephera appeared at Hotak's side and placed her arm in his, her expression more satisfied than anyone else's.

She looked to the gathered members and called out, "Let all children of Droka give their allegiance to their new patriarch . . . and their emperor."

The elders came forward and gave their allegiance, without hesitation. After Itonus's downfall, they knew they must.

Under a brisk morning wind, four battered imperial ships sailed into the fog-shrouded harbor. At first, to those at the dock it seemed Hotak had finally hunted them down.

General Rahm walked up to welcome a boat from the lead vessel. The captain, a gruff older female with cold, appraising eyes, knelt before the general. She dipped her head. Her crew, dressed in the kilts of the Imperial Fleet, raised their axes in his honor.

"Hail, General Rahm!" she bellowed. "I am Captain Tinza. The *Sea Reaver* and her sisters beg your permission to aid in the destruction of the murderous usurper, Bloody Hotak."

Rahm eyed her critically. "Strange words, considering your part in the downfall of Captain Veria. You left her without support."

The ships had been part of the Eastern fleet. When Hotak sought the execution of those officers loyal to Chot, the fleet had turned on itself. Veria, the senior officer, had died in the struggle.

"We were told by Hotak's emissary that the captain would be spared if we opened the way to her capture, that she would be allowed to prove herself to the new emperor and regain her position."

"And you believed that?"

The shame in Tinza's voice left no question as to her regrets. "Much ale was passed around that night. Strong ale." She looked up. "Let us atone for that disgrace! For Captain Veria, we demand the chance to battle with the usurper's forces."

He looked over the crew. "You'll obey in all things?"

"If you demand my life to secure the lives of the others, General Rahm, I give it to you."

"Just keep your crews away from the ale. Can you do that?"

She took his left hand and touched her muzzle to the black-jeweled ring he wore, an old minotaur custom of gratitude and fealty that most no longer recalled, much less performed.

With the four imperial ships came an equal number of catapults and more than two hundred and fifty fighters.

They brought with them new supplies of salted meat, wine, and more precise maps.

The arrival of the newcomers forced changes. More common houses were built. Jubal took charge of the ongoing procurement of food. Within a day's journey of Petarka lay two smaller islands. One had shallow shoals with an abundance of fish. The other, lush with vegetation, enabled the rebels to add to their storehouses of breadfruit and bananas. The ominous weather that had stricken so much of the empire had held off so far around Petarka, further aiding Rahm's followers in their efforts.

Over the next two weeks, three more vessels fought their way through storms to Petarka. Two came from Mito, including among their passengers a former militia commander named Ryn and almost half his fighters. The other ship had escaped from a small garrison on the remote southeastern colony of Hathan.

"Hotak wants a race of perfect, obedient soldiers," Rahm muttered to Jubal, going over the latest charts in the unadorned common room they had chosen as their headquarters. A pair of round brass lamps were set near Rahm. There were two windows facing the harbor, both shuttered to keep out the incessant wind. The door had warped and could only be kept shut by sliding an iron bar across it. "But he forgets that perfect warriors must trust their leaders."

"Will that help us?"

"If we act soon, yes." The general turned to a guard at the door. "You there! Tell all commanders to gather! Quickly!"

Within minutes, the room filled. In addition to Jubal and Azak, all seven other ship captains awaited his word. With them had come the commanders of the marine regiments that had sailed with each vessel and the chosen leaders of the bands of refugees.

"The *Sea Reaver* and her sister ships are ready at your command, General Rahm," Captain Tinza said. Behind her, the rest of the new captains nodded. Azak gave a slight snort at their enthusiasm.

"As are we," rumbled Napol, a hirsute warrior with a thick brow ridge and one broken horn. Like the other members of the marine regiments, he wore a padded kilt colored silver with one wide, sea green stripe running horizontally across the top. The silver around his sea-dragon badge marked him as the equivalent of a legion *hekturion*, a trusted officer in command of one hundred warriors, although only twenty of his original complement remained by the time his ship reached Petarka. He was now commander of all the marine units.

Rahm signaled for silence. "It pleases me to hear this, for we face no simple matter. We fight not only an enemy who outnumbers us but who is our own kin. Choices will be made—choices with regrets! We've got to strike before Hotak becomes too settled, before people come to think of him as the only power."

Captain Tinza raised a hand and roared her pleasure. "I have it! The Eastern fleet! We'll strike at 'em while they sleep!"

Her fellow captains rumbled their approval, and even Napol's officers added their voices.

"No!" Rahm smashed his fist on the table. "This is not some glorious death by futile combat! We fight to win, not to die! There is one plan for certain that offers us our best hope. It means at least a month of preparation and depends on you and your shipmates, Tinza, not to mention Napol and his fighters." Rahm gazed thoughtfully at Azak. "And it relies on you much, also, my friend."

"And what is this grand and dangerous mission?" The elder captain asked.

In answer, General Rahm lifted up the map so all could see.

The map displayed Mithas.

"We must strike at the heart of the empire," he said, his eyes meeting the gazes of each. "The very heart."

An uproar started.

After all his talk against suicidal missions, what more drastic plan could their leader have chosen than attacking the main island?

"To be precise," the determined commander went on, heedless of the confusion, "Nethosak, the imperial capital—and the palace of the usurper."

The heated discussion went on for over two hours, with suggestions and protests flung evenly. Rahm remained undeterred and finally dismissed everyone after giving them their new orders.

But two figures remained. One was Azak, now stone-faced. Another was a young officer from one of the last vessels to arrive, whose own expression bordered on fear.

"Rahm . . ." Azak began. "Rahm, there's news you should hear. This young officer told me just before you summoned us."

The general's eyes narrowed. "Ill news, I take it. And you are?"

"First Mate Rogan of the *Javelin*, General Rahm. My brother served under you about seven years ago. His name was Tyril."

The name did not register with Rahm, but he nodded nonetheless. "Go on."

"Tyril joined the fleet three years ago. He's first mate on *The Scorpion's Sting*. He started with—"

"Never mind that," interrupted Azak, his gaze never leaving Rahm. "Tell him what your brother told you."

Rogan nodded, his look all the more apprehensive with each passing second. "*The Scorpion's Sting* was escorting a supply ship to some of the more obscure colonies northeast. A strange, sudden storm slowed them, but they finally came to the last one on their list—and found nothing left but a big scorched rock, sir! Some sort of terrible fire had burned away everything. No houses, no people, no trees, no animals. General, even the *rock* was half-melted!"

"What happened?"

"The gods only know."

Rahm snorted.

Azak cleared his throat. "Tell the general the name of the island, lad."

"It . . . it was called Tadaran."

"No survivors whatsoever," the old mariner added softly. "No trace of any life at all. I'm sorry."

Face emotionless, Rahm looked at the first mate. "You're certain it was Tadaran?"

"Aye, general."

Staring down at the charts, Rahm quietly said, "Thank you for telling me. You can both go."

"Rahm—" said Azak.

"Go!"

The captain ushered the younger minotaur out, shutting the door behind them. For more than a minute, General Rahm eyed the map before him, staring at the place marked Tadaran. His breathing turned rapid. Every muscle grew taut. The whites of Rahm's eyes were engulfed by red.

With a roar of outrage, he tore the map into tiny pieces then scattered everything else off the table. The brass oil lamps clattered to the floor, both flaring briefly then dousing themselves before they could set fire to the room.

Heedless, Rahm roared again and turned the table over. He charged forward, head down, and rammed himself straight into nearest wall. The entire cabin shook with the force. Then he vented his anger on the shelves, ripping them off one by one and hurling the contents throughout the room, trampling everything. The chairs followed, turned quickly into splinters. Bereft of anything else to destroy, the general slammed his fists on the walls then, when he had collapsed onto his knees, the floor. Over and over he called out the name of his mate, Mogra, and their son Dorn.

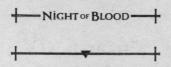
Captain Azak stood by the entrance to the cabin, waving off anyone who came near. Three hours passed, in which he listened to the destruction and grief loosened by his friend.

When the door opened at last, he turned to face the general, expecting the worst. Instead, although disheveled, Rahm met him with a strange, determined calm.

"Rahm . . ."

"I need some new charts," the general said. "And a table and some chairs, too. Can you see to that?"

"Aye, I can. But—"

Smoothing the black streak in his fur, the general continued, "I'm going for a walk. To clear my head. I have some ideas as to the specifics of our plan. I'll want to go over them with you when I return."

"Rahm, your family—"

Rahm's eyes flashed, but he quickly smothered the emotion. "My family is dead, Azak. They were on that island because of Hotak. As sure as if he had set fire to them himself, the false emperor's responsible for their deaths." The general patted his friend on the shoulder, expression never changing. "We have a war to fight. That's our concern now."

With that, he walked off, leaving the captain to stare and shake his head.

CHAPTER XIV

FATE AND CHOICE

The day came when Faros and Ulthar were assigned to the processing station.

"You two! Come with me!" Whip in hand, Paug pointed them toward a pair of wagons separated from the others. The prisoners there had an even more gaunt look, and their fur had patches where not only the hair had all fallen out, but their blistered skin burned red.

Ulthar's ears twitched. "In there?"

"That's right, barbarian! You recall the way, don't you? You spent three months there last time, didn't you?"

The mariner clamped his mouth shut and started forward. Eyes wide and unnerved, Faros trailed behind.

At the second wagon, Paug turned them over to a grim, thin guard with bloodshot eyes. "Here's the two replacements."

The other figure, his fur patchy, indicated the wagon's interior. "Inside with them."

"Get in!" snarled Paug, snapping the whip.

The prisoners seated themselves. Eyes deeply shadowed

and bloodshot stared back at them. Shivering, Faros dropped
his gaze.

Their first hint that they approached the station came
with the metallic odor that stung their nostrils. What seemed
a mist also pervaded the area, a mist that proved to be acrid
smoke created by the four constantly smoldering pits that
surrounded the two-story, ash-gray building.

The station had no windows, a wise precaution considering the foul haze permeating everything. Only two
wide wooden doors allowed entrance into the rectangular
stone structure.

"You two," muttered the soldier who had received them
from Paug. "You'll be working on Number Four."

Flames shot up from the pit in question. At the same time,
a harsh scream erupted and a thick-linked chain hanging
down into the fiery hole rattled madly for several seconds.

A furious overseer began shouting something into the pit
while other guards began forcing four prisoners down a pair
of ladders.

The guard steered them toward a long row of workers
standing just yards from the edge. The prisoners were bent
over a long table on which they appeared to be hammering
away at something.

"Over here!" a sentry shouted to a minotaur pushing a
full cart.

The prisoner maneuvered the cart next to the line then
took an empty cart away for the full one he left behind.

Atop the battered but sturdy iron table lay piles of ore.
Prisoners labored to reduce the ore in size. After chipping the
rock and earth away, blue-green copper glinted in the smaller
rocks that workers then tossed in the carts. Two sentries constantly patrolled the line. Nearby, a lone archer stood ready
to shoot on command.

"Unless you've got no brains in your head, you know what

to do," snarled the guard. The soldier who had brought them walked off, his part done.

Ulthar and Faros seized hammers. "Lucky we are," murmured Ulthar.

"It's so hot!" Faros gasped. "Even Argon's Throat can't compare."

"Could be worse. Could be down in the pit."

They battered away at the rock. Standing in one place, working steadily, was exhausting.

After some time, an elderly prisoner came by with a bucket of water. As Faros took a drink, he saw that the other prisoner had lost all but a few traces of fur. The old minotaur's snout was covered in lesions, and one eye looked unfocused. His hands had calluses and old burns. It was apparent that his right leg had been improperly mended after being broken. He had also lost two fingers on his left hand.

"That 'un worked the pit. Everything you see . . . the result of the pit." The mariner's eyes grew tinged with crimson, and the pace of his breathing doubled. "The pit. He was lucky."

By the end of the day, Faros could barely walk. Even the brawnier Ulthar was drained. Both could barely see, too; the mist and continual flaring of the pit made their eyes sore and weak.

Every jostle of the wagon hurt, and by the time they returned to the camp, Faros barely had the strength to eat. He joined Ulthar and Japfin outside of the bunkhouse. Japfin was his usual stoic self, but the other giant said nothing, digging morosely into the oat and fish mix they were served.

"What happened out there, calf?" the black behemoth grumbled.

"We pounded ore all day," said Faros.

"Hard enough work, but not hard enough to beat the life out of old Ulthar here. The barbarian's the toughest one here. Next to me, of course."

Ulthar raised his bowl and poured the remnants into his mouth. He swallowed then rose, abandoning the other two.

Leaning toward Faros, Japfin muttered, "You don't know what's eatin' him at all? Figured he'd tell you if anyone."

But Faros only shook his head. He watched the mariner walk off, wondering, too, what was troubling him.

After more than a week of sullen silence, Ulthar began talking again. Some things Faros knew, such as the mariner having grown up on Zaar. Ulthar's family had been prominent in trade, dealing in pottery and fruit—papaya, breadfruit, and mangos—which they traded with another colony more rich in metals. For the first fourteen years of his life, he had sailed among the islands, learning of each new place, gaining a new tattoo here and there to recall adventures.

"Sail with full load," Ulthar muttered, punctuating every sentence with a blow of his hammer. "Come back with raw iron and copper, which we sold for good profit." Briefly, he smiled at the memories.

Faros waited until the guard had walked past then asked, "So what happened?"

The family had done so well that they decided to expand their business to include distant places. Unfortunately, only a day away from home after a profitable voyage, a terrible storm overtook the ship.

"Only survivor," growled Ulthar, battering a rock into dust. "Floated for two days. All family dead."

Shortly after his rescue, his colony had become embroiled in a dispute with a neighbor that ended in blood, and Ulthar joined the crew of a ship determined to make the enemy pay. The feud went on one year, two, three . . . As it dragged on into a fourth and fifth, the crew began to lose track of their cause.

"Took a small ship with lots of cargo, not 'un from the other side, just a fool in the wrong place. Then another and another. Good hunting, good profit. Took to sacking any ship not ours."

Ulthar had become a pirate, for six years preying not only on vessels of the lesser races, but minotaurs as well.

Adding to his tattoos and gaining a reputation for his ferocity, Ulthar became one of the mates. He might have succeeded the captain if not for three imperial ships that put an end to his trade. One had acted as bait, the others closing in once it was too late for the pirates to pull out.

"We hunted our own. The worst crime of the empire. The captain and the first mate, they got the kiss of the axe. Me almost. Sentenced with the rest to the galleys."

Ulthar survived for four years until making good his escape. He wandered onto the mainland, running across a band of brigands who decided that a minotaur would be a welcome addition. But after two years, nostalgia had sent him back to the sea, back toward the colony he had left so many years before.

"Three days past Mithas," the giant rumbled, "imperial ships found me and 'un of the captains recognized these." With the hammer, he indicated his many tattoos.

This time, they had sent Ulthar to Vyrox—and almost immediately to the processing station.

"Tried twice to escape. Got whipped twice." The former pirate shrugged. "Thought they could do nothing worse, but I was wrong . . . wrong." He paused suddenly in his work, looking the smaller minotaur deep in the eye. "I will not go back to the pit, Bek! I will not."

Faros did not know what had happened in that fiery place that would unnerve a pirate, but it made him pray that he would never be assigned to the hellish hole. Better any other task, even death detail, anywhere but the flame-engulfed abyss where every day prisoners screamed.

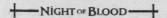
Anywhere but a place that could fill even Ulthar with dread.

Kolot sat before the campfire, watching the grime-encrusted representative of the Lord Chieftain. Clad in discolored goat furs and a rusted breastplate, the burly, stench-ridden figure slobbered blood and juice from the nearly uncooked haunch all over himself, but he seemed not to care. Near his left side rested a favored weapon of Blöde these days—a long axe whose handle had been wrapped tightly in leather for a better grip and whose single-edged, curved blade made it deadly. Etched across the inner edge of the blade were three marks—a half-circle flanked by two horizontal lines— signifying the old ogre belief that Sargonnas himself blessed the weapon.

Seated next to Kolot, Golgren maintained an air of patience and neutrality. He picked at his own, smaller piece of meat with care, almost as civilized as a minotaur. Compared to the fat, froglike Nagroch, Golgren looked almost noble.

The camp in which they supped was a temporary one. A dozen round tents made from dried goat skins dotted the area, a rocky enclave whose crevices and overhanging formations made it excellent for hiding. It had taken Kolot and the others days of strenuous travel over hills to reach the camp. The minotaurs would have never been able to find it on their own, so well did the landscape conceal it.

Forty warriors surrounded Kolot and his guards. The large band wore goatskins, scavenged leather jerkins and coats, gray cloth kilts cut near the knee, and flat leather sandals if they wore anything on their feet at all. Each wielded either a thick club or axe.

The minotaurs and Golgren had been allowed to keep their weapons, but all four realized that if things went bad with negotiations, their weapons would help little against such numbers.

"I hear your words," shaggy Nagroch grunted in his deep, hacking voice, food spilling from his monstrous jaws. The dark night combined with the fire to make his pockmarked visage more grotesque. "I hear things humans used to promise before they started burning villages, slaying children!" Under a thick, gray brow, bloodshot eyes focused on Kolot and Golgren. "I ask to me, 'Do these make same promises? Will Blöde be next after humans in black lay cut up like'—" He hesitated, looking for a proper comparison. Nagroch finally stared down at his ravaged meal, his brutish face stretching into a wide grin. "Like this goat?"

"You heard the word of the Grand Khan, Nagroch," Golgren responded politely. "And while you might question these," he indicated the minotaurs with a mild expression of dismissal, "the word of the glorious Khan is pure, a diamond in the sun."

The subchieftain belched, a putrid odor almost as bad as what emanated from his sweat-soaked body. He wiped his mouth with one hand, then wiped the hand in turn on his kilt. "I think I have more trust in bulls than ogres who dress like females."

"The word of the Grand Khan is inviolate," insisted the other ogre, speaking almost perfect Common. "That is proven, yes?"

Nagroch grunted reluctant agreement. His gaze returned to Kolot and something in it caused the young minotaur to stiffen.

"You know our offer," Kolot blurted. "We intend this pact to be favorable to all and a portent of doom to our common enemy."

Nagroch did not seem very impressed—either that, or he was still puzzling over the word "portent."

Golgren smiled at Hotak's son, revealing too much teeth. "Friend Kolot," he said in his smooth voice, "this one must explain. To ensure that peace is what ogres get, Kern had to make early promises to Blöde."

"Blöde made good promises back!" the subchieftain countered.

"Yes, that is so. But what Blöde and Kern find right does not work with your kind, friend minotaur." He leaned forward, poking at Kolot's chest with a leg bone. The two guards bristled but Kolot quieted them. "From you must come something else."

"Something else? What're you talking about?"

Golgren told him.

The eyes of all three minotaurs widened in disbelief.

"You can't be serious!" Hotak's youngest son sputtered.

The Grand Lord acted as if Kolot had just gravely offended him. "It must be so, minotaur, or not only will Blöde reject joining us, but this one fears his Grand Khan will rethink his own agreement to the pact."

"My father's offered you freedom from further attacks by the Knights of Neraka. He's offered you better weapons, supplies . . ." Kolot rose, his guards standing with him. Nagroch's warriors growled. "With all that, you still ask for this madness?"

Nagroch sat back, looking resolute. "Humans offered much. Humans took more. Blöde not be tricked again. Blöde demands proof. Minotaurs must pay right."

Kolot stared at the two, furious. He finally muttered, "I'll have to return to Mithas, then. I can only promise that I'll tell my father everything, not that he'll be willing."

"This must be settled now, son of Hotak."

"Now? But I can't promise on my own—"

The Grand Lord's eyes narrowed ominously. "You must."

Kolot's fists clenched. All of them knew how much Hotak desired this alliance. "Give me a moment to think on it."

"Of course," Golgren replied, smiling graciously yet

looking as if he planned to skin the minotaurs for a tent of his own.

Kolot pushed his way out of the circle. The other minotaurs stayed silent while he paced on the dark outskirts of the camp.

Growing desperate, he turned to his companions. "Well? You heard what he said. Any thoughts?"

The younger blurted, "It's barbaric! It cannot be done!"

"But if not," interjected the veteran, "it leaves us open to the danger that Kern and Blöde will still unite, push back the Dark Knights, and then fall upon the empire. Wouldn't be the first time ogre eyes beheld Mithas and hungered despite the water that separates us from them, eh?"

Kolot nodded to both of them. "Sound words, but no answer for me. What can I—?"

He paused as footsteps warned him of someone approaching.

"A pardon for this intrusion," Golgren said, his tone unapologetic. "This one thought to be of some aid, yes?"

"Don't trust him, my lord," growled the older guard. "He speaks much too cleverly for an ogre."

The Grand Lord bowed as if taking this comment for a compliment. "A solution is possible that might salvage matters."

"What sort of solution?" asked Kolot.

"May I approach?"

"Go ahead."

"You might do this to fulfill the pact. . . ." The ogre leaned close and outlined his suggestion.

When he had finished, Kolot swallowed. "I can't," he whispered. Shaken, he stared out at the black landscape, his gaze on something invisible. "If I don't?"

"Then you go home with nothing, son of Hotak."

As simple and final as all that. Kolot glanced at the other two, but they had no help to give him.

Steeling himself, the emperor's youngest confronted the emissary from Kern. Jaw set, Kolot replied, "All right. I have no choice. In the name of my father, I accept the terms."

"A wise choice. No regret," soothed Golgren, putting a companionable arm around the minotaur's shoulder and starting to guide him back to the camp. "Now come! Nagroch will want this news."

Kolot followed slowly, walking as if thrust through the heart by a sharp blade.

CHAPTER XV

PURSUIT

The salty smell of the sea mixed with that of fresh baked oat bread, broiled goat, fried fish, and a hint of sulfur from the distant peaks of Argon's Chain. Such smells had always been identified with good fortune and the stability of the empire.

But Bastion could not enjoy the day. A rift had opened between him and his father. There had been several unsettling catastrophes throughout the empire, some that hinted at magical influence, but Hotak had refused to take note. Even the recent rash of tremors along Argon's Chain, which had collapsed three viable shafts, damaged facilities, and set back the emperor's ambitious quotas, had done little to convince Hotak that unusual forces were at play and threatening his reign.

Then there was the recent incident of an unidentified minotaur slain in front of the palace. He had been watching the royal residence but was killed when he tried to evade the soldiers. Hotak had shrugged it off as an isolated episode, but Bastion could not let it rest. Today his search for the identity of the mysterious minotaur had led him to the lowliest neighborhood of Nethosak, situated in the southeastern section.

The captain of the search patrol saluted him. "We've a name, my lord. One Josiris. He stayed at this common house until three days ago then never returned."

Bastion blinked, the only sign of the depths of his pleasure at this unexpected intelligence. He peered past the officer, eyeing the rows of simple gray, nondescript structures.

"The badge he wore, the brown and black bear of House Ursun, was a forgery, my lord. Questioning of the elders proved without a doubt that he wasn't one of their clan."

"I never expected him to be." Bastion dismounted. "And his room?"

"He left nothing that would identify him." The brawny captain bared his teeth, adding, "But it appears he didn't live alone. Those we questioned indicated that another was seen with him, one who returned to the room this very morning."

Bastion's nostrils flared. "Why did you not say so in the first place, you fool?"

"He's here no longer! We've looked around. He must've been warned."

"How could he have been?" Hotak's son bristled. "Question everyone again! I want the port cordoned off and each block searched thoroughly. I assume you now have some description of this associate."

"Aye, my lord."

The patrol captain led Bastion to a faded door. The interior of the common house had a musty look to it. The corners and edges of the plank floor were filled with grime, and the original white paint on the walls had turned a rust-brown over the years.

"My lord!" One of the soldiers came running down the steps, a two-foot long map tube in his hand. "We found something! It was hidden in the rafters.!"

"Let me see." Bastion unrolled the contents. "Sea charts. Have these brought back to my quarters. I want to study them."

"Aye, my lo—"

Shouting came from beyond the rear of the building.

Bastion hurried past the soldier. Following the voices, he turned right around a corner leading into a narrow avenue shadowed by the city wall.

An avenue where Hotak's son found the corpse of one of his own search party.

Two other soldiers stood over the body, one of them just about to reach down and roll it over.

"Hold! No one touch him!"

The other minotaurs stepped aside. Kneeling, Bastion nudged the corpse so as to view the victim's face. His helmet rolled off, rattling.

The minotaur's muzzle had frozen in a death grin, its tongue dangling to the side. The faded brown eyes looked stunned. Someone had buried a dagger blade into the muscled hide at the base of the neck.

"That's Belrogh, my lord," muttered the lead officer, coming up behind Bastion. "I sent him out back when we first got here."

Bastion noticed blood on the nearby wall. "That is not Belrogh's blood. His assailant has suffered some injury."

Only one dagger lay nearby, and it had no shred of blood on it. Belrogh's sword remained in its sheath.

"Alert the others," Bastion informed the officer. "I want this area covered quickly. The assassin may still be nearby." To the first of the two soldiers, Bastion commanded, "You are to watch over this corpse until help returns. You," he added to the second, "come with me. Now."

As he headed up the avenue, Bastion drew his sword. Belrogh was no easy target. Their quarry was very dangerous.

They moved along for some distance, seeing nothing. Then, a speck of red on the ground caught Bastion's attention. He knelt to look it over.

Blood . . . and very fresh.

Bastion studied the buildings nearby. A towering gray storage house bearing the old imperial condor symbol stood on the right, and on the left, the back of a sailor's inn—quite crowded from the voices and raucous music coming from it.

The storage house was a more logical hiding place, but the inn drew Bastion's attention. A place full of strangers, the perfect spot for one who did not wish to be recognized.

"He may be in there. Be ready."

As they neared the back entrance, Bastion discovered a second splatter of blood.

At the door, a third sign of blood, which would have been missed by less-observing eyes. Bastion clutched his sword and entered. Voices rose from the front of the inn. Someone laughed, and the clinking of mugs indicated a toast. All seemed in order.

Bastion's gaze went to the floor, and he noticed something amiss.

"The floor," he muttered. "It has not been cleaned! Look at the grime." When the soldier still did not understand, Bastion blurted, "So where is the blood?"

"Perhaps he stopped bleeding, my lord?"

"Perhaps, perhaps not. Turn around. We have already lost valuable time." Bastion practically pushed the fighter back into the alley.

That was when a hefty oak plank struck the soldier on the head.

The stricken warrior collided with Bastion, knocking his sword away as both stumbled to the ground.

Bastion grabbed for some weapon and found the guard's

axe. He barely got the shaft up in time to block the sharp edge of a sword—his own.

Crusts of blood covered the assassin's short, wide snout and some flakes dotted his fur, but otherwise he appeared unhurt. Like the dead Josiris, this minotaur also wore the badge and kilt of House Ursun. Wiry and swift, he wielded the blade with veteran skill.

"Surrender," Bastion suggested, trying to maneuver. "There are soldiers approaching from every direction!"

The other minotaur brought the blade down again, barely missing Bastion's wrist. Hotak's son tumbled away, then righted himself.

"I've always admired you, Lord Bastion," the assassin hissed. "You're a true warrior. It would've been an honor to serve under you." He thrust, forcing Bastion to dodge. "Quick, too!"

Bastion tried to counter with the axe, but the nearby walls made him miscalculate.

"I thank you for your praise," he retorted. "Surrender now, tell us all you know, and perhaps I can have your sentence commuted. You might be exiled or—"

"Sentenced to Vyrox?" The other bared his teeth. "I wouldn't insult the memory of my master Tiribus." The scarred minotaur darted forward, coming under Bastion's guard. The tip of the blade cut a gash across the latter's chest. Bastion lowered his own weapon and used it like a lance, trying to stab his adversary in the chest.

His opponent deflected the blow but was forced back. Bastion pushed forward.

From behind came the sound of running feet. He glanced over his shoulder to see two legionaries closing in.

His foe attacked with greater ferocity, almost catching him off-guard. Managing to dodge to the side, Bastion called, "This is your last chance. Surrender or die!"

With a roar of desperation, the minotaur lunged.

But the assassin overestimated his attack, leaving himself open. As the sharp blade flew past his right ear, Bastion jabbed with the axehead. It dug into the other fighter's unprotected throat, sinking in with such force that his body was yanked inches off the ground.

From his twitching hand fell Bastion's weapon. As he dropped, the assassin let out a gurgle. His larynx—his entire throat—was impaled.

"Well aimed, my lord!" declared a soldier, running up.

"Not at all! I wanted to catch him by the shoulder. He shifted at the last moment. I wanted him alive so we could question him, find out what other confederates he might have . . ."

But they would gain nothing from this traitor, whose eyes stared vacantly, empty of life.

"He did mention Tiribus, though," mused Bastion. "There lies a clue, at least. We need a complete list of those who served the late councilor." He blinked. "I remember one. Nalhin . . . Nolhar . . . he was on a list of questionables my mother brought—" His ears stiffened as the name came to him. "Nolhan. Tiribus had an aide called Nolhan. Find out what has become of him, if he's among the purged."

"Aye, my lord."

Bastion retrieved his blade, wiping it clean before sheathing it. "If this Nolhan is alive and in the city, I want him. He will be desperate, willing to do anything—especially when he discovers that his comrades are dead."

It seemed remarkable that the ship had so far managed to evade the two sleeker craft pursuing it. The sails were half-torn, and the wide-bottomed vessel was designed to carry cargo, not fly swiftly. The hunters gave chase in ships made to cut low in the water. Yet somehow, the first ship stayed in the lead.

"The gap is closing," Captain Azak remarked from the deck of *Dragon's Crest* as he lowered his eyeglass. "Slowly, but it is closing, my good friend. The pursuers fly both the sea dragon and kraken banner, marking them of the Eastern fleet."

General Rahm snorted. "I've never seen ships like those."

"I'd heard tales of new craft being built in the shipyards of Mito. These must be the first. What do you want to do?"

The tiny rebel fleet had sailed out on maneuvers, but no one had thought that the empire would have vessels this far away from the capital.

The general tugged at his ebony-stoned ring. His glittering blue eyes peered at the ships. His good ear straightened as if he listened to words no one else could hear.

"I wanted to avoid a fight," he muttered. With reluctance, he then asked, "Any sign of other pursuit?"

Azak called up to the watch in the crow's nest. "Any other Imperials?"

"None seen, Captain!"

A crewmember approached and saluted Azak. "Captain Tinza asks to go aid the ship in distress!"

The wrinkled mariner let out a harsh laugh. "What Tinza wants to do is test herself in battle! The other ship could sink to the bottom of the Abyss for all she's interested."

Rahm leaned over the rail. "Have they seen us?"

"They're about to run down the stag. I doubt that one pair of eyes has looked our way."

"So we could sail on and forget what we saw?"

"Aye, we could."

Rubbing the underside of his muzzle, the general eyed the harried ship. "Do you think Tinza and her fellow captains still have their old banners?"

A toothy grin escaped the master of *Dragon's Crest*. "I'd wager they do."

In contrast to Azak's grin, General Rahm's expression had grown decidedly grim. The blue of his eyes had turned as chill as ice. Tugging on the ring, he said, "Then here's what we do."

As they cut the distance between themselves and their target, the two imperial ships separated, one seeking the port side of the fleeing vessel, the other the starboard. The captains intended to pinch their prey between them. This would be their first capture since their ships had been commissioned two weeks earlier.

When word came that more than half a dozen ships approached from the east, the captains worried only about opportunistic pirates. Then it was discovered that the sea dragon banner was flying on the lead vessel.

The fleeing ship slowed then began to turn back toward its two pursuers. She could not hope to win against so many, but still she would not lower her sails.

The new arrivals spread out.

Raising an eyeglass, the captain of the second imperial vessel studied the rival fleet.

"The four closest look all right," he muttered to his second. "Something's missing from the others, though." After a moment's consideration, he realized what. "There's no banners on the rest. Now why would that be?"

"Should I signal *Emperor's Pride*, Captain?"

The captain's wide, round nostrils flared. "I don't know. It doesn't look like anything's amiss." He raised the eyeglass again, studying the ships that carried the sea dragon banner. "If I could only . . . by the Sea Queen! 'Tis the *Reaver!*"

"Captain?

"The *Sea Reaver!* Damned Tinza's ship! Warn *Emperor's Pride!* Get the catapult ready! Be quick!"

From the *Sea Reaver*, a miniature sun darted high into the air, its arcing path sending it toward *Emperor's Pride*.

The vessel began to turn, but even with her swifter design, she moved too slowly. The fiery sphere—a heavy, oil-soaked ball of wood—plummeted toward its target.

The top of one of the *Pride's* masts broke away, sending burning rigging and sail down on the deck. Smoke rose.

"Orders, Captain?"

Minotaurs were trained from birth not only to fight, but to fight to the death. However, a futile death had little honor in it.

"Turn us about. Get us out of here. We must reach the main fleet."

"They're fleeing!" Azak crowed. "What cowards!"

"No coward," Rahm returned, eyes unblinking. "He seeks to warn the rest of the fleet of our presence in these far waters. Signal Tinza and the others to make sure that doesn't happen."

The weathered mariner looked for the *Sea Reaver*. "That will not be necessary. I daresay she already has that in mind."

Led by Captain Tinza, the renegade ships of the Eastern fleet were already closing in on the nearest vessel.

That left the first imperial ship.

"They're firing their catapult!" someone roared.

Fiery death rained down on *Dragon's Crest*. The shot itself missed, but burning oil flew everywhere. Crew members rushed around to douse the fires.

Dragon's Crest brought its own catapult into play. Unfortunately, the first shot went wide. One of the other ships tried but also missed, scorching a comrade instead.

The *Crest* veered in closer. Its next shot tore through the main sail, leaving a blazing hole in its wake. Sailors scrambled up to try to repair the damage.

From the other side, *The Horned God* moved in to cut off any escape. The impetuousness of the captain proved a mistake. This time the enemy's fiery ball soared with accuracy.

"Damned fools," General Rahm muttered.

The projectile struck the deck, smashing a gaping hole in the center. Flaming oil blazed. From the hold, smoke billowed out.

"Azak! Get us close. Force a boarding."

Dragon's Crest angled sharply. The enemy catapult fired again, but the flaming ball struck just past the *Crest's* stern.

Their catapult useless, some of Azak's crew readied bows.

"Come on, you old sheep!" the captain shouted. "Hurry before they pincushion you first!"

The archers braced themselves. Rahm raised his arm, awaiting the proper moment.

A storm of arrows whistled down upon Azak's crew. One crewmember fell dead. Another helped a wounded comrade, pierced with a bolt, stumble away. Bolts bristled like porcupine quills in the hull of *Dragon's Crest*. Several perforated the sails.

"Too soon," muttered General Rahm. "They shot too soon."

He lowered his arm in one swift movement. Now the sky filled with arrows coming from *Dragon's Crest*. Some struck the enemy's hull, others the sails. Cries arose from the other vessel and more than one body plummeted over the rail into the choppy sea. Several unmoving forms littered the deck.

"Again!" the general commanded.

A wave of return fire came first and three of Azak's crew perished. Their next volley, however, wreaked as much havoc as the first. One foe dropped from the rigging, his body hanging by his tangled foot. Two more slumped over the rail. The arrows that flew back were fewer.

The Horned God had pulled back, black smoke still billowing from its hold, but another ship had maneuvered near.

Several of the *Crest's* crew threw grappling hooks, securing the enemy ship. Rahm's eyes took on a fanatical look as he seized his axe. Raising it high, he leaped forward, crying, "For Honor! For Glory!"

Cheered on by the sight of the general, Azak's crew followed eagerly.

Rahm's axe quickly cut into a snarling sailor who leaped to confront him. Able fighters from both sides fell, and the already-grisly deck soon piled with the dead and wounded. Wood became slippery with blood. Smaller battles took place on the steps to the wheel and even on the rigging. Axes and swords flew. The two coupled ships rocked wildly on the water.

Fending off one opponent, Rahm paused to take a breath. He glanced to his left, eyes searching—

The edge of an axe blade nearly took his sole ear. Rahm whirled about to meet a hulking figure wearing a harness badge with a golden edge. The captain.

"Traitor!" bellowed the giant officer. Both his garments and his fur were matted with blood. "Renegade! I'll have your head!"

Their weapons clashed. "I'm no renegade," hissed Rahm, his tone cold. "I keep the oath I made to my emperor, Chot. Can you say the same?"

"My emperor is Hotak!" The axe came down again, the edge crashing into the deck.

Rahm scrambled away, then slammed the head of his weapon against that of his opponent's. Again and again their axes met while others fought all around them.

The captain's attacks turned more brutal, more relentless. Flecks of foam dotted his muzzle, and his eyes turned crimson. Rahm recognized the berserker fury overtaking the fleet officer. Even if his ship was lost, the captain would not stop the fight. He would struggle until his wounds were fatal.

"I'll hang your rotting head from the yard arm! I'll cut your flesh up to feed to the fish!"

The captain's axe came down with incredible force, chopping the rail to tinder. General Rahm swung his own weapon around, managing a strong cut into the other's forearm. Despite the streaming blood, the enemy officer showed no sign that he even felt his injury.

Once more Rahm barely avoided a blow. His strength flagging, he attempted a desperate tactic. He swung hard, pretending to aim for the chest but suddenly letting his weapon fly. The unhindered axe caught his foe's leg, the head shattering the knee cap in the process. Blood splattered them, and the captain was sent sprawling.

Even crumpled on the deck, the stricken captain refused to give in. He turned the spiked tip of his axe toward his victorious foe. The eyes that stared into Rahm's showed nothing but cold fury.

Grabbing away the threatening spike, General Rahm took the weapon and buried it in the captain's chest.

Soaked in blood—some of it his own, he realized—Rahm dropped to one knee. Around him, the few enemy crewmembers left had fallen to their knees, their arms behind their backs and their muzzles to the deck. Some of the victors roared in triumph while others attended to the remaining fires.

"The ship's in fair shape, considering," Azak said, coming up to Rahm, his own fur covered in blood. "We've got more than enough hands to take her under way."

"Good."

"Tinza's got the other ship sinking, but this prize makes it all worthwhile. Our first victory against Hotak!"

"A lopsided victory. We outnumbered them nine ships to two—ten even, if you count the one they were chasing." The general looked around at the gathering fighters. "A sloppy exercise. What if we hadn't come upon them from their blindside while they were preoccupied? There must be coordination, not every minotaur for himself." Absently tugging on his ring, he asked Azak, "What about the other ship? Did she flee?"

Azak snorted. "Now that would have been ingratitude! Nay, they not only have stayed, but I was just told that someone aboard desires to speak with you as soon as possible."

"Give me a few moments. I'll speak to him in my cabin aboard the *Crest*."

"Before you leave . . . there's still the question of the enemy crew."

The general looked over his shoulder, expression guarded. "How many?"

"Eleven, not counting three with mortal wounds."

Turning away from his comrade's sharp gaze, Rahm said, "We can't afford to keep prisoners, Captain."

Azak did not blink. "Aye, General. As you say."

Barely acknowledging the raucous cheers of his followers, Rahm returned to his sparsely decorated quarters and dropped onto the cot built into the inner wall. In a small recess in the wall by the head of the cot, a half-eaten loaf of round, unrisen oat bread and a nearly empty bottle of briarberry wine stood as the remnants of the general's last meal.

Rahm was just reaching for the dark bottle when someone knocked. With a grunt, he barked, "Enter at your own risk!"

A crewmember peered inside. "A visitor from the other ship, General. He insists to see you."

"Let him in." The bottle held tightly in one hand, Rahm waved the visitor in.

Clad in a green travel cloak and wearing the brown, shield-patterned kilt of a clan the general recognized as an ally of Hotak, a younger warrior with a long, narrow snout entered. Under a slim brow, he stared back at the general with troubled eyes. His silver-brown fur made him stand out from most minotaurs and caused Rahm to stir with interest.

"I know you, don't I?"

"We met twice. When you had lengthy business with my lord."

"Your lord?"

With an expression of intense earnestness, the newcomer dropped down on one knee and lowered his horns in submission and said proudly, "I am Nolhan, first adjutant to the former head of the Supreme Circle, Senior Councilor Tiribus—now dead."

The neck of the bottle cracked under Rahm's tightening grip, but before he could say anything about Tiribus, Nolhan continued.

"I sailed this way with a small crew based on word of refuge given to me by a trusted friend, but instead ran across the two Imperials you saw. You saved me when all seemed lost."

"I made a choice," the general replied.

The younger minotaur looked up at him. "And I am grateful. General Rahm Es-Hestos. For what I owe not only my master but now you, I offer my services in your campaign against the murderous usurper." From the confines of his cloak, he produced a pair of small, bound scrolls. "I offer you the names and locations of friends of my Lord Tiribus—important friends who will, the old gods willing, help us see this would-be emperor's head decorating the imperial gates."

Chapter XVI

Dance of the Dead

Surrounded by a fifteen-foot wall of gray stone upon which yard-high metal spikes were set, the imperial palace presented a vigilant façade. The wall surrounded a manicured lawn with groves of oak and cedar. Beyond the barred, arched front gates topped by the cast-iron countenance of a crimson minotaur, a wide, stone drive wound its way to the entrance.

Towering, groomed oak trees led to the broad marble steps. Four columns, carved to represent fearsome warriors, and two immense bronze doors, lined with intricate scrollwork, opened into a wide, torchlit corridor. The corridor led directly to two vast chambers, the first where the emperor held court and the second the main ballroom.

This night, the latter held precedence. Hotak's favored had gathered at his command. To the sounds of a small orchestra—round-bodied lutes, long, silver recorders, copper-kettle drums, and slim, curled brass horns—the guests of the emperor danced expertly.

Hotak and Nephera, too, glided across the floors, their sweeping movements and intricate stepwork marveled at by the others. The eyes of the pair never left one another and all present recognized the intensity of their attraction.

Hotak wore a gleaming helm and breast plate of the finest steel, a lengthy crest of crimson horse hair trailing behind. His flowing cloak complemented his consort's glittering silver and black gown. He thrust forward his right hand, touching his mate's muzzle. Her eyes flickered then, gazing at him, and she took two steps back, drawing him into her. Their feet moved in perfect unison, creating patterns based on the number five—five steps in line to the left, five in a swirl, then more in a line to the right.

As their muzzles grazed, the emperor whispered, "It's been too long since we danced like this."

"We've both been busy, my husband. The rule of an empire makes many demands, does it not?"

"But at times it causes a distance between us I don't like, Nephera. You are too often at the temple these days. Your place is here at the palace, my dear. Close by my side."

She gave him a brief smile. "I was with you last night. All night."

His hand stroked the underside of her muzzle. "I recall quite well."

The music drew to a close. The duo grasped one another's hands. Hotak bowed to his wife, his breath coming slightly fast, his fur tinged with moisture. Nephera bowed back. Her silken gown clung to her in a manner that further enticed the armored emperor.

An aide approached Hotak. The soldier said nothing, but the emperor nodded understanding.

"Your legion commanders," the high priestess said with a slight hint of reproval. "And now it is you who will leave me."

Dismissing the aide, Hotak whispered, "But I, at least, will return in short order."

As he departed, a voice behind the imperial consort

murmured, "An exceptional display of your grace as a dancer, my priestess."

Lothan hovered over her, his gray robe brushing the floor. A gold chain around his throat allowed a medallion with the symbol of the Supreme Circle to dangle over his chest. Nearly hidden by the cheek-high collar of his robe was a thinner, silver chain. Within the robe, the symbol of the Forerunner faithful rested near the councilor's heart. Unlike most of the minotaurs in attendance, Lothan had taken no part in the dancing, seeming content to watch.

"Indeed, the entire evening has been an exceptional and successful display. The might and wealth of the empire are clearly yours to command, my priestess."

"The emperor and I are quite pleased by the progress so far." She looked at the administrator, her eyes as intense as his own rarely blinking ones.

He moved closer, whispering to her alone, "It would be the perfect night to announce Lord Ardnor as heir."

She wanted that, but Hotak had cautioned her that tonight was not propitious. Her husband brooded over something, but over what, Nephera could not say.

"No. We can afford to be patient. I've told this to Ardnor more than once, although he, of course, has wanted it since the first day."

"The emperor has put it off several times."

"It will happen soon. I promise you that, Lothan."

Hotak returned. Lothan made a respectful retreat.

"My dear," Nephera's husband murmured, his good eye as intense as before, "I think I'd like another dance."

The music began the moment they started to move, a brass-dominated, almost martial piece. The talk among the dignitaries dwindled away, and guests joined in the dancing.

"I understand his devotion to your temple, my dear," Hotak said, thrusting one hand around her shoulder while pulling her close. "But at times the councilor places himself too near the imperial consort for my tastes."

"He merely wanted to be heard, my love. There was so much noise."

The scent of the sea touched Nephera's nostrils, and the shadowed form of Takyr materialized behind Hotak. Takyr closely followed them across the floor. Almost it seemed to the high priestess that she danced with two partners, one living and one not.

Mistress, came the voice in her head. *I return to you.*

Lady Nephera tipped her head slightly toward the ghost.

It is as you said. Lord Nymon is gathering support around him.

As she had expected, the powerful noble was seeking to formulate opposition to her son's declaration as heir. That would not do. She stared at the shade, knowing he would understand the course of action to be taken.

But Takyr did not depart just yet. *There is . . . there is no trace of the cloud creature,* he whispered, his face twisted and ugly. *It is beyond my ability to follow its path. It may still pursue its prey, but it may also have dissipated.*

"Are you all right, my dear?" Hotak murmured in her ear. "Has the long evening tired you?"

"It's nothing. Just a momentary lapse." Nephera had no desire to reveal the truth.

So once again Rahm had likely evaded her. Nephera had underestimated him. Maddening enough that he had escaped Hotak's soldiers and the usually thorough Bastion, but *how* had General Rahm kept himself hidden from the temple?

With a flick of her head, the high priestess dismissed the shade. Takyr drifted away, fading to nothingness. He would be nearby when she needed him.

"Nephera, my dear?"

She realized that the music had ceased. "I'm sorry, Hotak. My mind wandered."

He nodded, touching the underside of her muzzle. "I want you with me the rest of this night, my dear."

The high priestess nodded and even adopted a pleasant expression, but the fire she had felt earlier had dampened.

"Still up, I see," Azak called from the doorway.

Rahm looked up from his charts. "Yes."

"You need sleep."

"Sleep? Each passing day means the usurper solidifies his hold."

The graying captain shrugged. "But if you die from lack of sleep, what will it matter? Hotak will remain emperor, and your wife and son will go unavenged. Rahm, you're the lifeblood of this fellowship. Even Jubal looks to you for guidance. Besides, I thought Nolhan provided you with some very useful information."

"He did. So much so that I'm contemplating changes in our plans." Rahm tugged on his ring as he turned back to study the charts.

"Hmph. Well, see that you stop soon. As a boon to me."

Instead of agreeing, the general asked, "How are those new ballistae coming? We'll need them."

"There should be two ready soon. They are a little more awkward to build than we thought."

Rahm grimaced. "Only two? Then put one near the bow of *Dragon's Crest*. The other goes on the *Red Condor*," he added, referring to the imperial ship that had been renamed. "Have the crews work with them. I want them familiar with the ballistae."

"I will see to it . . . in the morning."

Alone again, Rahm went over the map, studying the best way to avoid garrisons and fleet ports. The twin isles of Thorak and Thuum were dangerous. To avoid detection,

Rahm's force would have to sail well south, adding days to an already-arduous journey.

A powerful yawn overtook him. As he stretched, Rahm noticed that the room had grown dim despite lit oil lamps. He blinked twice, but the dimness did not lessen.

"Azak was right," the general muttered. "Still, a few hours of sleep should remedy matters." Mogra and Dorn would forgive him this lapse.

Rahm unhooked his axe harness and lay it on the chair. The weapon itself he set within reach. As he released his grip on the axe, a tremendous sense of unease shook him. Rahm looked around, absently rubbing his ring.

To his horror, two savage, disembodied orbs that blazed like fire glared at him from the doorway.

"What in the name of the Abyss?"

Around the inhuman eyes began to appear a thick, black patch of mist—a body of sorts.

Rahm pulled back. The misty creature floated toward him.

Seizing the nearby axe, the general took a desperate swing. The blade passed through without effect. The mist around the malevolent eyes thickened. Thick, brutish arms formed.

"Sargas preserve me!" Rahm burst out. "Guards! Azak!"

No one responded, even though he heard voices beyond the door. Somehow, he had been cut off from the world. Desperately, Rahm swung the axe but accomplished nothing. The cloud creature had no substance.

A scent pervaded the room, one that reminded the general of a battlefield after the struggle, when the dead lay uncovered in great numbers, the elements already fast at work on them. The scent of death.

"Nephera!" he snarled.

Cursing, General Rahm edged toward the door. With comically-cumbersome movements, the cloud beast turned to follow. Rahm seized the door handle, but despite his efforts he could not open it. The general pounded on the wood and shouted.

The conversation outside continued unabated.

The scent of death grew overwhelming. The cloud darted forward, reaching for him. A hazy shroud covered Rahm's head, choking him. Try as he might, he could not close his mouth.

The fiendish creature sought to suffocate him. The axe fell from his weakening grip. Rahm flailed about as his body was lifted up. He gasped for air but only swallowed smoke. The general grasped at the fiery orbs so close to his own. His eyes bulged—

As his left hand passed through the shadowy horror, the ebony jewel on his ring flared, and a terrible screech filled the room, one that even those outside his room heard.

The door flung open, and Azak cried, "Rahm! What—?"

The dark cloud retreated, emerging swiftly from Rahm's throat. Before his astounded eyes, sparks of black lightning played around the screeching, twisting nightmare, eating away at the foul creature. The demonic assassin shriveled, its form breaking up into small pieces.

With one last, inhuman cry, the cloud beast dissipated.

Collapsing onto the cot, the general could only stare and gasp.

"Easy there!" Azak said, seizing a bottle and bringing it to his friend. "Here. Drink some of this first." As Rahm drank, the captain said, "Just catch your breath. Yes, we saw it, too, although what it was I cannot fathom."

"N-Nephera . . ." Rahm managed to spout. A fit of coughing struck him. Azak gave him more wine. "I could feel it coursing down my throat and into my lungs. Nothing could stop it." He gazed at his hand. "But something did. I think . . . it was my ring."

"Your ring." The captain snorted. "You really think so?"

"Yes. The moment it touched the monster's orbs."

Azak peered at it. "Not minotaur craftsmanship. Where did you get it?"

Rahm's brow furrowed. He stared at the glittering black gemstone, almost losing himself in its many facets.

"You know," he finally answered. "I don't remember."

Chapter XVII

Small and Deadly Worlds

A phalanx of twenty hand-picked warriors rode with Maritia to the mines of Vyrox—twenty more than she thought was necessary. Mithas was solidly in her father's grip. Certainly the miners, subdued by their harsh labor, would pose no danger to her.

Her mission to Vyrox was twofold. The recent destruction caused by the latest tremors—excessive even by the area's reputation—had made the imperium's prime source of raw materials fall terribly behind schedule. Hotak would not stand for that, not with his ambitions. Maritia's foremost mission was ostensibly to evaluate the logistics of procurement based on the remaining viable shafts and set new goals. Her second task was of a more delicate nature; she was delivering her own deposed patriarch to the camp.

Four legionaries wielding lances rode ahead of her. Maritia and another soldier flanked Itonus. The former patriarch was clad only in kilt and sandals and had his hands bound before him. Behind them rode the rest of Maritia's guard.

They reached the camp near dusk. Not for the first time, Maritia coughed in a vain attempt to clear the pervasive soot from her lungs.

A gigantic guard with savage eyes confronted the arrivals from inside the gates. "State your business or be off with you!"

Bristling, Maritia nudged her horse forward. "I trust you recognize an imperial officer, warrior."

The guard swore under his breath. "Forgive me, lady! They said you'd be coming earlier. When you didn't, the commander assumed you wouldn't arrive until tomorrow."

"We're here now. Your name, warrior?"

"Paug, lady."

"Well, Paug, please alert the commander that Lady Maritia de-Droka, imperial representative, is here. Be quick about it!"

As Paug hurried away, his compatriots pulled the gates open. Maritia rode in, following the retreating guard to the commander's quarters. The prisoners she saw seemed a dirty, surly lot. Few looked up as she passed. Instead, they kept their snouts close to their meal bowls. The smell of the food was such that Maritia put a hand to her muzzle in a vain attempt to wave the odor away. Even the sulfuric stench from the far-off craters was less noxious.

Paug exited the commander's quarters, followed by a worn-looking officer lacking part of one arm. He gave her a half-hearted salute and said, "Krysus de-Morgayn at your service, my lady. I apologize for our camp not being ready."

"Never mind that. I'm here now. Do you have accommodations for me and my guards? We can make due with an empty barracks, if need be."

Krysus looked aghast. "Lady Maritia, I will not dishonor you by placing one of your eminent position in squalid surroundings. You'll accept my own humble quarters and the use of my staff for as long as you must remain here." He turned to Paug. "Show them where they may stable their horses."

"Aye, commander."

"My lady, if you so desire, we can retire to my office now." He looked with curiosity at the prisoner. "As for this one—"

"As for him," she interrupted, "he will be joining us. At least for the moment."

"Your courtesy knows no bounds," Itonus remarked dryly.

Hotak's daughter glanced at him. "Don't push your luck."

The ousted clan leader said nothing.

As their horses were led away, a chained figure, who had been watching her, suddenly found great interest in his nearly empty bowl.

"My lady?" the commander whispered politely.

"I'm coming."

Krysus offered his good arm. Itonus followed, two soldiers flanking him. "I've all the information you requested. I think you'll find that Vyrox is operating at full efficiency."

"We'll see." As they entered, her nostrils wrinkled from a wave of airborne ash. The sooner she finished here, the better. Then could she return home, to the cleaner, tasteful climes of the imperial capital. Return and forget all the drawn, hopeless faces of the prisoners.

As he and the others headed to the wagons the next day, Faros could not help thinking about the imperial emissary. Faros did not recognize her, but she was certainly of very high rank. Her sudden appearance, coupled with the fact that she was the first female he had seen in months, made him stare at her too long. Fortunately, she had not noticed him. Faros had simply been one more prisoner to her, one more honorless, clanless worker. His secret was safe.

For all the good it did him.

Paug walked past in the opposite direction, the new prisoner beside him. The latter moved not like one of the workers, but as though he were a personage inspecting the facilities. The Butcher seemed to give him some respect.

"Name's Itonus," Japfin remarked quietly. "Turns out he used to be patriarch of Hotak's own clan. The new emperor's kicked him out—all the way to Vyrox!"

"The leader of his own House?"

"Aye, and what's more, that fine female who brought him here is none other than the daughter of Hotak."

Faros blinked. "That's Lady Maritia?"

"Aye, and savor any glance you get of her. She's likely to be the last female we ever see."

A guard came upon them, his whip already dancing. "Enough talk! Climb aboard!"

All interest in the emperor's daughter and the betrayed patriarch dwindled as the wagons rolled to their destinations. Faros stared at his arms and chest, where tufts of fur had begun to shed. Each day the patches grew larger, and he could do nothing about it.

Heavy piles of ore waited. Faros began hammering. Lean, yes, weary, certainly, but Gradic's once-soft son had become as well-muscled as most of the others.

Two hours into the day's labor, water was distributed among the prisoners. As Faros drank, he noticed a pair of guards approaching. He tensed. Such visitations always meant bad news.

The taller, a pinched-faced veteran with scars all along the right side of his muzzle, studied the group.

"That one," he indicated a minotaur with his coiled whip. The other guard moved to pull out of the ranks a worker even younger than Faros. "That one, too," the senior sentry added, indicating a brawny, older prisoner further down.

The whip pointed at Faros. "And that one."

From Ulthar's direction came a sharp intake of breath. Not understanding, Faros joined the others. The guards marched the three away—toward the fire pit.

Dismayed, he stopped in his tracks, an action which earned him a stroke of the lash. Stumbling forward, Faros eyed the hellish crater, the thick smoke, the fearsome flames. Within it, someone cried out in sudden, harsh pain.

"Down the ladder, you three! Down!"

The top two rungs of a heat-blackened ladder thrust up from the pit's edge. Despite the callouses on his hands, the ladder felt incredibly hot. As he descended, Faros peered down. He could see nothing but smoke and the glow of fire.

"Come on!" roared the guard above. "You'll see enough of it once you're down there working!"

Forced to move awkwardly because of the fetters, Faros descended into the choking haze. The heat he had found so unbearable above proved a cool breeze in comparison to the inferno below. Every lungful of air burned.

From the ladder he went to another and another, ten ladders in all, and each a twenty-foot descent. At the base of the last, a guard cautioned the prisoners to lean against the hot, ashen wall. Faros needed no warning, as the carved ledge upon which they stood was only three feet wide. Flames shot up past him. The smell of burning oil singed his nostrils.

Faros made out level upon level of stone walkways and, stationed at intervals, prisoners with long, iron-hooked staffs. One worker had the end of the staff around a chain from which hung a thick, oval container made of iron. From the way the shackled figure labored, the container carried in it something of immense weight.

A rock slipped out, plummeting into the abyss. Immediately a guard whipped the guilty worker, almost sending him over the edge.

The soldier guiding Faros stepped close. "A good lesson there, fool! Those containers're worth more than your miserable hides. You'll feel the whip for each spill. Now move it!"

"What're they doing?" he blurted.

"Smelting, fool! There's charcoal and ore in those containers." Faros knew that with the right heat but no fire inside, the copper and iron would separate. "The open containers are fresh loads sent down from above. You'll be catching those and passing them on."

Depositing the other prisoners as they walked, the guard at last brought Faros to his new station. One level down, a pair of minotaurs worked at a large iron container. Both laborers looked ready to collapse.

A new overseer took charge. Completely ash gray, eyes lined with red veins, and his arms covered in scabs and burns, he rumbled, "The chain system brings the bins of ore. You catch one off as it comes near, then use the hook to guide it down to that pair. Let 'em empty it, then take the hook and guide the empty one back up. The chains above will send it back for refilling."

Reaching into a shallow alcove carved out of the burned wall, he thrust a staff into Faros's sweating hands. Faros fumbled for a grip, nearly losing the staff to the pit.

The ghastly looking overseer chuckled. "Clumsiness isn't a good trait down here, lad, though we're always looking for fuel for the fire."

A grinding sound warned Faros. Out of the haze swung one of the cast-iron containers. Roughly the width and height of a wooden barrel, it proved surprisingly heavy. He struggled as best he could, catching a loop from the dangling chain and dragging his catch toward the waiting pair below.

No sooner had Faros sent the emptied bin back than another filled one came out of the haze. Barely recovered, Faros went back to work, discovering this time that the bin held charcoal.

Over and over the process was repeated. Ore would come, he would deliver it to the workers below, they would empty it into the ovens, then send off the container for more. Next came the charcoal and the same process began all over again.

Faros soon learned to calculate the length of each break, allowing him to sit for a few precious moments. And sit he needed to, whenever possible. The heat was dizzying. The ledge made his work precarious at all times.

Three hours passed. Breathing heavily, Faros was about to reach for yet another container, his hands shaking from effort.

A rumble below startled him, and he missed the loop. The container vanished into the haze, unemptied.

He quickly glanced down, but rather than being upset, the two prisoners there suddenly threw themselves against the wall. From the pit rose roaring, white tendrils of flame.

"Yaah!" Falling back, Faros barely missed being engulfed. He covered his face and curled in a fetal position. As quickly as they had come, the hungry flames withdrew.

"Get up! Get up you sniveling wretches!" roared the ash-gray overseer. To his latest minion, he rumbled, "When they add fuel to the pit, that happens sometimes. Listen for the rumbling, and you'll likely live through it. Understand?"

Faros managed a short nod.

"Hurry!" snarled his instructor. "Next one's coming."

A filled container materialized. Body aching and eyes still seeing ghosts of the flame, Faros started the cycle anew. Only after the overseer left did Faros finally look around to see if the other prisoners had noted his pitiful reaction. Only then did he realize that one of them was no longer there. He had not even heard the scream.

A chill night wind coursed through Nethosak, a wind that pervaded every building in the capital, no matter how well-sealed. Most who felt it huddled close to fires or threw on cloaks. A few with senses more acute felt their fur stand on end and looked around anxiously, certain that they were being watched.

Dark, green-gray clouds encompassed the capital, too. Within the foul murk, flashes of bloody crimson burst briefly to life, then perished.

The sky became a maelstrom, howling and whirling. Each moment, a storm of gargantuan proportion seemed ready to strike.

Within the temple of the Forerunners, the faithful acolytes hurried along their way, sensing more than most the strangeness of the night. They shivered as they raced along the corridors and glanced over their shoulders as they passed the ominous, towering statues.

For those whose tasks took them near the meditation room where the high priestess had secreted herself an hour earlier, the sensation of fear was strongest. Four anxious Protectors stood guard there, ears taut as they pretended not to notice how the shadows around them encroached. Within, Nephera's voice could be heard, but the few comprehensible words were in no earthly tongue.

As her voice rose, an endless multitude of ethereal, invisible forms flew up through the temple roof into the fiery sky, riding the winds and streaking with the lightning in all directions. For a time, they fluttered around and around over Nethosak, as if gaining their bearings, then in one sudden burst they spread out over the imperial capital, out over the entire island, and swiftly beyond.

Shrieking spectres in tattered garments coursed through buildings without pause, passing unnoticed by and even through those still awake within. Raging ghosts in rusted armor did battle with the elements as they soared over the Blood Sea.

Most had been sent with but a single mission in mind. The high priestess sought more than ever any clue, any word, of those plotting against her and her mate. From her latest lists, Nephera had underscored hundreds of names, countless locations. She could not yet reach the limits of the empire, but she could cover much territory.

On a ship departing Kothas for colonies southeast, the captain no longer dined alone in his quarters. Now a disheveled minotaur whose throat bore a six-inch gap at the center sat across the table, dead eyes intently staring at the ignorant mariner.

On Sargonath, the captain of the local militia led a patrol to investigate recent reports of nighttime activity by the ogres. Along with him rode twenty strong warriors and, floating alongside them, three apparitions. One was the captain's own brother, his crazily tilted head the result of an ogre club that had snapped his neck and crushed in his skull. Now he watched for possible seditious thoughts on the part of his sibling. The dead served only the high priestess.

On Mito, Governor Haab questioned a shipwright who had been found procuring materials for an unsanctioned vessel—a small ship with which he hoped to join his cousin, the former militia commander, at some unspecified location. The captive minotaur's arms had been bound behind him, and he had been forced to his knees. Despite pressure in the form of a prolonged whipping, the blood-soaked shipwright still claimed not to know his destination.

Haab leaned against his desk as one of the guards struck the prisoner across the muzzle. The governor tapped his fingers on the wood as he spoke. "If you do not know this place where you were to meet Ryn, then how could you possibly set sail? Did you plan to sail around the Courrain until you just happened to pass one another?"

When his guest did not reply, Haab had the guards whip him again and again. The governor was upset and rightly so. The flight of Ryn and much of the original militia was a black mark that would cast a shadow on his authority.

"Well?" demanded Haab. "Why does he not speak?"

One of the guards bowed, his ears flat. "The pain, sir. I think he's in shock."

"Let me see." Haab stepped up and seized the prisoner's muzzle, turning the gaze to his own.

The governor saw nothing within. The eyes stared, but his prey had escaped after all. Haab knew that he would not be coming back. With a snort of rage, the minotaur twisted the bound figure's head sharply to the side.

Letting the body drop, Governor Haab, his breathing short and his eyes red with fury, turned. "Dispose of it! Now!"

As they obeyed, he sat down at his desk, brooding. The throne expected a report, one with a satisfactory conclusion. Discovering the whereabouts of the traitors would have not only erased Haab's black mark, but it would have put him in good standing with his emperor.

He seized a blank parchment. If the trail was lost, it was best if it looked as if it had never existed in the first place. That would ease Haab's troubles.

Quill in hand, he wrote:

In the matter of the traitor Ryn, through careful work, he and his band were hunted down in the hills of Mito, where they had hidden. They refused to surrender, and when it was clear they could not escape, they committed suicide. Their bodies were burned as a signal to all rebels. A thorough investigation finds no link to any outside contact.

The governor nodded. A few more lines of explanation and his failure would be forgotten. His career would be saved.

However, the ambitious Haab would have been less confident had he been able to see the figure now draped over his shoulder. This figure's chest was ripped open and blood was congealed over the gaping wound. It was the husky shade of the late Governor Garsis, whom Haab had personally executed, and who now had been granted the duty of monitoring his successor's loyalty. Garsis could not lie about what he saw, but the truth was just as damning. Lady Nephera had chosen each of her spies carefully.

The undead streamed throughout the reaches of the high priestess's might, a thousand wailing shades silently haunting those on her lists. Most were set upon tasks identical to that of Garsis. Watch. Listen. Discover. Report.

But for a select few, there existed a different, darker task. The high priestess had a list of those minotaurs who had already been found wanting or defiant. To deal with such, Nephera had chosen among the apparitions those who were most suited to action. Although they were the last to emerge from the shadows of the temple, their mark would be felt most.

They had died violently, terribly, and their anguish and anger remained as virulent as ever in twisted faces and twisted souls. They hungered to share their pain, their deaths, and so she had granted them their desire.

The first of them came screaming silently into the luxurious villa of the patriarch of Clan Dexos, a sturdy, black-furred elder. He was vocally a supporter of Hotak, but behind the scenes, Brygar used the name of the new emperor as a way to skim profit from the farmers and herders of Kothas whenever they sent their shipments to the markets of the capital. In another time, Brygar would have worshipped the god Hiddukel, the Deal Maker.

He did not notice, of course, that he was no longer alone. Brygar stood in the vault kept hidden deep below, awkwardly carrying with him a sack of ill-gotten gains. One servant, a trusted guard bearing a torch, stood with the patriarch. Despite the bulkiness of his load, the elder always carried the gold himself. It made him feel close to his wealth.

The spectre, still invisible, swirled around Brygar's unprotected throat.

"What was that? Did you feel a chill wind?"

"I felt nothing, my lord."

Brygar shrugged. The vault was three levels underground. No breeze could reach down here, but it was always cold beneath the earth. He hefted the huge sack and dropped it atop the others. More than fifty large sacks and twelve oak chests filled the inner half of the chamber. No matter who was emperor, Brygar profited.

"Aaah . . ." the minotaur inhaled the imagined scent of riches. No one appreciated its bounty as he did. "Wealth is power, Malk. Wealth is strength. What you see here is worth a hundred duels, a dozen bloodings in battle."

"As you say, my lord."

The patriarch snorted at Malk's flat tone. "Give me the torch. I will stay. You may go."

The armed guard obeyed, bowing as he left.

Brygar stepped forward, touching one of the sacks reverently. He did not notice the flame flicker oddly. Nor did the older minotaur sense the wispy presence that circled him once, twice, and then drifted through him.

The elder swatted at his ear, as if a fly was harassing him. He inhaled again, admiring what his cunning had wrought over the years.

Something moved within one of the sacks.

Brow furrowed, the robed minotaur strode forward, feeling the bag. Nothing there. He snorted.

In another sack only a few feet away, there was more movement.

"What goes on here?" Brygar grunted.

Suddenly, he noticed several of the sacks shifting as though some creature within each was struggling to free itself. The patriarch leaned forward, his muzzle only inches from one of the bags.

And then that bag and every other one burst open. An eruption of gold, silver, and steel filled the vault.

Stumbling back, Brygar stumbled for the door, but it swung closed, the bolt outside locking. With his free hand, he banged on the door, shouting.

The coins and gems clattered harshly on the stone floor, then whirled about and spilled all over like a lava flow. His back to the door, the black minotaur gaped as his wealth danced about as if with a life of its own. It piled up before him, a huge, loose mound that spilled over his feet, burying them.

From the mound burst skeletal hands formed from the coins. They grasped at him and tore at his hem. The door behind him heaved as if some great beast were shoving against it. Startled, Brygar stumbled forward into the clutching fingers.

They ripped at his clothes, his fur. They pressed his face close to them, almost suffocating the minotaur. He floundered about as if lost at sea, his panic growing.

Mouths opened in the mound. Wide, hungry mouths. They rose high, forming muzzles, empty sockets—minotaur skulls created from glittering metal. All were identical, the very image of the shade that the high priestess had sent to haunt Brygar.

The ghoulish skulls melted together, creating one monstrous head. A neck and shoulders followed, the entire shambling corpse soon resurrected in gleaming detail.

The corpse had been eaten, torn apart by sharks on a voyage which a younger Brygar himself had organized. Great gaps in the torso and limbs attested to the horrific fury he had suffered before death had claimed him. Ribs of silver jutted out, and within them were mangled lungs of steel. Red rubies accented where the blood had flowed most. and the eyes were green jade, envious of the life the sprawled figure before it still retained.

As the patriarch attempted to crawl away, wave upon wave of coin drew him back toward the outstretched arms of the ghoul.

Desperate, Brygar grabbed for the torch, which he had dropped on the mound. With it, he tried to drive the spectre back.

The mouth opened wide. A hideous stench filled the sealed vault, the decaying of the flesh that had tormented the ghost since death. It choked the life of the flames and nearly smothered Brygar himself.

Gasping, Brygar dropped the dead torch. Darkness did not entirely claim the stone vault, for a dread illumination radiated from the mound and the ghost. The foul greenish light cast an even more terrible aspect on the fiend.

"Help me!" shouted Brygar. "Someone, help me!"

He was as brave as most minotaurs, but there were limits. One could not fight the dead, and one certainly did not want to share their monstrous fate.

The sea of coins dragged him relentlessly toward the cadaverous form. The ghoul's fetid smell permeated everything.

Brygar threw coins at his tormentor, threw the jewels he so coveted away in defense. They stuck to the spectre, giving it more substance.

As it grew, the ghost opened its maw wider. A horrific wind arose, one that pulled the patriarch forward faster. The undead creature inhaled, empty sacks and loose coins falling into a darkness more terrible to Brygar than the legendary Abyss.

With a fearsome moaning, the ghost's mouth stretched to encompass his billowing form. Brygar could not keep himself from being sucked into it. He rolled over, yet that only meant that his feet were pulled in first. The frantic minotaur clutched at the mound, but for all its weight his wealth gave him no hold.

Shrieking, the patriarch was pulled into the spectre's mouth.

It was more than two hours before Brygar's absence was noted by his household. The guard who had been with him was alerted. Torch in hand, the anxious warrior descended to the vault. He found the heavy door unbolted and open, just as he had left it. Cautiously, he pushed it wide.

His ears straightened. A strange, unsettling sound came from the back of the vault. Drawing his sword, the guard stepped in and held the torch forward.

In the midst of the neatly packed mound of sacks, Brygar Es-Dexos crouched, making an odd, keening sound. His knees were tucked into his chest and encircled by his arms. He rocked back and forth. His eyes stared ahead, never blinking, and a bit of drool escaped his slack jaw. The patriarch's entire form trembled. He would remain so for the rest of his brief life.

In such manner did most of those Nephera had condemned suffer. The bitter phantoms vented their rage through the minds of their victims, leaving in their wake empty shells.

For one name on her list, the high priestess decided to rely on more subtle measures.

Lord Nymon was a gruff old bull who had survived much intrigue over his career and had even capitalized on it. Now he controlled the political fortunes of enough other high-ranking minotaurs to give him influence over the affairs of the empire, and this time he intended to use that influence.

Nymon admired Hotak, even supported him in many things, but he did not care for these rumors of a hereditary line. It went against everything minotaur. However, Nymon also knew the dangers of protesting the emperor's ideas. Hotak's own patriarch, Itonus, was an example of what happened to those who believed like Nymon.

Itonus was a fool, though. The way to defy the new emperor was by open, unified opposition through legal channels. Confronted in his court by a petition presented by the strongest of the emperor's supporters, Hotak would have to not only hear the protests, but answer them openly before his subjects. That would kill any notions of his son Ardnor becoming emperor.

Although it was late, Nymon continued his writing. The others still needed some convincing, but tomorrow he would give them the proof. He had worked all evening to make everything perfect. On the table next to a knife were the cores of two apples, the only sustenance he had allowed himself.

An odor wafted past his nostrils. The scent of the sea. Nymon looked to the window, but it was shuttered tight to keep out the harsh winds blowing about Nethosak. Behind him, the shadows coalesced into the monstrous form of the ghost Takyr.

Takyr floated behind the broad-shouldered minotaur, white eyes looking over both the noble and his papers. The cadaverous shade reached out one bony hand and touched Nymon on the arm.

Nymon shivered and clutched the arm. He looked around the room.

Invisible to the mortal's eyes, Takyr leaned close, placing his rotting muzzle only an inch from Nymon's ear.

You have enemies . . . many enemies, Lord Nymon.

The seated figure shifted and looked up furtively before resuming his work.

Even the emperor is displeased with you. He knows your thoughts concerning his son and the throne.

Nymon started. He gazed at the wall and muttered, "Can Hotak know what I do? Surely not."

Takyr persisted. *Your enemies know the emperor will not protect you from them. Should they seek your death, he will let them.*

The quill snapped. Lord Nymon eyed the splattered ink as if it were his own blood. Had Hotak distanced himself of late? Nymon tried to recall their last encounter and everything he remembered he saw in a terrible light.

"Hotak knows. He must! By Argon! He'll—"

The ghost interjected into his thoughts, *Your enemies draw near. They come for you now, knowing that they will receive accolades from the emperor, not punishment.*

Gasping, the elder noble rose and rushed to the shuttered window. Flinging it open, he glanced outside as the wind threw back his mane and droplets of rain splattered his face.

"Nothing," grunted the minotaur, but he left the window open.

But again words of fear spread by the ghost filled his thoughts. *Your enemies are within your own home.*

A shutter creaked. Nymon jumped. A floorboard groaned under his feet. He jerked toward the door, certain that the sound was that of an approaching assassin.

Like a vulture circling a sickened animal, the spectre floated around his prey. He touched the minotaur on the cheek, making Nymon turn nervously.

The old warrior's heart pounded now. He started for the door then hesitated. Influenced by the shade's whispers, he saw in his mind a horde of armed figures wending their way up the stairs. Their axes and swords gleamed sharp.

Still Takyr was not finished. He breathed in the face of his victim, letting Nymon's subconscious taste the cold of the grave, the chill of death. His head was filled with visions of himself hacked up by assassins or—worse— dragged off to a public execution. Both would bring shame to his House.

"No, I can't let that happen."

Takyr grinned, rotting teeth and gums displayed for one who could not see him. *There is one way that will spare your family, your honor...*

The ghoul stretched forth his fleshless fingers, and the knife that the noble had used for the apples jostled just enough to catch Nymon's attention.

Clutching the blade, the minotaur brought it to his chest then paused.

"No, this isn't right!" Nymon lowered the knife. He put his other hand to his head, closing his eyes as he sought to focus his thoughts. "This is madness!"

Takyr touched the hand that held the knife.

The noble's eyes widened.

The hand sank the blade into his heart.

A horrified gurgle escaped Nymon. He twisted around, mouth agape. Dying eyes at last saw the foul spectre haunting him. Nymon reached out an imploring hand, but Takyr floated back, savoring the moment. Lord Nymon collapsed.

Drifting to the table, Takyr ran one finger over each line of his prey's writing. As he did, the words leaped from the page, jumbled around, and reorganized themselves. When the ghost was finished, the parchments now held a full and detailed confession to crimes against the imperium, along with a pleading for mercy for his family and House.

Nephera sat in her chambers, sipping wine and looking over a list. She did not raise her gaze when she sensed the presence.

Mistress.

"You've done it, Takyr?"

Yes. They will find him as you desire.

"Good." She lowered the list. Her eyes were bright. "Very good. Now nothing stands in the way of Hotak declaring my son as heir to the throne."

CHAPTER XVIII

BLOOD UPON THE HORNS

The foul weather, especially the fog, had enabled the ships to avoid any of the vessels patrolling Mithas's waters. It had taken a week of preparation and almost two more of cautious travel for the small flotilla to get this far.

A lightning strike was the ragged rebellion's best hope.

"We must strike at the heart," General Rahm had told the others. "We must slay Hotak himself. Cut off the head and the body follows."

"But a full honor guard protects him whenever he goes into the city, and the people follow him," Jubal had protested. "Attacking the palace is unthinkable. It's the most protected place in all the imperium!"

Hotak had smiled. "So it is. And who would know better than I?"

Passing Thorak and Thuum proved easier than planned, but Hathan, the small garrison island further to the southeast, proved more trouble, for four Imperials had docked there en route to some more distant location. Rahm had been forced to add two days to the journey by heading south around Hathan.

At last, they neared the southern coast of Mithas. In such close waters, Tinza and the other captains had raised their sea dragon banners and guided the other ships like an escort. Here, such a varying group of vessels did not seem out of place.

As they approached Mithas, Rahm did the unthinkable, splitting his forces and sending some off on a separate mission. Captain Tinza and the other three vessels from the Eastern fleet sailed toward the northern tip of the island, some two days from Nethosak. There lay the port of Varga, a small but significant landing used as a link between the far northeastern colonies and those in the innermost Blood Sea region. Tinza and her band would sail in under the banner of the fleet, strike, and create trouble, then escape to a prearranged destination.

With the exception of *Dragon's Crest*, the rest of the vessels were commanded by the general to sail to the mountainous eastern shores. They, too, had been given orders timed to coincide with Rahm's own plan.

Hotak's legion guarded the capital; Rahm's own Imperial Guard protected the palace. No one knew the layout of the city better than Rahm. He had memorized every street, every public building. He had studied every available blueprint of the palace, knew each winding corridor and alcove. The knowledge had enabled him to perform his duties and survive where so many others had failed.

Rahm knew the individual commanders of Hotak's forces, knew them well enough to predict their thinking. He understood their deficiencies.

"The merchant Nolhan spoke of . . . Bilario," Azak muttered, eyeing the hazy shore. Tall, wooded hills were all that could be made out—and the jutting rocks scattered dangerously just off shore. "He will be waiting for us at this location?"

"Aye. He owed Tiribus much—so Nolhan said—and the councilor kept him ready in case something happened. Since Tiribus did not see fit to make use of him, it will be our pleasure."

Silence reigned aboard the ship, the only sounds the creaking of the hull and the constant lapping of the sea. *Dragon's Crest* was sailing unusually close to the shoreline. The crew did soundings, and one sailor clung to the bow.

Two hours passed. Three.

A sharply carved rock thrusting out of the sea made Rahm stand up straight. "There!" he whispered, gaze intent. "That's the mark he said to look for! See how it juts up like a raised sickle?"

"Aye, and a wicked promontory at that. So now we head inland?"

"According to Nolhan, it should be safe here."

"Let us hope he was not mistaken, my friend."

The renegade ship slipped in closer. Azak commanded the crew to adjust the sails. "We will have to take a long boat in the rest of the way."

Six in all boarded the small craft. To Rahm, each stroke of the oars sounded like thunder. It seemed to take an eternity to reach land. When the boat neared the craggy shore, the general leaped out to help guide it in.

Everyone disembarked. Two young warriors, volunteers, stood by as the general said farewell to Azak.

"Thank you for all your aid," Rahm said, clutching the other's hand. "You've been the truest comrade, captain."

"And you, Rahm, have also been true, which is why I intend to go with you."

The general's eyes narrowed. "Don't be foolish, Azak. That's madness."

He looked over the captain's shoulder, realizing that the long boat had begun returning to the ship.

"You there!" he called. "Stop! Come back!"

"They have orders from their captain," Azak informed him. "And to me they owe their allegiance first and foremost." The captain adjusted his axe harness, the head of his weapon already covered by a cloth shroud so as to avoid any gleam from torchlight. "We waste time. This merchant is supposed to be found near Jarva, some four hours' journey by foot. I suggest we move on so that we travel as little as possible by day."

The other two looked to the general. In silence, Rahm took the lead, Captain Azak following a step behind.

Wild, grassy fields populated intermittently by copses of oak and cedar made up the landscape. On occasion, high rounded hills added variation. The minotaurs crossed a well-worn dirt road but saw no sign of traffic or patrol.

"What sort of merchant lives way out here?" Azak whispered.

"The sort whose dealings involve a swift flight to sea afterward."

"A smuggler?"

Rahm rubbed his muzzle as he gazed at the path. "Nolhan didn't use the word, but he certainly hinted at it. Master Bilario traded in everything, so he said. Absolutely everything."

They continued on through mist-covered fields, now and then struggling over uneven, muddy patches. At last, the four came upon a rise over which they spotted the shadowy outline of a provincial estate surrounded by a stone fence. What looked to be fruit trees dotted the area behind the main, flat-roofed, building.

"Doesn't seem like anyone's home," Azak muttered.

Rahm sniffed at the air but said nothing. His fingers strayed to the ring.

As they descended, the dim illumination revealed unsettling things. A wooden, slat fence designed to pen livestock had been shattered to kindling. Within lay several carcasses. Further on, an unhitched supply wagon lay tipped on its side, its wheels broken.

Rahm's nostrils flared. "Something's burning, and not just wood."

Crouching, they headed to the main house. Through the open windows, silken curtains of some light color fluttered. The disturbing scent grew stronger.

Across the front step lay a body.

The young guard had been stabbed several times in the chest and, judging from the blood pooled underneath him, more than once in the back. For good measure, someone had crushed in his muzzle, giving him an ogrelike mask in death. Near his feet, a small, single-edged hand axe lay unsullied.

General Rahm touched the body. "This didn't happen very long ago."

"Looks like Nolhan's information was a little old." The captain commented, stepping over the corpse and peering inside. A second later, he pulled back, coughing violently.

"Many dead in there?"

"I couldn't—" Azak coughed again. "I couldn't see much, but the stench was the worst I've smelled since the time the *Crest* had to fend off barbarians who'd boarded her at night. Someone set a fire in there, but it only did half the job. Think it was Hotak's warriors?"

"Who else?" Rahm looked around. "Let's look around and see if we can salvage anything." He grunted. "It's going to be a long walk to Nethosak, and we—"

But he got no further, for at that moment, the sounds of rushing hoofbeats came from the dirt road.

"Inside!" ordered the general.

Eight riders arrived at a breakneck pace. With one exception, they dismounted immediately. That one, clad in the cloak and open helm of an officer, bellowed, "Give everything a look, you blasted loafers! That herder said the ship was just leaving the coastline when he saw it! They may have come here!"

"Place stinks worse than a refuse pit!" grumbled another figure. "All this for smugglers?"

"Be glad you weren't one of them when the emperor's finest came through! Old Bilario should've surrendered to them right away instead of trying to bluff. I warned him enough times."

"Nothin' but a bunch of crow fodder here, Captain," returned a third warrior. "Can't we go on? I'm about dead on my feet!"

The others chuckled, but the captain did not find it humorous.

"You may be local militia, but you're still part of the armed might of the empire! By the throne, do your jobs."

The soldiers quieted down and began wandering about the premises.

"Kreel!" shouted the patrol leader. "Get your sorry carcass into that building! Go through every room on both floors!"

"Captain, have a—"

"Do I look like your mother? Get inside, or I'll throw you in myself! Darot, go with 'im and hold his hand!"

"It's not the bodies," growled Kreel, his voice growing near. "I have a sensitive nose."

Inside, Rahm turned to his companions. "Find a place on the floor. Play dead."

They did so, barely in time. Rahm lay down near an elderly female twisted into her robe. The fire had made partial work of her.

The harsh clatter of armor and weapons echoed throughout the otherwise still house. One came near Rahm, constantly sniffing. His companion was no more eager.

"Waste of time here," whispered Kreel, sniffing again.

"Stop whining," the other one, Darot, snarled back.

Further in, something shifted. Both searchers froze, then, more determined, edged forward, axes ready.

A young fighter near the militia members sprang up.

Rahm also jumped to his feet, swearing under his breath.

A dagger flew into Darot's throat. At the same time, a hand kept his muzzle tightly shut. A muffled grunt escaped the dying minotaur before he collapsed into his slayer's arm.

"Darot?" blurted Kreel, turning to see what was happening. He barely had time to register the figure hunched over his companion before General Rahm seized him and, with one swift movement, twisted his head to the side until his neck snapped.

"Kreel, you worthless excuse for a warrior!" shouted the voice of the patrol officer. "Are you two asleep in there?"

"Still lookin'!" came the answer from behind Rahm.

The general turned to see Azak, winking with a grin.

"Well, hurry about it! I'd like to get to bed before dawn!"

"For one seeking the hidden, he bellows too much," Azak remarked quietly.

"We need to find another way out of here." Rahm peered through the dark but detected no back entrance. "Spread out. Find an exit. Whoever does, alert the rest as silently as possible."

As the others vanished, the general made his way down a blackened corridor. He moved slowly, for the floors lay littered with obstacles. Rahm could smell the sickly odor of roasted flesh everywhere.

Pausing, he put his hand against a crumbling, charred wall—and suddenly noticed a brief glimmer. Rahm glanced at his ring then spotted a side hallway. Axe ready, the general followed the hallway.

A ruined door greeted him a short distance ahead. Rahm tugged on the still-warm handle. An abrupt, loud creak shattered the quiet as the door opened.

Cursing silently, Rahm peered out. Beyond the estate grounds lay a lightly wooded area. If he and his fellows could reach it . . .

"Thought I heard something," a tall figure bearing an axe grumbled behind Rahm. "Captain's tired of waiting for you two to—" He stopped and raised his weapon. "Captain!" the searcher roared. "I got one! Captain!"

Rahm barely got his blade up in time. The two heads sparked as they clashed, the force of the blow sending both stumbling back. Grunting, Rahm's foe swung again, a whistling swathe. Rahm brought his own axe under the other's outstretched arms. His blade dug deep into his foe's midsection. The minotaur teetered then made a wild swing that brought down much of the already-disintegrating wall.

Rahm caught his opponent in the side. The axehead sank deep this time. The other minotaur let out a moan then toppled forward.

Shouts arose from within the building, then the clash of arms. Hurling himself through the doorway, Rahm landed hard on his knees. His weapon flew just out of reach, and he stooped to pick it up.

"General?" The voice belonged to Tovok, one of his volunteers.

"This way!" Rahm commanded. With Tovok close at his heels, he charged around the building.

Rahm saw one of his men in combat against two opponents. Sending Tovok toward one, Rahm charged the other.

The general's target turned at the last moment, barely deflecting the axe. Rahm brought the axehead up and struck a hard blow under the soldier's jaw. As his foe staggered back, he thrust the pointed tip into his unprotected throat.

The second attacker fell quickly to Tovok and the still-unidentified rebel.

"By that short stance," the shadowy form chuckled. "It has to be you, Rahm."

"Azak! Are you injured?"

"Some small cuts, but nothing to boast of." The mariner's voice dulled. "But the lad who fought beside me . . . he perished after slaying their captain."

Rahm did a quick count. "Is one missing, Azak?"

From without came the sound of horses.

Rahm whirled toward the front entrance. "We can't permit him to escape!"

They burst out of the building to discover the last of the militia squad just mounting his horse. He kicked at the other mounts, trying to move them out of the way.

With a prodigious leap, General Rahm managed to grab him by the feet. The rider tried to shake him off then decided that his best course of action was to spur his horse and drag his assailant along with him.

The horse careened over the rock-strewn path, but Rahm refused to let go. The other minotaur swatted at him, then pulled free his axe.

Rahm twisted sharply. The horse whinnied as it lost its balance. The fleeing soldier gave a dismayed shout as he slipped off. Both combatants went tumbling across the harsh ground. Rahm freed his dagger just as he landed atop the other fighter. His adversary, seeing the blade, released his hold on his own half-drawn weapon.

"I yield!" he gasped.

General Rahm drove the dagger deep into the other's throat. His companions caught up just as Rahm pulled the crimson-drenched blade free. Azak offered his friend a hand up.

To Tovok, Rahm commanded, "Get us three of the horses. Scatter the rest. Leave no clues."

Azak glanced back at the house. "What about—"

"Leave him. By the time anyone comes, it'll be just one more body left for the carrion crows. None of us wore any markings."

"As you say."

Tovok rounded up the horses. The trio mounted, Rahm taking one last look at the darkened estate.

"More deaths to lay at Hotak's blood-soaked feet," he murmured, his tone so chill that his companions glanced at one another.

Urging their steeds, the three rode toward the capital.

Lady Maritia de-Droka had stayed for five days then departed with her retinue to inspect other facilities north of the camp. No one had expected to see the emperor's daughter again, and so it came as a surprise when, more than two weeks later, she returned. The reason for her second visit was a mystery to the prisoners.

"She should close down the processing station," Faros muttered to Ulthar as they climbed into the wagons. "There has to be a better way. A gnome couldn't have designed worse!"

"Can be abandoned or dismantled easy with little cost," replied Ulthar. "In case of eruption." He shrugged. "But I agree. Gnomework. Definitely gnomework."

Faros was thrust each day into the hellish abyss, and each day new screams assailed his ears. Several times he assisted in carrying out victims, their bodies black on one side, blistered on the other. Most died quickly, but some few were put out of their misery even when it was determined that they might survive.

It had been a fairly safe day so far. Only twice the flames erupted.

One bin, two, three, then ten. Over and over the cycle went.

The ground shook. Pieces of rock dropped from above, pelting Faros. The rumbling increased, becoming thunder. The earth shook with such violence that Faros fell to his knees. A small crack opened where he usually stood, and the edge crumbled into the vast pit.

On his hands and knees, he squeezed himself against the wall. Most tremors faded away after only a few moments, yet this one grew worse, becoming a full, violent quake within minutes. Faros heard screams and shouts. Several prisoners headed toward the ladders, many stumbling because of their fetters. One prisoner lost his footing, reached for the worker in front of him—and with a cry both plummeted into the abyss.

Ore containers swung wildly about, often colliding. A downpour of dirt almost buried Faros. Spitting dust, he abandoned the alcove, joining those converging on the ladders.

Ahead, a tall, graying prisoner fought to keep steady as he, too, edged to the ladders. However, as he put his foot down, the walkway collapsed, sending him slipping off the edge. The prisoner seized a handhold and tried to pull himself up. Reacting instinctively, Faros hurried forward.

"Your hand!" he shouted. "Give me your hand!"

The other did, almost losing his grip. Faros raised him up slowly until the latter could bring one leg up on the path. With further assistance, the elder prisoner climbed to his feet. As he did, Faros got a good look at his face and saw that he had rescued the ousted patriarch, Itonus.

Itonus nodded curtly then both hurried up the ladder.

As the pit workers reached the top, other prisoners bent to help the survivors up. The tremor began to subside, but no one trusted that another might not occur. Faros watched anxiously as Itonus moved up then took his own turn. Above, a strong, steady hand stretched out to Faros—a hand with tattoos.

Ulthar practically lifted the smaller minotaur up to the ground level. With a gasp, Faros fell into his arms.

"Had a cousin, Sardar," Ulther muttered. "Sailed with me for family, then as pirate and brigand. Everywhere I was, Sardar, too. Good comrade, good fighter." He snorted quietly. "Sent to the pit with me and died first day. Couldn't catch him in time."

Faros could say nothing but managed to nod. He stepped back to look at the pit, where the fires stirred up by the tremor had only just begun to drop back out of sight.

A hand touched Faros's shoulder. Too weak to be startled, he turned and once more found himself gazing at Itonus.

"You." Calculating eyes the color of charcoal shifted to Ulthar. "And your friend. You will be summoned. Be prepared."

He backed away, moving casually into the throng of prisoners. Faros glanced after him, but Ulthar quickly nudged his companion.

"Give no sign. It betters the chances."

"What did he mean? What could he want with us?"

Before Ulthar could respond, a guard approached. "Everyone to the wagons! You'll wait there until we know what's going on. Rest while you can. You'll have to make up for the lost work later!"

As they obeyed, Ulthar quietly responded to Faros's question. "Why else would 'un as important as he want us?" For the first time in days, Ulthar allowed himself a full smile. "I think he has a plan to escape, this patriarch does, and from the likes o' him such a plan might work."

Chapter XIX

Discovered

The apprentices working at the barrel maker's establishment on the northern edge of the imperial city had departed. Only Master Zornal, the chief cooper, remained, for he lived above his business. Despite his lean form, the dark brown minotaur had severe jowls, so much so that they gave him what many thought a decidedly canine appearance.

Zornal bolted the entrance then headed to the nearest work bench. There he glanced at the efforts of one of his newer charges. Incredibly impatient, young minotaurs tended to work the wood as if in a combat with it. They did not admire the wood's strength, work with it as though it were a comrade.

As he doused the oil lamps, a soft rapping came from the door. Rubbing his hands on his apron, Zornal called out, "One moment! One moment!"

Relighting the lamp nearest the entrance, he slid open the bolt and opened the door.

A compact but solid figure barged into him, pushing the barrel maker back into the workroom.

Another intruder darted in, immediately dousing the light. To Zornal's dismay, a third joined the others, shutting the door and quickly bolting it.

"Unhand me! I am a member of House Arun! You assault a good citizen of the empire! The State Guard will have your heads!"

"They would certainly love mine," remarked the one who had collided with him. "But would you give it to them, Zornal?"

"I know that voice!" the cooper blurted. "Rahm?"

"Aye, Master Zornal, but please, speak quieter."

"Of course, of course," returned the barrel maker in much softer tones. "Step back further, so we can converse in safety. Have you eaten?"

"Not in some time," Rahm admitted.

"Then come! I can certainly feed three worn, hungry travelers."

They settled at a squat table in the rear where the apprentices ate their meals and, over pieces of goat and some ale, the general explained the situation. Zornal listened intently, never interrupting. Only when Rahm had finished did he comment.

"You should've never come back! Assassinate the emperor all by yourselves? Better to have waited until you had an army behind you! I understand your reasons for wanting Hotak dead. I can even sympathize. But be reasonable!"

"Too many lives were put in jeopardy just to get us here, Zornal. I'll not leave. Not while the usurper lives."

Ears flattening, the barrel maker sighed. "Very well. I may be foolish, but I'll do what I can to help you. No friend am I of the new emperor! Many a good customer I lost through him."

"I'd hoped you'd help. That's why I came to you." Rahm peered at the rows of barrels. "More than enough customers still, I see. Including the imperial throne, by chance?"

"Aye, we sell to the throne. Always have. My father and his father before him. Would look strange, not to mention be unwise and unhealthy, if I ceased to do so now."

"So you still have access to parts of the palace, then?"

"What're you getting at?"

His good ear twitching, General Rahm stared thoughtfully at the darkness.

Morning came. At the sounding of the seventh hour, the apprentices, already at their stations, took up their hammers and other tools and began the day's labor. Quas, the overseer, a hefty minotaur with unkempt mud-brown fur and thick, blunt horns, directed the distribution of materials. He stood watching the workers, a long, pale pipe with a slim downward curve sticking out of the side of his mouth. Long favored by mariners, the pipe was as close to the sea as Quas had ever come.

Master Zornal joined his cousin. "Quas, I need you to come upstairs with me for a moment."

Removing his work apron but keeping the pipe in his mouth, Quas followed.

As they reached the top, the master cooper gestured to the empty rooms across from his own. Quas removed his pipe and paused, openly curious.

"In here," commanded Zornal, pointing to one of the rooms.

With slight reluctance, Quas entered. However, when he saw the two figures standing within, the overseer immediately started to back out, a wispy trail of smoke in his wake.

Tovok, stationed behind the door, shut it, blocking his way.

"Be at ease, cousin. These are friends."

"Zornal, that's . . . that's General Rahm Es-Hestos!"

"Then I need not introduce myself," remarked the shorter minotaur.

"Zornal! How long—?"

"Only since last night. They came for help."

Quas swallowed, then quickly recovered from his initial shock. He thrust the tip of the clay pipe back in his mouth. Expression calming, he finally said, "Of course! The honor of our clan wouldn't permit otherwise. Forgive me, general. They said you'd escaped overseas."

With no furniture in the room, Rahm and his companions had slept on the floor using woolen blankets. The barrel maker had also provided empty cedar crates for them to sit upon. Rahm offered two of these to the pair.

Zornal sat, but Quas chose to stand, clearly unnerved despite his seemingly calm demeanor. He puffed on the pipe over and over, as if he hoped to fill the room with one vast cloud.

"Your cousin speaks well of you," the general began. "He intends you to inherit the cooperage, I understand."

"If I'm worthy of it." The overseer's puffy, black eyes brightened. Despite his humble words, he clearly enjoyed hearing of his good fortune.

"He also says you deal with the throne. You even go to the palace on occasion."

"Aye, but only the kitchens. Master Zornal has an agreement with the merchant Detrius. We provide the barrels, he the grain, and I deliver it to a cousin of ours who runs the kitchens."

General Rahm stroked the ring. "Better and better. The old gods must watch over us. How soon before you make your next run, Quas?"

"Another week."

"Would a few days earlier make a difference?"

Zornal answered for him. "Olia—she runs the imperial kitchens—might think us a little eager for coin, but she'll not have a problem with that."

"Just what do you plan?" asked the overseer.

Rahm indicated the far corner of the room. There stood one of Master Zornal's largest barrels. "You'll have some extra barrels with you this time and, because of that, some assistance. Say that Detrius sent the new grain because he discovered he charged too much on a previous shipment. Have them placed with the others."

"Y'mean to enter the palace yourself in one of them, don't you?"

Rahm's face grew grim. "It is better if you don't know."

"A daring plan." Quas fiddled with his pipe.

"Perhaps."

Someone called from downstairs. Rahm and his companions stiffened, but the master cooper shook his head. "Just one of the apprentices. Quas, we'd better get back to work. General, I'll see to it that you get some food later on."

"Thank you, Zornal. And you, too, Quas."

The overseer shook his head, still dumbfounded. "A daring plan."

Day gave way to evening. Quas remained behind to work with Zornal on the barrels. Although the work went well, the pair did not finish until late into the night.

Quas straightened, groaning. "Cousin, I must go."

"Go, and with my thanks."

"And mine," added Rahm quietly.

After Quas had gone, Zornal led them back upstairs. The master barrelmaker bid them a good sleep then departed for his own chambers.

So near to his goal, Rahm could not sleep. He lay staring at the ceiling for some hours then quietly rose, a slight unease touching him. The sound of snoring came from Azak's direction, but neither the captain nor young Tovok stirred.

The general crept to the lone window, feeling the sudden need to peer out. Shadowed buildings met his gaze, shadowed buildings on a street barely illuminated by one tired lamp. To the south, a faint aura radiated from one quarter of the city.

A flicker of flame below caught his attention. Rahm looked and saw a lone minotaur whose attention seemed to be focused on Master Zornal's facility. Under the pale light of the lamp, the commander recognized the face of Quas.

Someone stirred behind Rahm. Azak's voice hissed in his ear, "Is something amiss?"

"Look there. Before he vanishes."

"Looks like . . . it almost looks like Quas."

"It is."

"What would he be doing here so late?" asked Azak. "Come to see Zornal?"

"When the barrelmaker's sound asleep?"

They continued to watch. At first it seemed that the overseer had left, but then Captain Azak caught sight of him, still watching. "There! See his foot? Just barely out of the deepest shadows?"

Quas stayed for a few moments more then retreated. The pair waited, but the overseer did not reappear.

"What do you make of that, Rahm?"

"He plans to betray us."

"But that would bring danger to his own cousin."

"Aye. And it would bring Master Zornal's establishment to Quas." A movement outside caught the general's attention. "Hold! He comes back!"

Sure enough, Quas not only had returned but now looked to be intent on getting inside. From below, they heard the slight creak of a door.

The two fugitives looked at one another. "We can't take a chance," said Rahm. "We must find out what he is doing."

Rahm led the way to the stairs. A dim light shone from the vast workroom. Oil lamp in hand, Quas was inspecting the barrels. He appeared to be looking for something.

Carefully Rahm descended, Azak close behind. The overseer, intent on his activities, did not even turn. The general approached him. Quas muttered something under his breath, then nodded.

Rahm, now only a few paces away, reached for the other's arm.

With a startling roar, Quas swung the oil lamp at the general's face.

The flames came perilously close. Rahm instinctively backed away, the only thing that saved him from the jagged knife that Quas drew from his belt.

Instead of following up on his advantage, Quas made for the door. Azak started after him, but the overseer threw the knife, sending the captain diving for cover.

Rahm leaped for the retreating figure. Quas gaped, and then the two collided. The lamp flew from the overseer's grasp, crashing to the floor. Oil spread and with it came hungry, eager flame.

Quas was a slippery foe despite his girth. He twisted around, putting Rahm within inches of the growing fire.

Azak ran to contain the flames as best he could. Quas struck Rahm on the jaw and broke the general's grip. The overseer put his calloused hands around his foe's throat.

"You've lost, general," Quas growled. "You've lost your run, and now you'll lose your life!"

"And . . . you're losing . . . your inheritance," Rahm managed.

Quas looked up, finally registering the fire. Seizing the advantage, General Rahm pushed with all his might, broke his adversary's hold, and threw the other off. Unable to control his momentum, Quas rolled to the side and nearly collided with Azak.

Flame shot over Quas's oil-drenched leg. He tried to brush the fire out with his hand, only to have the flames race up his arm. Quas snorted in fear, trying to douse himself. He screamed.

Rahm could not save him. The fire did its terrible work in short order. Quas slumped to the floor, his entire body ablaze. He twitched once, twice, then stilled.

"Rahm! We need your help!"

The general hurried to where Captain Azak and a bleary-eyed Tovok were attempting to smother another part of the inferno.

"What is it? What's happening?" roared Zornal. The barrel maker came running down the steps. "By my ancestors!"

From outside came raised voices.

"Upstairs!" demanded Zornal. "Go!"

"We can't leave your workroom!" said Rahm.

Outside, someone struggled with the bolted door.

"Hurry!" demanded the barrel maker.

With great reluctance, the three fugitives ran up the steps. Moments later, shouting voices filled the building.

"More water there!" roared Master Zornal below. "Hurry!"

"It's too late for this one!" someone called out. "He's burned nearly to ash!"

"Who is it?" yet another voice asked.

"Quas!" Zornal roared. "The poor lad thought to smother the flames, but they caught him instead! I could do nothing! He was dead in moments!"

Zornal and the others fought the fire. Once, it seemed they had beaten the flames into submission, only to have them flare up again. In the end, nearly an hour passed before the situation was under control.

"Throw out what can't be salvaged," Zornal said. "Get that refuse out of here! Modron, I'd be beholden if you could bring Quas to our clan house. The patriarch will have those who can better attend to him."

Several anxious minutes passed, then Zornal came up the steps. Rahm and the others had retreated into their room, ready to fight their way out if need be.

"They're all gone," said their host quietly. "All is in order."

"I'm sorry about your cousin," the general returned.

Ears flat, Zornal muttered, "Tell me what happened."

The barrel maker listened close then, eyes closed, he nodded.

"I understand," Zornal said. "I never thought him capable of such treachery. You have my sincerest apologies."

"And you have my apologies about the fire, Master Zornal. We tried to put it out."

"The damage is repairable. 'Tis you I'm fearing for. We can't take any more chances. Come the morrow, I'll make certain that a wagon's readied and you're on your way out of Nethosak. This nonsense about the palace and Hotak must be put to an end."

"No." Rahm gave the sturdy cooper a stare that made him back down. "Send the captain and Tovok away, but I will not go. You'll understand that, I trust."

"I will not be going back without you, Rahm," growled Azak.

"Before you argue," their host interrupted. "Recall that you no longer have a driver. I can't take Quas's place and, after what happened, we dare let no one else know that you're here."

Rahm nodded, his expression calculating. "A good point. I suggest that we settle all these matters tomorrow. No campaign's well-planned that's planned without sleep."

"As you like, then," Zornal grumbled. The cooper departed, returning to the cleanup below.

Tovok and the captain settled down quickly, but Rahm toyed with his ring, thinking about the morrow. No matter how many obstacles fate put in his path, the general swore that he would have the usurper's head.

Either that, or Hotak would have his.

CHAPTER XX

VISITOR IN THE NIGHT

As day struggled to supplant night, a narrow two-masted galley bearing the rearing-horse banner fought the stormy waters and docked in Nethosak. Set lower than the ocean-crossing ships of the imperial fleet, she traveled only in the Blood Sea. The stocky, pointed bow of the galley gave some indication of its value in battle, for she could readily ram less agile opponents and send them to the bottom.

Her arrival initially interested no one. Only when an old mariner lighting his pipe spotted a certain passenger standing defiantly at the rail did word spread like plague to the port watch. The watch at first refused to let the passenger disembark. Only after invoking his father's authority three times did Kolot manage to gain access to the capital for his guest.

And so, in a manner befitting a visiting dignitary, the Grand Lord Golgren marched into Nethosak.

Alerted by swift messenger, Hotak prepared for the unorthodox visit. Servants clad him in the majestic armor he had worn for his ascension, girding him now for a war of diplomacy. Ogres respected strength, courage, and readiness for battle.

On the wall behind Hotak hung the portrait of the emperor and consort seated in repose by an open window overlooking a hill-strewn vineyard. Hotak looked proud in his legion armor, his helm resting in the crook of his arm, while Nephera, her gown one of dark emerald elegance, looked lovingly in his direction.

Nearby, a circular bed of red-stained oak had taken the place of the one chopped up during Chot's pathetic fight. Nephera's side was untouched.

If the high priestess had not slept in their bed this night, word nonetheless quickly reached her of the galley's arrival. She entered the imperial quarters, fully dressed for a proper greeting with a foreign dignitary—even one of ogre persuasion. The flowing silver and black robe not only emphasized her figure but also her high rank.

"My husband, I see you are already prepared to meet our unexpected guest."

A soft, fresh wave of lavender wafted under the emperor's nostrils. He inhaled it, recalling simpler times. "May I say how lovely you look?"

"You may," she replied with a knowing smile. With practiced hands, she adjusted his cloak and brushed off a loose thread on his breastplate. "You realize what his coming here must mean?"

"Of course. Golgren's gotten his miserable khan to accept our pact. It was a foregone conclusion. We both knew that."

"But this unexpected visit . . . that speaks volumes."

"Kolot did his job well," Hotak said, the comment almost an afterthought.

"He had little with which to fail," Nephera responded. "We planned everything for him."

The emperor fought back his annoyance. "Give him some due. True, he is not as efficient as Bastion or as loyal to you as Ardnor, but Kolot's brought no shame on this family. Only honor."

"Yes, he has brought no shame. And I am aware of his strengths."

An anxious officer entered, going down on one knee before Hotak. "My lord, your son Kolot and the ogre emissary, Grand Lord Golgren, await you in the planning room."

Hotak clapped. "Excellent! I trust someone has seen to Lord Golgren's needs?"

"Aye, my lord. As best as we could." The soldier showed some distaste at having to treat an ogre so courteously.

"I see no need to wait any longer." Hotak extended his arm toward Lady Nephera. "My dear?"

An honor guard of a dozen attentive soldiers armed with axes materialized as the pair stepped into the hallway. Aides and guard officers silently closed in behind them. By the time Hotak and Nephera reached the framed doors of the planning room, they were surrounded by more than fifty minotaurs—certainly enough to give the ogre a memorable first impression.

At the center of the room stood one of the strongest, thickest oak tables in all the imperium, for minotaur commanders had a habit of banging their fists against the nearest surface when arguing. Two golden chandeliers, each with twenty-five candles spread along their five upcurved arms, illuminated the chamber. Wooden grillwork covered the white plaster walls, and in the frames created by the grillwork hung detailed color maps of the major islands and colonies of the Empire.

On the far wall, in a frame spanning the length of the chamber, Hotak had hung his masterpiece. Upon a turbulent ocean of blue-green, with hints of crimson where the Blood Sea lay, were marked each of the over three-dozen official colonies. The huge, vividly marked map could not help but draw the eyes, and so it did not surprise Hotak to see Golgren, seated and with a chalice of wine in one hand, perusing the display with much interest.

A helmed herald stood to attention as the imperial couple appeared. The minotaur's stentorian voice announced, "The Emperor Hotak de-Droka and his consort, the Lady Nephera!"

The brief flaring of her eyes was the only sign of Nephera's anger that her own title was omitted.

Kolot, seated across from the ogre, rose and bowed toward his father. The younger minotaur looked worn and uncomfortable. Golgren, on the other hand, appeared quite energetic as he rose from his seat to bow gracefully to the duo.

With Golgren and Kolot stood ever-watchful Bastion.

"My greetings, Grand Lord Golgren!" the emperor roared cheerfully. "It's been a long time, hasn't it? More than a year since we last met face-to-face. Where was it, Zygard?"

"Not so long, not so long," grunted the ogre, standing. "Yes. Zygard it was," he added, referring to the ogre settlement nearest Sargonath. As Golgren spoke, his gaze drifted to Nephera.

"How is the Grand Khan?" asked Hotak.

"The lord of all he surveys," Golgren responded, still eyeing the consort.

Hotak held back a frown. "Your visit, while welcome, is entirely unexpected. Dare I presume to think that this means acceptance of our offer?"

Golgren smiled, revealing far too many teeth. "More than you think." The tall figure raised one meaty fist in salute. "But first, my friend Hotak must be congratulated on his ascension! The Grand Khan sends his best wishes and regards in this matter."

"You are too kind."

The ogre chuckled, a harsh, grating noise.

Now the emperor frowned. He signaled for his retinue to depart. "Come, let us talk."

The Grand Khan's ambassador was staring directly at the Lady Nephera, and his look was not admiring.

Only then did Hotak recall that ogres did not accept females in leadership roles.

"My dear," the emperor said in a voice aimed to be as pleasant as possible, "it occurs to me that we'll need to present our guest to the Supreme Circle in a formal ceremony."

She blinked, not understanding his hint. "Of course, my love."

"It would be best if perhaps you would see to it now."

"Hotak—" she began, indignation rising.

"A good idea, Father," Bastion interjected, cutting off her protest and taking her arm. "Mother, I will be happy to assist you."

Nephera's eyes went briefly to her husband again, then a mask of courtesy spread across her features. "Of course. I shall take care of everything." She gave Golgren a polite look. "So good to see you again, emissary."

The high priestess strode gracefully out of the room, Bastion at her side.

Kolot also started to rise, then dropped back into his chair.

"I should probably stay, Father," he muttered.

"Your consideration is noted, lad, but you're dismissed. Go and relax."

"Yes, Father." The muscular figure bowed his horns low in respect as he passed.

Hotak again indicated the chairs. "May we proceed now?"

But Golgren preferred to look at the vast map again, inspecting it intently. "So many little islands. So large the areas of water between them. How proud you minotaurs must be of your realm."

"Indeed we are. Our nation is a diverse one, with every type of land imaginable. We have farmland to cultivate, forests for timber and fruit, hillsides for herding, and mineral-rich quarries necessary for the making of tools and weapons."

Finally seating himself, the emissary gazed steadily at his host. Hotak sat across from the ogre and waited. From the confines of his cloak, Golgren brought forth a thick, rolled parchment.

"My Khan offers this treaty, but only if certain conditions are met." The ogre placed the parchment down on the table. "Your son assures me they will be."

"Of course." Hotak reached for the parchment, only to be stopped by Golgren, who removed yet another document from his voluminous mantle.

"You will want this, too, Great Hotak."

"What is it?"

"A pact between Kern and Blöde, including your people."

The emperor's one good eye widened.

"Kern and Blöde are mortal enemies," Hotak remarked as matter-of-factly as he could manage.

"As ogres and minotaurs have always been."

Hotak unrolled the treaty involving Blöde. He read through it, struggling with the barbaric ogre script. Only a handful of ogres, most of them in the ruling caste, actually knew how to read and write.

Hotak looked up, his one eye widening further. "What is this? Surely my eyes deceive me!"

"No," rumbled Golgren.

Hotak thrust the parchment at the ogre. "Explain this now."

Golgren shrugged. "The son of Hotak did what was necessary to save the pact. Blöde would not accept otherwise, and if Blöde would not, neither would Kern." The emissary smiled in a manner he no doubt thought sympathetic, but to Hotak he looked like a hungry, grinning beast. "If it is not acceptable . . ."

"I have not rejected it." The emperor said nothing more, gathering his thoughts.

Golgren downed the last of the briarberry wine in his chalice. He glanced with interest at the dark green bottle sitting on a nearby stand, but satisfied himself with toying with the empty goblet.

"It would take much convincing. Even my most loyal generals would balk at such an alliance." Hotak rubbed his jaw. "Yet the possibilities . . ." He slapped the pact on the table, his expression resolute. "By Argon's Chain, it shall be done!"

Golgren showed his teeth. "My Khan will be most pleased."

"This must be done properly, though. To ensure that all goes smoothly, I'm going to have my son—Bastion, that is—take command of this matter."

"We are agreed then?"

"This will satisfy Kern and Blöde? No land exchange?"

"Ogres have little use for dots of dirt scattered in the water. Yes, friend Hotak, all will be satisfied."

"Good." Hotak rose. "What I've agreed to risks an insurrection, you know."

He offered his hand. Golgren, still seated, took it. The Khan's ambassador had a powerful grip, but so did Hotak. The minotaur had the pleasure of seeing Golgren wince slightly.

"We are agreed, then." Hotak's mood brightened considerably. The momentous pact had become a reality. There would be some difficulties in implementing the ogres' demands, but nothing insurmountable. "Golgren, your chalice is empty. Join me in having some more wine. We shall drink to the partnership of our peoples and talk of our aspirations for the future, eh?"

"This one would never turn down such a generous offer."

The emperor poured Golgren some of his finest wine then raised his chalice in a toast.

"To the day of destiny, my ogre friend."

As the imperial capital played host to one unexpected visitor, the port of Varga welcomed others. The four ships sailed into the windswept harbor, the banner of the Eastern fleet waving high over each. Staffed by a small garrison and expecting no trouble, Varga believed the ships were here either to deliver messages or important passengers, or to restock supplies.

The officer on duty, First Dekarian Ilos de-Morgayn, signaled the ten soldiers under his command to stand down. Ilos stood on the dock, watching the first long boats draw near and wondering if they would bring any news of interest.

As more and more long boats filled the harbor, the First Dekarian grew suspicious.

When the first landed, their passengers swarmed toward the port, their weapons drawn. Startled, many of the dockworkers stood transfixed. The First Dekarian seized one of his soldiers.

"By the Axe! Alert the commander! We're under attack! Go! We'll try to delay them!"

As the messenger hurried off, the officer ordered the rest of his fighters off the dock. The simplest way into the heart of the city was a street between the two largest shipping warehouses. If necessary, Ilos would torch the wooden structures. The invaders had to be coming for their contents. Why else attack Varga?

"Halt!" he shouted at one of the invaders, a female dressed as a captain of the fleet. "This port is closed to you!"

She laughed. "This port closed to us? By you? I'll do you one better! I am Captain Tinza and, in the name of General

Rahm Es-Hestos, I order you to surrender! You'll be treated fairly. That's my first and final offer."

"Stand ready!" the First Dekarian shouted.

The captain tightened her grip on her axe, all humor fleeing from her expression. "You're a fool. And a dead one."

She raised her axe high, and with a great roar the invading force descended upon Varga.

The watch fell in seconds, First Dekarian Ilos perishing almost instantly. His soldiers crumpled under the onslaught, all cut to ribbons by eager blades. Not a scar was suffered among Captain Tinza's warriors.

More boats came ashore, one of them carrying gruff Napol. With a nod to Tinza, he marched his marine fighters in the direction of the keep where the larger garrison was stationed.

Captain Tinza's force, more than two hundred strong, marched on the town itself. They soon had the majority of the citizenry under control. She then broke up her command into two groups, one taking stock of the available supplies and the other embarking on a building-to-building search.

Ilos had at least succeeded in warning his superior. First Hekturian Goud could not abandon his post. His honor dictated that he defend Varga as best he could. Instead, he sent five of his best riders to warn the capital.

Napol approached the small fort with several hundred trained marine fighters. Marching up to the gates under a flag of truce, he shouted, "Surrender, and you'll be incarcerated with the locals! Fight, and may your ancestors watch over your souls!"

The gates remained closed. Hekturian Goud did not even bother to reply.

Napol signaled for the assault to begin.

Three rows of twenty archers lined up, their ash bows pointed toward the southern sky. They fired the moment the marine officer waved his axe. The rain of arrows arched up, then descended toward the garrison.

Cries arose as bolts pierced throats and buried themselves in shoulders, legs, and torsos.

"Res!" Goud shouted to the Second Dekarian, now positioned up on the wall. "Return fire!"

The defenders replied. Not nearly so many in number, the imperial archers managed to pick off only a handful of the invaders.

Napol brought ladders into play on every side of the fort. The archers above responded, slaying a few attackers, while other soldiers pushed off the ladders.

Napol signaled a second volley, which caught the defenders in the open. Many fell.

Several long ropes with hooks on the end were tossed up on the walls. Hands gripped the lines, and armed climbers began their ascents.

"Let's go!" the marine commander shouted. "Get up there! You archers! Give them cover!"

Inside, Hekturian Goud removed his helm to wipe his forehead while he considered what to do. A third of his force had been slain, and the walls were becoming impossible to defend.

"Res!" he called. "Tighten up the port side!" More whistling filled the air as he relayed his desperate commands. "Send three to the west wall! Get—"

Four arrows struck the hekturian, one through the calf, another in his shoulder, and two plunging into his neck. Eyes already glazed, the commander crumpled to the ground.

The first marine fighters poured over the top. A few perished, but the rest held their positions. Pitched duels took place along the walkway.

The port wall fell first. Napol's fighters descended, attempting to open the main gates. Arrows rewarded the first two with quick deaths, but under the protection of shields, two more removed the brace.

With Napol leading, the attackers poured into the stronghold.

A few minutes later, Second Dekarian Res, Varga's acting commander, surrendered. Horns low, he knelt before the marine officer, holding his axe up for Napol to take. In all, the Battle of Varga had lasted only three hours.

As the prisoners were herded into the warehouses, Captain Tinza rejoined Napol.

"A battle well fought!" The captain congratulated him. "Not even noon! I hope the others have as much luck." She referred to the other ships that had separated from *Dragon's Crest*. The attacks by both forces had to come within only a few hours of one another.

"They'll do it, Tinza. They'll do it."

She nodded and watched her crew bring supplies aboard the ships. "We should be done before long." She rubbed her jaw. "Did you account for everyone? Did anyone escape?"

Napol lost some of his good humor. "Aye, at least three or four riders fled. Maybe more." He clutched his axe tighter. "They'll go and warn who they can."

Tinza's gaze narrowed. She stared toward distant Nethosak and bared her teeth in satisfaction. "Good. Then everything's gone just as planned."

Chapter XXI

No Escape

Word came quickly that Varga had been attacked, but no earthly messenger delivered the dire news. Instead, Lady Nephera, in the midst of preparing for the reception for Golgren, suddenly stared off into space.

"Varga . . . Varga . . ." she whispered. "You are sure? Northern port . . . four ships? Fleet banners!"

Though the rounded eyes of her two imperial servants could see no other, the high priestess gazed at the deepening shadows swirling before her.

"Leave me!" she commanded her attendants. As they gratefully exited, Nephera wrapped her arms around herself.

"Ships in the east, Varga to the north . . . what is this?" she snapped at those who had brought her the information. "Piracy or rebellion?" Whirling, the high priestess swung open the door through which the servants had fled, crying, "Hotak!"

Through the lofty halls of the palace Nephera raced. The high priestess's spies flew before her. Nephera went straight to the throne room, where Hotak had brought Golgren to flaunt the grandeur of minotaur power. The pair turned in puzzlement as Nephera burst through the great bronze doors.

"My dear—" began the emperor.

Her steely gaze cut him off. "Hotak, my love, we must talk. Now."

Sensing her urgency, Hotak bowed slightly to his guest. "If you will excuse me for a moment, Lord Golgren?"

The ogre nodded, pretending indifference. Only a slight narrowing of his eyes indicated his curiosity.

The emperor led his consort out. Neither spoke until they had entered the planning room, and Hotak, looking around, had made certain that no one else was near.

"Tell me," he ordered her. "Tell me."

"Varga fell barely an hour ago. The ships are still in port, loading imperial supplies aboard. They fly the banners of the Eastern fleet!"

He ground his fist into his palm. "The four that fled. It has to be them!" Hotak rubbed his jaw. "I expected something, but nothing this audacious! What can those fools hope to accomplish?"

"They've stripped a port on Mithas itself! Think of what the people will say!"

"This can't be allowed." He swung open the door and shouted at a startled guard, "Summon Captain Gar!"

Gar appeared a moment later. The dusky warrior went down on one knee.

"My lord?" he grunted.

"Vagra has been attacked. Send a detachment of my personal legion there. Alert the Flying Gryphon Legion. Have one naval contingent set sail for the port. Watch for four vessels bearing banners of the Eastern fleet. I want those ships!"

Gar nodded. "Most of your legion," he said, "is already spread out over southern Mithas and one contingent was, by your order, shipped to reinforce General Xando on Kothas."

"Then take what's needed from Nethosak."

"It will leave the capital in the hands of the State Guard. For your own protection you'll only have the Imperial Guard, my lord."

"Do what must be done. Control of all security in Nethosak will be in the hands of the Imperial Guard, then. Bastion will not be available, but Kolot will serve well in this capacity. Any threat pertaining to the capital should be reported to him."

"Aye, my lord." Captain Gar rose and backed out of the room.

Lady Nephera approached her husband. "If there are any disruptions, you can be assured that the Protectors will be available."

"I'd prefer to keep them out of this. Nethosak is secure."

"As you say." She frowned. "It might be wise to hold off about Golgren and the pact for the moment—at least stall before making any announcement—until we know more about these matters."

"This must be Rahm's doing. Strike here, strike there! Harry my legions everywhere, trying to find my weaknesses!" Hotak snorted, a hint of crimson touching his eyes. "A fatal mistake. There is no weakness in my empire."

Lady Nephera patted his breastplate. "Well put, my husband. Now, might it not be best to return to the ogre, lest he wonder what terrible fate has befallen the empire?"

"You're correct as always, Nephera." They touched the tips of their muzzles together. Hotak inhaled deeply, taking in the lavender scent of his wife. "Thank you for your quick action."

"The temple exists to support you. I exist to aid you."

She watched as he left to placate Lord Golgren. "You may be right about Rahm, my love," she murmured, "but I fear you may also be wrong. This is too direct for the general, too rash. Something else is brewing, and I must find out what it is."

A pockmarked prisoner found Faros and Ulthar as they ate their morning meal and, with a nudge of his foot, indicated they should follow him. He led Faros and the mariner around several barracks, beyond the wooden watchtowers, and past parties of occupied prisoners. A few pairs of eyes glanced at the trio with dull curiosity.

They slipped around another corner, passed an unsuspecting guard in one of the towers, and suddenly confronted a sinewy, narrow-eyed prisoner who looked each of them over, then let them inside the barracks behind him.

Two figures stood in the shadows at the far end. To Faros's surprise, one proved to be Japfin, who had found reason not to eat with them this morning. The other was Itonus.

"You know who I am," Itonus said. "Once master of a powerful House. A foolish mistake has robbed me of that role, but not of friends on the outside. I have waited, and now they have acted." Itonus leaned toward them. "Arrangements have been made. I will escape this foul pit, but the way requires some trouble, some strength, and certainly some allies. I think you two fit my needs."

"Heard plenty of plans before," Ulthar said. "None worked."

"Mine shall. What do you say, both of you? This one you evidently know, he says I can trust you. He has already agreed."

"What about the Butcher?" Faros asked. "I've seen you rub shoulders with him. Is he a part of this conspiracy?"

"The—" Itonus chuckled. "Oh, good Paug." He waved his hand, dismissing the question. "Useful enough for keeping the trash from disturbing me, but certainly not a part of this scheme. Too volatile, too untrustworthy."

Escape. It had seemed such an impossible goal, but if anyone could succeed, it had to be the patriarch. Faros dared not turn down such a precious chance. "I'll do it."

Beside him, the tattooed mariner slowly nodded. "Also me."

"I had hoped to wait until the treacherous Lady Maritia left. However, I have to act in concert with the outside. Tomorrow morning, be prepared to travel in a different wagon. The choice will be clear. Do not hesitate, and once you are inside, look under the benches. Tools will be hidden there that can unlock our manacles and fetters. I will tell you nothing more, but act boldly. These steps must be followed without hesitation or error."

"What do you need us for?" Faros asked.

"To be blunt, as decoys. The wagons are the only way out of here, but if I try to ride alone, someone will notice. One prisoner is too obvious, but a wagon almost half-full, they will not bother to scrutinize. If there is trouble, I want comrades who'll follow orders. I expect you to obey me to the fullest. Now, if there are no more questions, this discussion is ended."

Itonus leaned back, eyes closed in thought. Japfin joined Faros and Ulthar, and the three departed the barracks.

Horns sounded, summoning the prisoners to the wagons. For once, Faros moved with some energy, some optimism. None of the three spoke. The key to freedom had been offered them by one in whom they could all believe.

As they neared the wagons, however, a sharp stinging blow suddenly sent Faros to his knees. While Ulthar moved to help him up, the Butcher wound up his whip. "Get a move on, you scum! The wagons aren't going to wait forever!"

Faros gritted his teeth, reluctantly obeying. He could not afford to show his emotions. Just a little longer and all Vyrox would be nothing more than a fading nightmare, and that included Paug.

Maritia stared at the departing prisoners, seeking one in particular. She stood alone in the room save for her bodyguard, the towering charcoal-colored Holis. "Are you certain of this information, Holis?"

"It came from a reliable source." Holis stood as still as a statue.

"I hope so. I wouldn't have lingered in this miserable place otherwise. I'm looking forward to seeing the last of it."

Maritia finally noticed the one she was seeking. Itonus glided toward the wagons as if still walking down the carpet toward the ornate chair he had used as patriarch. He did not look at all like a minotaur who had lost all his power.

"Father was wrong not to have him slain outright, Holis."

"As you say, my lady."

Maritia stepped away from the window. "I understand his reasoning, but he should've acted decisively."

"The political landscape can be a dangerous battlefield, my lady. Circumstances warranted imprisoning the elder, leaving open a possible use for him as a bargaining chip."

"Well the time for such concerns is past." She turned, her hand stroking the hilt of her sword. "If what your source says is true, Itonus might vanish from this place if we are not careful. That cannot be allowed, Holis."

"Your order, my lady?"

Her hand slipped from her sword to his chest. "No order. More a suggestion of duty to your master."

Holis bowed his head. "Tell me what must be done, and I shall do it, my lady. For the emperor, the realm . . . and you."

More shadows accumulated about the high priestess as she leaned over her desk, but Nephera paid them no mind, her attention completely fixed on her task. When she needed them, they would still be there. They had no choice but to wait.

Her words fell onto the parchment like water tumbling down a waterfall. Nephera's raven eyes wore a fanatical look, and the hand that held the quill moved as though another guided it. Names, places, and phrases erupted from the rich red ink. Varga, Tinza, Napol, Jubal, others.

The renegades had made a terrible blunder by returning to Mithas. They had given her the opportunity to identify them. She had new names, many names. More important, she could now follow their movements, for the ships departing Varga carried with them unseen passengers. Each rebel named would be attended to by one of the shadows serving her.

Nephera had so many under her command. She could monitor the thoughts and actions of anyone serving her husband to make certain they were as loyal as they claimed. Even Hotak had ghosts who attended him—a safety precaution in Nephera's mind. That he did not know of these sentinels was beside the point.

Pausing, the priestess exhaled then surveyed her quarters, her sanctum. Here in the temple her authority was absolute. Her acolytes followed her every word. The faithful knelt at her feet. The ghosts obeyed her commands and fed her power beyond the emperor's imagining.

Lady Nephera glanced at her list again. Before long, Nephera would be able to present to Hotak details of the rebels' organization, including the locations of their bases and those giving them valuable support.

Then . . . then finally, her husband would have to acknowledge the contributions of the Forerunners.

"What of Rahm?" she demanded of the air. "What of Rahm?"

His name had been mentioned, but his exact location was still unknown to her. She suspected that he worked at some goal separate from the attacks—and that made Nephera all the more wary.

"Takyr!"

Immediately, the hooded shade appeared. *Mistress.*

"General Rahm continues to be elusive. Why?"

Some force, some power must protect him from my view, mistress.

Nephera frowned.

He is as the dead are to the living. . . .

"In life, you were rare among our kind, for you dabbled in magic."

I was . . . touched by magic, mistress, the hooded phantom said. He raised his right hand, and for the first time Nephera noticed that two fingers were missing and the rest had been scalded. *And that touch led to my . . . alteration.*

He did not explain further. Ghosts either tried to forget their demises or went about proclaiming their stories to any and all who would listen. Some of the first shades to swear allegiance to the high priestess after the Dream had wailed endlessly of their downfalls until she had commanded that they never again speak unless so ordered.

"So you can tell me nothing at all?"

Nothing, mistress.

With undisguised irritation, Nephera turned on the deathly throng, looking down at the milling shades contemptuously. "Useless! None of you can tell me anything! None of you can find the worst traitor!"

Whatever they had been in life, at this very moment they were less than the dirt beneath her feet. Even Takyr had the good sense to retreat, his expression shrouded by his hood.

"No one?" Nephera sneered. "No one can tell me where General Rahm might be?"

They moved about in uncertainty, faces passing through faces, bodies through bodies. Their numbers filled the room.

Then one lone shade drifted hesitantly toward her. He had died violently, judging by his blackened, blistered flesh. Most likely he was a victim of fire. The odor of ash permeated him.

"You have something to say?" Lady Nephera urged. "You have something worthy of my time? Come closer and tell me."

In life, mistress, I was called . . . Quas, the ghost managed to emit from his charred mouth. Despite the savage damage to his face, he also managed an expression that the high priestess thought resembled hatred. *And I may know . . . where General Rahm might be.*

Chapter XXII

Revolt

An *ogre* in their midst.

Rumor had it that there had been an invasion up north, that hundreds of minotaurs had been slaughtered by unknown villains. Who else but their taskmasters of old would dare such a vile, cowardly strike?

The minotaurs summoned by Hotak stared warily at their emperor's unwelcome guest.

"Dress it up like a doll," muttered one general, "give it a hundred baths, and it'll still look and stink like an ogre."

"Would look a lot better with his head off and decorating a pike," replied a companion, fingering the hilt of his sword.

"Could keep old Chot company there, eh?"

The group of officers laughed harshly, but they stilled when Golgren glanced their way. The emissary nodded at them, then gave the minotaurs a strangely cheerful grin.

The officer who had been fingering his hilt shook with anger. He gripped his sheathed blade and would have stepped forward if not for quick, restraining actions by the others.

"Your majesty," muttered the senior councilor, addressing Hotak. "It might be best to conclude the matter quickly so that this . . . your *guest* can return to a more secure venue."

Hotak signaled for attention. His audience, some forty of the empire's finest, included members of the Supreme Circle and other senior officials. They drew more closely together.

"First," said Hotak, "the rumors of battle are true." As angry murmurs arose and reddened eyes fixed on the ogre, the emperor quickly continued, "The villains are traitors of the realm, renegades under the command of Rahm Es-Hestos."

He went on to explain all that was known. Some of the rage against Golgren faded, but the warriors still watched the emissary, and their hands never strayed far from their weapons.

Satisfied that he had made himself clear, Hotak cleared his throat and indicated the ogre. "All the more important that, in such uneasy times, hard decisions be made. Old enmities must die. Warriors of the realm, I am proud to tell you that a pact of alliance has been agreed upon with the lands of Kern and Blöde."

Eyes bulged; gasps of denial escaped gaping mouths.

"Your majesty! *Ogres?*"

"Better the human vermin!"

Hotak's one good eye stared his followers down. "Silence! I do not ask your permission for my decision! This is an imperial edict. I have honored you with my reasoning."

Many quieted, but some still could not accept matters.

"How can ogres be trusted?"

"What guarantees have we that they won't betray us?"

The emperor drew himself up. "Do you think we go into this alliance blindly? This excellent emissary has risked his life coming here to sign the pact and prove their intentions."

"But what guarantees do we have?" one of the generals persisted.

Hotak clamped his mouth shut, finding himself unwilling to disclose the terms by which the allies were bound. He was not helped by Golgren, who whispered, almost blithely, "They will know the truth soon enough. Speak, friend Hotak."

Before a single word could escape him, the emperor was interrupted by shouts from outside. Turning on his heel, he pointed to a guard. The guard rushed out to see what the commotion was about, and a moment later burst back into the chamber.

"Your majesty! Another galley's entered the harbor! It bears *ogre* markings!"

A renewed roar filled the room. One officer drew his sword and rushed toward Golgren. The ogre would have defended himself but Hotak drew his own weapon, deflected the other's blade, and trapped it point down. The stunned officer dropped his weapon with a clatter and knelt before Hotak.

"Forgive me, my lord! I didn't mean—"

With a snort of anger, the emperor dismissed the impetuous minotaur from his thoughts. He looked to Golgren. "Explain!"

"They were to follow behind your son's galley, great emperor, and were not to enter the harbor until my signal." The emissary shrugged. "The journey was not an easy one. Perhaps the captain did not trust the weather. My apologies, but the ship is necessary for my return home. And is intended to carry vital cargo, yes?"

Hotak frowned then nodded. Sheathing his sword, he turned and shouted to the guard, "Have our horses ready! Warn the escort that they should be ready to fight!"

One of the generals who had protested earlier snarled with satisfaction, "Fight the wretched beasts, majesty? We will come—"

But as Hotak pushed past him, Golgren at his side, the emperor shook his head fiercely. "Fight *them*? I'm thinking we might have to fight our own people!"

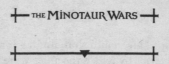

A single ogre in the capital almost started a riot. A *crew* of ogres arriving on an ogre galley—even under a flag of truce—was more than enough to ignite a bloodbath.

The port watch could do little to restrain the growing crowd of minotaurs. Recent events and rumors had stretched the nerves of the populace thin. Now, here appeared an historic enemy, and in numbers that suggested treachery.

Rocks, empty barrels, harpoons . . . whatever could be found, the furious mob threw at the ogre galley. Most of the objects landed short, the ogres not having docked, but a few struck the decks. One harpoon even managed to thrust through a sail, which brought raucous cheers from the onlookers.

Doing themselves no favor, the ogres for their part enjoyed taunting the minotaurs. Cries of *"Uruv Suurt!"*—accompanied by other grunted words in the ogre tongue—fueled the mob's outrage. Few among the minotaurs understood much of the language, but they knew what names they were being called by ogres and guessed rightly that they were being vilely insulted.

But the minotaurs could not reach the ogre galley, and likewise the ogres could not escape. Two massive warships had slid in behind them, blockading the low-slung craft. Aboard one ship, a crew was already manning the catapult. The mechanism had been wound, and all they needed was word from the captain. At such close range on an unmoving target, they would strike hard.

Not content to leave matters in the hands of the imperial fleet, a few minotaurs clambered down into rowboats and set off toward the ogre galley. One watch officer who attempted to block them was shoved into the harbor

Aboard the galley, an ogre cast a spear at the attacking rowboats. More out of luck than aim, it landed in the first boat and pierced the leg of a minotaur. That minor bloodletting opened the floodgates. As the one boat rowed back to deliver its wounded passenger, scores of other minotaurs armed with clubs, axes, and more crowded into any available craft. Someone with a bow began shooting at the galley. With a cry, one of the ogres tumbled over the rail, a shaft through his chest. As he hit the water, the mob let loose with a roar.

As if on cue, the warship fired the catapult. Only the lurching of the galley spared it from terrible damage. By chance, the stone glanced off a rail, causing only superficial breakage, but the incensed crowd roared again.

The ogres moved to repel boarders. The crew gathered at the rails, heavy clubs and long spears at the ready. They looked as eager as the minotaurs for a fight.

At that moment, a contingent of soldiers on horseback drove into the rear of the crowd. Rather than attacking with axes or swords, they whipped at the rioters, cutting a path through them.

"Make way for his majesty, the emperor!" shouted a crested hekturian. "Make way!"

The crowd did not immediately understand, not until horns began blaring, and Hotak himself, helm on and cape flowing behind him, drove through their midst. The emperor's name spread like fire throughout the area. The mob faltered. The port watch finally began to make its presence felt.

"Commander Orcius, signal those ships to hold their fire!" Hotak shouted. "Hekturian, seize the weapons of any who refuse to lower them! Someone get those boats back to the docks!" Turning to the ogre by his side, Hotak said, "Golgren, you're with me. Stay close."

Despite his calm demeanor in the face of possible catastrophe, the ogre emissary remained near to his minotaur host. The mob recognized that the emperor rode among them, but an ogre was still an ogre, and many pointed and glared at him. Golgren was within tempting reach. Two guards had to whip some ambitious minotaurs away before they could pull Golgren down.

With a wedge now formed before them, the pair—emissary and emperor—rode ahead of the rest toward the end of the docks. In the distance, the warships quieted, but the catapults remained aimed at their targets. Several of the boats intent on attacking the galley had turned away, but a few still were trying to board.

From the docks came new vessels, longboats filled with groups of soldiers. At the head of the foremost, a dekarian shouted at the rest of the boarders, commanding them to cease or suffer the consequences.

Either not understanding or purposely ignoring the turn of events, some of the ogres attempted to spear their rescuers. One lance buried itself in the side of the dekarian's vessel just inches from the soldier.

Hotak dismounted and looked to Golgren. "Make it clear to your people that no minotaur is to suffer harm. I won't be able to stop my followers if that should happen."

Nodding, the emissary dismounted. With the emperor and his wary guards protecting his back, Golgren marched to the water and waved.

One of the ogres onboard noticed him and alerted the others.

"Kreegah!" Golgren called. "Suru talan Uruv Suurt! Kreegah! Yarin suru ki f'han! Ki f'han!"

The ogre scurried away then, after tense moments, he reappeared, accompanied by a larger, duskier figure in a kilt and rusted breastplate.

"The captain?" asked Hotak.

"No. The first mate. A good fellow."

Golgren repeated his commands. The first mate grimaced then nodded reluctantly. He barked orders to the ogres still defending against attacks. When that did not work, the mate began battering heads until the fighting stopped.

"Your galley cannot be allowed to stay," the emperor informed his guest. "My people have not been made ready."

"They will not return to Kern without this humble one. To do so would cause their heads to be removed, yes?"

Hotak rubbed his muzzle. "There's only one place for them to wait for you, then. Commander Orcius, I've a message for the captains of my two warships."

The emperor quietly spoke to Orcius, whose eyes widened, but he refrained from any protesting remarks. "I have two good soldiers who can be trusted with this, majesty."

As the messengers were rowed toward their respective destinations, Hotak's good eye fixed on Golgren again. "Now, emissary, I believe you need to send a similar message to your ship."

"Are you ordering me to leave?"

"You know our task is not yet done here, Lord Golgren. Rest assured, when you depart Nethosak, you will do so as befits your status as my honored guest."

The ogre grinned, displaying his filed teeth. "The great Hotak is too kind."

"Give them their instructions, my friend. The sooner the galley is out of here, the better."

With a slight flourish of his cloak, the emissary turned back to the vessel, where the first mate still waited. Golgren barked at the other ogre several times in his guttural language.

Hotak listened intently. While not completely fluent in the bastardized tongue of his ancestors, he understood well enough to know that Golgren spoke true.

The mate vanished.

The crowd had quieted now that it was clear that their emperor had the situation well in hand. What Golgren was doing with Hotak they still did not understand, but as the ogre seemed well-guarded, many took that to mean he was under some kind of arrest. Hotak did nothing to dissuade this notion.

The longboats began returning from the warships. Within minutes, the two minotaur vessels began to turn about, maneuvering to either side of the harbor and keeping a safe distance from the ogre galley.

With a groan, the ogre ship slowly rowed away from the docks. On deck, crewmembers worked the sails. A few onlookers jeered them. Some of the ogres appeared ready to restart the fight, but the mate and other officers moved among them, hitting them on the heads, even whipping them, until the sailors bent to their tasks.

Oars creaking methodically, the galley slipped in the waters between the two minotaur ships. The three sailed in unison, sails rippling in the harsh wind. Thunder roiled, but all three vessels had their orders and, as though part of the same fleet, sailed away.

As the last glimpse of them faded in the distance, Hotak and Golgren remounted. The emperor noted that most in the crowd now looked subdued, even puzzled at what had happened. Many clearly wondered if he intended to punish them for their actions.

Instead, he saluted them. A new cheer arose from the crowd. They called the emperor's name over and over, as if by his hand alone he had brought victory over their ancient foes. Golgren, surrounded by the crowd, couldn't contain his grin, even as most glared at him.

Horns blaring, the escort paved the way for the emperor and his companion.

"That was too close," Hotak muttered under his breath. "A good thing we were able to get the people under control."

"Truly they are yours to command, my friend," Lord Golgren returned as they started off. "You could attempt *anything* with them and they would obey."

The smile that Hotak gave to the crowd faltered imperceptibly. He knew to what Golgren referred, and it gave him pause.

"Yes, they would," he responded. His good eye narrowed on the ogre. "Something to think about a bit, isn't it, emissary?"

For the first time in months, Faros slept well. When the guards woke the prisoners that morning, he almost smiled. It took some effort to keep his expression sullen and not to appear eager. Even the slightest hint that something was amiss could send the entire enterprise to ruins.

Ulthar acted like his usual self, but with a glint in his eyes that Faros had never seen. Japfin was the worst of them, almost ready to sprint to work—and freedom.

They finished their bowls and waited for the horns. Only then did Faros whisper, "Shouldn't someone have signaled us by now?"

"Maybe there was some delay," Japfin muttered.

Ulthar quieted them. "A guard approaches."

They knew the coarse-furred figure walking toward them only by his face. Hand on the hilt of his sword, his expression the usual one of disdain, he said, "You've got new orders for today. You three are goin' on wagon number twelve. Understand?"

"Yes," Faros replied.

"Make sure I don't have to tell you again, because I won't." With that, he left them.

Ulthar rubbed the underside of his muzzle. "Only a few minutes left until the horns. Maybe time enough. Come!"

"Where're we going?" Japfin snarled.

"Back to barracks. Forgot something."

As they approached the building, Ulthar nodded to the black minotaur. "Japfin, watch."

Japfin took up a relaxed position near the door. Faros and

the other prisoner slipped inside. Ulthar shut the door behind them then headed down the rows of bunks.

"What're you doing?"

Ulthar stopped and moved some of the bunks out of the way. Faros helped him. Together, they tugged at the floorboards underneath.

"The other. Hurry!"

In moments, they had a shallow hole cleared.

Ulthar bent down, looking past a pile of half-ruined trinkets saved by prisoners. Twisting his hand around, he reached far underneath the wooden floor.

"Must still be here!" Faros heard Ulthar say. "So long . . . but must be here. Aah!"

The tattooed minotaur struggled to free his hand. He held up a dagger, which even in the dimness appeared to shine.

The rusted blade was a good six inches long. Faros recognized it as the type carried by the guards.

"Found it on a body during a collapse. Hid it, then, when no 'un looked, hid it down here." He bared his teeth in a savage grin. "Didn't know what to do with it. Thought about using it on good friend Paug." Ulthar snorted contemptuously. "On Paug, in Paug, all over Paug. Never did, though. Wanted better use . . . and have it now."

The door opened, and Japfin leaned inside. "Aren't you two through yet? Let's go before we miss our chance!"

Ulthar started forward, but Faros pointed. "What about this gaping hole? We can't leave it here like this!"

"What's the point?" grunted Japfin. "By the time they notice it, we'll be gone!"

"But it'll get the others in trouble! They'll whip them all." Even the slightest infractions earned punishment.

Ulthar shook his head. "Not enough time."

Faros knew he spoke the truth. With one last, regretful look, he followed the others.

The horns sounded as they returned to the main yard. All around, workers rose and headed toward the wagons.

Itonus's wagon stood off to one side. As Faros and the others neared it, they saw five other prisoners—two of whom they recognized—along with the guard who had alerted them minutes earlier. Of Itonus there was no sign. The guard looked more nervous than the prisoners.

"That's all of you, then," he said upon their arrival. "Now all we need is the patriarch, and we can go."

"He'll be along, Harod," snarled the prisoner who had stood guard for Itonus yesterday. "Just be patient."

"Patient? You know the risk I'm taking?" Ears flat, Harod continued to fidget. "You lot better get inside already. When Master Itonus appears, we'll be all the quicker."

The prisoners obeyed. Joining them, Harod pointed at the twin sets of bars across the floor. The bottom one on each side had two-inch high teeth while the upper ones had drilled holes for those teeth, plus indentations on the lower side. "Link those chains over the spikes."

After the prisoners had obeyed, he lowered the upper bars. Harod used a key to lock both sets of bars, then tested them.

"Once we're on our way, I'll get those unlocked."

The guard slipped out of the wagon. The prisoners shifted uncomfortably, the locked braces reminding them of the life they detested.

Trying not to worry, Faros leaned back and closed his eyes. As he did, though, he heard a sharp intake of breath.

"Paug's coming with two others!" Harod hissed.

Faros peered through a small rip in the wagon cover. Sure enough, the Butcher led a pair of grim, sword-wielding guards toward them, his thick brow furrowed in a manner that made him look even more piggish.

"Unload that wagon for inspection! Right now!"

"It's almost time to leave," insisted Harod, playing the loyal soldier. "My orders—"

"Your orders?" snapped the Butcher, cutting him off. He thrust his whip toward the insubordinate guard. "And what orders are those?"

One of the guards with Paug stepped up to the wagon. Glaring at the prisoners, he reached in and shook both sets of braces. With a grunt, he returned to Paug and announced, "They ain't goin' anywhere. They're locked good and tight."

Some in the wagon grew nervous, fearing that the plan had been abandoned and they were heading for the usual slave labor. With the guards no longer looking, they started tugging uselessly on their fetters

"The benches!" Faros whispered, recalling what the patriarch had told them. "There's supposed to be something underneath!"

Everyone began searching. Outside, Paug was haranguing Harod.

"So where is Kalius, your driver, eh? Funny thing, Harod. They just had a meeting with Kalius—the commander, her ladyship, and a nasty dark friend of hers—and he said some odd things! Talked about fake orders before he died. Talked about another guard, same clan as him and one of our newest workers."

Faros touched something on a ridge underneath his seat that at first felt like a bent nail. He pulled free a short, iron key.

"Hurry!" Ulthar stuck out his manacles, which Faros quickly opened. One of the prisoners on the other side located a second key and immediately set to work on his neighbor's chains.

Wrists and legs freed, Ulthar helped Faros with his own chains then directed the younger minotaur to assist Japfin.

Outside, Harod protested. "I don't know what you mean. My orders came directly from—"

"From the grand and glorious former patriarch of Droka, I'll wager! Funny thing about him, too, Harod. They found him lying in his bed after morning meal. Seems he crawled in there and just died. His eyes were bulged out, and he was sprawled on his cot like a doll. Almost looked like he couldn't breathe right, if you ask m—Look out!"

The prisoners froze—all save Ulthar, who, knife in hand, dove out of the back of the wagon. Seizing a loose pair of chains, Faros followed. As he landed, he saw Harod on his knees, Paug's hand squeezing tight on his throat. A dagger lay half-buried in the dust. Nearby, unnoticed by the Butcher, Ulthar had grabbed one guard from behind and was burying his rusting blade in his back.

The third guard grabbed at the mariner just as Ulthar's victim fell dead. Faros swung the chains, stunning the sentry and making him stumble past Ulthar.

Breathing rapidly, eyes red, Paug looked up as he released his hold on the limp Harod. Through his fiery haze, he saw Ulthar lunging for him.

Paug dodged away, only to feel a strong arm circle his neck and press against his throat.

"Planning to leave us?" snarled Japfin, who had come around from the front of the wagon. "You want to go so badly? Here! Let me help you on your way!"

"No!" Faros gasped. "We might need them." He turned to the guard he had stunned only to find that another prisoner had emerged to strangle the unfortunate sentry. His gaze returned to Paug.

Ulthar cocked his head. "You have an idea, Bek?"

"I . . . I think so. But we must be quick. Hide the bodies in the wagon!"

The others obeyed. Japfin eased up on Paug—slightly. The Butcher gasped for breath.

"I see it!" said Japfin. "This one might be able to help our wagon past the gates!"

"No escape—" gasped his captive. "Death? Aye—" He was cut off as Japfin squeezed against his windpipe.

"They must know about the wagon," said Faros. "When Paug doesn't come back . . ."

"Then *what*?" grunted Japfin.

"We need weapons. And more of us. It's our only hope. We've got keys. Let's free as many as possible, then use the fetters and manacles to overcome the guards and grab their axes and swords! Then, as soon as we have the armory open, we can get more."

Ulthar nodded his approval. "We do it."

Armed with daggers taken from the dead, two volunteers hurried toward the prisoners heading for the other wagons, their lack of chains going unnoticed. As they left, Faros had another idea. "Let's change clothes with the dead guards! From a distance, the sentries won't notice. We can head straight to the armory and open it up to the prisoners!"

Japfin snorted. "It'll work! They don't even look at our faces that much!" He glanced maliciously at Paug. "This one, too. We'll need all the garments we can get."

Paug struggled as they forced his clothing off. Ulthar made him put on the worn, faded kilt of a prisoner. He rubbed ash onto the Butcher's scowling visage. "No tricks now. Guards likely to stab you first before looking too closely at who's causing the commotion."

Because of his slim build, Faros could not pass for anything but a prisoner. He and the one other slave flanked Paug. Ulthar, Japfin, and the two remaining prisoners dressed as guards. Ulthar rubbed ash over his tattoos.

Japfin checked to see if the way remained clear, then the party abandoned the wagon. They walked slowly, almost trudging, to avoid drawing the attention of the sentries in the high towers. With few uprisings or successful escapes in its history, the soldiers of Vyrox had become somewhat set in their routines.

"Won't be long." Japfin hissed. "Somebody'll start something soon."

"Best to move fast, then," said Ulthar.

With Paug kept out of sight in the rear of the group, they headed to the gray windowless structure that served as the main armory. Two bored sentries wielding heavy axes attended the bolted iron door.

"No prisoners allowed within one hundred feet," commented the senior guard. "You should know that."

Paug trembled with frustration but said nothing.

"Orders from Krysus," Ulthar informed them, the mariner speaking precisely and timely to conceal his accent.

The young sentry looked over the mariner, then his eyes widened as he made out the tattoos under the ash. "You're not a—"

Ulthar lunged, his blade catching one warrior under the ribs before he could react. Japfin moved to grab the other sentry. Paug started forward, but Faros brought his dagger up to the Butcher's throat.

"Cry out and you die!" Ulthar warned the surviving guard, who dropped his axe. "Open the door!"

With haste, the guard obeyed. The moment he had done so, Ulthar struck him on the back of the head with the hilt of his sword. The guard dropped, sprawling on the ash-covered ground.

Faros's excitement grew. The way to the weapons was theirs. Truly luck was with them.

"What is this? What's going on here?"

Lady Maritia de-Droka and a sturdy, charcoal-colored minotaur stood a few yards away. Both carried packs.

"These prisoners shouldn't be allowed here!" Maritia said to Ulthar, not recognizing him at first. She then glanced past him and saw Paug. "You! What's—"

The Butcher tore himself free from his captors and cried, "They're prisoners! Look at their wrists!"

She looked and saw that, despite having removed their manacles, all the prisoners still bore abrasions from their confining grip.

The dark figure with Lady Maritia dropped his pack and pushed her behind him. With swift, practiced movements, he pulled his axe.

Paug dashed away. Lady Maritia turned and followed. Her bodyguard stood there threateningly for a moment, then whirled to follow his mistress.

"She's gone to warn the others!" Faros blurted.

"Aye, but does that matter? Get the weapons! Need as many armed as possible before the guards discover the truth!"

A horn sounded. Faros and the mariner glanced at one another. When the horn sounded again, it did so with obvious urgency.

The insurrection had begun in earnest.

The sentries attending the wagons were caught completely off-guard. The complacent prisoners turned into a savage pack. Many still chained swarmed over their captors, pummeling them with their fists, choking them with their thick manacles. Freed laborers took weapons from the dead.

A driver was torn from the seat of his wagon and thrown headfirst into the thick ash. Four enraged figures leaped on him, killing him and stripping him of all weapons and valuables.

An overseer with a whip tried to drive back a small group. He fended them off three times before one, risking the lash, seized the end of the whip. The overseer disappeared under their charge with a brief, piteous wail.

Some prisoners with foresight began to use the freed axes to smash away their remaining chains. With each passing second, more of Vyrox's slaves moved freely.

Faros armed himself. Gradic's son grabbed a sword from a

dead sentry. An axe he could have wielded better, but amidst such chaos a sword would be easier to handle.

Another horn sounded.

In the distance, a worker still struggling with his chains fell over, his back pierced by a well-aimed bolt. Seconds later, two more perished in a similar fashion. The counter-attack had begun.

Archers in the towers, on the walls, and on rooftops toiled with deadly accuracy, cutting down dozens of the prisoners, who could not hope to reach them with their hand weapons.

"We've got to stop this!" Faros called.

"I can use a bow well," a prisoner clad as a guard said. "At least, I used to. There must be some inside the armory."

"Go!" urged Ulthar. "Go!"

The minotaur nodded, vanishing into the weapon cache. A moment later, he emerged with a bow and a quiver of arrows. Several other freed prisoners rushed toward the armory.

Again a horn sounded, this time from the opposite direction.

"Grab whatever weapon you wield best!" Japfin shouted. "And bring something for the others! Hurry!"

"Bows!" Ulthar added. "To use against the archers!"

Faros eyed the towers. "Ulthar. maybe there's a way we can topple those towers. The wagons might do it!"

"Aye, they could! Japfin—"

But the black minotaur, having absorbed Faros's idea, had already dispatched some eager recruits to do just that.

More prisoners came running. Ulthar ordered several to stand guard, knowing that the armory was vulnerable.

Faros saw first one then a second archer on the outer walls plummet, transfixed by shafts. Shots now came regularly from below as more prisoners took up bows.

The ground was littered with blood-soaked bodies—guards but also many inmates. Scattered battles continued throughout the yard. A small band of soldiers in one corner fought a deadly swathe through the area.

"Krysus!" Faros yelled. "Ulthar! Japfin! We've got to find the commander!"

As they raced toward the officer's residence, other prisoners joined them. Krysus was the lord of Vyrox. He it was who let Paug beat the workers. Even though he kept mostly to his quarters, the commander was hated for the atrocities he tolerated.

"We need Krysus alive!" Faros shouted, hoping others would pass the word. They needed the commander as a bargaining chip.

Ulthar reached the officer's quarters first. As he leaped up, an axe nearly severed his head. A soldier lurking to the side swung his weapon in an arc. Ulthar blocked the second swing, but was caught momentarily offguard.

Faros tried to advance, but the sentry turned ferociously on him, nearly cutting him in the chest. The distraction enabled Ulthar to thrust, catching his foe in the side. The wound only slowed the guard. He fended off the mariner again until Ulthar caught him in a backswing, driving the point of his sword through the other's throat with such force that his writhing body was pinned against the wall.

With grim satisfaction, Ulthar let the guard's limp form slump to the ground. Turning his attention to the door, Ulthar kicked it open then charged inside. Faros and the others followed.

An empty room greeted their surprised eyes.

"He's gone!" snarled Japfin.

"Some time, too," Ulthar pointed out. "All neat. All orderly."

Before he could say more, one of the other prisoners barged in, eyes wide, breath heavy. "They're coming! They're coming!"

Faros's fur stiffened. "Who?"

The sounds of hoofbeats and the cries of prisoners filled the air. Above them all a harsh but authoritative voice could be heard shouting orders. A female voice.

Hotak's daughter had taken command of the defenders.

Chapter XXIII

The Protectors Unleashed

The coals glowed a brilliant orange, signaling perfect heat. In their center, the long iron brand flared bright.

Here, in an underground chamber in the Forerunner complex, the final initiation into the Protector ranks took place. Here, the First Master held court. Here he welcomed those who had passed the tests—those who had survived them.

The initiate knelt before the brazier, eyes straight ahead, ears erect. Sweat soaked his fur even where his mane had been shorn off. He had survived fire, water, depravation, and combat, and had sworn his allegiance to the order and to the high priestess's son. Now all that remained was to mark him as one of the guardians of the faithful.

"Beryn Es-Kalgor," rumbled Ardnor, reaching for the iron. Like the others, he wore only his kilts. In part, that had to do with practicality, for the chamber was stifling. However, those in attendance also wished to reveal to one another the sign of their brotherhood, the sign of their dedication: the axe symbol burned into their chests.

"Beryn Es-Kalgor, all tests of the body and mind have been passed. You have proven yourself worthy."

"I give thanks," returned the low voice of the initiate.

"You are welcomed into the fold." Ardnor approached Beryn with the burning iron. "Prepare now to receive my blessing."

He thrust the hot brand against the minotaur's chest.

Beryn did not move or breathe as the iron seared his flesh. His eyes stared impassively ahead. Ardnor watched him close. This was the last, ultimate test.

The vein in Beryn's neck throbbed furiously, but he uttered no sound. After a long moment, Ardnor withdrew the brand. Wisps of smoke danced about Beryn's chest. The blackened symbol of the axe stood revealed in all its terrible glory.

The First Master raised the brand for all to see, at the same time indicating that Beryn should stand and be recognized. The newly initiated Protector obeyed, with only a slight wobble of his strong legs. He stepped back into line, joining the other successful initiates.

Placing his fist over the axe symbol burned into his own chest, Ardnor began the closing litany. "The people are the life of the temple."

The initiates repeated his words in perfect unison.

"Keep a wary eye," Ardnor finished. "The day is coming."

They did not ask what day that might be. They never did. But when the First Master announced its arrival, told them what was required, all were prepared to sacrifice themselves.

Ardnor departed first, as always. The rest would wait a respectful interlude before exiting.

The lord of the order had almost reached his quarters when a robed acolyte came rushing down the corridor. The messenger fell down on one knee. "First Master, the High Priestess has been seeking your presence for some time! It is most urgent, I'm told!"

"Then get up, you fool!" he snapped at the underling. "Lead the way! Lead the way!"

He found his mother in her private chambers, her expression pensive. He felt her anger focused on him.

"You sent for me, Mother? Is it important?" Ardnor eyed the bottle of wine on her desk, but thought better than to reach for it.

"Important enough that you have already caused a dangerous delay!"

"I was detained by duty. I didn't expect any business at this hour of the morning."

"Well expect it when it is least expected from now on," Nephera said. The wall tapestries fluttered with her displeasure.

Noting his dumbstruck expression, she added triumphantly, "Rahm's been hiding in the workplace of one Master Zornal, a cooper of some repute, but clearly an enemy of the throne."

"But how did you—?" Ardnor clamped his mouth shut, going down on one knee. "Give the command, and I'll do what you desire."

"Attacks on two different parts of Mithas have forced your father to divide up his legions, leaving only a small contingent led by your brother to police the capital."

"Kol's a good soldier," Ardnor said grudgingly.

"But this task is above his . . . station." She took her son's muzzle in her hands and looked into his eyes. "The Protectors must act. Your father must understand. Rahm intends to assassinate your father, the emperor, in the palace itself!"

Ardnor rose, an expression of grim pleasure crossing his countenance. "Bastion will not like it that I'm involved."

"Your brother is away on other business. There is no choice but for you to take the reins and bring this enemy to justice."

He tipped his horns to the side in respect. "Then I go to serve my emperor . . . with your blessing, of course."

She kissed the top of his head. "Always, my son."

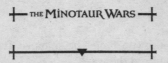

Maces at the ready, the black-helmed Protectors filled the streets. Grim, cloaked officers on horseback led each company. The dark army ignored the stares of onlookers.

At the head of the forbidding riders rode Lord Ardnor. His cloak, lined in gold thread, pulsated in the light wind. At the First Master's side hung a gilt-edged mace with a head resembling a tall, layered crown. The handle had been hollowed out in order to make better use of the solid iron head.

"Let no street or avenue from the northern sector be unattended!" he shouted as his followers spread out.

Citizens along the way stepped back hurriedly into their homes or businesses. What could draw the Protectors out in such force, none knew, but they sought no part of it. The old days when the temple of Sargonnas had ruled with an iron fist had been not very long ago, yet even the temple of Sargonnas had never produced a force as zealous or fanatic as the Protectors.

The heavy, persistent pounding on the door caused everyone to look up. Hes, the new overseer, rushed to see what was going on. As he reached for the handle, however, the door burst under the blows of two huge axes, and the cooperage filled with ebony-armored forms.

As the temple warriors fanned out, the helmed officer in charge demanded, "Where is the master of this establishment? Where is Master Zornal?"

"Right where he should be!" Rubbing his hands angrily, Zornal approached the intruder. "And wondering by what right you come smashing your way into a sanctioned crafthouse! My clan patriarch shall hear—"

The Protector smashed him across the muzzle with one gauntleted hand.

"He shall hear of your traitorous activities, barrelmaker. Harboring enemies of the throne and aiding in their attempt to assassinate his majesty." The officer turned to those warriors nearest to him. "Take him outside."

Several apprentices moved to aid the shocked and dazed Zornal. The cooper shook his head vehemently as he was dragged from his establishment.

Outside, Ardnor, still mounted, awaited. "So this is Master Zornal?"

"I am. The temple has no right to do this! You are usurping the power of the throne."

"I am the son of your emperor," the First Master reminded him. "I do my duty not only as his eldest, but also as a loyal servant of the empire."

"I, too, am a loyal servant of the throne."

"So loyal that you not only let two known fugitives hide within your workplace, but willingly aided them in covering up the death of your own cousin, Quas?"

As Ardnor uttered the dead minotaur's name, Zornal's expression changed. "I know nothing about any fugitives!"

"What about marked barrels?" Ardnor pointed to the street.

Zornal was forced to his knees. One of the Protectors removed a whip from his saddle then stood over the barrelmaker, waiting.

The First Master glared at his prisoner. "How long ago did the wagon leave? What route did it take? Who drives it?"

"There is nothing I can tell you."

Ardnor nodded. The whip tore into Zornal's back. The cooper grunted but did not confess. Ardnor signaled the officer to strike repeatedly. This time Zornal let out a short cry. The First Master leaned forward, waiting, but the prisoner remained stubborn.

"Again!"

This third time, Ardnor was rewarded with a cry of pain—but still no declaration of guilt.

Someone tugged tentatively on the First Master's arm. Ardnor turned his baleful gaze on the young fool. "You dare touch my person? If you think to defend your master, I'll—"

"Great Lord Ardnor, forgive me! My name is Egriv. I . . . I'm one of the faithful."

Ardnor had no time for fawning worshippers. "Be gone with you!"

"But master, I helped send off the wagons this morning!"

Now he had Ardnor's complete attention. The officer whipping Zornal paused, but an idle wave of Ardnor's hand returned him to his task. "Which way? How long ago? Who drives this wagon?"

Egriv was decidedly uncomfortable. "I don't know. There's five wagons, master! I don't know which one it might've been!"

"Do you know their destinations?"

This Egriv did—at least in part. One had headed toward the north gate, two others to the east, and one each had gone to the southern and southwestern parts of the capital. He listed two clans that had been mentioned in his presence.

Ardnor was furious. "It could be any one of those!" He considered further. "The assassins wouldn't go directly to the palace. They'd try a more roundabout trek. Aye, that's Rahm's sort of thinking."

"My lord?"

He turned back to the officer who had been whipping the barrelmaker. Master Zornal sprawled facedown on the stone street, his breath ragged, and his back a crimson maze.

"He finally confesses," the Protector informed Ardnor. "And verifies what this apprentice said."

"Did he add anything else of use?"

"Aye. The wagon we want will head to the west to pick up grain then turn south toward the palace. The barrels can be identified by the mark of a gryphon stamped on the top and sides."

Ardnor bared his teeth. "Clear a path! All riders to me!"

"What about this one?" the officer asked, indicating Zornal.

The First Master did not have to think long. "He's an enemy of the throne. You know what must be done."

The other Protector put away his whip and reached to get a sharp axe handed to him by one of his comrades.

Urging his mount forward, Ardnor roared. "Follow me!"

The black riders abandoned the cooperage, tearing through the streets. Only their lord shouted his eagerness. Ardnor already pictured his capture of the elusive Rahm and, after that, presentation to his father of the rebel's head on the end of a pike.

The wagon moved too slowly. Tovok, dressed like an apprentice, drove the wagon, following a route that would avoid regular patrols and guard stations. Captain Azak, too old to look like an apprentice, rode a short distance behind the wagon. Rahm, clad as a cooper, lounged in the back, his attitude casual.

Their route took them past smiths and glassblowers, the common houses, and then more stately villas. Everywhere markets abounded, crowds of minotaurs haggling for goods and services which slowed their progress. The delays frustrated Rahm.

At last, the general saw the palace coming into sight. Soon they would be at the back gate, used for deliveries to the kitchens. There would be guards there, but they would be relatively relaxed, never anticipating a plot as desperate as the one Rahm had hatched.

The cart jostled hard, shaking Rahm. He gripped the two barrels nearest him tightly, not wanting them to tip over. Their contents would aid his plan.

Near the base of the barrels, a two-foot long coil of string was carefully secured. The cord extended to a bunghole that had been plugged up with wood-colored clay. When lit, it would burn rapidly, igniting a small amount of explosive powder that would in turn ignite the oil that made up the contents of the three barrels.

The barrels would destroy the kitchens, killing many. The loss of innocent lives could not be helped. The explosions would distract from Rahm's true goal. During the chaos he would slip into one of the passages he knew, secreting himself until things had settled down. In the dark of night, when Hotak slept, Rahm would enter his chambers and repay him for what he had done to Chot.

Chot . . . and Mogra and Dorn.

Of course, Rahm expected to die. Tovok and the captain, though, would flee as best as possible after lighting the fuse. They would wait at a designated location for two days, then, if he did not show up, they would rendezvous with *Dragon's Crest*. The ship would not wait for any latecomers.

Closing his eyes, the general touched the dagger hidden beneath his apron, thinking of the blood it would soon spill—Hotak, Nephera, and if he could accomplish it, also the two sons Ardnor and Bastion. Of Hotak's children, those two were the most dangerous.

The wagon jerked, causing the contents in the back to jostle so harshly that Rahm had to struggle to keep from being crushed. His ring finger twinged. The general peered through a crack between the wooden planks near the rear, seeking a reason for the disruption.

In the crowds behind them, an ebony wedge pushed toward the wagon. Minotaurs hurried out of the way as armored figures swinging maces struggled to catch up with the wagon.

The Protectors had discovered him.

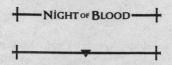
"When everything is settled, you must depart, Golgren. Out of sight, out of mind, you see. It'll take the people a little time to reconcile themselves to our agreement."

Golgren made no reply, but studied the contents of his cup. The ogre had a propensity for strong drink that rivaled any of Hotak's own people, yet Golgren never seemed to lose control of his faculties.

Hotak raised his goblet—only to be interrupted by an anxious officer barging into the chamber.

"Forgive me, my lord, but I have news!"

Hotak winced and glanced at Golgren. "Excuse me, emissary. Once again, a matter of state."

The ogre poured himself more wine.

Hotak stepped out into the hall then whirled on the messenger. "What news is of such import that you dare interrupt my meeting?"

"My lord, I was ordered to interrupt. The Protectors are loose in the city!"

His mate and son flashed in Hotak's mind. He frowned. "My son is leading them?"

"So it seems. They've already broken into the establishment of one Master Zornal, a cooper." The officer explained everything in detail, not only the cooper's supposed crime, but the punishment he had received for it.

"The fool!" Hotak roared. "Zornal should've been put into custody so that we could render proper judgment. His clan would've understood that. They will never accept a summary execution!" The emperor's eyes blazed. "Where is my son now?"

"In pursuit of the wagon. They were headed in the direction of the northern gate."

"Order the State Guard out. Get them after Ardnor and his band of fanatics before there's blood on the streets."

The officer saluted. "Aye, my lord! And General Rahm?"

Hotak fixed his good eye on the warrior. "Run him down, of course! Make certain that the guard commanders know that I want them, not the Protectors, to have the honor of capturing Rahm Es-Hestos. Go!"

The minotaur hesitated. "What if the Protectors resist? What if they disobey the Guard? Matters have always been bad between them. . . ."

"Use whatever force short of bloodshed—and use a bit of that, too, if need be. Leave my son alone, of course, but I want the Protectors off the streets."

The officer departed in haste. Hotak watched him go, aware that Ardnor was acting on behalf of the temple and Nephera. The people might misunderstand. He suddenly realized that he might have made a mistake dispatching the State Guard to deal with the matter. The throne had to take a hand in the matter.

"Find my son Kolot!" Hotak shouted toward a sentry. Golgren waited for him, but the emperor had no time for the ogre now. Ardnor's recklessness had to be stopped.

Moments later, the hulking warrior joined him in the corridor. "You sent for me, Father?"

Hotak told Kolot the situation, emphasizing that the Protectors had overstepped their bounds. "Make your brother understand. Your presence will lessen any shame for him when he's forced to stand down. Tell him this is my command."

Kolot straightened. "You can rely on me, Father."

"And Kolot, bring me Rahm's horns. You hear me?"

"It shall be done!"

Snorting in frustration, Hotak turned to the sentry and commanded, "Now go to the temple and inform the Lady Nephera that I wish to see her. Immediately. Tell her I will await her in our quarters. She's to come without fail. Do you understand?"

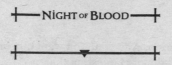

He sat waiting for her, hands steepled, good eye staring directly at the door. It occurred to Nephera as she entered that Hotak had slain Chot here. There were still stubborn traces of blood on the floor.

"What were you thinking, my dear, sending your Protectors into the streets?" the emperor calmly asked the moment they were alone. "I'm curious."

"I was thinking of the empire's future. I was thinking about us, and of our eldest son, who shall be lord of the realm after you."

"You couldn't wait long enough to discuss it with me?"

Nephera faced him, her manner befitting the mistress of the temple. He was speaking freely. Well, so would she. "How many times have your soldiers failed to catch Rahm? Who was it who finally dealt with Tiribus? How did we gather the intelligence necessary for you to make such a decisive strike against Chot on the Night of Blood? Who keeps an eye on those who might harm you?" She loomed over Hotak. "The temple has done much for you, my love."

"I'm aware of all you say, Nephera, but our history is against your religion being so closely involved with matters of state. I cannot permit even the temple that claims my mate as its high priestess to look as though it dictates law and new traditions."

She glared. "Am I to cease giving you counsel?"

"No. But this incident goes beyond counsel."

"Rahm is intent on assassinating you, husband!" Nephera said. "He planned on slitting our throats while we slept."

"You want Ardnor to capture Rahm, so *he* can be hailed as a hero."

"You are in danger!"

"Pfah! Not from Rahm. It seems I am in more danger from

my son's ambition. And you! You want him on the throne so badly! More and more I question that. . . ."

Lady Nephera drew back in shock. "He must be able to show others he is worthy! How better to do that than by this noble service?"

"Do you know what he did with one of the conspirators?" With a distasteful expression, he told her of Ardnor's actions against the cooper.

She was unmoved. "Zornal was a traitor. Ardnor acted accordingly. Should we expect anything less from our own son?"

Hotak turned to the balcony. "I've been forced to rectify the situation. The State Guard has been sent out to control the damage and turn back your followers, Nephera."

"You'll shame our son. In public! Your heir!"

"I've sent the Imperial Guard led by Kolot to meet with Ardnor. One brother aiding another will seem quite appropriate. I wish it could've been Bastion, but he's away on important business." The scarred emperor shook his head. "I sometimes wish it were Bastion who stood first in my shadow."

Paying his last words no mind, Nephera spoke sharply. "You must do something to keep Ardnor from being humiliated. There will be those who recall this episode when you name him your successor."

"You should have thought of that before you set him loose, my dear." He looked over his shoulder at her. "Go back to the temple now. I'll keep you abreast of matters. And I'll expect you to do the same, from now on."

Wise enough to pick her battles, Nephera bowed slightly and backed away. She had nearly reached the door when the emperor called her back. "Nephera, my love, you'd best pray that Ardnor redeems himself and captures Rahm. Pray very hard."

CHAPTER XXIV

VYROX IN CHAOS

Maritia and the commander of Vyrox rallied their forces—roughly a hundred foot soldiers and two dozen on horseback, most of the latter from Maritia's party. Krysus had the reins strapped to his maimed limb. In his hand he wielded a mace.

"You don't need to kill 'em all," Paug insisted. "Just the worst troublemakers. The rest'll mill around like lambs, then."

"You know which ones?"

"Aye! A black giant named Japfin, a huge barbarian covered in tattoos called Ulthar, and a sneaky little one called Bek! Take them out, and you've got the rest on the run."

Maritia nodded and turned in the saddle to face her troops. "Keep your ranks intact! Don't be drawn out! Mounted fighters first, followed by the rest!"

The soldiers listened. They knew the odds were against them but would follow her to the end.

"All right, then!" Maritia shouted, intentionally imitating her father. "We fight for the empire!"

With a roar, they charged.

From the walls and towers, archers continued to plague the rioters, but they themselves had suffered losses. One tower was empty. Some enterprising prisoners had tied ropes to another tower and were using one of the wagon teams to pull it down.

The prisoners began to torch various structures. The fires spread randomly, igniting the barracks.

Maritia's riders plowed through the first line of rioters. Inmates screamed as sharp blades sank into them. Bodies fell in twisted piles. Blood splattered everyone.

A ragged prisoner exchanged blows with Maritia then fell back as the foot soldiers swarmed. Stunned by the appearance of an organized force, the prisoners retreated.

But then a black giant rose among them—Japfin armed with a huge axe. He swung the weapon in a shrieking arc. Roaring orders to those nearest, he pushed them back into the fight. Urged on by Japfin, many prisoners stood their ground and began to force the mounted soldiers back.

The camp had become an inferno. The fires spread unchecked in every direction. Some of the prisoners abandoned the struggle and sought to climb their way to safety over the burning walls. Arrows stopped them.

The mass of prisoners finally gave way to Maritia's steed. Emboldened by her push forward, some of the other riders swung closer to her, helping to create a wedge. Closer and closer she fought her way to Japfin.

A shaggy figure darting in upon her from her left almost pulled her from the saddle. His jagged nails gouged into her leg, ripping flesh and drawing blood. Using the pommel of her sword, Maritia beat his hands off, then swung at him. He fell back into the wild throng.

As she turned from him, Maritia found herself staring into the raging eyes of Japfin. He snorted furiously and charged toward her, pushing aside prisoners and soldiers alike.

Holis stepped between them. The two dark-furred combatants threw themselves at one another. Axe struck axe with a tremendous storm, throwing sparks into the air. Maritia tried to reach the two, but the enemy line solidified to block her.

Japfin caught Maritia's bodyguard in the side. Holis cried out as the axe bit him deeply, his lifeblood spilling out. He dropped his weapon and clutched the open wound but could do little to stem the flow.

Japfin hit him again and again.

Badly wounded, Holis slid off the right side of the saddle, landing amidst chaos. Prisoners swarmed over him, ripping with their bare hands. He cried out once then vanished beneath them.

With a roar, Maritia saw an opening and urged her mount toward Japfin. The trained animal kicked at those in the way.

Japfin waved his weapon in mock greeting. "Come closer, pretty one!" he roared. "Come taste the kiss of my axe!"

Her horse reared. Japfin sidestepped the animal's assault, but as he did, Maritia swung, her sword cutting a shallow wound on his forearm. He laughed it off, swinging the axe still wet with Holis's blood.

Maritia deflected a second strike then thrust. The tip of the blade fell just short of Japfin's jugular. He laughed again then attacked with more fervor. She twisted away, but Japfin's axe struck her horse.

The stallion shrieked as the blade sank deep into its neck. Blood splashed its mane as the animal dropped to its knees. Disoriented, Maritia tumbled to the ground, trying to hold onto her sword.

A shadow loomed over her—Japfin, come to finish her. He raised his blood-slick axe high.

The mace struck him hard in his wounded arm. Japfin roared and dropped his axe. He spun and came face to face with Krysus, preparing a second strike. As the commander lunged at him, Japfin, ignoring the pain in his blood-drenched arm, reached out and seized the mace.

Krysus struggled, but Japfin tore the mace free and pulled the officer from the saddle.

"Everyone sent to Vyrox dies, commander!" he roared. "Your turn!"

Japfin struck the officer in the throat with his own mace. The crack of bone could be heard several feet away. His larynx crushed, the commander slumped in Japfin's arms. The black minotaur gave him a cursory shake then tossed Krysus's body aside like so much refuse and turned his gaze back to Maritia.

"You're definitely a pretty one," the giant rumbled as he neared. He hefted the mace with a practiced hand. "Maybe if you're real nice, I'll save your hide from these others."

"I promise to be very nice," she retorted, spitting blood from her mouth. "I'll give you a quick, clean death—unless you would prefer to surrender."

He laughed then tried to take off her head with the mace. Maritia ducked, jabbed unsuccessfully at her foe, then rolled away as the mace came around again.

"You dance well, my lady!" Japfin jeered.

She did not respond. Instead she rolled toward him, surprising him and coming under his guard. Her roll ended in a kneeling position from which she thrust her blade into Japfin's chest just below the ribs. He let out a cry of pain and shock.

"I'll cut ... you . . . to little . . . pieces!" he gasped.

Eyes flooded with crimson, nostrils flaring, he brought the mace up as high as he could and put his full weight into one final swing.

Maritia threw herself forward. Her blade buried itself deep in Japfin's stomach.

Japfin tumbled backward. The weapon fell from his grasp, striking the ashy ground an instant before he also fell, dead.

A thick cloud of dust rose. Coughing, Maritia prodded the massive form with the tip of her blade, but Japfin did not stir.

"One down," she muttered. Her gaze shifted to survey the rest of the battlefield, where desperate figures on both sides fought with all the energy they had left. "One down, too many left."

While a few prisoners had made it over the walls, the gates remained barred and protected.

Staring at the wagons, Faros hit upon another idea. He forced his way toward Ulthar and called out the mariner's name.

Ulthar retreated to his friend. Blood drenched the mariner from head to foot.

Gasping for air, the brawny figure muttered, "What?"

"The wagons! Maybe we can drive them through to the gates. You and I might be able to open the way for the rest!"

"The battle is not over yet! Too many guards still live!"

"But what about escape? Now would be the best time."

Ulthar shook his head. "If we flee now, the guards will regroup and follow. We cannot leave until all are dead!"

"Ulthar—"

"Vyrox owes us, Bek," he returned, his eyes half-red from growing bloodlust. His breath continued to come in gasps. "Vyrox killed many, many of us. Now we must kill Vyrox."

With a snarl of contempt, the mariner turned his back on the younger prisoner and headed back into battle.

Faros stared after Ulthar. A small part of him screamed that he should try to escape on his own, but he fought the shameful feeling down. Surely Ulthar had the right of it. The fight would end soon. The soldiers, outnumbered from the start, had expended themselves. Vyrox already belonged to its inmates. All that mattered now was finishing the task.

Gripping his sword tight and taking a deep breath, Faros raced after his comrade. Ulthar fought like a demon, and for the first time all the tales he had spun of doing battle with sea monsters and pirates seemed to be truth. If he survived, Ulthar would surely add a new tattoo to his garish collection.

Smoke shrouded everything. The gates disappeared, and the combatants became half-seen ghosts. Whether or not the prisoners triumphed, they certainly had destroyed the mining camp. There would be little left but stone walls surrounding a blackened interior.

Faros battled, hoping only to survive until he could spot a way to freedom. Again and again his blade met the weapons of ghostly enemies in an endless clash of metal against metal that left his brain and arm numb.

An enemy who was not a ghost burst through the ranks to confront him. He held a mammoth, blood-stained war axe in one hand.

"You!" Paug rumbled. Once more he wore the kilt of a guard. "Been looking for you and your friends. I wanted the barbarian first, but you'll do for a nice warm-up before I take his head."

The axe came at Faros with horrible swiftness, biting into the ground inches from him and sending up a cloud of ash. The area around the pair seemed to empty out, as though no one cared to be too close to the Butcher and his prey.

Faros managed to deflect the first few blows, but where his strength flagged, Paug's was undiminished.

The Butcher laughed. "Is that all? Might as well stand still now. I'll make it nice and quick, I promise you!"

Once more he brought the axe down, this time nearly cleaving the arm of his smaller foe. Stumbling out of the axe's path, Faros fell back.

"Pfah! It's like fightin' a child! Might as well offer your neck now! I'll only cut you up into three or four little pieces!"

Still teetering, Faros took a reckless lunge and came up short. Worse, he lost his footing. He tumbled forward, his snout burying itself in the smothering ash.

A heavy foot nearly crushed his sword hand, causing Faros to cry out. He tried to pull free.

"Let go!" Paug shouted. After Faros had obeyed, the overseer pressed down even harder. Pain wracked Faros.

"I'm going to deliver you to the lady," the Butcher mocked. "Your arms, your legs, then your ugly head as the big prize."

At that moment, a wave of other struggling fighters swept into the pair. Paug cursed as a falling body pushed him to the side.

Faros struggled to keep from being trampled to death. He rolled away, only to be kicked in the stomach by a soldier who jumped over him to get to another foe. Managing to catch his breath, Faros got to his knees.

A hand seized him. He struggled—

"Nay, friend Bek! 'Tis only I!"

Ulthar helped Faros to his feet then handed him his sword.

"I'm all right," Faros said. He looked around, but of Paug he saw no sign.

Ulthar grinned. " 'Tis almost won, Bek! Their numbers shrink! The imperial cow still fights, but she's tiring! What a mate she would've made! Pity she'll die with the rest, eh?"

"We did it?" It was too hard for Faros to believe.

"See for yourself! They are lost!"

A wind had blown away some of the smoke, enabling Faros to see clearly. Wherever he did, he saw that Ulthar spoke the truth. The manic fighting had died down into little desperate groups. None of the mounted escort remained—at least not on horseback—and those walls and roofs not aflame were swept of archers.

Indeed, it seemed they had won. The last vestiges of the

foul penal camp seemed either ablaze or in the process of being ransacked.

It was the end of Vyrox.

Then a horn blared far beyond the camp walls—a horn immediately answered by another from within.

Most of the remaining combatants did not notice at first. Only when a third blast echoed throughout the camp did the noise finally alert the prisoners.

"What is it?" Faros asked, ears taut.

Ulthar's gaze shifted to the main gate. Two guards were trying to unbolt the entrance.

Again a horn sounded, this time from just beyond the walls.

"Reinforcements from the females' camp?"

"I doubt it," said Ulthar, who started toward the gate. "Couldn't afford to leave them alone. Prisoners there'd riot, too."

"Who, then?"

The gates swung open, and a column of armed riders, the black warhorse banner held high, burst through the entrance. Their loud cries and shrill horn sent chills through Faros.

From out of nowhere, a contingent of Emperor Hotak's own legion had arrived.

Chapter XXV

Blood Chase

"Out of the way!" Ardnor roared, nearly trampling an elderly female crossing the street. "Move or be run down!"

Zornal had not misled them. They had sighted the wagon just as it turned toward the palace. Somehow, though, the driver had managed to lead them on a zigzagging chase through every side street of the northern quarter. The Protectors had lost, found, lost, and found their prey repeatedly. Now they spotted it heading toward the northern gates.

People scattered as they roared past. Wagons toppled over, shattering their contents, spilling wheat and barley everywhere. Still the rebels' vehicle kept ahead of its pursuers.

Ahead, a bottleneck of wagons waited for soldiers to inspect them before they left the city—a security measure put in place by Bastion. The First Master looked around but could not spot the one he believed to be carrying Rahm and his confederates.

The officer in charge looked up from inspecting a sack of walnuts as the Protectors hove into sight. For a moment, he seemed tempted to draw his weapon, but instead abandoned the cart he had been investigating and stepped up to meet the newcomers, "I am Captain Dwarkyn! Explain this!"

The Protectors bristled. Ardnor leaned forward, crimson-tinged eyes narrowed dangerously. "Is it possible that you don't recognize the eldest son of your emperor?"

Dwarkyn frowned, but held his ground. "I've had no word of your coming, my Lord Ardnor. Forgive me. What brings you and—" he surveyed the rest of the Protectors with thinly concealed distrust— "these others to the gates at such a hectic time? Had we known, I would have arranged a formal—"

"Be still!" interrupted the First Master. "We have reason to believe that one of these wagons bears enemies of the state seeking to assassinate the emperor."

"I've heard none of this!" Dwarkyn looked at another guard, who shook his head. "But if such is true, you can rely on us." His eyes narrowed. "There's really no need for the temple to assist—"

"These enemies have escaped your State Guard more than once. It's time for more thorough measures. Step aside! My brethren will search these wagons now."

"My Lord Ardnor, I must protest—"

The First Master glared at him until the officer clamped his muzzle shut. "Then go make your protest and leave us to our work, Captain Dwarkyn."

The latter backed away, signaling his soldiers to follow. They stood to the side, wary but unwilling to interfere with the emperor's son.

All the wagons looked maddeningly alike. Ardnor's followers began to search with ruthless determination. They tore off protective tarps, threw out materials in their way, and smashed apart barrels. Though within minutes the contents of several wagons lay strewn over the area, no sign of Rahm was uncovered.

"Stop!" Ardnor commanded, frustrated by the obvious failure. "They have eluded us! Pryas, make sure that—"

An explosion rocked the right side of the gate.

Fragments of the high stone archway dropped upon the clustered wagons. One Protector was thrown back against the wall. Shouts rose as dust and masonry rained down on everyone. One of the gates swung open with a long groan, nearly ripping off its iron hinges. Burning oil splattered several wagons, creating scattered fires that further panicked the animals.

Through stinging eyes, Ardnor saw a short, brawny figure leap on one of his riders, knocking the startled Protector from the saddle. Nearby, a younger minotaur abandoned his wagon for a horse brought to him by an older fighter already mounted.

"Mount up! Mount up!" cried the First Master.

It was pandemonium among the wagons and horses. Pushing past the melee, the first of the Protectors reached the battered archway.

That was when a second explosion went off, followed immediately by a third, even more powerful.

The force of the blasts scattered everyone and sent fiery oil raining down upon the ground. Horses screamed, and bodies dotted the area. The broken gate tore free, collapsing on a pair of Protectors. On the wall above, sentries scurried to abandon their posts as the arch collapsed.

Ignoring the carnage at the gate, Ardnor led the remaining Protectors out. Ahead, General Rahm and his compatriots raced along the road. The landscape beyond the gate was flat, grassy, and thinly populated, but shortly beyond, thick wooded hills beckoned.

Led by Ardnor, the Protectors' powerful steeds slowly cut the gap. They entered a small, outlying settlement, racing through it with abandon and scattering all in their path.

Tents were flattened. Wares flew. At least one rider was thrown from his horse and left behind.

The village vanished behind the pursuit, the landscape giving way to groves of black oak, cedar, and birch. General Rahm turned the trio east, taking a fork. Dust rose behind the fleeing renegades.

Rahm had taken a short cut to the first of the hills. The First Master quickly surveyed the area ahead and spotted another side route winding up toward their quarry. "Pryas, take some of the others and ride up that way! Ride hard! Cut them off!"

The other riders split off as Ardnor watched Rahm and his companions urge their mounts up the trail. Rahm had committed himself to a path that led in only the one direction, where Pryas would be waiting. The great general had finally outfoxed himself. The renegades were trapped from above and below.

Suddenly Rahm and one of his companions veered their horses into the thickening woods, a place of brambles and untrustworthy footing. The remaining rider reached for the axe harnessed at his back and urged his horse ahead to confront Pryas's group. Ardnor ignored the suicidal fool and spurred his followers ahead after Rahm and the older minotaur.

The two fugitives vanished in the woods. Ardnor tried to judge the best path. Around him, the Protectors battled their way through clinging, low-slung branches, narrow passes between trunks, and sudden gullies hidden by old brush. One horse stepped wrong, sending both it and its rider crashing against a huge trunk.

The Protectors gradually spread out, creating a jagged line of silent, resolute riders. Above the search, large, angry black birds cawed their complaints, but otherwise the forest was eerily quiet.

A horse emerged from ahead, a riderless horse recognized by the small axe brand at its flank as the one ridden by the general. Ardnor signaled for a halt as the animal approached. Taking to foot, his foe would be limited as to the distance they could cover but better able to maneuver and hide.

"So, you play the cowering rabbit," Ardnor mused quietly. "I'll still find you." He rose in the saddle in order to direct the others.

Somewhere far to his left, one of his followers let out a muffled, short-lived cry.

There was a brief clash of arms, raucous sounds that sent the black birds fluttering into the skies, their complaints renewed more violently.

"There he is!" someone shouted.

The Protectors split up, some turning toward the second cry.

Ardnor led one party. They found the prone figure of a blood-splattered Protector. A blade had left a great, moist gap in the dead fighter's throat. Off in the distance his horse stood waiting. Ardnor started to order someone to regain the beast, then hesitated as all heard the clash of arms from another direction.

"Don't let him get away this time!" the chief Protector roared, twisting on the reins. "Catch him!"

As they neared the struggle, he made out two Protectors battling an obscure figure. One of the Protectors had dismounted; the other was maneuvering on horseback. Maces clashed against a short, sturdy axe. Their adversary kept backing away, using the trees for interference.

Ardnor raised his mace and rode in, letting loose with a wild shout.

The half-glimpsed figure turned at the cry just as Ardnor struck hard with the solid, five-pound head of his weapon.

His opponent deflected the blow upward. The mace smashed him on the temple. Ardnor heard bone crack even as he was swept past by his horse's momentum.

Approaching the body sprawled on the ground, the First Master frowned. Ardnor knew what Rahm looked like, and this dead minotaur did not match his description. The general had been short but muscular—and not so gray-furred.

Leaping down, he bent to study the battered features. The wrinkled snout and and weathered face could never be mistaken for the general's.

"It must be the sea captain, Azak, my lord," one of his followers offered. "He matches the description given us."

"Do I care who it is?" Ardnor raged. "It isn't Rahm!"

As he shouted, a band of riders approached from the road. Expecting Pryas, the First Master turned, only to be confronted by a contingent of the Imperial Guard—and, worse, his brother Kolot.

His eyes blazed. "What do you think you're doing here?"

Kolot looked defiant. "I have orders from Father. You're to leave this problem in our hands. The Protectors are to return to the temple immediately."

"I will not!" Pryas and the remaining Protectors rode up. Ignoring Kolot, Ardnor asked his second, "What happened to the third fugitive?"

"He refused to surrender. We were forced to slay him."

"Take everyone and scour the woods to the north of here. Rahm must have escaped. He can't run that fast. Hunt him down."

"Ardnor!" Kolot shouted, this time making certain that not only would his sibling hear him, but everyone else, too. "You must put an end to this! By Father's orders—"

"Damn Father!"

Kolot leaned toward him. "Ardnor, stop this disobedience. There's already been too much damage because of the Protectors' interference! The northern gates are in ruins. They're still trying to put out the fires there. We've—"

"Be quiet!"

Kolot threw himself off his saddle—mere moments before his brother's mace would have struck him in the chest. Kolot's soldiers drew their weapons. In turn, the Protectors, just about to depart, swerved around to shield their master.

"My horse!" commanded Ardnor as though nothing had happened. Mounting, he glanced contemptuously at his sibling. "Go back to Father, Kol. We'll finish this task without you. Understand?"

But Kolot got back on his horse and followed after his brother. After a wary hesitation, the soldiers and Protectors followed after the pair.

The two brothers surged ahead of the rest, riding deep into the thick brush. Kolot rode alongside Ardnor now, continuing to insist that his elder brother listen to reason.

"You'll get Father in a rage! He's already having to deal with protests from some of the patriarchs!"

"Then he can do with those whining fools what he did with old Itonus! He's emperor, brat! He can do whatever he wants!"

"You know it's not that simple!"

Ardnor reined his mount to a halt. He turned on Kolot, fighting the impulse to strike his brother again. "By our ancestors! How were we ever born of the same mother? Go back to the palace, Kol! I'll bring back the general in chains to Father! I'll prove to him—to all of you—that I'm worthy to follow him to the throne!"

Kolot snorted. "That's all this means to you. You don't care how this looks for our father. All you want is to gain—" His attention shifted upward. "Look out!"

Kolot leaped at him, shoving Ardnor off his horse.

Ardnor struck the uneven ground hard, the wind and most of his sense knocked from him. He tried to rise but was too groggy.

Trying to focus, Ardnor spied two figures in combat, one of them his insipid sibling. The other his drifting mind eventually identified as General Rahm Es-Hestos.

On foot now, Kolot and the renegade commander traded blows. Kolot had long reach and great strength, but Rahm moved more nimbly than his bulkier foe, ducking Kolot's axe and diving in with his blade.

Ardnor tried to rise, but some incredible force held sway over him, and the only movement he managed was ludicrously sluggish.

Just yards away, Kolot brought his axe around, trying to catch the general in the side. Rahm rolled back, landing in a crouching position, and instead the axe buried itself deep in a tree trunk.

Leaping forward, the general tried for Kolot's stomach, but Ardnor's brother deflected the blade with the axe's handle, receiving instead a shallow wound in the shoulder.

"This isn't between us," growled General Rahm. "Surrender and Father might spare you! He admired you once!"

"As I did him. But we're long past that."

Kolot's face took on a savageness. He charged. Again and again, his axe came at Rahm in deadly, shifting arcs, pressing the general back. Rahm tried to defend himself but slipped down on one knee. Seizing his advantage, the larger minotaur raised his weapon.

Then Rahm did something completely surprising. Lowering his sword, the general held up his empty fist so that the black-gemmed ring he wore was aimed at Kolot.

The gem flared.

The light blazed bright in the minotaur's eyes. Kolot let out a gasp and tried to shield his face while at the same time swinging his axe.

General Rahm thrust his blade into Kolot's throat.

Ardnor's brother stumbled back, the dripping blade sliding free. A stream of red poured from the wound, spilling over his breastplate. Kolot dropped his axe, his hands twitching madly.

General Rahm thrust again, stabbing his adversary in the same place.

With a slight grunt, Kolot crumpled to his knees. He stared at his foe—then dropped to the ground.

Ardnor finally managed a shocked grunt, which only served to remind Rahm of his presence. Still trying to rise, Ardnor stared into the calm face of his brother's killer.

General Rahm took a step toward him before shouts in the distance made the renegade glance to the west. Turning from Ardnor, Rahm seized the reins of Kolot's horse and leaped into the saddle. Kicking hard, he urged the animal into the woods.

The First Master reached one futile hand toward the fleeing fugitive, but the general vanished among the trees.

Seconds later, a force consisting both of Protectors and soldiers arrived. All looked stunned by what they beheld.

"What're you . . . waiting for?" snarled Ardnor, pointing east. "Go find him!"

"But First Master," one of his own blurted. "Your brother—"

"Go after him, you fools!"

Pryas and one other Protector stayed behind to assist Ardnor. A Guard officer dismounted and went to Kolot's side.

At last able to stand, Ardnor stared at the soldiers. "Well? Why are you standing around? We might still catch Rahm!"

With a hint of distaste, the officer remarked, "Should not some of us stay behind to guard Lord Kolot's body?"

"Of course, of course! You deal with it, then!" Feeling more himself, Ardnor mounted his horse. Without a second glance at his brother, he started off after the others.

The officer watched the First Master vanish into the woods. He snorted derisively.

"Prepare a proper framework," he commanded, removing his cape and laying it over the body. "At least we will see to it that our lord is brought back to his father with full honors." His eyes flickered to where Kolot's brother had vanished. "Which is more than some others deserve."

CHAPTER XXVI

CATASTROPHE

The mounted column charged into Vyrox. Their numbers spread out in perfect order. At their head, a tall, slender, black-furred figure pointed his axe at the prisoners.

"Form ranks!" Ulthar shouted. "Our numbers are strong!"

The prisoners obeyed, creating ragged lines facing the newcomers. Others sought to fend off the remaining guards and soldiers led by Lady Maritia, who fought with renewed confidence.

The first of the new riders collided with the lines. Minotaurs again screamed as battle-axes and swords dealt death. The struggle turned against the prisoners.

One inmate, his shoulder ripped open, dropped to his knees and was trampled by a pair of massive warhorses. Axes wielded with veteran expertise made short work of two other prisoners. Another worker who dropped on his knees to surrender was skewered through the throat by a zealous rider.

Shouts arose behind Faros. Maritia and her small host pressed close, pushing the back ranks into those trying to hold off the mounted onslaught. A badly wounded prisoner collapsed into Faros's arms. As he tried to pull the inmate to safety, a camp guard darted near and ran Faros's charge through the chest.

Furious, Faros exchanged blows with the guard and managed to cut him deep on the arm. The sentry lost his sword, but Faros hesitated a second too long, giving the other a chance to flee.

Faros pushed forward, trying to catch up with the sentry— and instead nearly collided with a minotaur he had hoped never to see again.

Paug.

The overseer's grotesque visage brightened as he saw who stood before him. With a loud bellow, the Butcher attacked. The smaller minotaur darted back, barely missing being cleaved in two. Paug's weapon buried itself deep in the dusty soil, sending a spray of stinging ash into Faros's face. His eyes tearing, Faros retreated further, trying to recoup.

"Hold stil, vermin," the overseer rumbled. "Time to die!"

He swung at Faros's unprotected chest. Another axe met his with a resounding crash. Ulthar glared at the sadistic guard, snorting his disdain.

"Yes," he growled back at the Butcher. "Time to die."

Ulthar elbowed Faros aside. He and Paug traded swift, numbing blows without success. The mariner could not get past Paug's guard, but neither could the overseer break through Ulthar's skilled defenses. They battered away at each other, seeking some opening, some fatal mistake.

Faros would have come to Ulthar's aid, but just then a mounted soldier broke past the line, nearly running him down. Faros rolled to the side, but the rider quickly steered his horse around for a second try at him.

This time, the soldier also swung at Faros with his axe. Faros tried to deflect the blow, but only partially succeeded.

The tip caught the side of his muzzle and cut into the flesh, making Faros bite down to keep from crying out. Trying to ignore the taste of his own blood, he looked around for his adversary. The mounted fighter had wheeled again.

The soldier swung low. Faros flopped on his back. Taken by surprise, the rider missed by a wide mark. As his adversary rode past, Faros jabbed at his horse's rear leg. The animal stumbled and lost its footing.

The rider leaped, barely escaping being crushed. Faros charged him and, gripping his sword with two hands, ran the gaping soldier through the abdomen.

Ulthar and Paug still dueled. Ash drifted all about. Both fighters breathed heavily, and their eyes blazed red. Sparks flew whenever the heads of their two axes collided. They had shifted away from the rest of the struggle. Only the dead gave the pair any company, and neither paid the littered corpses any mind.

Paug slipped. He fell down on one knee, teeth bared. Ulthar battered him harder, at last breaking through and cutting the Butcher on his arm. Paug swung wildly.

Confident, Ulthar moved in. He had the Butcher where he wanted him; all that mattered now was to make a quick end of it.

A slight movement to the side of Ulthar caught Faros's attention. To his horror, he saw a bloody, ash-covered soldier push himself up from the dead and reach for a sword.

"Ulthar!" Faros shouted. "To your right!"

The battle drowned him out. He started to run toward Ulthar—only to have a pitched struggle between a soldier and a prisoner suddenly materialize to block his path.

Once more he shouted. "Your right, Ulthar! Look out!"

Ulthar's eyes narrowed, and he swerved to the side.

The soldier's blade sailed harmlessly past Ulthar's twisting form. At the same time, the tattooed prisoner's axe bit solidly into the attacking minotaur's chest, sinking deep. The soldier crumpled, his weapon dropping. That was when Paug leaped.

Ulthar had no time to defend himself. Paug's strike tore at his mid-section, ripping apart his stomach.

Ulthar staggered back, tripping over a body. He fell and landed in a limp heap. Blood pooled around his body.

Stepping over Ulthar's motionless form, the Butcher raised his drenched weapon again.

A rage enveloped Faros, a rage fueled not only by the sight before him but all the horrors he had experienced. He let out a maddened shout and threw himself at the murderous guard, managing to stab him in the shoulder.

Momentum sent both tumbling over the bodies. Faros's sword went flying, but Paug, too, lost his weapon. The pair ended in a tangle of arms and legs, colliding with other pathetically struggling combatants.

Paug put a hand to Faros's throat, intending to snap the latter's neck. The Butcher snorted, "I'll—kill—you!"

Faros managed to push the hand back. His strength should have been no match for Paug's, but the overseer's wounds finally began to take some toll. Straining, Faros seized Paug's throat with his other hand.

"I'll . . . die," he gasped. "But not . . . before you!"

Paug's crimson eyes widened. He gagged. The hand that had tried to strangle Faros dropped to his side—

And came up, a dagger held ready.

"Pathetic calf . . ." Paug rasped.

Faros nearly lost his grip. Once more he had failed those who had sacrificed themselves for him, and this time his mistake was fatal.

But suddenly Paug faltered. His body jerked, and he swayed. The overseer blinked. With all his might, Faros shoved, sending the guard tumbling. Faros rolled away.

His hand fell upon Ulthar's axe. He seized the weapon just below the head then swung the axe around.

The sharp edge of the axe drove into the guard's left leg. Paug dropped his dagger and, with a guttural roar, collapsed.

Tossing aside the heavy axe, Faros seized the dagger. He dragged himself to where the larger minotaur lay writhing and moaning. The axe had cut to the bone, and rich red blood covered not only Paug's limb, but the hands he used to try to stop the flow.

The piggish face turned as Faros drew near. One hand searched for the knife. Faros held up the dagger for his tormentor to see.

Despite his condition, the overseer threw himself at his smaller foe.

Gritting his teeth, Faros thrust. The dagger plunged through the Butcher's chest just below the rib cage.

Paug gasped then fell back, the blade sliding free. He stared where the dagger had sunk in. His baleful gaze turned to his slayer.

Pure hatred radiated from those dying orbs. "You damned—"

His head slumped back, and the eyes closed. Paug stilled.

As if touching something leprous, Faros hurled the dagger away. Paug's blood stained his hands and chest. Forgetting all else, Faros made his way back to Ulthar. Even though shouts and the clang of weapons filled the air, the younger prisoner heard only the reproaches of the dead.

"Ulthar . . ." he called, touching the mariner on the shoulder.

The tattooed figure could not answer him. Glancing at the wide, monstrous wound dealt by Paug, Faros could see that death had been instantaneous.

He had never revealed his true name to the former brigand. Now that filled him with regret. Faros made certain that Ulthar's eyes were closed then slid the axe that his friend had wielded so bravely into the dead prisoner's hands. Bowing his head over the body, he recalled Ulthar's favorite song.

"You're going home finally," Faros muttered. "Back to the sea . . ."

The thundering of hooves put an abrupt end to his mourning. Faros glanced up then barely leaped out of the way as another band of mounted soldiers tore through what remained of the prisoners. Many of the surviving inmates dropped to their knees, lowering their horns in surrender. A few others still fought, but their situation grew dire.

One rider, his mount driven to the side, now headed directly toward the mariner's body. Heedless of the danger, Faros stepped in front of Ulthar, waving his arms in a desperate attempt to turn the rider aside.

The warhorse rose up on its hind legs. The rider, the tall, slim figure who led the imperial soldiers, shouted something at the animal.

Refusing to back down, Faros yelled at the mount. The horse's hooves came down sharply, kicking at the minotaur before it. One hoof caught Faros on the side of the head.

He struck the ground hard, the layers of ash providing little cushion. The sounds of battle, the sounds of ignominious defeat, ceased . . . and with them went all consciousness.

Maritia and her forces had been certain of death yet they struggled on. Hotak's daughter had lost many fighters. Only a handful of the camp's guards still lived. Despite that, no one thought to surrender. Then the horns had sounded and a column of Hotak's finest legionaries had burst through gates, trampling the astounded inmates without mercy. The warhorse banner had galvanized Maritia's weary fighters and sent them back into the fray with renewed hope of glory.

The rebellious prisoners tried to hold, but they had reached their limits. The frantic strength they had mustered faltered, and with it went any vestige of order. The battle became retreat and slaughter. Mounted soldiers encircled small bands, slashing away at stalwarts in the front. Around and around the legionaries rode, whittling their foes down. The last finally dropped to his knees and bent his horns to the dusty soil.

Thick smoke still covered much of the yard, and Maritia moved with caution. Shadows formed in the mist, fatalistic rebels trying to kill as many soldiers as possible before being slain themselves. She battled with one such ghoul, a ragged-eyed, ferocious barbarian who leaped out of the smoke, slaying the guard who had been her guide.

She felled the ghoul, but more shadows coalesced. One of her escorts pulled her back, shouting, "My lady! Stay behind us! We'll withdraw toward the gates. The smoke's not as thick as here."

"Go!" she snapped.

Out of the smoke—almost on top of the rioters—came half a dozen legionaries on horseback. Two prisoners ran before them, only to perish—one neatly beheaded by a quick, almost casual swing of an axe.

In the lead rode Bastion. He did not stop, but gave his sister a brief nod before vanishing back into the mist. The surviving prisoners dropped their weapons. Two of the riders remained, circling them. Several of Maritia's soldiers moved to help secure the enemy.

"We're gathering them in the center of the yard," one of the pair on horseback informed her.

Maritia followed the soldiers and their captives. In the center of the yard, she saw that several dozen prisoners knelt under the watchful gaze of legionaries. To the right lay rows of wounded, some moaning horribly.

The trickle of surrendering workers quickly became a flood. There remained little hope of escape, and most realized it. Soon, row upon row upon row of prisoners, snouts turned to the ashy ground, knelt before the triumphant legion.

Some of the camp guards taking part in the watch began muttering about executing everyone. Maritia confronted them.

"There will be no more talk of that! Their fates will be decided by your emperor. Do you understand?"

"But we were just—" started one, only to fall silent under her stern gaze.

"Well said, Mari," remarked a familiar but weary voice.

She turned to find her brother leading his horse toward her. "Bastion! Only you could create such miracles. How did you manage this?"

Other than his coating of ash, he looked orderly and in command—as always. Bastion gave her a tired smile as he handed the reins to a subordinate.

"You may thank Kol for this miracle," he replied. "I am in this area on a delicate mission for Father. When I saw the smoke rising in the distance, I feared the worst, knowing that you had last been in this region. I had the horns sounded, hoping that someone remained who would open the way for us—but I rode in not even knowing if you were still alive."

"It was very close, Bastion. The commander of the camp, Krysus, was slain early on. The audacity of the prisoners caught everyone by surprise. I did have warning from one of the senior guards, an otherwise disreputable fellow by the name of Paug."

"Paug's dead, my lady," blurted a wounded camp guard. "I seen him fall—but not until he bravely slew the tattooed one!"

" 'Tattooed one?' " Bastion said.

"One of the insurrection's leaders. A giant of a fellow. There was another giant with him, very dark-furred. I killed him."

She looked at the guard. "What about the third one Paug mentioned, a younger minotaur?"

"No idea, my lady."

"I'd like to see this 'tattooed one,' Maritia."

"Aye, I can show you," the guard said.

He led them to where the worst of the fighting had taken place. The mangled, gaping corpses of soldiers and prisoners lay intertwined. Unattached limbs littered the area. The ground had been soaked by blood and gore.

They found Paug and his adversary close to one another. The dead guard's expression seemed bitter.

Bastion leaned down to inspect the dead prisoner. "From the outermost islands," he remarked. "Zaar, I believe. Exceptional sailors and fighters. Curious that he would end up in a dry zone like this."

"I would've much preferred that he had not, believe me. I doubt the rest of the prisoners would've fought half so well without such fanatic leadership."

"Minotaurs are all good fighters," her brother returned, dryly. He stood, gazing around at the detritus of the struggle.

"Is something wrong?"

"This revolt makes my task a little harder. Vyrox would have been strained as it is by my new imperatives."

"What do you mean?"

He eyed her. "The reason for my 'miraculous arrival' is that I came to this area to fulfill our new pact with the ogres."

She looked at him in wide-eyed surprise. "So they weren't satisfied with all that we offered? They want more raw materials as well?"

Bastion's brow furrowed. "You do not understand. The ogres want proof of our allegiance. They've known treachery in the past. Golgren says we must pay our way into their trust." His countenance darkened. "I do not like the ogres any more than you do, but . . ."

"If Father is willing to pay the cost . . ."

His gaze swept across the lines of kneeling prisoners. "Vyrox must be shut down for a time, but that cannot be helped."

She nodded, understanding. "Then . . . we must do whatever is necessary."

Her brother turned away, stepping over the dead. Maritia followed. The fires, bereft of much else to burn, had begun to settle, causing the smoke to thin. Shattered towers and the skeletons of barracks greeted their eyes, along with endless mangled bodies. Already the burned stench of decay rose high above the camp, and the carrion crows gathered in large, hungry numbers.

Bastion paused, his eyes shifting to one of the bodies at his feet. He touched the shoulder of one prisoner who lay face down.

"This one lives," Bastion informed a soldier. "Check to see how many others like him there might be."

"Aye, my lord."

"We will need every last slave."

"It'll take some time to get everything back in order," Maritia murmured. "Eventually everything will return to normal, Bastion."

Her brother stared at her. Then, gaze shifting so as to take in all Vyrox—from the scorched walls to the ruined buildings, the numerous dead, and lastly the rows of defeated prisoners—he muttered, "You believe that, Mari? Do you really?"

CHAPTER XXVII

OF THINGS TO COME

General Rahm kept his appointment with *Dragon's Crest* only an hour before she sailed. The first mate, Botanos, peered into the darkness, looking for the others, reluctant to leave.

"Get underway, Captain," Rahm commanded. The normally jovial mariner was silent as he absorbed his new title, and turned to his duties.

Rahm retired to his cabin, his only order to have someone bring him food and, especially, ale or wine. He shut the door behind him then fell back onto the cot.

A knock on the door interrupted the general's dark thoughts. To his surprise, it was the newly appointed captain carrying in his meal.

"Bread, salted goat meat, and one of the captain's favorite wines," Botanos announced.

"You're the captain now," Rahm snarled, seizing the bottle.

"Did he die as a warrior?"

"He died for a fool . . . but he died a good warrior, yes."

The mariner sat down without invitation. "I'm sorry your plan failed, general. If you'd been able to slay the emperor . . ."

Rahm took a long drink then said, "I killed one of his sons. A start, at least."

"Well, that's fine, then. That'll weaken the throne."

"Pfah! I slew a boy in a warrior's body. I slew Kolot de-Droka when I really would have preferred to kill his brother, Ardnor." Rahm stoppered the bottle. "I failed everyone. Perhaps this rebellion should have another leader—providing the others are not dead, too."

Botanos leaned back. "As to that, all went well both east and south. I'll let them tell their own tales when we meet up with them again, but I think you'll find that Captain Tinza performed well, general."

"Small victories."

"But it's a start." Botanos took the bottle and put it on the table. "Best eat some food first, then sleep. Things'll look better in the morning."

Rahm toyed with his ring, finding something fascinating about the way it glittered. "Will Azak be alive in the morning?"

Botanos clamped his mouth shut. Turning, he left Rahm to his contemplations.

Shouts awoke the general as he struggled through a nightmare in which everyone around him turned into Hotak. Rahm rose and realized that the shouting augered trouble.

Racing up on deck, he found Captain Botanos peering north.

"We've friends, General. Imperial friends."

Barely noticeable in the dark, two shapes rose and sank with the waves.

"Can we outrace them?"

"We shall see, General. We shall see!"

Dragon's Crest coursed through the waters. Botanos barked orders at the crew, yet they could not seem to lose the two hunters.

"Let's try something different." To the sailor at the wheel, he shouted, "Head toward shore, but closer this time! I want to be close enough to count the leaves on the trees!"

As *Dragon's Crest* drew near to the shore, a groaning sound came from its port side.

"Starboard!" roared Botanos, moving quickly toward the bow. "Starboard! That's good! Keep straight ahead! Now port! Port!"

Rahm peered over the rail. Just visible above the water he saw several jagged mounds. Botanos might be able to safely steer his ship, but then his rash strategy might also accomplish just what their enemies desired.

"Starboard!" shouted the captain. Again came a groan. "Forgot that one!" Botanos glanced back at the two pursuers. "Hope they forget, too."

"Would they even come after us here?"

Botanos pointed at Mithas. "If we keep on this track, we'll be around the island long before them. Either they follow or they lose us."

Giving up appeared not to be an option for the hunters. With one taking the lead, they entered the dangerous waters.

"Captain Azak once told me no one knew the waters of the empire better than he did," Botanos commented. "And he taught me everything he could—hey! Hard to port!"

As expertly as their vessel navigated the area, the pair giving chase seemed to be doing just as well. The second ship imitated the route of the first with precision.

"That first captain's sailed here before," grumbled the massive figure next to Rahm. "But how often?"

"They're getting nearer." Rahm considered. "The catapult. Could you hit the lead ship with it?"

"Not very likely, even if the weather was better, and it was daylight out. Probably just stir up the water near their bow."

"Get it ready, anyway! Hurry!"

Scratching his head, Botanos gave the command. The crew quickly had the catapult prepared for firing. The captain called for oil, but Rahm countered him.

"I don't want them to have any forewarning."

"But if we hit them, the flames'll do extra damage."

"It should do damage enough without hitting. On my signal!" Rahm watched the first ship maneuver. "A little closer—now!"

The huge ball went soaring into the night.

"I can only promise that it'll land near, General!"

"That's all I want."

The black waters exploded with the sound of the huge missile striking. The lead ship immediately lurched away from where the missile had crashed into the sea.

Even from *Dragon's Crest* the groan of wood against rock as the hunter ran aground sent shivers through everyone.

"You tricked her onto the rocks!" roared Botanos merrily.

The first pursuer seemed to stop dead in the water, her bow turned to the shore. The second vessel came in behind, gradually slowing.

The crew cheered General Rahm. Botanos ordered them back to their posts.

"Time to get out of these waters," the captain rumbled. "Should be clear sailing from here."

Behind them, the stalled imperial vessels gradually vanished in the darkness.

The next night, under cover of darkness, *Dragon's Crest* met up with the other ships. Captain Tinza requested permission to come aboard. Several minutes later, she and Napol climbed onto the deck of Rahm's ship to cheers from the crew.

"A wonderful adventure it was!" she announced. "All went as smoothly as can be. Not only have we struck a blow against the usurper, but we stocked each of our ships."

"Losses were minimal," informed the marine commander, looking quite proud. "You should've seen it, General Rahm! We did as good as any of Hotak's legion— by the wild seas, better than that!"

"I'm glad," Rahm responded with less enthusiasm. "I'm glad all went well for you."

"Not all went well with you?" returned Tinza, her attitude becoming more subdued.

"They slew Hotak's son, Kolot," Botanos interjected. "The emperor himself proved to be too well guarded. I regret to say that my captain was killed during the mission."

"But he died a true warrior." Napol looked around as if he intended to fight anyone who said otherwise.

"What matters," said Tinza, "is that the usurper has shown weakness. Now we should sail out of sight and begin the next phase."

They eyed Rahm with great expectation. He could not help draw strength from their confidence.

"You heard Captain Tinza," he declared. "We set sail for Petarka. Our first strikes have let Hotak know that we exist. The next one will teach him that we intend to endure."

The others cheered. Rahm kept his gaze steady, strong, the very image of a commander who believes that victory is ensured.

Captain Tinza and Napol departed, leaving Rahm with Botanos. The heavy minotaur roared orders to get the ship underway.

"How long will it take us to reach Petarka from here?" the general asked.

"If all goes well and we sight no patrols, four days."

Four days. Such a long time. Rahm already dreamed of his return. He intended to bring the House of Droka down.

The information Tiribus's former aide, Nolhan, had brought would prove useful. Hotak might sit on the throne now, but Rahm swore that the dynasty would end in blood.

At Hotak's insistence, the unveiling of his statue had been delayed twice. The first delay everyone understood, for the emperor had commanded five days of mourning for his son, to be followed by a funeral ceremony such as those reserved in the past only for emperors.

On the first day of mourning, horns throughout the capital sounded twice, then the bells in the central towers rang five times. At noon, the bells rang again and at that point all minotaurs stepped out of their homes and businesses and went down on one knee. There they knelt as riders bearing the warhorse banner rode slowly by. At intersections a trumpeter would blow two mournful notes, then the soldiers would move on.

At the ninth hour of the sixth day, mourners filled the area surrounding the palace grounds. Four soldiers stood behind copper drums flanking the open entrance. In the wide pedestrian square, a vast, wooden pyre had been built.

At the tenth hour, as the bells sounded, four legionaries carried out an oak platform bearing the body of Kolot. His axe lay propped in his arms. Blood stains still matted his fur. Sheaves of horsetail grass had been carefully arranged around him, and a shield lay at his feet. His fur glistened from the oils applied to make the body more flammable.

After climbing a ramp, the legionaries set their burden atop the pyre, each afterward slapping a fist to their chest in homage. Once they had descended, workers removed the ramp. Nearby, more soldiers, these carrying torches, awaited the signal.

At midday, the emperor's family stepped forth from the palace. Dressed as they had been for the coronation, they now also wore a dark red sash from their right shoulder to the left side of their waists, the honor marking the death of a leader. Escorted by the Imperial Guard, they walked to the beat of the drums to a position before the pyre, where Hotak would give his speech.

The emperor solemnly surveyed the throng, nodding as if such a show of respect was expected. "Today, a great warrior passes from us!" he shouted. "Today, a worthy son leaves!"

Nephera stood by his side, face utterly emotionless. She had already given a eulogy at the temple on the first day of mourning and had also hired Tyklo sculptors to do a special statue for the Forerunners, one that would be mounted in a place of honor.

For once, Hotak had not argued with her.

"Kolotihotaki de-Droka, warrior of the empire, officer of the Imperial Guard, beloved son, gave his life in the pursuit of his duty! He performed as we all hope to perform, sacrificing for the good of all! In his final moment, Kolot chose the ultimate course of action, and in doing so, he saved his own brother!"

Ardnor, Bastion, and Maritia stood at attention behind their parents. Maritia's eyes were red. Bastion wore a look of calm, but his left hand remained tightly clenched throughout the ceremony.

Next to Bastion, Ardnor, helm in the crook of his arm, glared almost defiantly at the crowd. He had sworn publicly that he would capture or slay his brother's killer. Some within the imperial circle thought that he spoke too publicly, as if he sought to deter any criticism for the chaotic actions leading to Kolot's death.

Hotak turned to the pyre. "A warrior is dead! Let us sing of his victories, recall his glory! Let us now honor his passing— and pray that when our time comes, we are as worthy!"

He signaled the four torchbearers. They bent down and lit the base of the pyre.

The flames leaped up eagerly. They burst high into the air, snatching at the body.

Falling to one knee, the emperor bowed his head. His family and the crowd followed his lead. The fire burned lustily, in short order enveloping everything. The bells sounded slowly.

When the flames had reduced the platform and its contents to near ash, Hotak and his family rose. Accompanied by their honor guard, they returned to the palace. Only when the imperial family vanished through the tall doors of the imposing edifice did the crowd rise.

For five days after, the warhorse banner hung upside down throughout the capital.

As to the true cause for the second delay in the collossus's unveiling, many had their suspicions. Some suspected Hotak waited to make his announcement about the empire's goals of expansion. Other rumors held that Hotak would announce his eldest son as heir, something once unthinkable.

Only the emperor knew the real reason.

The great square where Chot's titanic statue once stood was cordoned off. Able warriors, attentive eyes focused on the crowd, lined the rope barrier. Sentinels and archers watched from the rooftops.

At the sound of the horns, Hotak led his wife into the square amidst cheers. Gone were the sashes of mourning.

Behind the royal couple came Ardnor, followed by Bastion and a still-subdued Maritia. On this special day, the eldest son of the emperor dressed as an officer of the Imperial Guard. The suggestion that he wear such garb had come from his mother, who felt that any announcement of succession would be better accepted by the populace if he did not flaunt his position in the temple.

The glittering Crown of Toroth atop his head and carrying the majestic Axe of Makel Ogrebane, Hotak nodded to his subjects as he and his wife made their way to the platform set up before the veiled statue where other dignitaries, including the Supreme Circle, waited.

A hush swept over the crowd as Hotak raised the axe. Hotak nodded, quite satisfied by the adoration shown by his people. The bloody night of months before was a distant memory to most, the end of a long, bleak age of stagnation, and the beginning of a grand new era of conquest and glory.

"Citizens of the empire!" Hotak said. "You come here today, I think, with the intention of saluting me!" He shook his head at this. "But in truth, it is I who must salute you!"

He waved the axe high again, causing the crowd to roar.

Ardnor led the cheering, waving his fist in the air and urging the people on.

"An emperor leads, but he cannot lead without the people!"

Hotak looked to a waiting officer. The latter signaled the soldiers holding the ropes of the massive tarps draping the huge statue to stand by.

"Today we unveil a likeness of your emperor, but it is not displayed here to set the fear of the throne into your hearts! No, rather it will stand here to remind all that now an emperor rules who serves the wishes and dreams of his people, who will see that his people take their rightful place as the foremost power in all of Ansalon—nay!—in all of Krynn!"

The officer nodded to the soldiers.

The tarps fluttered off, revealing a giant shaped in Hotak's image. The statue wore the uniform of a legionary and in one hand held the helmeted head of a Knight of Neraka. The entire statue had been meticulously carved and exquisitely painted from sandaled toe to tip of the towering horns.

Trumpets wailed, and the emperor's honor guard let out a war cry. A satisfied smile spread across the Lady Nephera's face.

The emperor signalled for silence.

"For decades, the reign of Chot meant decay and disarray. He led us to new depravity and disaster—and all for his own corrupt gain. The empire stagnated. But no more! Ours is a vibrant race! Our population has more than tripled since our war with the foul Magori. We now threaten to overtake our ready land and resources. If we are to flourish, we must expand!" He took a deep breath. "It is our destiny!"

The emperor extended his hand. Stepping forward, Bastion gave him a copy of the pact.

Hotak held it up for all to view. "You see here the future of the realm. No more will we be satisfied with meager colonies on the edge of the Blood Sea, planting ourselves on bits of rock throughout the Courrain Ocean." Passing the axe to Bastion, he unrolled the scroll. "On this occasion, I am proud to inform you that an alliance has been forged, a pact with the lands of Kern and Blöde, lands awash in blood spilled by the Knights of Neraka, lands seeking our aid. In return, they give us the foothold on the mainland we have so long desired."

Uneasy rumblings greeted this announcement. The crowd was not angered by the alliance, but neither were they pleased by a merger with their ancient foes.

Undaunted, Hotak added, "Kern, Blöde, and every land adjacent shall be cleansed of the Knights' taint! The ogre kingdoms, weakened by war, invite our aid. Later, they will have no choice but to accept our continued presence in their territories—a presence that surely must, in the name of vigilance, multiply over time."

Which meant that once welcomed into the lands of the ogres, the emperor had no intention of departing.

The citizens understood. Hotak's farsightedness moved them to cheers that built to a cascading roar. Hotak stretched his arms out to his audience, as if embracing each as a brother.

Rolling up the scroll, Hotak turned solemn. "At this moment, the first ships are being made ready. Rumor tells of a distant war brewing among the humans and the elves. The Overlords, who have never dared face minotaur might, are said to be squabbling with one another, losing their grip over their domains. The time is at hand!"

As the first voices rose, Hotak cut them off with a wave of his hand. "This is a time of change akin to the First Cataclysm, when the old gods sank decadent Istar beneath the sea and ripped our homeland free from the continent! This is a time when traditions must make way for expediency, for necessity!"

"It comes!" hissed Ardnor, eyes bright, body bristling with anticipation.

"Be still!" Bastion said quietly.

Lady Nephera's smile grew as Hotak reached again for her hand. Their children stepped up, Ardnor edging in front of Bastion and Maritia.

The emperor drew himself up. "I cannot ignore the possibility that, in the midst of this glorious campaign to come, the crown might have to be passed on swiftly. If that happens, it must done with the utmost urgency, else we face catastrophe. Therefore, for the continued stability of the empire, I will hereby declare this day an heir, a successor to the throne!"

Although stilled by Hotak's words, the crowd waited with eagerness.

"Should something befall me, I now declare as my chosen successor . . . my son, Bastion!"

Bastion's name spread through the crowd with as much speed and consternation as it did through the royal family.

Lothan and the other councilors eyed one another in absolute bewilderment. Maritia stared wide-eyed at her dark-furred brother, giving him a look of pride that slipped away quickly when she glanced at their enraged mother.

At first, the Imperial consort could only gape at her husband. She soon recovered her poise, but her eyes blazed red at the emperor—and his announced successor.

Bastion wore an almost puzzled expression, but he calmly stepped forward, going down on one knee before his father.

Behind him, Hotak's eldest snorted furiously. Every muscle in his gargantuan body wished to act upon the brother who had stolen his birthright. Maritia quickly moved between her brothers and grabbed Ardnor by the arm. He shook her off, trembling.

"Do not kneel before me," a seemingly unaware Hotak declared, reaching out with both arms. "Rise, Bastion!"

The dark-furred warrior stood still as his father embraced him. "Why, Father? Why me?"

"For the sake of us all," the elder soldier murmured.

As Hotak backed away, Nephera also stepped forward and hugged her son. She said nothing to Bastion, however, and the embrace was a cursory one. When she had retreated, Hotak brought his chosen heir to the edge of the platform, pushing his son in front of himself and presenting Bastion to the crowds.

A murmur arose. None could deny Bastion's reputation and record. He was widely respected as a capable warrior loyal to his comrades, and such traits were valued by the minotaur people.

And so the crowd roared its approval.

Bastion solemnly waved. Hotak waved, too, then signaled the rest on the platform to come and greet his heir.

Maritia clutched Bastion's hand. "I had hoped . . ." she began, tears falling free. "I had always thought . . . Kol would've been so proud of you!"

But Bastion did not respond, instead staring past his sister. "Where is Ardnor?"

Maritia frowned. "He left. He was very upset."

Bastion's eyes grew veiled, but he said nothing, instead turning to accept the plaudits of other well-wishers.

As Bastion basked in the moment, Nephera pulled her husband aside. Her countenance hid her true emotions, but the words she spoke for his ears alone revealed her deep displeasure. "We never agreed on this. Never even discussed it! Ardnor was meant to be emperor!"

Hotak waved at onlookers. "I thought long about it, but after this last debacle, I can't permit such a thing. He's been careless, overzealous, and without regard for honor. You favor him, but he's proven himself unfit. I had to make my own choice on behalf of the empire. I judged my sons on their merits. Bastion is more deserving."

"But we agreed upon Ardnor, and now you shame him without warning, shame him before everyone!"

His countenance darkened. "This is not about Ardnor, my love. This is about the empire and what is needed to see that it does not weaken again. I've done what must be done for our race—as I have since first I took up a weapon to defend it."

"Our son—" Nephera began.

"Our son will be emperor," Hotak remarked, moving past her and waving at the crowd again. "But his name shall be Bastion."

He left her alone, glowering. Nephera glanced around, looking for Ardnor. The high priestess could only imagine that he had departed as soon as it was possible for him to do so without drawing attention. After all the promises, she could not blame him.

But she blamed her husband. To reject his eldest son before the eyes of thousands . . . what was Hotak thinking? It was not just Ardnor who felt humiliated and betrayed.

A faint shadow formed next to her. Takyr stood silently by his mistress, seeming to wait for some command. But the high priestess had no command for him. Not yet.

Her eyes swept over the fawning crowd. She—more than anyone—had guided Hotak's rise. To show his gratitude, he had rejected the temple over which she ruled, the advice she had wisely given, and the child she had nurtured from birth to be his successor.

"My son will yet be emperor," Lady Nephera whispered behind Hotak's retreating back.

Trailed by her darksome servant, the mistress of the temple left the others to their celebrating.

CHAPTER XXVIII

STORM-TOSSED

The ogre galley bulled its way toward the coast of Kern, its sails straining amidst the intense, unnatural storm. High waves rocked it about and threatened to engulf it. The crew struggled to keep the lines set and the square-rigged sails from ripping. Already two hands had been lost to the crashing waves.

Sequestered serenely in his cabin, Golgren sipped some of the fine red wine he had received among his parting gifts from Emperor Hotak. The minotaurs made excellent wine as well as axes and swords. Years of battling minotaurs made Golgren admire their craftsmanship, almost as much as he detested those who wielded them.

It had taken some doing for Golgren to convince his fool of a khan that this alliance would be a worthy one. There were rumors of late of some human—a female, if the tales could be believed!—seeking the goodwill of Blöde, which was why Golgren had worked quickly to add his brutish cousins to the pact. The ogre emissary envisioned himself as Grand Khan of a combined realm, one day. No more Kern. No more Blöde. And, in the end, no more minotaur empire.

Superior among all ogres—at least in his own opinion—Golgren understood the likes of Hotak and believed he could manipulate the new emperor to his advantage. Let the minotaurs think they would rise to the top of the alliance. When Golgren was finished, the beasts would be what they were always meant to be—slaves serving the ogre race.

Someone banged on the cabin door. Golgren barked a command in the crude language of his kind, and a moment later the simpleton who acted as captain squeezed his gargantuan frame through the doorway.

"Shut the door, fool!" the emissary said in Common. He insisted that those who served with him maintain some knowledge of Common to prove to minotaurs and other potential allies that ogres possessed more than rudimentary intelligence.

"Storm pushes wrong," the hulking figure said in the terse speech of most ogres. "Sails almost torn apart."

Golgren cursed the inexplicable nature of the Blood Sea. If the wind and sea both fought against them, what could he do?

Of course! The answer was in the hold. What else was their cargo good for? Let them earn their meager bits of food.

"No sails, captain. Rely on oars—and oars alone."

"Oars?" The thick brow of the other ogre furrowed. Golgren knew that in such storms, the captain would be reluctant to use the oars for fear they would break, and the ship would capsize without sails for balance.

"Yes, oars." Golgren poured more wine. "Our new guests must work until they bleed. It will prepare them for their future, yes?"

The ogre captain grunted reluctant agreement then departed. Master of this ship he might be, but the Grand Lord could have his head if at all displeased with his obedience.

Alone again, Golgren sat back and, wine in hand, dreamed of glory.

Chained to the oars, the dour minotaur slaves struggled to push the galley forward. Monstrous overseers wielding multi-barbed whips grunted orders only half-understood. On a big brass kettledrum near the aft, another ogre used his wide, thick palms to beat the rhythm of the oars.

Weakened and defeated, the minotaurs rowed.

The back-breaking work they had performed in Vyrox had been cruel, life-stealing—but any minotaur would have returned there if given the slightest choice. When they had seen the long, flat ogre galley and the tusked figures standing armed and ready, the defeated workers had sagged with fresh despair. Three days of forced marching had already sapped their strength. Whips had ended mutterings and urged the dumbstruck prisoners into the hold of the vessel.

In the foul, parched realms of the ogres, they could only expect worse shame, torture, and an honorless, wasting death—all to fulfill the dreams and ambitions of Emperor Hotak.

Blöde and Kern had demanded no land. The ogres wanted something more precious as a sign of Hotak's faith. Minotaurs were taught to slay one another in ritual combat, but when faced by outsiders, they traditionally united as one. To prove that Hotak valued their partnerships, the ogres had demanded of him minotaur slaves to work their own mines. They had demanded the unthinkable, that minotaur deliver minotaur into foreign slavery, and Hotak had done so secretly but with little hesitation. After all, these minotaurs were brigands, traitors, or worse.

The hull groaned. Water seeped through the oar ports, requiring constant mopping and bailing. One set of slaves, fighting to keep their oar in the water, suddenly fell back into their fellows as the straining timber cracked in two.

The overseers whipped them hard for their failure, then out of frustration whipped other slaves nearby. The minotaurs snorted in hatred. Chained and broken, they lacked the will to do more. The rowing continued on.

One among them cared not a whit about storms, whips, or even, if the vessel survived, his inevitable destination. Faros pushed and pulled at the oar as if no life remained in him. When ogres barked at him, he did not blink. When whips bit into his matted and bloody hide, he did not flinch. For all practical purposes, he might as well have been one of the walking dead.

His mind, however, was far more active than any guessed. In it swam visions of the people and events that had led him down this dreadful path. He saw over and over his father, mother, siblings, Bek, Ulthar, the Lady Maritia, Paug, and so many others. Faros relived the nightmare of his life endlessly in his mind.

Throughout it all, he recalled the voice of Gradic pleading with him to be cautious, to flee to safety so that some day he might return to avenge clan and kin. The pleadings pounded madly into his mind with the steady beat of the drum. In truth, the voice might have been that of his father, but the words demanding justice were Faros's own.

Return? Could he ever hope to return, much less see justice done? It seemed so unlikely, so impossible. Ulthar, a hardened pirate and brigand, had survived Vyrox far longer, just to die when it looked as though he might at last seize freedom. Now, not only had Faros been condemned to serve the enemies of his people, but he was being sent to a land that made the mines of Vyrox seem a paradise by comparison.

Return? He had no hope of returning. Only death would garner Faros his freedom and perhaps end his shame at last.

The beat of the drum continued. The minotaur slaves rowed on, edging closer and closer to their destiny.

Glossary

The Abyss — Netherworld supposedly at the bottom of the Maelstrom in the Blood Sea. A place of evil and death ruled by the goddess Takhisis.

Amur — Agricultural colony northeast of Mithas, noted for corn and wheat.

Ansalon — The southernmost major continent of Krynn.

Ardnor de-Droka — Eldest son of General Hotak de-Droka and Nephera. First Master of the Protectors, sentinels of the Forerunners.

Argon's Chain — A tall mountain range, along Mithas's eastern side, rich with many minerals and replete with several active volcanoes.

Argon's Throat — The most dangerous mining shaft in Vyrox.

Arun — Prominent House known for craftwork, such as barrel making.

Astos — General and member of the Supreme Circle under Chot.

Aurelis — Colony located on eastern perimeter of the empire.

Axe of Makel Ogrebane — Ceremonial weapon representing the favored axe of the legendary hero and emperor, who freed his people from slavery. Jeweled yet functional.

Azak de-Genjis — Captain of *Dragon's Crest* and comrade of General Rahm.

ballista — Weapon used on some minotaur vessels. Launches two eight-foot, iron tipped javelins with great force and accuracy.

Bastion de-Droka — Second son of General Hotak de-Droka. Officer of the legions.

Bek — A servant in House Kalin. Loyal companion of Faros. Name adopted by Faros in Vyrox.

Belrogh — Soldier slain by one of Tiribus's aides, Frask.

Beryn Es-Kalgor — An Initiate within the Protectors.

Bilario — A merchant, possibly involved in smuggling.

Blöde — One of the ogre realms of Ansalon. Ruled by a Lord Chieftain.

Blood Sea — A sea northwest of Ansalon, so named because of the water's blood-red tint, due to the silt deposits once stirred up by a vast whirlpool in its center.

Boril — A member of the Supreme Circle under Chot. Betrayed by Lothan.

Botanos — First mate of *Dragon's Crest*.

Breath of Argon — Invisible, poisonous gases seeping through the mineshafts of Vyrox.

breathing sickness — Lung disease caused by the constant inhaling of a combination of dust and fumes during mining. Victims lose fur and weight, their flesh grows pale, and they vomit constantly.

briarberry — Rich red berry used primarily for wine making.

Broka — Small colony at the geographic heart of the empire, noted for timber.

Brygar Es-Dexos — A dishonest merchant, who is patriarch of Clan Dexos.

The Cataclysm, also The First Cataclysm — The catastrophic event when the gods sent the nation of Istar to the bottom of the Blood Sea and caused the minotaur kingdoms to be ripped free from the mainland.

Challenger's Roost — Disreputable tavern in Nethosak, where games of chance are played, including those in which body parts such as ears may be forfeited.

chemoc, or Feeder of Chemosh — A rare, part feline creature, almost as tall as a horse at the shoulder, used by the minotaurs in combat sports. Chemocs have two heads, vestigial wings, and their tail is spiked. Related to manticores.

Chot Es-Kalin, also known as Chot the Terrible, Chot the Invincible, and Chot the Magnificent — The minotaur emperor who rose to power in 368 AC and ruled through the Summer of Chaos. Overthrown by General Hotak de-Droka on the Night of Blood.

cloud creature — A demonic assassin created by Nephera.

common house — Multiple-dwelling building for low-rank minotaurs.

cooperage — Barrel-making establishment.

Courrain Ocean — The vast ocean east of Ansalon.

"cow" — Derogatory term. Ultimate insult to any minotaur. Minotaurs refuse to accept that they so closely resemble the said animal.

Crespos Es-Kalin — Eldest son of Gradic of House Kalin.

Crown of Toroth — Ceremonial piece recreating crown worn by legendary emperor who expanded minotaur maritime interests.Used primarily at coronations.

Darot — Militia fighter from Jarva.

dartfish — Thick, yard-long, deep-sea fish with pointed noses. Predatory. Considered a delicacy.

de — Designation in minotaur clan name that indicates clan originating from Kothas stock.

dekarian — Sub-officer serving under a hekturion. Generally commanding ten soldiers.

Delarac — Clan allied with House Droka.

Detrius — A grain merchant in the imperial city.

Dexos — Prominent House which supports Hotak.

Doolb — A captain in the Imperial Guard under Hotak.

Dorn Es-Hestos — Son of Rahm Es-Hestos.

Dragon's Crest — Ship owned and commanded by Captain Azak de-Genjis.

Droka — Clan of General Hotak.

Duma — Colony located in the southern region of the empire.

Dus — Colony located east of Mito.

Dwarkyn — A captain of the Imperial Guard.

Eastern fleet — The largest of the imperial fleets, with general duties of maintaining security in all waters east of Mithas.

Edan Es-Brog — High priest of the Temple of Sargonnas.

Egriv — An apprentice at Master Zornal's cooperage and a member of Forerunner faith.

Emperor's Pride. A warship of the Imperium's Eastern fleet.

Es — Designation in clan name indicating clan originating from Mithas stock.

The Eye — Large, irridescent pearl used in special ceremonies by the high priestess of the Forerunners.

Faros Es-Kalin — Nephew of Chot Es-Kalin.

Firemount — An iron-rich island just to the south of Kothas that has been colonized for mining.

First Master — Title given to Ardnor de-Droka as leader of the Protectors.

five — Number considered good luck by minotaurs. Any multiple is also considered to be lucky.

Flight of the Gods — Minotaur term for the departure of the gods after the Summer of Chaos.

Flying Gryphon Legion — Legion noted by its banner, a golden gryphon ascending upon a field of silver.

forerunners, or Forerunners — According to the tenets of the sect, those minotaurs, either ancestors or loved ones, who have died and now watch over their living kin. Also, those who follow the faith.

Frask — Aide to Senior Councilor Tiribus.

Gaerth — Tall, slender captain of a mysterious ship aiding General Rahm's escape.

Gar — A captain of the guard within the imperial palace.

Garsis — The former governor of Mito. Executed by Haab.

Gask — An island to the east of Mito that has been colonized for mining.

Genjis — Clan house of Captain Azak, represented by trident and ship symbol.

Gol — Island colony on eastern edge of the minotaur empire.

Golgren — An ambitious Grand Lord of the ogres.

Gorsus — Prisoner who died in Vyrox.

Goud — First Hekturian of the port city of Varga.

Gradic Es-Kalin — Younger brother of Chot. Father of Faros.

Grand Khan — Symbolic ruler of Kern.

Great Circus — The vast, oval arena, seating thousands, in which by rite of combat duels, emperors, and more are decided.

Grisov Es-Neros — Patriarch of House Neros and counselor to Emperor Chot.

Gryphon's Wing — Minotaur ship plying the Courrain. Commanded by Captain Hogar.

Gul — A distant island colony, not to be confused with Gol.

gully dwarf — Sub-race of dwarves generally found living among squalor and having limited intelligence but some cunning.

Haab — Provost captain, later colonial governor of Mito under Hotak.

Habbakuk — The Fisher King. Benevolent god of the sea.

Halrog — A prisoner in Vyrox.

Han — A blacksmith on the isle of Tadaran. Friend to Mogra Es-Hestos.

Harod — A guard at the Vyrox mining colony.

Hathan — A remote island colony to the southeast of Kothas, location of a garrison.

hekturion — A legionary officer in charge of one hundred warriors.

Hes — An overseer of Master Zornal's cooperage.

Hestos — A prominent House which supports Chot. Clan of General Rahm.

Hiddukel — A god, often called "the deal maker," who trades in souls. Patron of greed.

Hila Es-Kalin — Wife of Zokun Es-Kalin.

Hogar — Captain of the ill-fated Gryphon's Wing.

Holis — A member of Maritia de-Droka's personal bodyguard.

Horned God — Rebel vessel.

horsetail grass — Grass with herbal abilities, revered by minotaurs as a symbol of strength and honor. Bound sheaves are tossed during processions or laid by the bodies of the dead at funerals.

Hotak de-Droka, also known as Hotak the Sword, Hotak the Avenger — General of the legions and emperor following coup against Chot. Commander of the Rearing Horse Legion.

Hybos — High-ranking minotaur living on Kotha. Supporter of Chot.

Ilionus — Prisoner in Vyrox.

Ilos de-Morgayn — First Dekarian of the port of Varga.

Imperial Guard — Elite legion whose chief task is to protect the emperor.

Imperial Legions — The military might of the empire. Each legion serves under a general. Noted by their banners, such as the Rearing Horse Legion, and their silver kilts with red tips.

Irda — According to legend, the beautiful, glorious ancestors of both the ogres and the minotaurs.

Istar — Powerful nation once located where the Blood Sea now exists. After its ruler, the Kingpriest, proclaimed himself the God above Gods, a mountain fell from the sky and plunged Istar beneath the waves. At the same time, the minotaur kingdoms were separated from the mainland, becoming islands.

Itonus — Patriarch of House Droka.

Japfin — A prisoner working the Mines of Vyrox.

Jarva — Town located on Mithas, near the villa of the merchant Bilario.

Javelin — Rebel ship.

Jhonus — Protector skilled at hand-to-hand combat.

Jolar — Husband of Tyra de-Proul. Sea captain.

Josiris — Aide to Senior Councilor Tiribus.

Jubal — Raspy-voiced governor of the colony Gol under Chot.

Kaj — Prisoner in Vyrox.

Kalin — Clan house of Emperor Chot. Clan colors are crimson and black.

Kalius — A guard and wagon driver in Vyrox.

Kaz Dragonslayer — Legendary hero and renegade. Companion of Huma Dragonbane.

Kazelati — Descendants of Kaz's followers. Their hidden domain lies beyond the empire.

Kelto — Bodyguard to Grisov Es-Neros.

Kern — More dominant of the two ogre kingdoms. Blöde is the other. Ruled by a Grand Khan.

Kernen — Capital of Kern. Once the seat of High Ogre might, now ruled by the decadent descendents of that fabled race.

Kesk the Elder — Member of the Supreme Circle under Chot.

Kesk the Younger — Member of the Supreme Circle under Chot. Son of Kesk the Elder.

Kiri-Jolith — Bison-headed god of just cause. Rival of Sargonnas. Second most prominent deity among the minotaurs until the Flight of the Gods.

Knights of Neraka — Human military organization derived from the defunct Knights of Takhisis. Recognizable by their black armor, they seek the conquest of the continent of Ansalon. Sometime ally of the empire, especially during the reign of Chot.

Kolotihotaki de-Droka — Youngest son of Hotak de-Droka, commonly known as Kolot. Officer of the legions.

Konac — Imperial tax master under Chot.

Kothas — Twin island of Mithas and nominally its equal. Major importer of meat to the empire.

Kreel — Militia fighter from Jarva.

Kroj — General and commander of the empire's southern forces. Hero of the battles of Turak Major and Selees.

Krysus de-Morgayn — One-armed commander of Vyrox.

Kyril — Young officer with duty to capture or slay Rahm on the Night of Blood. He attempts to atone for his failure by entering the Great Circus.

lavender — Scent favored by female minotaurs. Used in perfumes and potions.

Lord Chieftain — Title of ruler of ogre kingdom of Blöde.

Lothan — A member of the Supreme Circle. Appointed Head of the Supreme Circle following Hotak's coup. Also one of the Forerunner faithful.

Luko — Drunken young minotaur whose ear is shorn off in game of chance in the tavern Challenger's Roost.

Maelstrom — The vast whirlpool set in the midst of the Blood Sea. During the Summer of Chaos, it fell dormant.

Magori — Aquatic crustaceans who warred against the minotaurs during the Summer of Chaos.

Majar — Father of Luko.

Makel Ogrebane — Legendary hero and emperor who freed his people from slavery. See Axe of Makel Ogrebane.

Malk. A servant in House Dexos.

manticore — Monstrous, human-faced feline found in some rare parts of Krynn.

marine regiment — Contingent of naval fighters, as distinct from the crew of a warship. On imperial vessels, generally up to one hundred warriors.

Maritia de-Droka — Only daughter of Hotak. Officer of the legions and Imperial Guard.

meditation room — Secluded chamber in the Temple of the Forerunners where the high priestess communes with the dead and casts spells.

meredrake — Horse-sized, savage lizard used by ogres as attack animals and trackers.

Minotaur Empire — Sea realm consisting of some thirty-plus islands of varying population (Mithas and Kothas are the most populated) spread over the expanses of the Blood Sea and the Courrain Ocean. There are also a few minor colonies on the northeastern peninsula of the continent of Ansalon.

Mirya — Ghost summoned by Nephera during outdoor ceremony.

Mithas — Foremost of twin islands. Location of Nethosak, seat of the imperium.

Mito — An island colony that is third in population and the third largest builder of ships in the Minotaur Empire. Located three days east of Mithas. The chief settlement is the port city of Strasgard.

Mogra Es-Hestos — Wife of Rahm Es-Hestos.

Morthosak — Chief city and capital of Kothas.

Mykos — Eldest son of Tyra de-Proul.

Nagroch — Subchieftain of Blöde.

Napol — Commander of the marine regiments serving Rahm.

Nemon de-Droka — Father of Hotak.

Nephera — Wife of Hotak de-Droka and high priestess of the temple of the Forerunners. Mother of Ardnor, Bastion, Maritia, and Kolot.

Neros — A prominent House which supports Chot.

Nethosak — Capital of both Mithas and the empire as a whole.

Night of Blood — The horrific night of carnage in which Emperor Chot and his family and those most loyal to Chot are struck down by the supporters of General Hotak.

Nilo — Prisoner in Vyrox.

Nolhan — First adjutant to the head of the Supreme Circle, Senior Councilor Tiribus.

Nymon — Noble seeking to fomulate opposition to Hotak's plans to create hereditary rule.

Olia — Headmistress of the imperial kitchens and cousin to both Zornal and Quas.

One True God, also One God — A deity rumored to exist on the mainland.

Orcius — Commander serving Hotak.

Paug — A warden in Vyrox. Also known as "the Butcher."

Petarka — Mist-enshrouded island far to the east, beyond

official boundaries of the empire. Utilized by followers of
General Rahm.

Polik the Pawn — Corrupt emperor from the time of Kaz
the Dragonslayer. Kept in power by the secret manipulations
of the red dragon Infernus.

processing station — Dangerous, fiery location where the
ore from the Vyrox mines is prepared for shipment and use
to the empire.

Protectors — Martial arm of the Forerunners, noted by
their black armor with gold insignias and the maces they
generally wield. Commanded by Ardnor de-Droka.

Proul — A prominent House which supports Chot.

provost captains — Military liaisons appointed as acting
governors under Hotak.

Pryas — Protector officer.

Quar — Obscure island colony just beyond official boundaries of the empire.

Quas — Overseer of Master Zornal's cooperage. Cousin of
the master cooper.

Rahm Es-Hestos — Commander of the Emperor's elite Imperial Guard under Chot. Later, rebel leader against Hotak.

Rearing Horse Legion — Legion commanded by Hotak,
noted for its banner — a black, rearing warhorse on a field
of red.

Red Condor — New name given to former imperial warship captured by rebels.

Res — Second Dekarian of the port city of Vargas.

Resdia — Daughter of Gradic Es-Kalin. Younger sister of Faros.

Rogan — First Mate of the *Javelin*. Brother of Tyril.

Ryn — Militia commander in Strasgard.

Ryog — A prominent House which supports Chot.

Sardar — Cousin of Ulthar. Pirate and brigand killed in accident in Vyrox.

Sargas — See Sargonnas

Sargonath — Small colony on the northeastern peninsula of Ansalon created as a sign of alliance by the empire, the Knights of Neraka, and the Kazelati after the Summer of Chaos. Its chief resource is timber.

Sargonnas, also called Sargas, Argon, and the Horned God — Chief deity of the minotaurs before the Summer of Chaos and the Flight of the Gods. Consort but also rival of Takhisis. The red condor is his symbol.

Scorpion's Sting — Imperial vessel escorting supply ships to outer colonies.

Scurn — First mate of the ill-fated Gryphon's Wing.

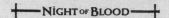

sea dragon banner — Banner of the imperial fleets.

Sea Reaver — Former imperial ship commanded by Captain Tinza.

Selees — Lush, southern island noted for historic battle.

shadow sellers — Disreputable merchants plying their wares in the torchlit areas of the Great Circus. They will sell anything.

Ship Master — Appointed head of a clan's maritime affairs, overseeing most sea merchant functions.

State Guard — Military force with primary function of overseeing police duties in all major settlements. Their armor is gray.

Strasgard — The port city of Mito. A chief shipbuilding facility.

Summer of Chaos — Minotaur term for the Chaos War, when the gods fought over Krynn.

Supreme Circle — The august governing body under the emperor. Consisting of eight members, they deal with the day-to-day functioning of the realm.

Tadaran — An island colony in the northeast of the imperium. Hiding place of General Rahm's family.

Takhisis — Powerful, manipulative dark goddess who is constantly seeking control of the mortal plane. Sargonnas is her consort, but also her rival.

Takyr — Sinister ghost serving Lady Nephera.

Targonne, Morham — Leader of the Knights of Neraka.

Temple of the Forerunners — Central temple of the dominant religious sect in the empire, following the Flight of the Gods. Its tenets preach that those who have passed on watch over their loved ones left behind. Their symbol is a bird ascending over a broken axe. The main temple, in Nethosak, was formerly used by the priests of Sargonnas.

Tengis — Distant tropical colony noted for foodstuff such as breadfruit.

Thorak — An island near Thuum.

Thuum — A wooded island colony on the southeastern edge of the imperium.

Tinza — Female captain of the *Sea Reaver*, former ship of the eastern fleet.

Tiribus de-Nordmir — A Senior Councilor and head of the Supreme Circle under Chot.

Tohma — General and member of the Supreme Circle under Chot.

Toroth — The emperor instrumental in expanding minotaur maritime interests beyond the Blood Sea. See Crown of Toroth.

Tovok — Young rebel fighter.

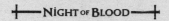

Tremanion — Prisoner in Vyrox.

Tupo — Youngest son of Gradic Es-Kalin. Younger brother of Faros.

Turak Major — Southern island. Location of historic battle.

Tyklo — A House whose tradition in stonework has made them one of the most respected clans among the minotaur. Chief artisans of the throne.

Tyra de-Proul — Imperial administrator of Kothas, appointed by Chot.

Tyril — First mate of *Scorpion's Sting*. Brother of Rogan.

Ulthar — A prisoner working the Mines of Vyrox. A tattooed, former pirate and brigand from the distant colony of Zaar.

Ursun — A prominent House which supports Hotak.

"Uruv Suurt" — Ancient ogre words meaning "minotaur."

Varga — A small but significant port in north Mithas used as a link between the far northeastern colonies and those in the innermost Blood Sea region.

Veria de-Goltyn — Chief Captain of the imperium's eastern fleet under Chot.

Vyrox — A harsh mining community, worked mostly by prisoners, located in Argon's Chain. Iron, copper, lead, and zinc are some of the minerals found here.

Warhammer Point — A harsh island to the east of Mito that has recently been colonized for mining.

Xando — A general of the imperial legions. Stationed on Kothas.

Yarl — Prisoner in Vyrox.

Zaar — A remote island colony that lost contact with the minotaur empire for several generations and has only recently been rediscovered. Home of Ulthar.

Zeboim — Volatile dark goddess of the sea.

Zemak — The Colonial Governor of Amur under Hotak.

Zen — Governor of Amur under Chot.

Zephros — Heavyset elder of Clan Droka and rival of Itonus. Patriarch of Droka under Hotak.

Zokun Es-Kalin — First cousin of Emperor Chot. Ship Master of House Kalin's merchant fleet.

Zornal — A master cooper in Nethosak.

Zygard — An ogre settlement near Sargonath.

The original Chronicles

From *New York Times* best-selling authors Margaret Weis & Tracy Hickman

These classics of modern fantasy literature – the three titles that started it all – are available for the very first time in individual hardcover volumes. All three titles feature stunning cover art from award-winning artist Matt Stawicki.

DRAGONS OF AUTUMN TWILIGHT
Volume I
Friends meet amid a growing shadow of fear and rumors of war. Out of their story, an epic saga is born.

DRAGONS OF WINTER NIGHT
Volume II
Dragons return to Krynn as the Queen of Darkness launches her assault Against her stands a small band of heroes bearing a new weapon: the DRAGONLANCE.

DRAGONS OF SPRING DAWNING
Volume III
As the War of the Lance reaches its height, old friends clash amid gallantry and betrayal. Yet their greatest battles lie within each of them.

Collections of the best of the DRAGONLANCE® saga

From *New York Times* best-selling authors Margaret Weis & Tracy Hickman.

THE ANNOTATED LEGENDS

A striking new three-in-one hardcover collection that complements *The Annotated Chronicles*. Includes *Time of the Twins*, *War of the Twins*, and *Test of the Twins*.

For the first time, DRAGONLANCE saga co-creators Weis & Hickman share their insights, inspirations, and memories of the writing of this epic trilogy. Follow their thoughts as they craft a story of ambition, pride, and sacrifice, told through the annals of time and beyond the edge of the world.

THE WAR OF SOULS Boxed Set

Copies of the *New York Times* best-selling War of Souls trilogy paperbacks in a beautiful slipcover case. Includes *Dragons of a Fallen Sun*, *Dragons of a Lost Star*, and *Dragons of a Vanished Moon*.

The gods have abandoned Krynn. An army of the dead marches under the leadership of a strange and mystical warrior. A kender holds the key to the vanishing of time. Through it all, an epic struggle for the past and future unfolds.

Before the War of the Lance, there were other adventures.

Check out these new editions of the popular Preludes series!

DARKNESS & LIGHT
Sturm Brightblade and Kitiara are on their way to Solamnia
when they run into a band of gnomes in jeopardy.

KENDERMORE
Tasslehoff Burrfoot is arrested for violating the kender laws of
prearranged marriage – but his bride pulls a disappearing act of her own.

BROTHERS MAJERE
Desperate for money, Raistlin and Caramon Majere agree to take
on a job in the backwater village of Mereklar, but they soon discover
they may be in over their heads.

RIVERWIND THE PLAINSMAN
A barbarian princess and her beloved walked into the Inn of the
Last Home, and thus began the DRAGONLANCE® Saga.
This is the adventure that led to that fateful moment.

FLINT THE KING
Flint Fireforge's comfortable life turns to chaos
when he travels to his ancestral home.

TANIS: THE SHADOW YEARS
When an old dwarf offers Tanis Halfelven the chance to find his father,
he embarks on an adventure that will change him forever.

Strife throughout the land of Krynn

CITY OF THE LOST
The Linsha Trilogy, Volume One
Mary H. Herbert
After the near-disaster chronicled in *The Clandestine Circle*,
the Knights of Solamnia send Linsha Majere to an outpost in the
backend of nowhere. But trouble seems to run in her family, and
Linsha soon finds herself involved in a war between two dragon
overlords, the Knights of Solamnia, the Legion of Steel,
and invaders from across the sea.

DARK THANE
The Age of Mortals
Jeff Crook
Beneath Thorbardin, a spellbinding fanatic preaches revolution,
turning the hearts of those who are caught up in the cause. The ancient
dwarven nation is bloodily divided, and the true leadership banished.